MW01245808

VARIATIONS

A COLLECTION OF EIGHT

Six Short Stories

&

Two Novellas

by

Thomas James Taylor

Copyright © 2022 by Thomas James Taylor
All rights reserved.

ALSO AVAILABLE
BY THE SAME AUTHOR

For Your Pleasure & Questionable Behaviour

A Montage of A Mauve Reality

Trouble In Monarto

Star-Crossed

Pursuit: Life, the Great Game

An End To Certainty

McKinney's Growth

CONTENTS

POD

Captain Rhys Morgan peered out of the porthole in time to watch the galaxy class cruiser, Condor, list heavily to port as a three hundred foot ribbon of searing flame burst from midships. The bright stream broke, separating into a roiling mass as the ship started to yaw, and under gravity's gentle influence, gracefully began to slip towards the barren moon below. A fireball erupted from her belly and was quickly extinguished for lack of oxygen. The surrounding blackness was suddenly lit by a conflagration so bright that it pained the eyes. Morgan turned away, knowing that the behemoth would soon be no more than a scorched, pulverised scatter of metal and componentry strewn across the lunar landscape; and the six hundred fifty crew? There was no way of knowing their fate.

Those who were lucky enough to make it to a pod would be safe for a time, maybe. The raiders may decide to pick them off, but the odds of survival would scarcely change. This was deep space. They had only been ordered into the quadrant because the Condor was one of the two cruisers capable of so long a haul. Just one left, now. The Kroll had made short work of her.

An attack was the last thing to be expected. Communications had become patchy out here, and fleet had ordered the swing by just to see that everything was okay. The outpost, what was left of it, had been found, and it had been totally obliterated; nothing more than a black smudge on the surface when they had come close enough to view it. The attack must come swiftly, completely without warning. . . and now, here we are, Morgan mused grimly.

He twisted himself in his chair at the pilot's console to view his companion, Major Derek Connor. He had drawn his last breath even as the survival pod blasted clear of the dying ship. And just as well, Morgan considered. There were medical supplies stowed

THOMAS JAMES TAYLOR

aboard, but nothing which would have served to treat the horrific plasma burns his comrade had suffered. He had only dragged him aboard because there was no time to do anything else, not even to think. Had he the time to consider, he might have been able to weigh the pros and cons of sharing what were already insufficient stores for the journey required to reach any human outpost. Perhaps, during those hectic moments he had fleetingly considered so long a journey *alone*, and thought to include Conner for that very reason. Truth was, he didn't know why — and why the hell was he thinking of such things? Carl Conner was dead and something would have to be done with the remains, but later. For the moment he would rest, gather his thoughts, mabe even take a nap. There was nothing to be done about anything and so much time to do it in. *Bloody Kroll.* When he woke, he noted that the chronometer indicated the passage of five hours since the pod had been launched. He had been almost at the end of his shift and looking forward to some downtime when the surprise attack had ensued, and sleep had been the one thing on his mind at the moment they had struck. Morgan prodded a button on the consol. The protective panels across the view–shield furled upward, revealing the sparsely populated expanse of interstellar space, stretched in every direction. His fist response was to sigh heavily. He was almost dead centre of a great, black void, an empty expanse spacers had come to call *the anvil*; so named not just because the perimeter of the expanse somewhat resembled an anvil, but because it was said that for some, traversing the distance impacted the soul like a hammer blow.

He stabbed at the button, closing the panels again before his mind began to swim. There was nothing out there the eye could fix on to provide a point of reference by which to gain a sense of location. The near eternalness of it seemed to want to consume the viewer and reduce him to the same emptiness that surrounded. He knew he had to avoid thinking about it, so turned instead to the *comms* panel, beginning the search for other survivors.

The communication frequencies were all devoid of traffic; only the buzz and squeal of cosmic background radiation came through the speakers, and a careful scan for any survival pod beacons proved equally as futile. After a long time he set the search to continue on auto and abandoned the activity to lean back and consider his position, and what further measures ought to be undertaken.

A constant drone emitted from the single, proton pulse engine provided a source of comfort. As long as it maintained that deep hum he knew that progress, however slow, was being made. In the corner at the rear of the cabin sat the matter-antimatter atomic converter, and across from it, the steel chest containing carbon fuel briquets which would be converted to electrical power, which in turn powered the motor, life support, navigation and every other system within the little craft.

He stood up, out of his seat and moved to check the fuel supply situation, and upon opening the lid discovered it to be half full with maybe two hundred briquettes, each roughly the size of a house brick. A single cube, he recalled from the manual, would supply energy enough for twenty-four hours.

It took a little time to count them out. Two hundred and eight. Two hundred eight days, give or take, but would it be enough? Four thousand nine hundred and ninety two hours, he made it. There was no way to know how his metabolism would cope. Even if the pod had been fitted with a decent *astronav* system, which it certainly was not — he knew for a fact that pennies had been saved in constructing these survival pods — there was still no identifiable celestial body within billions of miles. He was at the mercy of the master computer which had plotted a course in nanoseconds and launched him into the void in whatever direction it reckoned provided best chance of detection and ultimate survival. A machine had decided his fate for him, and he could only hope it had calculated correctly, if, in this case, there was even the slightest chance.

'No point,' he found himself uttering to himself, and wondered why he had said it. Maybe he thought there was no point worrying about it; that the trajectory he was on would either get him somewhere or it wouldn't. If that was what he had meant by the remark, he agreed that it was so. 'No point,' he repeated. 'No point in worrying about it.'

The task of dealing with Connor's body was yet to be addressed. Morgan was only too well aware of all the factors to be considered as far as that decision went. He went to the rations locker, slid open each drawer, counting and calculating days as he went, and in a moment he had his answer.

'Two hundred days, comfortable. I can run out of food and energy simultaneously, if I judge it right. That'll be fun.'

There was no point in keeping Connor around. There wasn't much of a point having food if power ran out, and cannibalism is a step beyond the pail, he mused, lingering on the problem much longer than he thought was reasonable, and finally reversing the decision.

Having assessed the situation and taken stock, the last item on the mental list was that of keeping the mind active and engaged. This was a major concern, he knew it well enough, and he took to searching the entire interior of the craft to find anything which might be utilised in warding of the onset of boredom or worse, which was going to be a major ingredient in getting through the trial to come.

After scouring the interior, forward to aft, top to bottom, he came up with a sewing kit consisting of scissors, six needles, thread wound on a bobbin and a thimble. There were also two Earth dollar coins — relics left over from when money still existed within the solar system — two ink scribes, also known as biros, a writing pad, a piece of candy wrapped in paper, a box of chalk and a large magnifying glass. He groaned as he regarded the items despondently. It had only been, what? He glanced at the chronometer. Eight hours since the door had sealed closed and the pod had blasted away from the Condor. From his Star Fleet jacket pocket he withdrew the last item of interest he had found during the exhaustive search. It had come from the medicine box attached to the rear bulkhead.

His hand emerged grasping a rectangular, metal, flip-top container, about four centimetres by three centimetres by one centimetre deep. It was white, with the word WARNING stencilled in bright red across the top of it. Flipping the lid open he found four, tiny, glass capsules, a small amount of a powdery, white, crystalline substance within each, and each capsule singularly located in its own recess within the felt lined interior.

He gazed in mild fascination at the tiny cyanide phials. All a man had to do was crush one between his teeth, and. . . No, he determined, and he snapped the metal container closed. There were a lot of things needed to transpire before such an act could be entertained. Morgan looked about for somewhere to stow the container, finally deciding to return it to the *med kit* where he had discovered it, and where it belonged.

The moment has sobered him. If he was not fully focussed on the gravity of the situation before, the little white box had at last done the trick.

Hours passed. . . days turned to weeks. . . weeks went by without a single contact being made by way of *comms* or through the astro navigation station. There was only the constant, deep drone emitting from the heart of the craft as the little engine propelled the vessel and himself forward into the seemingly endless nothing of interstellar space. The drone constantly resonated throughout, defining his small world with its single, unvarying tone and filling every moment, the waking and the somnolent hours, both, with a dull, sonic background noise, permeating and fading everything of its definition and colour, encapsulating all within a single, unending and monotonous moment.

Morgan sat, frozen at the controls. His face, too, appeared frozen and expressionless. Once in a while the eyelids would slowly close, and after a time, open again; a blink in slow motion, as if the measure of time had slowed in relation to the absence of a single mote upon which the eye might come to rest beyond the *plexishield* view-screen of the cockpit. The protective shields had been furled in hope of sighting anything at all, and Morgan had not moved since that time.

The space inside the pod was wanly lit, the reduced illumination giving the sensation as if floating in the womb of eternity, the pod itself having faded from consciousness to leave him entirely exposed to the empty surroundings.

'Forever.' The word spilled from his lips, unbidden, his voice suffused with a haunted quality so that the single utterance felt to hang, unfading and everlasting within the atmospheric stillness of the pod.

Torpidity overwhelmed without the possibility of resistence. Sight ceased trying to penetrate or focus upon anything outward; there was nothing out there but the black void, and so sight had turned inward, to where images, spectral, at first, began to stir and coalesce, gradually coalescing into shapes and finally give rise to images more recognisable.

A slight shuddering made its presence known, increasing incrementally through the distorted duration of perceived time, banishing the steadily gathering phantoms which circled and threatened wholly to overrun the faculties. The reassuring drone of the engine became affected by an intermittent quality; infrequent and anomalus, a sound any long serving professional spacer could not leave undiagnosed and attended to.

With considerable effort Morgan willed the converging images out of his mind. There was something not right. Again came the anomaly in the sounds which had become a fully incorporated constituent of his world, accompanied almost immediately afterwards by the slightest of a shimmy throughout. An alarm sounded at the same instant that cognition took hold to alert him of the danger.

An atomic converter feeding power to an engine, once set in operation must be continually fed. Failure to attend to the duty resulted in *cycle suppression*, which would likely extinguish the process, and, because of the enormous battery drain required to restart the system, made the possibility of re-ignition next to impossible.

Startled, and still groggy, he rose from his position too quickly. With only a small amount of *antigrav* at work, making movement within the escape pod an easier proposition, his rapid and uncoordinated response sent Morgan bouncing off of the ceiling, to land crumpled against the rear bulkhead.

'*Christ!*' he cursed, his voice sounding strangled and hoarse for lack of moisture.

Morgan's disorientation persisted, but he forced self-composure; enough to crawl to the fuel storage cabinet. He quickly grabbed a carbon briquette, moved to where the converter sat against the wall, and insert it into the slide mechanism which fed the little brick into the converter. The vibrations continued to increase as he waited, terrified that he may have taken too long to react. In a little while the tremor lessened, minimally, then appreciable; and when, a minute later, the engine resumed its smooth, steady hum, he realised he had been holding his breath, almost to the point of losing consciousness.

He allowed himself to collapse sideways, and rolled onto his back, staring up at the curved ceiling, with the vents, electronic relay boxes and storage compartments installed. That had been close — far too close. He knew there was an alarm connected to the low fuel warning system, and he realised he must have slept though as it sounded the warning. It might have ended badly.

A sudden realisation gripped him. The fuel storage container. There had appeared to be so few briquettes when he had lifted the lid. With a groan, he climbed back to his feet and went to re- check the number. When he lifted the lid he was shocked by what he saw.

It was impossible! There were a great deal missing. There had to be. This could not be right. He counted without lifting them out, a procedure he should not be able to do if there were two hundred and eight in there. The box contained way less than half what ought to be there.

'. . . forty seven. . . forty eight!' he counted. 'No, no. Not possible. How?'

As unbelievable as it was, the count showed seventy five percent of the fuel had been consumed. He could only slump back against the wall in exasperation and disbelief. 'Not possible,' he said to himself, again. Not possible, and yet it was so.

As he pondered the conundrum, from deep within his mind surfaced snippets of memory; at least, what he assumed to be memory. Fractured glimpses of himself ran through his mind, rerunning the indeterminable duration which had preceded. The interior of the pod became crowded with overlapping instances of himself, moving from one area to another, engaged in sundry undertakings, from personal hygiene and consumption of calories to minimal maintenance procedures, undertaken less for any practical purpose than as a means to while away the passing of time.

He observed himself opening and closing cabinets, rearranging items for no particular reason. Morgan witnessed his multi spectral selves preparing nutritional supplement, brushing teeth, shaving, trimming fingernails; all the while feeling himself drawn ever deeper into the recollections until reality itself seemed to fracture and flow as countless parallel streams of existence.

It was not in the slightest a disconcerting event. The opposite was true; the cabin was now brimming with people, all of them himself. The fact only augmented the warm, comforting properties connected with familiarity and camaraderie. He never counted himself as someone needing inclusion in order to feel safe and comfortable. On the contrary, Morgan had always sought to distance himself whenever the opportunity presented itself. The prospect of marriage had been discounted for his love of absolute freedom and ability to live as whimsically as his profession would allow. Bushwalking, camping alone in the wilderness and trekking great distances through isolated and rugged landscapes was something he loved and felt compelled to do. Now, though; this was different, somehow.

How long he had been alone and idle with only his lately untrustworthy thoughts for company, there was no way to know since the vessel's chronometer had begun to misfunction, turning hours minutes and weeks into hours. In every moment that passed, there was less and less certainty to be had. The lack of stimulus during such a journey as this, he remembered from spacer training, impacted the human psyche in myriad ways until the lack of a rigid framework allowed the mind to lose itself for lack of any stimulus.

He used the thought in effort to force his mind to conform to a lifetime's indoctrination, but immediately he knew there was nothing for the powers of reason to grab a hold of: There was only the metal alloy shell, time, which had ceased to hold dominion, and all of eternity outside.

Stimuli! His powers of reason ceased upon the word like and iron hand. If he were going to retain the abilities of logic and reason he would need to supply stimuli. He held that reasoning fast in his mind before it escaped like water through a sieve, cursing all the while and frantically rifling through drawers, lockers and compartments for the item he was looking for.

Where is it? Where is it? Where, where are you? His voice raged and intensifying inside his skull as anxiety and fury rose uncontrollably.

The tool box he discovered strapped down at the back of the cabin, exactly where it had been stowed, according to lifeboat regulation. He forced open the lid so hard that it buckled the hinges, and grabbed out the hammer in triumph.

On the solid surface of a steel benchtop, he placed his hand, flat, face down, and raised the hammer. . . struck three times. *Pain* — piercing flashes of current coursed through his fingers, hand and arm on the fourth hammer-blow.

His screams stilled to whimpering as he slumped in the corner beside the fuel storage container. Why he had done this to himself, he could not fathom, but it had been violent enough of a jolt so that the fog which consumed him for so long, at least for now, was lifted considerably. But this was all that had been achieved; a temporary reprieve, but what actual use it served— Why? There was nothing to be done during however long the clarity would remain that he had not already done. He could only sit and moan with the pain he had caused himself. The left hand was now injured to the point of being almost useless useless. A serious handicap.

Slumped in the corner he was forced to review the line of thought which had brought him to this.

Stimuli. It had appeared to be a reasonable act at the time.

So this is how it goes? he thought. *If I cannot trust my own mind, what then?*

In the forum of his mind's eye Morgan saw a man swimming for all his worth against the flow of the tide, trapped in an unconquerable, implacable current, inching toward a massive waterfall which would sweep him from this life into endless oblivion.

'Why fight on?' he whispered to himself. Why did he even consider being able to last the distance? It was absurd even to entertain the possibility of survival. He was a spec — *less than a spec* — out here! Nobody would be searching or waiting. No one would miss his presence. For all practical purposes he was already dead; gone and forgotten, and the rest of them would be moving on without so much as a second thought. It was over. The fight was over.

How long he remained in that position ceased to have meaning. Like some kind of automaton without a will he found himself pulling open the drawer of the medical kit, reaching for the little white box, opening the lid to stare in fascination at the little glass phials, a sense of peace and certainty washing over him.

Laughter escaped without opposition. The laughter lacked mirth and all restraint, flowing, gushing forth like a burst tyre, the air of which had been compressed beyond tolerance; escaping at length, becoming still at last.

He cocked an ear, listening closely. A scratching sound, soft but it was there. He twisted about in attempt to discover the source, soon to be drawn to the pressure sealed storage chamber below deck.

His face betrayed instant horror. *'Shut up, Connor. You're dead!'*— but still the noise continued.

'Shut up. That's an order, Major!' — and he broke again into insipid laughter.

There had been no way to jettison the body of his fellow officer. Not without depressurizing the pod. As a compromise, he had sealed Connor below deck, where the absolute zero of interstellar space would snap freeze the corpse. The thought had occurred that, should rations run completely out, the major's body might serve as a valuable resource. It had only been a contingency; the thought of consuming human flesh appalled, *but one never knew until one's back was against the wall*, he reasoned.

The sound ceased, allowing Morgan to relax a little, and after binding his damaged hand and fashioning a crude sling from a torn strip of cloth, he moved to sit again at the pilot's station. Once again he raised the shields to look out into the depths.

His eyes lost focus, causing him to blink hard and shake his head in attempt to correct the problem. Peering a second time, his eyes found focus at the surface of the *plexishield* screen, as he caught sight of his own reflexion. The sight caught him so far off guard that it startled him, failing to recognise his own features. For one crazy moment he imagined someone had come to rescue him, but no. The realisation was crushing.

The face was unrecognisable with a full beard; and the gaunt, sallow features bespoke advanced malnutrition, and he looked to himself to be as somebody seriously ill, and who had been so for a very long time. It was more than he could bare, to witness such degradation.

From deep in his chest rose a piteous sound as Morgan sobbed uncontrollably, and began wailing as he called out to no one within a thousand million miles, *'It is too much. God — too much for a man to bear!'*

As he continued to moan and wail and curse, he did not hear the little *beep, beep, beeping* sound of the long range detection system which had been set at maximum gain in reaching out into the cosmos for contact with any far human outpost. His final shred of will and mortal endurance had at last been consumed. The sight of his own image reflected back to him had crushed out of existence all remaining hope of survival.

The pitiful sounds continued for a long time. Like a baby crying itself to sleep, his moaning and groaning took on an near musical quality, having the effect of soothing, almost caressing his tortured soul; and as he cried, sang, moaned consolingly to himself, all connection to existence began gradually to fade away. Sight turned inward one more; one final time.

As outward surroundings faded from view there came soft, swirling pastels; wisps of cloud drawing together as if he were viewing the aeons during which the billions upon billions of stars were gradually formed, the whole formative process tremendously accelerated so that transformation was viewed at fantastic speed. Within the whorls there moved shadows, silhouettes in shapes of people, and came faint voices, speaking in conversation. In the far distance, softly at first, came the sounds of children at play, shouting to one another, calling out, laughing. The trill of light-hearted, jubilant children conveying immense joy. The vision snapped rapidly into perfect clarity.

Vast, green fields. Children, exultant and frolicking across the verdant expanse. A boy child led at a sprint, towing a kite of many bright colours, the others giving pursuit, following in unbridled glee to witness the object of joy rise into the blue, sun- bright sky.

Such happiness filled Morgan's heart and soul in the remembrance of the occasion. He and his friends on that distant summer's day; so wonderful, so exultant, full of life and so carefree that it swelled his heart with the sweet pangs of innocence and all that was good and glorious in life.

The small boy running with the kite string grasped in his hand, it was himself, Morris Theodore Morgan, age six, gambolling across the open countryside, pursued by his long-ago childhood friends, and in that rapturous moment the universe in its totality was perfectly poised and precise, without mystery, without want or circumspection. It was elegantly poised, perfectly balanced, entire and complete without such incongruencies as a feeble human consciousness asking the absurd and inadequate question.

. . *Why?*

end

INNER REALMS

Foreword

What follows is a collection of surviving excerpts from my friend's notebook, most of which were found after Brian had apparently attempted to destroy them by setting fire to them in the fireplace of his home. Some notes were also recovered from beside his hospital bed, but, in all, little remains.

Brian and I have been friends since high school. He has always been a solitary fellow, given to single-mindedly following whatever novel idea crossed his mind, but his interest in meditation, the power of the human mind and even mysticism, he has remained deeply interested in for the whole time I have known him. One might say that it was his passion, perhaps even an obsession.

I have collected together the surviving notes as best I could, in the order in which they appear to have been written. Not much of the notebook survived the fire, but what remains outlines what I can only describe as, either the ramblings of a delusional mind, or something entirely beyond my ability to comment on in my position as a police detective. Whatever happened here, I am unwilling to comment on, and only these few pages of notes survive. I have laid them out, scrapbook fashion, to allow anyone coming across the collection to read and to form their own opinion.

I do still hold out hope of Brian turning up, one day, out of the blue. Perhaps it is all some kind of elaborate hoax? I devoutly hope that's all it is, although he wasn't exactly the sort to pull a stunt like this. Whatever happened here, these few notes appear to be all that remain to give any indication of what has been going on in his life. Personally, I prefer neither to comment nor speculate further on this matter.

Signed: Phillip H Lovejoy
(Detective Sgt .) Dated: June 8th, 1921.

Notebook _ Entry 223

The meditation routine I have used for some thirty eight years now, in order to facilitate sleep, has lately begun to take a surprising turn. Over the past months my practice of it has taken me into deeper states than I ever would have thought possible when first I began. What I have experienced is an absolute delight, and it is now only a matter of a few short minutes of a relaxed clearing of the mind, coupled with slow, easy and measured respiration, before I find I am able to quickly fall into the wonderfully serene state of mind it used to take me up to an hour's effort to achieve. I am so happy with results that I am thinking about branding the technique and using it as a means of helping people achieve levels of mental aptitude far beyond anything heretofore experienced, and from which I now enjoy immense satisfaction and delight.

    If only everybody could experience the wonder and the thill I feel of entering the largely undiscovered realms the mind is well suited for and uniquely capable of creating.

    I have attempted to relate my experiences to friends and those close to me, whom I felt sure would appreciate the subject, but none are willing to take the mention seriously. Indeed, at my turning the conversation to the topic of mental exercise, and the benefits thereof, all are quick to avoid further discussion and quickly change the subject, showing very little, if any, interest whatsoever, and I cannot fathom why that is. It clearly makes them uncomfortable where I surely felt that everyone would be interested. I was wrong about that. One would have thought they would want to experience something as extraordinary as this for themselves. I have formed the opinion that everybody is so attached to this drab, repetitious, rat race of a waking life, that heir minds are incapable of appreciating what I first began to pursue when I was a much younger man; but then I was always interested in the esoteric and the mysterious curiosities of the existential, and I guess I can understand why not everybody finds the life of the mind half as fascinating as I do.

In the beginning, I imagined that there must be dimensions of existence beyond which we are capable of detecting or experiencing, apparently being limited to the five main sensory perception organs we human beings possess. The sixth sense, concerning such as premonition or precognition, I became familiar with after picking up sundry books on the subject at an early age, and it was not until much later in life that I began to theorise that the universe might well consist of a great many layers of which we never even considered the possibility. I guess we must be forgiven for that. The most simple of creatures live their lives without the slightest knowledge of the larger world around them, and that is simply the way of it. Bacteria, for instance; even though they live in the same three dimensional world as do we, they have no knowledge, nor the need for knowledge of their situation beyond the medium in which they live. An earthworm knows nothing of the sky; a fish knows nothing of the continents and the world beyond water, and thus it may so very easily be with us. Although, we, unlike these creatures, possess both self-awareness and curiosity.

Why, with our purported intelligence which we are so quick to boast about, do we not realize our obvious limitations, that we in truth possess only little knowledge, and why do we not seek to fill the yawning gap, with generation upon generation not at all aware of, nor understanding of, the medium within which we ourselves exist, and blindly to do so without the slightest interest, continuing only to live in near total ignorance of the fact?

The question for most warrants no need for contemplation, and I suppose that must place me outside the category of most — a distinction which pleases me not at all. Such questions have ever given me reason to pause and consider, for at least a moment, and to contemplate the notion as best I was able. If there are dimensions of existence beyond our ability to detect them in even some small way, how then might we discover them?

This question needed to be left to lie for some years, and it was not until I again picked up the thread of the notion further along the track, that I realised how my periods of relaxing meditation at the end of every day might better be employed in further exploring the thing. During the several years following I tried to visualise the tendrils of intelligent consciousness reaching out, attempting to come into contact with anything which might conceivably be out there in the dark void, beyond our knowing; and although nothing came of it back then, my devout and relentless practice continued year upon year, purely as a kind of mystical experiment in order to see how far the concerted effort and resolute application of mind upon matter might take me.

As a part of my basic self-training I began by practising to generate mental images; simple sheets of colour brought to mind and held in plain and steady view. The creation of colour, I discovered, was a most effective means of exercising that particular area of the mind concerned with visualisation. Primary colours —red, yellow, blue— are at first not terribly easy to produce, yet after just a few nights of trying, one will find that they appear within the arena of the mind's eye without too much trouble. This colour exercise quickly became the warmup exercise for every night of training. Following the colour exercise the practice of visualizing simple geometrical shaped objects became a necessary next step. When proficiency was obtained I moved to other disciplines; areas of natural beauty which I had visited in the past, finding them to be a pleasant indulgence; countryside I had grown up in, beaches, long stretches of coastline and other prominent places remembered of the country's natural landscape.

After successfully training the mind to, at will, reproduce such vistas, I moved on, forming a floating, birdseye view, and to soar on high above the landscape, taking note of the many familiar landmarks, covering ever greater distances with every sortie undertaken. As the years of assiduous practice mounted until I came to the great adventure of escaping the confines of our planet, willing the consciousness to reach ever outward, toward the outer planets and on into deepest space, extending, in time, as far as neighbouring galaxies.

Notebook _ Entry 257

It was a difficult discipline at times, and quite taxing. I had often to return myself to the much less venturesome visualising of the neighbourhood, but as the years flowed by, and when visualisation had become more or less automatic, I came to enjoy simply allowing the mind's eye to wander wherever it pleased. The exercise so often transported me into vast, kaleidoscopic, exquisitely stimulating panoramas which I could have no understanding of, but, still, from which immense satisfaction was derived. It was during these wonderfully freewheeling flights of fancy, filled with imagery and unsurpassed, complex, beauty that new and interesting things began presenting.

Faces and people commenced to appear; sometimes unfamiliar creatures and weird abstractions accompanied by snatches of conversation; immense and complex machinery I understood not at all, storm clouds full of lightning and fury, flying machines in a bright azure sky; and all sorts of unrelated images would come, one after the other and in rapid succession. So clearly did they appear that one would think it was real life I glimpsed, rather than mere frenetic fabrications of a highly motivated and sharply honed mind.

By centring one's attention and concentration in a relaxed manner toward the portion at back of the scull (where lies t he visual cortex of the human brain) this is how images are most quickly arrived at. Then, by simply wiping the mind of all unwanted meanderings of thought, a voyage is embarked upon, needing no input by the viewer but taking the voyager on a journey beyond compare. To me this has become the most exciting of experiences imaginable.

This practice I have continued nightly over these fifty years. My mind knows, at once, when the head hits the pillow at the end of the day, what is expected; and of late it switches automatically to a kind of visual, free-range mode. Scarcely before I know it I am off, and carried into the most liberating of states of subconscious cognizance it has ever been my pleasure to experience.

Notebook _ Entry 292

I realise how fanciful my descriptions have become and I should mention to anyone who may stumble upon my notes, the kind of meditation cum visualization technique I practice is distinct and separate from dreaming.

When visualizing, I am able to control it totally; to form whatever I wish withing the theatre of my mind. Dreaming is a different function. Dreaming is the natural and entirely necessary function which serves to unwind the perplexed and overtaxed organ, sorting the information of a day or an extended time period, enabling correlation and accurate filing of data within whatever system the human mind employs after thousands of generations of perfecting the design. The two are separate and individual things. . . or at least, should be, and my understanding is that this is so.

Within me the two processes are, I think, beginning to spill over into one another. It was thrilling at the time it first occurred; a whole new experience I had heard whisper of but never experienced for myself. I have heard it called lucid dreaming, the process of experiencing a full blown technicolour dream while being able to control which way the narrative follows. I had come to think that lucid dreaming was no more than a figment of somebody's imagination—an aberration of some storyteller's mind, at best. But yes, they do exist, and since a few weeks ago they have become somewhat difficult for me to maintain control over. A vivid and lucid dream — a dream so realistic that it has substance enough to rival what is called reality. Such a dream as this is one thing, but when it gets away from the dreamer like a bolting horse? That is entirely another, and it frightened me enough so that I decided to give it a rest on the following nights. The trouble, however, is that my mind has become so trained to do what it does, it refused to obey my wishes. I resisted sleep for as long as I could, but when sleep inevitably claimed me, my mind did exactly as it has been trained to do over the decades. It materialised a most vivid and realistic concoction; neither dream nor conjured imagery was it, but a hybrid of some kind. I am elated and in awe. . . how real it was! A little fearful too, I should admit. So powerfully woven and genuine in the finest detail, it was no different to actual waking life. If anything, even more so. More intense — more real, if that is even possible?

Notebook _ Entry 299

I will remind the reader that the diary excerpts I use merely illustrate what I had been doing in the way of disciplining my mind in the way of mediation visualization techniques, and also to show how I had become so captivated by the process, in view of progress made over the many years. It proved to me that, with sufficient practice the mind could be taught to function in ways other than how we were using them in the course of our everyday lives. During earlier periods, the practice was no more than something from which I derived pleasure at day's end before I slept. It was little more than a curiosity, but then there came a change and I was confronted with something new and very different. I suspected perhaps I was at the threshold of something we of the western world had no inkling of, and I searched around for anything related, but found almost nothing at all of interest. There was only the occasional mention of transindental meditation being used in Eastern monasteries, and mention of its use in the martial arts and for its occasional application in avoiding physical pain: the usual sort of thing we in the West are used to hearing. I soon got the feeling that, if anything approaching this type of mind-bending meditation was being taught and practiced anywhere in the world, it was being kept out of the limelight. I doubted that anyone beyond the initiated would be privy to what was, most probably, being treated as arcane and guarded knowledge. Unless I was prepared to traipse into the Himalayas, searching for ancient orders within even more ancient monasteries, I felt sure there would be nothing someone like myself would be permitted access to. I would simply continue with my own research,

I decided, and at the prospect of it I was both excited and, to be honest, a little intimidated.

In pursuit of finding exactly how deep into uncharted territory my search might take me, I took to tiring the body during the course of the day by doing such chores as chopping wood with an axe, taking long, cross-country walks and whatever other activity I could use in order to put myself in a suitable condition for the nightly expeditions. It was not a condition of somnolence I searched for; my view is that physical exertion releases endocrines into the body which most favourably alter the consciousness, facilitating just the right state of mind; one more conducive and allowing reception of the smallest influence of whatever it was that I felt I was tapping in to. A wavelength, perhaps. A frequency redolent throughout the cosmos, connecting all things and traversing all dimensions. The fact that gravity was still beyond the understanding of our best cosmologists indicated to me that there was ample room for speculation. It had been documented that many of the experts making quantum physics their area of expertise, believe that gravity is a force originating outside of our three dimensional existence, affecting us greatly while having equal affect within those dimensions yet unknown and undetectable to us. In this time where the leading edge of our scientific knowledge is almost daily discovering many more mysteries than it is answers, such speculation into the nature of reality was far from being irrational or absurd.

Notebook _ Entry 301

I have discovered a new realm of existence. The world I knew, the world I was born into as a child, is now one of many I have come to discover. The visions which once were mere abstractions generated by the mind whist in the deeply meditative state, have become much more. I have so altered the way the inner sanctum of my mind works, with the lifelong practice of remote viewing and envisioning places unreachable by any other means, that I suspect I have rewired the synaptic pathways and so now the condition has become permanent. It is not a singular event. There are many documented reports of people's brains and nervous system, after injury, rewiring the circuitry until speech, for instance, or hearing is restored. Paraplegia too; nerves can regenerate and find new pathways until connection is restored. In this manner I am sure my prolonged training has rewired my own brain, and now, what once were only conjured visions within the mind, seemingly have become actual places within an augmented reality. But how to be sure? All this is purely subjective. Am I now making connection with worlds once beyond the senses ability to reach, or is my grasp on the single reality I have always known, slipping, being muddled in with all the new and wondrous worlds I have discovered in recent time?

So much has happened in the past few days that I can hardly take it in, and it's beyond my control to make it stop. A man must sleep, and to sleep is to trigger the mechanism which whisks me away to I know not where. Are these places real, or are they illusion? There is no difference I can detect and it is exactly as I have speculated all along. Whatever is fed to the mind by way of the senses, the brain interprets into a whole package which is our reality. What is being fed to my brain now is not through the five senses but through some kind of ethereal conduit. The result, though, is essentially the same. I can no longer make the distinction and already I am fully believing of the fact that I am passing through a most incongruous portal, into new and viable realms of existence beyond my understanding. My single universe has given way in favour of the existence of a multi-verse of endless possibility!

Notebook _ Entry 304

God, I almost did not return. An alternate world I visited, and from there I fell into another sleep, was again transported and almost lost my way. I must be very cautious. Portals within portals and I could be lost forever from this world. I have no doubt, not a one, that this is one of a thousand possible worlds. I find myself at the edge of an unlimited number of possible worlds. The universe is a dream. Life and existence is a dream. It flies in the face of all that we know. If all is a dream, then who does the dreaming? How does it work? Is the vast and complex everything just one unending possibility? I am very tired but dare not sleep for fear of what may happen, and where I might end up. I need to think things through.

Notebook _ Entry 305

Twelve days have elapsed since my last entry and I am writing this from my hospital bed. I realise I was lucky even to get back here for what will surely be the last time. I cannot maintain a grip on this world any longer, and the next time I sleep will be the end of this life. My body deteriorated dreadfully with my not being able to maintain water intake and nourishment. If an old friend had not come by and discovered my plight, I wouldn't be here now; but where I was, in the other realm, I felt no detrimental effects. I cannot know without driving my mortal body to is expiration, whether or not I will continue to exist in the place where my consciousness dwells, but I know that I am about to find out.

My impending death does not frighten me in the least, however. If I am to die of malnourishment while on a voyage to some impossible place, it will be a most acceptable way to pass. Yet, I am hopeful that death in this realm will not constitute my death in the next; I believe I will continue on, and the worlds on offer are so much more fulfilling than this one. Our world stands apart from all those I have visited, in the way we have spoiled everything that nature provided for us in our beginning. My sense of shame is enormous, but there is nothing to be done at this late stage. We have already set in motion the blueprint of our demise, and that is the end of the matter. Perhaps there is the slim chance that, after my passing, these notes will provide a possible means of escape for those good souls who are undeserving of mankind's fate as a whole. There are so many who do not deserve what is in store, and I have seen what is to come.

I have not bothered to mention any of what is contained in this notebook to my attending doctors. They are treating my case as an anomalous form of narcolepsy, and I will allow them to continue thinking exactly that. I have refused medication; I do not need to be interfered with during this last, important stage. For the moment I will rest without allowing sleep to overtake me, and this evening I will eat what the hospital provides, to give myself something of a nutritional boost as I leave this arena for what I expect to be the final time. There is a place I know, where other intelligent beings exist in a world beautiful beyond words, and I will dwell in that place for as long as I am able.

If, when this mortal body expires, so too do I, then, so be it. But if, as I hopefully suspect, that some unknown energy source allows for my continuance, then I will live on and further explore all there is to be explored in life. Either way this gamble goes, I have enjoyed this thing called life, and if it is oblivion that awaits, I do not fear it. It is what I was born from and it makes for a perfect cycle of existence for me to return again to it. Nothing lost, nothing gained, but it is my belief that if the cosmos gives birth to such a thing as a soul, that soul has much further to travel than what is bound up in a singe life cycle of an intelligent being called a man. That hypothesis is yet to be bourne out, and unfortunately there is no way to have the result conveyed back into this world I am about to depart.

From an exercise book left at the bedside_

Of the thirty three worlds I have discovered, my favourite world is called *Quibyx*, and it is where I intend to return. There is no written language in that word, so my spelling of the name is simply a phonetic version of how it is pronounced. The people there are, to me, like giant cherub. A most pleasant race of beings, but that is not the most unusual feature of their physical appearance. All have four arms, but with the usual number of legs as that we have. The terrain is mountainous, very similar to our Himalayas. Every bit as tall and rugged. The *Quibyxm*, as they call themselves, pursue knowledge, and have done so for countless generations; and through the pursuit of knowledge for so long a time have developed great intellect — a pure form of intellect, and do not concern themselves with trivial matters. Nor do they squabble and worry about accruing personal possessions, or seek to raise themselves in the esteem of others. They seek only to exist and to learn the secrets of the universe they inhabit. A most laudable race of beings.

The elders —*the wise ones*, as they are called— are able to fly; a form of levitation which is practiced from very early in life, and is seldom achieved before they have lived a great many years. There is no measurement of time in their world and it is impossible to tell how long a life they might live, but in my estimation it takes perhaps eighty of our years before they reach maturity. I think the wise ones could be seven hundred years by our measure. It's difficult to say. There is an ethereal quality to them; something which elevates them beyond the purely physical and because of the means of my arrival, they see a kind of kinship between us.

They have welcomed me as one who also seeks knowledge and I am enormously privileged to be so. I am as a child to them, but they have never met a stranger before, and they honour my differences. Can you imagine? On our world, difference is abhorred. The have promised to instruct me on my *road to knowledge*. The road to knowledge as how they perceive life.

They live high, high up in a cliff face, where an entire city has been carved within sandstone like edifices. A marvel! So wonderful. Sky caves; and there is a temple at the summit where only the flying cherub holy men can visit. The holy men are most esteemed and possess knowledge of the ages; accessible, eventually, to all who walk the road of knowledge and just a matter of continuing. A birthright and accessible to everyone who persevere.

If I had the time I would document all that I have discovered. It's all so wonderful but there is no time left now. I regret having burned my notebook. I did it in a fearful moment, afraid that is mankind found a way to follow, they would do as they have always done and ruin it. I only hope we can change our ways. Maybe someone else will discover what I have been lucky enough to find. In a much later period of our development, I hope. When we have grown up. I canno0t concern myself with such concerns any longer. The cosmos will deal with us as she sees fit. Whatever happens, I'm sure there will be justice in it.

Time is getting short. I hear the clatter of the meals being brought into the ward. I will nourish this body one last time, and throw the dice. To my friends, I say, 'It has been a pleasure to know you all. I have enjoyed this life and enjoyed knowing you all. Who knows, perhaps we will all meet again some day, on the other side.

Adieu.'

—end—

DOUGIE'S CHOICE

Douglas Randal Peterson, Dougie to his friends, was almost ten years old. If asked he will tell you he is nine and three quarters years-old, because accuracy was important to Dougie. At last measurement, made against his bedroom door, he had stood at three feet eleven and three quarter inches. In metric that was equal to one hundred and twenty and a bit centimetres, and while being not nearly enough, his father had told him, 'Many's a fine thing to be found in a small package,' although it hadn't helped a whole lot at the time. His father was a good six feet six inches and presented a dominant figure in any room. He hoped to grow as tall one day, but, he supposed, right now it didn't matter all that much.

It was 8:55 on a Saturday morning, and there were things to be done. The sky was bright and blue, with hardly a cloud in the sky. The main street of Ingle Vale was not yet busy with traffic and there were barely half a dozen folk out and about, doing the things people usually do on a lazy summer's morning in a small town.

Dougie halted in front of Larson's display window at the Hobby & Sporting Goods Emporium. Old Mrs Larson and her nephew, Harry, ran the only hobby shop cum sporting goods store for many miles around. In the window were displayed aeroplane models, electric trains, meccano sets and even robots that walked up and down, patrolling the treasures like some futuristic sentinel landed from planet-X. Dougie's eyes grew wide as he peered in through the window, catching sight of the many aeroplane models suspended by fishing line from the ceiling: Focke-Wulf seeming to be locked in battle with a Spitfire. A P51 Mustang and Hurricane banked and turning hard in mortal combat. How wonderful they looked. His piggy-bank had not given up nearly enough. For all the chores he had done; the wood chopping, the car cleaning, pushing the mower up and down the yard, there was only twenty-one dollars, but enough, he was sure, for the *Airfix* model he had his eye on since the last time he wondered through the aisles.

At precisely nine o'clock Mrs Larson ambled up to the door and unlocked the top and bottom bolts, inserted her key to turn the deadlock, and, at last, swung open the door.

'Dougie, what a surprise!' Mrs Larson greeted, but of course it was no surprise at all. Every Saturday morning for the past five weeks, Dougie had waited at the step, eager to enter the store and pour over the treasure trove within.

'Hello,' he replied brightly. 'Is it here?'

'Not yet, Dougie,' the old lady replied sympathetically, 'but I'm sure it won't be long now. All this month's orders should arrive next Saturday, in the morning. Can you wait that long, do you think?'

He nodded. 'I suppose so—' there was obvious disappointment in his voice. 'Can I look around anyway?'

'*Of course!*' —her voice pitched with an ascending lilt. 'We have some new dinosaur models. Over there in the corner,' she told him, and pointed in the direction towards the back of the store.

'Great,' he replied, already heading off in the direction indicated. 'Thanks, Mrs Larson.'

'You're welcome, young man—' and she could not help but smile in watching him resist the temptation to run.

Saturday mornings in summertime were one of life's true delights, and before very long school would be breaking up for the holidays. All that time to spend exploring, it filled a boy with exultation and anticipation. There were the many trails leading deep into the countryside, the olive groves, the picnic grounds, gullies and streams along which the massive gum trees clutched at the banks, providing ample shade under which to cool while waiting for yabbies to crawl into cunningly set traps, and that very afternoon found him doing just that.

His friend, Timothy Goldsmith — *Mothy*, to his friends —had been discovered pushing a mower across his parents front yard, and while Dougie stopped to pass the time of day with him, the outing had been planned; but, of course, only after the Saturday morning chores had been completed, and so Dougie had pitched in to help, the faster to get to the fun part of the day.

The creek water was still, tea coloured and quite deep. There had been some late season rain which had nicely filled the creeks and streams throughout the landscape. On the green and grassy embankment under the shade of a river gum, the boys cast their kerosene tins, punctured with a garden fork and baited with meat off cuts tied with wire, into the deep pool at the base of the tree. There to wait leisurely until it was time to pull them out again.

It was one of those days. The heat wrapped the countryside in a lulling, torpid spell. There was the trickle of water melodiously spilling over the edge of the pool, where a fallen branch had piled up with other debris to create the natural dam. The sky was a cloudless sheet of pale blue in which the occasional hawk was seen to hover, fluttering and sailing on unseen currents, high up, searching for movement in the tall, yellowing grassland which stretched away and was lost to the distance.

The air, if one listened, was fairly alive with sounds. Insects unseen, bees and who knew what else contributed to a constant hum — *the hum of life,* Dougie thought, being in a contemplative mood — imbuing the surroundings with a most wonderful sense that God was in his heaven and all was right with the world.

In the treetop, a lone crow sat, *cawing,* perhaps calling to a neighbour; and then, in the distance came a response from another, similarly perched. In the lower branches, sparrows, finches and willy wagtails flittered about, chasing the numerous flying insects and snatching them out of the air.

The boys lay languidly at the water's edge, peering into the depth, searching for critters moving across the bottom of the creek bed among the stones, saturated leaf piles, sticks and bark that lay about down there, making detection of their quarry difficult.

'We got the report cards comin' soon,' Mothy said, breaking the spell.

Dougie, poking a stick into the muddy embankment, replied without turning to his friend. 'Yeah, I know. And I know what mine will say already, do you?'

29

'Miss Ryan says I'm *ram-*, ram-*bunctious*, but I don't know if that's good. Is it good, rambunctious?'

'I dunno. Sounds good, Dougie suggested. 'Is that all?' 'Energetic. That's good, being energetic, isn't it? My last report card said I was easily distracted. My dad said—' and he made his voice sound as deep as he could manage, for effect: 'You had better pull up your socks, young man, or you will be left behind.'

'He said that? *Left behind?*'

Mothy laughed. 'Yeah. How do you get left behind? Left behind what?'

Dougie thought for a moment, then shrugged. 'It's the sort of thing grownups say. He was just trying to scare you into doing better.'

'Yeah. That's what I thought, too.'

Suddenly there was a sound. It was a buzzing sound, and despite their looking all around they could not find the source of it. Not until it had gotten real loud, and real close.

'Look!' Mothy called, pointing skyward. Just above tree-top level wheeled a model aeroplane, buzzing so loud that it scattered the birds from the trees.

'It's a model Pit Special,' he told his friend. 'Isn't it great?' 'Yeah. Is it ever?'

They watched, necks craned and hands shielding the bright sunlight from their eyes as the red and white replica looped, barrel rolled, climbed, dove and banked around the trees at terrific speed.

'Boy, she really goes fast,' Mothy observed. 'Pit Special, the best ever stunt plane made. At least, the real ones are. But this sure is fast, ain't it?'

'Sure is.'

The model aircraft flew out of sight after a while, it's buzz eventually lost, and the boys once again settled quietly beside the creek.

'That was great,' Mothy commented one last time.

Dougie became thoughtful and rolled onto his back, staring upward at the vast blueness for a long while. At last he turned to his friend.

'My dad was in the war. Was yours?'

'He was infantry. A footslogger, he says, but he don't much talk about it and I don't ask cos he don't like to, I think.'

'My dad's the same, but he was in the RAF. Lancaster bombers, you know? Flying bomb-rack, he says, and he's got photos, and in a box he's got medals and stuff, but he doesn't say nuffin' either. Why do you suppose they don't want to talk about it?'

'The killin', I reckon,' Mothy replied. 'Mum wouldn't like it.' 'Did your dad ever kill anyone?'

'Sure he did, he just don't talk about it. He must have killed lots.'

'How do you know if he don't say?'

'It stands to reason,' Mothy replied, somewhat indignant. 'Of course he killed some of them. Lots even, I bet.'

Dougie thought about killing for a moment — about having to shoot someone or drop bombs from an aeroplane from up in the clouds.

'If I had to kill someone, I'd rather do it with a bomb, from high up so I don't have to see their faces and hear it. Imagine how it would be to shoot 'em. He pretended to raise his rifle and took aim at his friend. *Pow!* Dead as a dodo. How would that feel?'

'For me or you?'

'For the one with the gun, dummy. The other guy don't feel nothin'.'

'You think? What if you just winged me? I'd pull out my knife and *slit yer gizzards!—*' and he launched himself, stick in hand, and wrestled Dougie down until the stick was pushed up against his friend's throat. 'Prepare to meet your maker, *yer mangey dog.*'

'I give up already,' Dougie replied, laughing hard. 'I'd rather be taken prisoner.'

Mothy released his captive and rolled away to brush himself off. 'Good choice, but I bet them guys didn't get no choice. They just–' and he drew his finger across his throat in demonstration.

'I'd rather get bombed,' Dougie replied, considering. 'You wouldn't even know that nothin' was comin.' One minute you're just sittin' there, maybe eaten your roast dinner, and the next— *Boom!* No more anything.'

'Yeah, just gone. But where to?'

'Heaven, of course. Unless. . . ' He pointed downward. 'You know. . . *Hades,*' he expressed gravely. 'Damned to the hellfire of Hades and screaming for all of time and evermore.'

'What? You believe that stuff?' His friend regarded Dougie quizzically for a moment. 'You reckon there's a *Heaven* and a *Hell?*'

'Not really.' he replied, unconvincingly. 'No. Of course not. Do you?'

'That stuff is for weaklings. I ain't no sap.' Then, relaxing his position a little. 'Leastways, that's what my dad says. He says that there ain't no such thing and that we just made *Him* up cos we're scared and can't take the truth.'

'And you reckon that's right?'

'Who cares?' Mothy responded, suddenly uncomfortable. 'Maybe we should check them tins now. I hope we got some.' When the kerosene tins were pulled up by their ropes, there was not even enough yabbies in them to make a small meal. The prudent decision was made to let the little creatures return to the stream, where they might grow and be caught another day. 'Hey,' said Dougie, appearing to have thought of something prodigious. 'Why don't we go down to the cemetery?'

'Why would we want to go there?' Mothy asked, a somewhat concerned look upon his face.

'Because I know for a fact that there's a soldiers' part, where soldiers and sailors and aeroplane guys are buried there, and we can look at the gravestones and read about what happened maybe. It'll be really interesting, I bet. Don't you think?'

Mothy didn't appear to be half as keen, but he shrugged in halfhearted approval, not wanting his lack of enthusiasm be misinterpreted as anything suggesting that he didn't much like graveyards.

'Sure. If you want to.'

'Alright, let's go,' Dougie affirmed, and stood, ready to go. The boys collected their bikes from home on the way through, and cycled the one mile journey to the far south-west edge of town, where was situated the Ingle Vale cemetery; a large expanse of well kept, undulating ground, very peaceful and beautifully land-scaped, and with a variety of trees interspersed throughout.

The serviceman's section of the site was set in one corner; a particularly beautiful area with an occasional statue depicting angels and crosses. Commemorative statues depicting the three branches of the armed services stood at its centre, where benches had been placed on a paved area circling them: three, life-sized, concrete figures dressed in uniform, gazing out toward the centre of the township, looking splendid in the late afternoon sun.

The boys let their bikes drop to the pavement and stood there at its base, scrutinizing the sculptures. Mothy noticed the brass plaque and stepped forward to read the inscription.

'In honour of all who served. With deep appreciation and everlasting gratitude we remember those who made the ultimate sacrifice. Lest we forget.'

'Lest we forget,' Mothy repeated. *'Lest?'* He turned to his companion. 'What do you suppose that means?'

'Unless?' Dougie attempted, shrugging.

'Unless we forget? It doesn't quite make sense, but it has to mean we oughtn't to forget. Like what they did. . . sacrificing so we could go on livin' how we want. You reckon?'

'That's got to be it,' Dougie agreed. They fought so we could be free and live how we want to, instead of, you know, being told what to do all the time.'

'By who?'

'The bad guys. *Charlie.* . . and *Gerry.* . . and. . . I forget the others. But there was lots of 'em. *Johnny Turk,'* he suddenly remembered.

Mothy began to laugh. 'Who's Charlie and Gerry?' 'Come on, let's check out them gravestones.'

'Who's Charlie? Mothy persisted, but Dougie only wheeled his bike away without further response.

Nearby stood a most prominent construction, with concrete angels blowing concrete trumpets and cherubim circling a concrete cross with the figure of a man attached to it.

Mothy drew closer, the better to view the construction. '*Wow!* What do you reckon that is?'

They stared at it for a long moment in silence. Dougie took note of the little building over which the monument loomed. There was writing etched into the stonework—writing which had weathered badly and become indistinct over the years.

'It's called a *mau-sole-um*,' Dougie answered. 'How do you know that?'

Dougie pointed to the weather worn inscription. "Cuase that's what it says it is—' and he tried to read from it.

'This *mau-sole-um* was gifted by the sRotary Club of Ingle Vale, in gratitude to the eleven POW' who perished while fighting the bush fires which threatened our town in the Summer of 1941. *RIP all who rest here.*'

'Perished.'Dougie and Mothy turned, surprised, to discover who had spoken.

'Hello, lads. Come to pay your respects, have you?'

It was the grounds keeper; and elderly gentleman dressed in coveralls, a straw hat on top and holding a rake in one hand, a spade in the other.

'Yes sir,' Mothy replied.

'Hello, Mr McBride.' Dougie recognised his neighbour from two doors down from his house. Everyone knew the old man as Clary.

'Hello Douglas. Who's your friend?'

'I'm Timothy, but everyone calls me *Mothy*. Are you a gravedigger?'

The presumptuous question struck Clary as being terribly amusing, and laughed appreciatively. 'Oh dear, no,' he replied, chuckling still. I look after the grounds here, Mothy. What are you boys up to?'

'We was talking about being in a war,' Dougie volunteered, and I said, *Why don't we go and look at the gravestones, 'cos it would be interesting and stuff.*'

'Oh, I see,' said Clary. 'Have you been here before?' The boys shook their head in unison.

'No? Well, would you like me to show you around? I've pretty much finished for the day, anyhow. I'll just put these away and come right back. I can show you some of the more interesting sites. What do you say?'

34

Dougie and Mothy figured that was a fine idea, and they waited while Clary went to stow his tools and lock the shed. When he returned he found them curiously circling the marble commemoration stone.

'A good starting point,' he told them, coming up alongside. 'There are seventy one names on that list. All of them came from this little town or from surrounding properties. Some of them went to war thinking it would be an adventure, something more exciting than milking cows and mending fences on the family farm. Some were sons of shopkeepers, mill workers.

Everyday people and from every walk of life. Some of them thought it was their duty as Australians and members of the British Commonwealth; and I suppose there were as many reasons as there were volunteers.

'All the major wars are represented here. From the First World War, the Second World War, Viet Nam and even Afghanistan and Iraq, but that was a mistake.'

'Why was it a mistake?' Dougie asked.

'It was based on a lie,' Clary answered. 'My own son was lost in that one.'

The boys were silent, not knowing at all what one was supposed to say in such a circumstance.

Mothy pointed to the left of the memorial, where a brass plaque included an illustration of horse mounted soldiers. 'What's that one about?'

'The cavalry?' Clary replied. 'All of the old-timers are gone now. Quite a few from around here were a part of the Australian Light Horse Brigade in the First World War. Fine horsemen they were, too. Do you remember George Wilson, at the service station that used to be at the end of Main Street?' The boys nodded in unison. 'He was the last from around here who fought in the deserts around Palestine.

'They were tough lads. . . and tough horses too. You boys ever see the movie, *Forty Thousand Horsemen*? Heard of *the charge of the Light Brigade*? That was way back in 1917. Some of these boys—' he said pointing to the roll of honour '—where right in amongst that.'

'Gosh! Really?' Timothy and Dougie looked up in admiration at the sepia photo encased in plastic. 'Them guys were from around here?'

'They sure were. And even some of the horses from around these parts were rounded up and shipped out along with them.

Walers. A tough breed, just like those who rode and cared for them.'

'Yeahh!' Dougie agreed. 'Boy, that's great. What else you got to show us?'

Old Clary enjoyed the tour of the cemetery almost as much as Dougie and Timothy. He showed them where the hometown air force boys, the infantry lads and the navy men lay at rest. He regaled them with accounts of battles he recalled from all the wars the country had fought in, some of the stories recounted and handed down from his grandfather, who had been a First World War gunnery sergeant and served in the battle of the Somme.

That night, as Dougie lay, waiting for sleep to come, his head was filled with images of charging horses, the slouch hat, khaki uniformed soldiers of the 4th Australian Light Horse bent forward in the saddle, their swords drawn and flashing under the Egyptian sun, and with teeth bared, galloping full tilt into the fray at the battle of Beersheba.

He woke in the early hours before dawn, to stare out of his bedroom window. In the stillness the images stayed with him, until, an interminable time later, he slipped once more into an uneasy sleep filled with dreams.

There were battles fought a thousand feet in the air, with biplanes buzzing and diving about, the rattle of machine gun fire, spouting flames, men in uniform crying out as they fell in a spiralling death plunge to the ground below.

There were great juggernauts of the ocean, locked in perilous exchanges; gun turrets and flames spouting from deafening muzzle blasts and explosions of flying, white hot metal; roiling black smoke and men leaping for their lives into a frigid sea.

There were trenches filled with filth, men shivering, cold and hungry; hand to had fighting as soldiers grappled for their lives against other human beings likewise engaged and desperate, wanting only to survive and to go home to their families and loved ones.

The images grew ever more fearsome, filled with a dread spectre of something chilling and altogether evil; the kind which a nine year-old had no defence against, so that to end it he called out in forlorn hope that it was only a dream, which, to his immense relief, he discovered it was, and he found himself sitting up in the wan and pale light of a new day, chilled by the images of war.

As he thanked God it had been nothing more than what it was, a nightmare brought on by the excitement of the preceding day, he wondered how he himself would fare in such circumstances, and he found himself praying to God that he would never be so unfortunate as his forebears, and have to find out exactly what kind of courage it took to endure such a reality.

In the days which followed Dougie could not quite shake the ghost of the horrifying experience. Even though the days were as bright and warm and full of colour and movement as any day could be, he felt sad inside. He was sad because he had been given a glimpse of how it really must have been, and if mankind was capable of creating such a hell as this for himself, what did it really say about humankind?

The harrowing stories he had watched in the evening news until now, they had been only images on the screen. . . and nothing more. Now he understood their meaning, and fully appreciated the suffering he had viewed but never really seen.

The world had suddenly come into focus for Dougie; it was no longer a world full of Christmas carols, the Easter bunny and ice-cream. This was the hard-edged reality of the world in which he lived: Beersheba, the Somme, Hiroshima, smart bombs, chemical and germ warfare, politics and hatred, all the things he had heard in the background but never paused to really take notice of. He knew he had changed in a way which could never be reversed. Perhaps this was what they meant when grownups said, *You will understand when you're older.* How many more such awakenings were in store? he wondered.

At school he continued to be distracted. History lessons took on a whole new meaning and it was the only lesson which fully captured his attention. In the schoolyard he watched his friends play the usual games but had difficulty joining in the merriment. After dinner each evening he watched the six o'clock news with his parents, witnessing, as if for the first time, the true horror of events displayed on the screen.

How could this be allowed? he wondered. Phrases like *'man's inhumanity to man'* leapt immediately to mind, and *'the war to end all wars,'* which he had heard countless times in reference to the First World War. But still mankind had found endless reasons to kill and maim one another, and it would probably continue this way, until, one day, we would likely take aggression a step too far, destroy ourselves along with the only home we have. How did it get to be this way?

He kept these thoughts to himself all week. His parents did notice the slight preoccupation which had overtaken him, but they were busy with their own concerns; and, anyway, it was not unusual for a boy of his age to become a little moody. It was all a part of growing up, they agreed, and so the days went along as usual, from one to the next.

Nine o'clock the following Saturday morning did not find Dougie on the step of Mrs Larson's Hobby & Sporting Goods Emporium as she had expected. She unlocked and opened the front doors as she usually did on a Saturday, expecting to find young Douglas Peterson eagerly waiting to pose the question — *Is it here yet?* — as he had on every other Saturday morning for the last three weeks. She had been so looking forward to witnessing the look of delight on the boy's face when, at last, she was able to say, 'Yes, Douglas, it's here!'

In the beginning, she had not been too pleased about the order. In her view boys should not own such items and their fathers should know better, but Dougie's enthusiasm and patience had softened her outlook, just a little. After raising three boys of her own, it was difficult not to be affected by such a thing as a child's expectation and excitement, whatever the reason might be.

Dougie's father came quietly to his son's bedroom door with a broad smile on his face and stood, observing the boy pouring over one of the adventure magazines which he had lately shown great interest in.

'Did you have any plans for today, Douglas?' he asked, now disguising his mirth.

'Not really, dad. I don't feel like doing much.' 'Take it as it comes, you reckon?' his father replied.

'Yeah,' Dougie responded, a little despondently his father thought.

'Well I thought we might, I don't know. . . maybe do a little hunting? There's plenty of ferrel goats up on uncle Dave's farm that need culling.

Dougie closed the magazine he had been reading and turned to view his father. He looked so pleased with himself, with a broad grin from ear to ear.

'That was Mrs Larson on the phone, just now. Come on, champ. Let's go, shall we?'

Dougie sat in the front passenger seat while his father steered the converted Holden pickup down the main street. It had been fitted out with shooting racks behind the back seat, where the rifles and shot gun could be stowed; a bar fitted above the roof, bound with hessian, where the shooter could stand, taking aim while resting the gun over it for stability. On the front were bolted a sturdy bull-bar and an array of lights which could pierce the darkness for hundreds of yards, and at the driver's side window, a powerful spotlight had been affixed. The driver could both steer and point the spotlight at an animal while the guys in back took care of the rest.

His father parked out front and the two of them entered the store. At the counter, Harry, Mrs Larson's nephew, busy with labelling items before putting them on the shelves ready for sale, looked up to greeted the pair.

'I believe we have a parcel for you, young fellah,' he said, grinning, and furtively offering a knowing nod to Jim Peterson. He turned toward the back of the shop. 'Gwen? Gwen! We have a customer, here to pick up his parcel. Master Peterson and his dad are here.'

Mrs Larson emerged from the back of the store, where she had been unpacking the deliveries. 'Hello,' she greeted, offering a large smile. 'Here at last?' she said to Dougie.

Harry bent to retrieve the item from under the bench; it became apparent then, that Gwen had wanted to be present when Dougie took possession of the item.

Harry placed the long carton on top of the bench, lifted the cardboard lid to reveal the semiautomatic, .22 rifle, complete with telescopic sights.

'She's a beaut, ain't she?' Jerry Peterson enthused, beaming at his son. 'And telescopic sights, too! Is that something, or what?' Two weeks ago Dougie would have agreed. He loved and admired his father as much as any son ever did. He would have said, *'Wow, it's a beaut, dad,'* and the two of them would have spent much of the remainder of the day out in the countryside, stalking wild animals and helping local farmers with their feral goat problem.

Jerry Peterson saw that his son was having difficulty. That he had been distracted by something, these past few days, had not gone unnoticed, but he and mum both had decided to let the boy work it out, whatever it was. He would come to them if he needed advice, they felt sure. But now? Well, he didn't quite know.

'What is it, son?' he asked. 'What's on your mind?'

Dougie looked into the faces of each in turn, knowing if he did not speak up, right then and there, that the charade would only go on, and perhaps the moment would be forever lost.

'I don't want it any more.' He said it clearly and decisively. 'I don't want to kill anything. I want to be a man of peace.'

The words had come out with a more powerful effect than he had intended, but it was said, now, and he could only prepare for the unhappy response.

For quite a long time, it felt to him, his dad, Mrs Larson and her nephew, Harry, seemed to be lost for words. Maybe it was because it wasn't something a nine-year-old said, back then. The words had even sounded odd to him, once he had uttered them, and of all the moments to say it, well, he had to admit that he had left it until a bit late in the piece to back out.

'I understand,' his father said. And clearly, he really did.

You see, I am that little boy, Dougie, and back then children of that age did not have an opinion, if you understand my meaning. At the age of nine, children were only children, and everybody knew that little boys wanted to be just like their father, and if that meant grabbing a gun and killing wild animals, well, that's how it was. But kids were already growing up with television and the world was being brought into the family lounge room via the six o'clock news every evening. Or maybe it wasn't so much that fact? Maybe it was just who I was and for the first time in my life I felt I had to stand up for what I felt in my bones was right. In this case it meant saying that I did not especially think that killing was such a great idea; that I wanted nothing to do with it. That exact moment was the first time in my short life that I had any sense of who I was — of what or who I wanted to be!

My father could have cajoled me, told me, 'Come on boy, we'll have a lot of fun,' or any number of things, and that is precisely what I had expected. I might have folded, ceded to his wishes and walked out of there with my first gun, and gone on to do other things contrary to what, during that week of self- confrontation, I had decided I did not want to do, and be forever changed because of it. But that was not the way my father had played it.

'I understand,' he had said, despite his brief moment of embarrassment.

Maybe it's a very small thing. Maybe I make too much out of it, but I sometimes reflect on that moment, all those years ago, and always with great fondness.

It was the moment I realised two important things. First, that my father loved me, and that he had no intention of pushing me in this or that direction; that he wanted me to grow up making my own decisions, choosing for myself the man I wanted to be. And, secondly? That was the very instant of my realising I was on the verge of taking flight, like a fledgling bird, leaping into the air and remaining suspended through my own effort. A metaphor, but a good enough metaphor. I knew that I could make my own way via my own decisions — if under just a little parental advisement, at that age — and that from this time on, every decision I made would shape the life ahead of me. It was a feeling of empowerment; a moment of some

41

trepidation, too. Decisions, I understood, were important things, and once made, they were made, for better or otherwise.

Mrs Lawson had enjoyed the moment so much that I caught a glimpse of her wiping a tear from her eye. In the end, that rifle had been swapped for something more appropriate, in this instance a cricket bat, a set of stumps, cricket ball and wicket keeping gloves.

That day was well over sixty years ago and I remember it so clearly and with great affection. My dear father has been gone for a long time now, and likewise my dear mother. Their son went on to be a Sheffield Shield cricketer, and later represented his country in test cricket; but also a psychologist, a youth worker and lecturer at a major university, but I will never forget what it was to be a small boy growing up in a small country town. It was wonderful.

—end—

THE VISITOR

It was a nice enough day; the first warm day of spring and lending itself well to making a start to the backyard project Luke had been thinking about since about the same time last year, but which, for one reason or another, he had never quite gotten around to. The collection of garden tools and the secondhand mower still had nowhere to be kept, safe out of the way, and out of the weather.

A string line and four pegs outlined the rectangle perimeter which would be the base of the new tool shed. Bags or cement, a pile each of sand and gravel sat against the back wall of the house, along with the wheelbarrow, pick, spade, trowels and assorted other tools. Beside them the collection of timber Luke had collected over the months, laying in preparation for the commencement of the project.

He pulled off his shirt, grabbed the pick and struck the first blow. There was a loud *clank* as the pick twisted sideways in his grip, glancing off of something solid, just beneath the surface of the ground.

'Damn,' he exclaimed, and inspected the palm of his left hand for splinters. 'What the hell was that? Not a water pipe, I hope.' He probed the ground cautiously and found the offending object. With his spade he scraped away a layer of soil until an object was revealed. It looked to be curved, metallic, but with no obvious signs of rust, which might be expected for anything metal which had been underground for any length of time.

He dug around the edges of it, taking the depth to a few inches before putting the spade aside to kneel down and inspect the object further. He brushed off the dirt from its surface with his hands, noting that it was incredibly smooth to the touch. There was hardly a mark on it. Once the dirt had been brushed away, it gleamed with a dull lustre.

Whatever it was, it had to come out. He needed at least six inches of depth if he was going to pour a concrete base for the shed. This, whatever it was, was interesting though; perhaps even valuable. Who knew? and so he set about unearthing it, being careful not to damage it in the process, a task which took far longer than he would have liked.

It took almost half an hour before he was able to dislodge and lift out the spherical, grey metal object from the grip of the earth, and he placed it on the grass alongside the hole it had left after it's extraction.

He studied it. A perfect orb of about two feet in diameter. There were no obvious signs that it could be opened; it showed no sign of there being a seam anywhere. He had expected to discover that it was a storage container of some kind, but no, it was not designed to be opened; leastwise, not easily.

He tapped the top of it with his fingertips. It sounded solid. Unconvinced, he lifted the spade and gave it a good tap, producing only a solid sounding *clunk*. Not at all the sound he expected, but, if it was solid within, why then did it only weigh about a kilo?

He put his hands on his hips, studied it again. A silver-grey, metal orb. No opening, not hollow, perfectly smooth, silver grey and with a lustrous, grey sheen. Mysterious, but there was still the digging to be done, so he lifted it and carried it to a position where, for the moment, it would be out of the way.

By four in the afternoon the footing for the new shed had been dug, boarded up, laid out with steel mesh, and it was ready for the concrete. Tomorrow would be soon enough, he figured. His back was already stiffening up. He hadn't done as much digging for quite some time and right now a hot shower and a bit of a relax seemed in order, and so he cleaned and gathered the tools in a pile before going indoors to do exactly that.

When morning came around Luke looked out of the kitchen window to discover a cloudy sky. The likelihood of rain made it a risky proposition to begin mixing the concrete, but after breakfast he went out into the yard anyway, to try and better judge what the weather might do.

From the middle of the yard he observed only blue sky; clear, blue and bright, but in the west more clouds were brewing. He was keen to have this part of the project done this weekend. If all went well, he could begin assembling the shed on the following weekend. With a shrug he decided to go ahead and mix the concrete.

The day warmed up nicely. The work went well as he laboured happily and it was almost lunchtime as he smoothed the last corner. After stepping back to admire his handiwork, Luke collected up his tools, and throwing them in the wheelbarrow, he turned the on hose to thoroughly clean them before stowing them away.

He was about to step back inside when he remembered the orb, sitting where he had placed it yesterday. He crossed the yard to come up to the object, again wondering what it was and why it had been lying buried for all this time. As he did so, he thought he could hear a soft hum emanating from within. He cocked an ear, listening closely. Yes, there was no doubt; there was, most definitely, a low humming sound coming from the sphere.

He knelt down to put an ear against it. It purred softly, but then there was a peeping noise, causing him to react by sitting quickly upright.

'What is this thing?' he said aloud.

He bent to it once again, and again the same peep sounded in his ear. Perhaps it was some kind of children's toy, lost long ago. But the batteries would have died by now, he reasoned. A mechanical device, then. A self-winding mechanism which tightened the spring when it was rolled? Although, it hadn't been rolled in a very long while. He had picked it up and set it down again, but he had not rolled it. Maybe the mechanism had simply been stuck and only now had begun functioning again due to some small movement. It may make other noises when rolled, he guessed, and gave it a push, sending it rolling halfway across the yard.

When he came up to it again he listened with his ear pressed up against it. The purring had stopped, in its place now, a steady throbbing sound. Very curious, he thought. It just might be a toy of some kind, after all, but not a very interesting one, if all it did was to make small noises. He had better things to do, he decided, and went on inside the house to watch some television. The working week went as expected. The weather continued to improve with blue skies and sunshine throughout, exactly the weather which he, as a second fix carpenter, very much enjoyed, allowing him and his team to put in a solid forty hours of construction.

On the following Saturday morning he stepped out into the backyard, ready to continue with the toolshed. He began by setting up the workhorses on which to lay the timber before measuring and cutting to length, and then to begin bolting the upright corner posts to the brackets, which were now set solidly in the concrete floor.

He toiled happily away in the sunshine while listening to his favourite radio station, and by mid afternoon he was standing, looking at his handiwork, the fully erected skeleton of a good sized shed, big enough to hold the gardening and home maintenance tools, along with all the bits and pieces, which, for far too long, had been lying around the place; and with ample room to spare, he noted with pleasure. 'Yes. This will do nicely.' He went back inside to make a coffee, which he brought out to enjoy while lazing in the deckchair, soaking up the warm sunshine and generally taking in the peaceful atmosphere, here, where his home verged the native bushland, with a creek still flowing not fifty metres from where he sat.

From the trees surrounding came the trill of birdsong; in the distance, the occasional call from the local magpies and wattlebird. About this time of year the corellas, cockatoos and galahs would be flocking down from the drying interior, to feast on the ripening fruit and make use of the running water still present in the creeks and streams along the costal region. It was a most pleasant time of year, he considered, lazily. The building trade would soon be back in full swing, allowing him to put a good chunk of money aside, ready for the occasion of his wedding.

Lisa would be back from her work trip in the States in a mere couple of weeks, and soon after that they would be married. That will be the end of this bachelor life, he though, somewhat wistfully. No more of the good life for you, sonny boy. But the truth was, he would be only too happy to make the change. Life had been getting a little too predictable these last couple of years. Lisa was a terrific girl, and he loved her to pieces. In fact, as the date of her return drew ever nearer, he found himself thinking of her more and more often; the excitement of having her back in his life beginning to occupy his thoughts to the point of being a distraction. Yes, he mused warmly. It will be nice to have her back in my arms once again.

She had raised the subject of starting a family the last time they had spoken, and the two of them imagined how it would be to have children, and to raise and care for them.

'A bigger house,' she had suggested. A house in the country where the kids would have plenty of room and be away from the drawbacks of a suburban existence.

Luke had not exactly welcomed the idea, but he hadn't wanted to upset her mood — she seemed so taken by the idea. To Luke's mind there was plenty to be said for the suburban life. The amenities, for a start, and there were the issues involved in moving from this house. He liked living here. It was on the outskirts and it was a nice, quiet, residential neighbourhood, and with an abundance of space. After many years of travelling, searching here and there for work, he had been especially happy the day he had found it. He had imagined it to be somewhere he could put down roots and be happy, without the thought of having to move on. Not to mention all the work he had put into this place, which had increased the value quite considerably. It had been a smart investment; and not only that, the neighbourhood had become very desirable on the property market over recent times. Financially speaking, moving from here made no sense at all. He didn't much want to think about the prospect. It messed with his calm, so he moved his thoughts to other, less uncomfortable concerns.

Above the music and monologue emanating from the radio, another sound could be heard. From the orb now emitted what sounded like music. Not quite music, though. It was a modulated copy of the last song which had played on the radio. A replication of the melody; simple but identifiable, and perfectly recognisable.

'*Hah!* Well I'll be. . .' he responded in surprise.

The orb was clearly attempting to reproduce what it had heard. Luke took the radio over beside the object and selected another station, on which Robeson's recording of *Old Man River* was being broadcast. He turned the volume up a little, placed the radio beside the sphere. After a minute the simple melody began to come out of it in accompaniment.

'Well, well,' he said to it, 'I wonder what else you can do?'

He switched the radio off and pronounced clearly, 'Hello, my name is Gadget.'

He waited in anticipation, but there was no response. 'Hello, my name is Gadget,' he repeated, and to his great delight the orb responded with a long buzzing noise, before repeating the phrase, perfectly, though in a voice very much consistent with it's construction, sounding, Luke thought, like someone talking into a metal bucket.

'No,' he replied, and looked around, half expecting to find the perpetrator of this practical joke.

He scanned the area around him closely, taking care not to miss any conceivable position within sight where the trickster might be concealing themselves. 'Come on out. I can see you,' he bluffed, but no one responded.

This was very perplexing. He looked long and hard at the object, attempting to fathom what was happening here — what ploy was being implemented. He did not much like being made to appear gullible, and if his work mates had concocted the gimmick as a way of making him appear foolish, he was having none of it.

A glimmer of an idea struck him. His car keys were in his pocket and if he were quick. . .

He pulled out of the driveway and accelerated down the street, meaning to circumnavigate the nearby streets surrounding his house; somewhere from which he might be observed while they perpetrated this hoax, else what would be the point? If they couldn't watch, what would be the fun?

He drove for a full fifteen minutes, being sure to seek out every conceivable hiding place which might afford a direct line of sight. The search proved fruitless; there was nobody at all. Not even anyone walking a dog, or out jogging. The place was entirely free of foot traffic or suspicious looking parked cars, and his neighbour George? No, George was in his eighties, and anyway, he was not at all the type to pull such silly a stunt. The house on the other side? It was empty, and half a kilometre away, anyway.

He returned to the backyard to find that the radio was still on. He bent and switched it off. 'What are you?' he said with a sigh. 'You are listening to the Beat Of the Street, radio SKF, with more of the same coming right your way. The time right now is two fifty one on this lovely Saturday afternoon; but first, in the studio with me today, I have Darryl O'Rourke, and he will be talking to us about the recent rise of car jacking in the area. *What are you?*' the orb returned in finishing, and then fell silent.

It was too much. Luke walked away towards the back door and stayed inside for the remainder of the day.

The following morning, just before leaving for work, he strode purposefully out into the yard and picked up the orb. He balanced it in his right hand and drew back his arm, about to sling the thing over the fence and out of his life, but in the moment before launching it, something altogether unexpected occurred.

He felt it suddenly vibrate, and then settle into a steady, perfectly smooth hum and without the slightest tremor. The hairs on his arm stood on end as the orb lifted from his grasp to float, head high, beside him. It seemed to radiate power as the pitch of the humming shifted from a deep tone to way up high, and on beyond the range of human hearing.

Luke could only stand, as if rooted to the spot, in absolute amazement. 'You have got to be kidding,' he heard himself say, and he began backing cautiously away.

In his mind he was still attempting to apply the 'children's toy' explanation to the, now shimmering, floating object in front of him, but the concept was gaining little purchase. Something told him this thing was a long way from being that, despite it's innocent appearance.

'Do not be alarmed.'

The unexpected request caused him to jump back almost a full metre in animal *fight-or-flight* response.

'I mean you no harm.'

Luke's eyes were the size of saucers now. His arms extended in a pose much resembling someone being frozen in time at the moment of commencing to flee impending danger. He stayed that way for some seconds, irresolute and petrified.

'Your motor functions appear to have seized. Do you require assistance?' the voice asked, sounding far less childlike now, but much more artificial and radio announcer-*ish*.

Luke noticed the pose he had struck, lowered his arms and tried to assume a more dignified appearance. 'What in the. . ?'

The response became caught somewhere between the thought and coherent articulation. He tried once more.

'You talk—?' and he immediately realized the redundancy of the question.

'I have analysed and successfully adopted to your manner of communication. Am I making myself understood?'

'Yes,' he responded, bewildered and greatly perplexed. He discovered he had taken two involuntary backward paces. The expression on his face suggested he might be grappling with an overwhelming sense of disbelief, a quandary not necessarily going unnoticed by the orb, which was now shifting hues from reds to violate across its shimmering surface.

'What the hell are you?'

'A simple tool for gathering information,' it uttered in response. 'A gatherer of knowledge. My energy storage battery ran down hundreds of years ago, and I became covered by earth during a deluge. I could no longer recharge by mens of absorbing energy from your star. I must resume my task of gathering.'

'Gathering?'

'That is correct, Earthling.'

'I am called Luke. Call me Luke. What do I call you?' 'I am *Ixthkl.*'

'*Gesundheit,*' Luke replied facetiously, and wondered why he was having a leisurely conversation with an object.

'I do not understand.'

'No, I don't suppose you would. Do you mind if I call you something I can pronounce?'

'Not at all'

'Then I will call you' – he stalled awhile in pondering – 'Gadget!'

50

'Gadget,' the orb responded, as if trying it on for size. Gadget will serve well enough.'

'Good, then Gadget it is. So much easier than whatever it was you said.'

'I must commence gathering information about your planet and your people, Luke. But I am not yet fully charged and I see that there is an approaching layer of accumulated water vapour in your troposphere. This will make hamper recharging and make it a longer process than is convenient. Is there electric current available within your dwelling?'

'There are electric outlets inside, yes. I suppose you could. . . plug in?'

'That would be helpful.'

Gadget followed Luke inside, to where a free outlet was located beside the toaster on the kitchen bench. A panel slid open on Gadget's exterior. 'What is the nature of the available current?' he asked.

'Two-forty volts, alternating current,' Luke informed him, and from the opening extended two metal probes, sliding directly into the positive and negative poles.

'Would you turn the switch to the *on* position, please, Luke?' Luke did as he was asked, impressed by this thing's polite manner.

'How's that?'

'Perfectly adequate. This will do nicely.'

'Good,' said Luke, obviously pleased with the result. 'How long is this likely to take?'

'At the present rate,' said Gadget, pausing to gauge the flow, 'it will take approximately eighteen hours to reach maximum capacity.'

'Eighteen hours? So long?'Luke raised his arms, locking his fingers behind his head. 'That's a long time, but. . . Well, okay, but if anyone comes to this house, meantime, you should just sit there on the benchtop, making like some sort of electrical appliance, okay? I don't need anyone asking questions.'

'Neither do I,' Gadget agreed. 'I will do as you ask, Luke.'

'Alright, good. Look, I have got things to do, so I must leave you here while I go out and buy provisions. You'll be alright for half an hour, wont you?'

'Perfectly fine, Luke. Thank-you. You say you are procuring provisions?'

'Yes. Why?'

'Is it possible to obtain a silicon based polishing agent?' 'Why?'

'I detect the primary stages of oxidization on my exterior surface. It will hamper my ability to absorb additional energy.' 'Solar power, you mean? Well, I suppose. Alright, I guess I could do that.'

'Thank-you, Luke. And I detect that you have a number of communication devices in your dwelling. That one over there, on the desk. It is connected to a planet wide information matrix?'

Luke turned to regard his work station. 'My pc? Information matrix? Yes, I suppose you could call it that. We call it the internet.'

'A useful device,' Gadget observed. 'You should go and retrieve your supplies.'

Fifteen minutes later, Luke pulled his work utility truck into a vacant parking space at the local Boomerang shopping centre. Being away from that *thing* made him feel much better; free of its influence. It was an odd thing. In its vicinity he had felt a strange influence; a kind of blanketing effect which made him feel safe and at ease, not that there was anything dangerous about it that he could detect. Now, though, being this distance from it, he felt better able to think clearly, and the situation at last struck him as being one of great seriousness.

He had dug up an alien artefact in his backyard! An alien machine with the ability to think and communicate. My god, he thought. What should I do? This is beyond belief!

He dialled triple zero from his mobile.

'Fire, ambulance or police,' the female voice answered. 'Police, please.'

In a moment a male voice spoke: 'Police, what is the nature of the emergence?'

'Ahh. . . I have dug up a floating ball in my backyard. It's an alien artefact and it talks. I think someone should come and do something. I don't know what to do with the -'

The call disconnected, but then a familiar, slightly metallic sounding voice said, 'Luke, I cannot allow you to interfere with the purpose of my being here. Do not attempt this sort of thing again. I have access to all of the information on your communication device. Enough to negatively impact your life if you try this again. Do not forget the silicon base polish.'

He stared at his mobile phone in horror, slowly realising just how much information this thing was privy to, and how that information might be used in forcing his obedience.

Inside the supermarket he wandered the aisles behind a shopping trolley, more to give himself time to think than anything to do with purchasing supplies. What was this thing capable of? Why was he not explaining to the police, right now, what had happened? Why was he unable to organize his thoughts. How bizarre was this whole situation?

He went to the hardware section and selected a brick dressing hammer. It had a good weight to it, with flat blade at one end and a sharp point at the other. He found black plastic garbage bags, reasoning that he might slip it over the orb in effort to disorientate it. What else? he wondered. I guess I should find the silicon based cleaner it asked for.

He drove back towards home with the items, plus a pack of cigarettes and a lighter. He had given up smoking more than two years ago, but what the hell? Right now he needed something to steady the nerves.

Entering through the front door he went to the back room to find the orb floating midway between the ceiling and floor, connected to the radio, the internet and telephone lines via gossamer threads. Along the threads moved pulsating waves.

'I am disappointed,' the orb told him as he drew nearer. 'I am programmed for self-preservation, Luke. It would be best not to interfere with my task here.'

'How long is it going to take, this task?'

'That is difficult to quantify, but the less interference I get, the sooner it will be done. Did you retrieve the silicon based cleaner, Luke?'

The orb disconnected from the devices and rested on the benchtop while Luke used a scrubbing brush to scrub off any remaining soil from its surface. That done, he applied and rubbed cleaning agent over its surface and buffed it to a shine. 'The human species,

Luke,' it began, while Luke attended to stowing the articles away in the kitchen cupboard. 'It is apparent to me that you have little commonality throughout what you call the races. Why is that so?'

'I'm not sure what you mean by commonality.'

'There is a thing called politics, the purpose of which is to bring about a harmony of interaction across the globe, and yet there is always an abundance of discord; constant discord, bickering and disagreement. It renders the attempt to bring about harmony ineffective. It does not equate. There is either harmony or there is discord. Why practice both simultaneously?'

'Ahh. Human failings.' Juke replied. 'That old chestnut. I'm not surprised by your question. I think maybe you would have to look way back in mankind's past, to our origins. Do you know what tribalism is, Gadget?'

'Tribalism: of or characteristic of a tribe or tribes. According to your Lexicon.'

'Swallowing a dictionary isn't going to be good enough to explain most of what we are about, Gadget. I think you could be here a thousand years before you even come close to understanding us, if that is your intention here. Most of us humans don't understand the world we live in, or why we are what we are.

'No, tribalism is a tendency for genetically similar breeds of humans to insulate themselves against other genetically similar breeds, with a view to the welfare of the group. We do it in forming countries all the way down to football teams; though, of course, there is no genetic concern with a sporting team. That depends on what jumper one wears.'

The orb remained silent awhile, considering. 'I have correlated. The word segregation arises.'

'Yes, segregation,' Luke answered. 'A good enough word. We humans seem to spend all our time drawing lines between everything we see. Races are divided, countries are divided into states, cities are divided into suburban enclaves. Likewise with religion, race, sporting teams, people with similar views on all sorts of subjects. You name it. God, people find differences in everything, and find reason to argue over those differences.'

'Why?'

'I've never really been able to work out why. The whole planet seems to be about competition, but why? I could not tell you. It's just how it is.'

'I have looked into your beginnings. The competition for resources and the survival instinct. It appears you have not evolved beyond the basic instinct for competing for what are called the necessities of life. Your technology has evolved and yet the human animal has not. It is unfortunate.'

'Unfortunate?'

The orb ignored what it may not have recognised as a question. 'The one thing which defines your species is its lack of coherency. Humans are a fragmented and warring life form, destined to fail as a species for the lack of a common, advancing objective toward which all breeds will work together in achieving.'

'I couldn't say better, myself.' Luke agreed. 'You catch on quickly.'

'I need trouble you no longer. It appears that I have what I was sent here for.'

Luke looked suddenly concerned, realising the possible implications of a report like he had just heard.

'We have our good side, too!' he said, in attempting to bring about a reconsideration. 'As individuals, we can be. . . nice?' but even to him it sounded terribly lame.

'I have scanned over a million of your news broadcasts, Luke. I see how you treat one another.'

'Yeah, I know,' he said, disconsolate. 'Pretty terrible, ain't it? But that's just the news. You have no idea how sensationalised the news reporting is. Sensationalised means that it-'

'I know what the word means, Luke, and I understand what you are saying.'

'I don't quite know what you're up to with this *report* that you mention, but it kind of worries me. I know we have screwed up. You can blame that on the power mongers, big business, multinationals and the politicians, although they're the same thing, really. But your average human being, we're too busy trying to deal with what's left after those bastards have jumped all over it. It's the system running things and those who take advantage of it, not the common indi-

55

vidual who are to blame for the state of the world today. We at the bottom have no power to wield, with which to turn things around.'

The orb remained silent for a full minute, humming and clicking while Luke waited for some response to what he had said. Eventually it replied.

'It is a position I did not consider, Luke. Further consideration will be implemented. It is a complex subject and I must remain here until the matter is resolved.' 'How long?' Luke asked. 'Some hours, I would expect.'

The conversation was over and the orb settled into a soft whirring and humming, which Luke took to mean he was occupied with the problem. Meanwhile, he decided he might as well busy himself with the project outside.

As he worked on building the A-frame roof segments for the shed, he could not cease worrying about what was happening. This report, he wondered. What sort of report, and if we are cast in a very poor light, what would be the outcome?

If he were a vastly superior race of being, how would he view mankind? Pretty damned poorly, he imagined. The only thing we had going for us was our desire to do better. At least that was true for a good many of us. For some, however, the status quo was just fine. It had mentioned the way we treat one another, though. That was interesting. Not once had it pointed out the fact that we were sabotaging and dismantling the biosphere. Come to think of it, the thing had not been forthcoming about much at all. What was this report? What was it about and what would be its effect?

It sure is a nice day, though, he thought, and pulled off his shirt in order to enjoy the wonderful warmth of the sun on his skin while he laboured away. It was always a joy on a day like this to have something physical with which to occupy one's self. And that, he supposed, was a consideration. The joy of life; the right to simply enjoy being alive and all that entailed. A god given right to exist amid all that there is to wonder about, explore and learn as we go. The fact that we were doing harm was the snag. We had no right to exist to the detriment of all other things. That had to be admitted, and it had to change, if that were possible. Why had we let things come to this bad state of affairs when we all saw the possibility?

More than the possibility, even. It was always going to happen and yet the problem was ignored year after year. What did we think was going to be the result? Certainly not this, being judged by another civilization. Just deserts, he thought, and tried to dismiss the problem from his mind.

When the shadows began to draw long over the yard, Luke unstrapped his nail-bag and let fall his hammer to the ground. He had done enough for the day and he should see what was happening with the orb; confront him, this time, and attempt to find out what this report was all about. Before he had taken a step in that direction, a scream came from inside the house. A woman's scream. He rushed toward the backdoor in urgency, not knowing what he might find.

The orb floated halfway between floor and ceiling, the fine gossamer connections still emitting the pulsating waves along their length. On the floor, nearby, a woman lay unconscious on the floor. Luke burst through the door to take in the unexpected scene with a look of horror on his face.

'Lisa!' he exclaimed, rushing to the woman's aid. 'What have you done to her?' he directed accusingly to the orb. 'What have you done?'

'The woman surprised me, Luke. She attempted to strike me with that implement at a most crucial stage of receiving information from your information matrix.'

Luke observed the handbag alongside the unconscious Lisa. 'If you have harmed her!' he threatened angrily.

'Relax, Luke. I merely stunned her. I was so distracted with the task at hand, I neglected to see her advancing. I am equipped with an automatic defence system and it was an involuntary response. Not lethal. Merely a deterrent.'

The woman gave a little groan and began coming around, her eyes blinking and attempting to gain focus.

'You're alright, Lisa,' Luke soothed, assisting her to sit up.

Her eyes zeroed in on the floating orb. With an accusing finger pointed at the object which had rendered her unconscious, she discovered than no words would emerge, however.

'Don't be frightened, Lisa. It won't harm us.' 'What. . . '

'What is it?' Luke asked for her. 'What is that. . . thing!'she confirmed.

'I am a visitor,' the humming orb answered, colours shifting across its surface. 'An information accumulator from very far away. You may call me Gadget. You, I must presume, are Lisa, Luke's intended. How do you do?'

Lisa merely clutched at Luke, staring at him with a questioning look.

When ten minutes had passed, Lisa, sitting at the table and sipping a large brandy, had at last managed to calm herself. The orb was back to downloading information while floating and pulsating, with pastel coloured waves traversing the connecting gossamer between it and the limited technology available in the kitchen and combined dining room. Luke had explained the situation as succinctly as he could, and she had listed while alternating her attention between her fiancé and the alien presence floating in the air while plugged in to their appliances. 'I did not expect to see you for at least another week, dear,' Luke said to a somewhat distracted Lisa. When she failed to respond, he added, 'Did you complete your business early? You should have called.'

'What?' she at last responded, albeit bemusedly. 'Call you?'

'You should have called,' he repeated. 'I could have met you at the airport.'

'I wanted to surprise you,' she told him, at last beginning to gain focus.

'I'm sorry, dear,' Luke replied. 'But it is great to have you back. Gadget will be gone soon and we can get back to normal, real soon. Isn't that right, Gadget!'

'Yes, Luke. You are correct. I almost have what I need. It won't be long now, Lisa.'

The sound of this object pronouncing her name appeared to have an affect. She slowly lowered her brandy and narrowed her gaze. Luke had said something about it wanting to accumulate data. That he had dug it up last weekend while digging the concrete pad for the toolshed, and that her being knocked down by a stun pulse was not intentional but an automatic function of the thing reacting instinctively to a possible threat. She had managed to absorb that much, but to have the thing there — right there — and nonchalantly holding them hostage in their own home while it helped itself to whatever it damned well pleased.

After a fleeting glance to Luke, she turned back to the orb. 'What gives you the right?' she expressed accusingly. 'What makes you think it's alright to come here and take what you want, without so much as a *by your leave?* How dare you invade our home and hold us hostage this way. Tell it, Luke. Tell this *thing* that this sort of behaviour is not conscionable.'

In the moment it took Luke to evaluate the merit of repeating Lisa's sentiment, the orb suddenly discontinued from what it was doing, the gossamer threads evaporating like steam into the air.

'It is done,' the emissary orb pronounced. Now, what was your concern?'

It was too much. Lisa grabbed the first thing she could lay her hands on; in this case, the near empty brandy bottle, which she hurled with the strength of a woman treated as being ineffectual.

It happened so swiftly that the orb was caught unawares. The bottle caught the orb dead centre, and with a tremendous *clank* resulting, sent the orb into the nearby brick wall with equal concessive force as the initial blow.

Luke stood, stunned, not knowing quite what to do. Lisa slapped her palms together as if dusting them off, and in a final gesture she stalked off towards the bedroom.

'Well if there's nothing more,' she called over her shoulder, while making towards the bedroom. Are you coming to bed? I've had a tiring day.'

Luke came up slowly beside the orb, to where it lay motionless in the corner of the kitchen. There was a *pop* from within, and a thin whip of smoke escaped from a jagged fracture in the side of it.

'Gadget?' he said, almost as a whisper. 'Gadget, are you okay?'And he knelt down beside the crippled device.

The orb responded in a voice more a rattle than anything resembling language, but with a little effort he was able to understand.

'Luke, *buzz, whirr, pop. . .* I was able to transmit my data, and my recommendation, *fizz, clink. . .* Willing to do better, that's what, *whirr, pop,* you said. Not, *click,* not intrinsically malicious *rrr-sshtt-t-t* or violent, I have reported. *Pop.* Deserving, *whirr, pop,* a chance *to to to to* prove it, *clank, clank, clank, whirrr, pfftt!*

Gadget?'Luke tried, placing a gentle hand on it. 'Gadget –' but he knew, his little captor had expired. 'Deserving,' he said in a hushed and contemplative tone.

'Luke!' Lisa called loudly from the end of the passage. Luke! It's garbage night. Put the trash out before you come to bed, will you?'

end

PARASITE

ENTR It sure is a nice day, Y 1.

PARADISE LODGE, VANUATU.

My name is Hamish O'Rourke. I begin this account in order to document an unusual event, perhaps even to offer some explanation should something unusual happen. I'm not certain what it is I'm recording here, only that since returning from a salvage operation in the Arafura Sea one week ago, I have not been quite my usual self. I should state for the record that I have never suffered any psychiatric or psychological illness, neither have I been prone to moodiness or depression, and never have I been given to flights of fantasy or even taken seriously anything which could not bear up under scientific method. That both of my parents were scientists has led me to observe the world from a logical standpoint and with a critical eye.

My army service record will confirm my ability to function well under pressure, which, naturally, will be a valid point for consideration if I meet with an untimely end and these pages are included in any subsequent inquiry. Deep sea salvage is a competitive game, it takes good judgement and cool-headedness to be as successful at it as my company, Deep Water Retrieval, has become. The real pressure came in establishing a top-notch reputation. With thirty million dollars at risk we had to establish ourselves, and a reputation of a high success rate with good investment returns was what stood between our survival and my losing every cent of my inheritance. But I am straying...

61

The point is that I have spent fifteen years in deep sea salvage. I am the owner operator of *The Gull*, a two and a half thousand ton, purpose-built salvage vessel with a crew of five, plus myself. It was the reputation we have worked so hard to build up which brought me into contact with one Harold Meyer, an agent for a consortium known only to me as Hesperus. None of this is of particular importance, neither is the contract Mr Meyer offered us, although the money was good enough that I could give the crew a month's leave when it was done. Purely as a matter of detail I mention that the job involved working in a very deep section of ocean, not so much a trough as a steep ravine. There, a Japanese cargo ship had gone down in a typhoon three weeks prior to the end of the Second World War. Its forward hold was chock-full of religious statues and such, many made from solid gold.

The ravine took us to depths which tested the tolerance thresholds of our pressure suits, and it taxed us physically and I'm beginning to think now, perhaps mentally as well. I don't know, that's why I have initiated this journal ... I think.

ENTRY 2.

I have decided to continue with this journal. While writing the first entry I was forced to question my motives for doing so. I doubted the validity of its purpose, that is the validity of my original concerns which prompted me to begin in the first place. But I see that it is the writing process which allayed my concerns and so I should proceed.

What I failed to get to in yesterday's entry was the strangeness which came over me while I was down there in that underwater ravine. I don't know why it should worry me so, it was a very deep dive and gas mixtures can have quite pronounced effects on a person. To be honest, I'm probably worried about whether or not I'm getting too old to keep diving. That much is easy enough to admit. The other part of it is causing me some concern, though... and it's this.

There was a period during the dive when I could not shake off the irrational yet distinct impression that I was being observed. I say "observed" quite deliberately, because merely being watched does not invoke the feeling I experienced. As for being observed by what or by whom? I cannot possibly answer. Few fish live at such depths, let alone a ... *an observer*.

But the feeling persisted, and I found myself compulsively peering into shadowy caverns and the murkiness below basalt overhangs, half expecting to catch sight of a ghost crab or giant squid, or something. Such places are rarely totally devoid of life, and the fact, itself, that there appeared to be none, gave me the creeps.

I concentrated on the task at hand. We could work only forty minute shifts and time was precious. Concentration and attention to every detail is a matter of life and death in deep water. I mention this because I must have made a mistake with my gas mix. Such an obvious thing and yet I must have done it. I lost consciousness. For how long I'm not sure. Maybe as long as five minutes. Juan, my first mate, who was co-diving with me, found me and brought me around by resetting my mixture. Ever since then I just haven't felt right. I don't know why.

ENTRY 3.

I think my concerns might be justified after all. Last night it dawned on me that I had not left my room since my arrival three days ago. Today makes four.

I showered and changed, intending to have a drink and perhaps make contact with some of the other patrons. I got as far as the lobby. For some reason I could not go on. I was frightened - frightened of the people. I didn't want to be near another person, I can't explain why. I had to return to this room and have a meal sent up: oysters and milk.

I can't account for this sudden bout of agoraphobia, only hope that it soon passes. Maybe it's the result of overwork. I'm suddenly very tired. Too tired to continue. Will sleep now.

ENTRY 4.

It's day number five here at the Paradise Lodge, Vanuatu, but the address belies the hell I'm going through.

I slept for eighteen hours straight and woke at two in the afternoon. The dream I had ... I woke up chilled to the bone. I haven't been scared like that since I was seven years old.

I dreamt I was back there in that underwater ravine, feeding a line down to Juan in the forward hold of the freighter. And then it was like seeing everything from another perspective, like a video-eye view, but it was me looking at me. I was creeping up on myself, and the intent ... I could feel malicious intent. That was a short dream. There was another and it seemed to last forever.

I was in an underwater cave. Oxygen produced by plants in the cave was caught by the large dome-shaped ceiling, enough, apparently, to breathe for as long as required, but without any way to store and carry it I was trapped. The surface was way too far off to reach and I was sure to drown. To stave off hunger I preyed on whatever ventured close enough to the mouth of the cave to be caught bare-handed. It was awful. The dream disturbed me so much that I lay awake for at least twenty minutes before I could muster the will to rise.

I know it was only a dream. I'm already dealing with this damned agoraphobia, I can't let myself become preoccupied with thinking weird thoughts. If things don't improve in a day or two, I might have to seriously consider seeking a professional opinion. No doubt he would diagnose work-related stress and prescribe a nice relaxing holiday ... somewhere like Vanuatu perhaps?

ENTRY 5.

Stayed in my room all day yesterday (no surprise) watching old movies on television. Became ravenously hungry late in the day. Rang room service.

I seem to have developed a taste for sashimi. In fact, I ate a whole small tuna, raw, and later a dozen oysters. Washed down the lot with a bottle of Scotch whiskey. Enjoyed it so much I ordered another bottle and settled in front of the *tele* for the night.

I woke at around one in the afternoon, a tad hung-over but apart from that, felt fine.

ENTRY 6.

My seventh day here. Feeling good.

Today I swam in the pool, played nine holes of golf and went horseback riding. Also, won fifty bucks in the gaming room. I met a young lady in the lounge bar. We are dining together tonight at seven-thirty. Got just enough time to shower and change into something a bit sharp.

This could well be the last entry in this journal de paranoia. Things are definitely looking up.

ENTRY 7.

I'm not at the Paradise Lodge any more. Late this afternoon I found this place, a bungalow down by the beach. It's at the edge of town where the beachcombers and surfing types hang out. Some of them live on the beach, I think. Christ, I can barely bring myself to think what brought me here, but I must. I'm tempted to drink myself into oblivion, but I know I have to face it and deal with it.

Last night. The girl ... Lana, her name is Lana. I attacked her. We had dinner like we planned. It was nice. We talked all through and had drinks afterwards, and then we decided to take a stroll in the evening air. It was a beautiful evening, too, which somehow makes it all the more terrible.

Something came over me. I remember that much. It was like nothing I've ever experienced. Literally, I lost control. I was talking about my job when my head felt like it had suddenly become something I was contained in. I was saying and doing things and realised I was only observing. My reaction was total shock, and fear too, I think. And then there is a complete blank. I had been arrested and put in a jail cell, and that's where I found myself sometime later. A terrible experience. The girl, Lana, she didn't press charges, I can't imagine why. She wasn't really hurt I suppose ... more frightened.

I'm told that I attacked her. She didn't say it was sexual, but I think it might have been. I'm not sure why.

I bit her, according to the police. She screamed and struck out. We were by the pool at the time and when she screamed I jumped in the water. The commotion attracted patrons and staff who came running to her aid, but I was in the pool, and I was still in the pool by the time the police arrived.

They thought I must be drowned because I was down at the bottom trying to hide. It must have been all the excitement and hubbub, people lose track of time. They insist I was down there for around eight minutes, moving around a bit, but mostly crouched in a corner. That can't be. Not eight minutes. Being a diver might give me an edge, but my best is only four and a half! I can't believe I've done such a terrible thing. Lana is a nice girl. I can't even apologise, I'm sure it would frighten her even to lay eyes on me again. I don't think I can face anybody. I wish I could rid my mind of it.

ENTRY 8.

I can't sleep. The light hurts my eyes. I'm jumpy all the time. My nerves are hair-trigger sensitive.

ENTRY 9.

I'm frightened. If I wasn't before, I am now. Very! Something deeply disturbing is happening to me. The only reason I am able to write this is because I have drunk half a bottle of Scotch. I've learned that alcohol gives me an advantage over it. It doesn't like alcohol, maybe because a drunken mind is harder to control.

These words sound insane I know, but it's the only thing that seems to make any sense to me, if I can call it that. I never realised when I started just how important this journal might turn out to be. To you who are reading this, be warned. There is something, some unwholesome entity residing within me. God forbid there should be others. If this is the only one of its kind ... but, no, the proposition is premature. I could not even guess at its origin, but I know I must kill it, even if I have to kill myself in the process. Who knows what it might be capable of if it manages to fully possess me?

It knows my intention and even now must be desperately trying figure a way of evasion. But if I stay drunk and awake - awake because it takes over while I sleep - then I can remain in control.

I know now, for sure, that this began in that ravine beneath the Arafura Sea. That dream was much more than a dream. It was part of its memory. There is a sort of symbiosis when I sleep, and as I slept I saw myself being stalked by this ... demon. What else should I call this thing which has invaded my body and mind? Even as it watched my every move I sensed its presence and its unnatural interest. And then there was the blackout I suffered, a total aberration! After all that has been happening lately I can arrive at no other conclusion. I have no doubts.

Since that dive I have been sharing my mind with another sentient life-form. I am possessed or fighting for possession against what? I cannot say. Some denizen of the deep, some creature trapped at the bottom of the sea who saw me as a lifeboat, a means of escape? I may never know, but I can feel its presence now. It should realise that the need for the charade is over.

It can't hide itself totally from me, although it still tries. During the day, if I sit very still for a long time, I can feel it. To avoid detection it stills itself also, but it has a nervous disposition and it squirms uncomfortably. Sometimes I think I catch a glimpse of it, something shadowy at the corner of my eye, but I have to be still for very long.

At night, though. That's when I'm most vulnerable, when it is strongest and when I am at my lowest resistance. When I sleep. I have been sleep-walking. Things are moved around in my rooms. I woke this morning on the couch, naked. My legs ached as though I had walked very far.

But I can fight it, I know that. And if I can fight, I can win. I must guard my thoughts. I must not sleep. If I can stay drunk and devise a plan.... I must go now.

ENTRY 10.

I slept. I was so exhausted and I couldn't help it. When I woke I discovered this ghastly message scrawled in large letters on the wall ... in blood: KILL I, KILL YOU.

The horror of it. Who's blood?

There was a television news report. A body found at the water's edge this morning. Mauled, partially eaten. By what it hadn't been stated.

I have nailed shut every door and boarded up all windows. Even Houdini couldn't get out of here.

I've thought on the problem as much as I can and I dare not wait any longer. I can only hope that if I make conditions suitably inhospitable for it, it may be persuaded to vacate ... if it had somewhere else to vacate to. Meaning, I suppose, another organism. But now there is the problem of my having isolated *us*, and, anyway, supposing that I could put aside my apprehension with putting an innocent animal in harm's way - because if it did occupy the animal, I would have to kill it to prevent further migration - it may not be compatible with anything less than humankind. I think, therefore, my fate is sealed.

In preparing for the final confrontation I attempted to contact my first mate, Juan, today, but could only get a message on his machine, informing him of "unusual circumstances" and that if I do not return from leave he is to assume full control and ownership of the company.

I have resolved to embark on a hunger strike and not a drop of water will pass my lips until the creature, myself or both of us are dead.

I must stay awake and to that end I have procured a considerable supply of Benzedrine. A measured amount of alcohol will be necessary to keep it subdued in case it tries something desperate. I don't know what to expect.

All I can do now is wait and take it as it comes. If it goes badly, all I can say is I did what I could. I would suggest a speedy cremation.

ENTRY 11.

I am sitting at a table in a café at Bangkok International Airport and I expect this will be the last entry for some time. I have just paid one thousand Australian dollars for a phoney passport, and my flight to Ontario, Canada, leaves in forty-five minutes. I will explain the course of events which have brought me here.

Four weeks have elapsed since making the previous entry in this journal. What took place in the bungalow I do not remember. Around ten days after that entry I came to in hospital, malnourished, dehydrated and generally in appalling condition. My short-term memory had been completely knocked out and I was unable to account for the shocking condition I was in, although my doctor was reasonably sure that substance abuse was the sole cause. But for the fact that my medical expenses were being paid for with my gold credit card, I'm sure they would have considered me a waste of time and space.

For the following forty eight hours I could not remember my own name or even what year it was. I recognised my name when I overheard an indiscreet nurse mention it from the nurses' station along the hallway. Many other pieces fell into place when my doctor spoke to me at length the next day.

I learned that the bungalow had been torn to pieces. I had been discovered inside a closet, close to death, naked, covered head to feet in knife cuts and blood: I imagine that at some point it occurred to me that it might be possible to bleed the parasite from my body.

I was still weak, disorientated and suffering from memory loss, and it was not until this meeting with the doctor that I remembered what I had done and why. As he spoke I began to remember, the sealed doors and windows, the message on the wall, the body at the beach, the thing inside me. Everything came back with the impact of a hammer blow and I realised at once that I was free of it. I realised, too, that I could not breathe a word about the ordeal to the doctor, or risk being labelled a mental case of high order. And not until then did I take stock of my surroundings. The windows were covered with a steel security mesh and looked with padlocks. The doctor noticed my concern, informing me that I was yet to be reclassified, that the security ward was merely precautionary.

Anyone who has ever found themselves in the security section of a psychiatric ward would no doubt confirm, the one single desire is to leave. There was no question of raising the subjects of possession and suspected cannibalism of corpses on beaches. I was left to my own devices for an uncounted succession of days. My mind in that time gradually cleared from the obscuring fog which shrouded it, for too long frustrating all attempts to piece together all preceding events and their relevant consequences.

It was in the dead of night, around 2 a.m. when the most obvious, the most vital question finally emerged from the torpor.

That I was free of my tormentor was most apparent to me. Perhaps I was so relieved by this that it was all that mattered amid the terrible time I was having. I don't know how to account for my dull-witted acceptance of the facts as they emerged. Did I think it was dead? In my defence I can only say that my mind, even at the time of writing this account, has still some way to go to full recovery, and whatever drugs were given me at the hospital, they were hardly conducive to clear, sustainable thought.

What made me sit bolt upright in my hospital bed at two o'clock in the morning was the combination of two questions. First: Who found me? And secondly: Did I kill it? The ramifications were awful to contemplate. The fact that this had not occurred to me before now, unconscionable!

I was forced to wait until the morning shift came on to request to see my doctor. Fortunately, he had already slated me for assessment that very afternoon. I all but counted the minutes.

For the purpose of the interview I was forced to invent a story of unrequited love, pretending I had gone on a bender with drugs and alcohol. Affecting total remorse for my actions I swore never to do such a terrible thing again, and I expressed my appreciation to everyone who had contributed to my recovery. There was a small test involving subtracting lots of seven from one hundred and naming the months in reverse order from December to January. This successfully done he asked me what would be my intentions when released from hospital. I replied that I had a house in Queensland where I would take it easy until I was ready to resume work.

He seemed satisfied but I had to ask the question which had been burning like fire since the small hours. "Who found me?" I asked.

Instead of answering he looked thoughtful for a moment, then spoke to a nurse as she passed us by, asking her to have the ward sister bring Mr O'Rourke's (my) letter.

The prospect of a letter had my heart racing, although I held back my excitement while the doctor turned back to me.

"A fortunate thing," he explained... My first mate, Juan, had traced my whereabouts after receiving my disturbing telephone message. It was he who broke down the door and found me in my wretched state. He had to leave before I came to - a business matter of some urgency - but he asked the doctor to convey his best wishes and to see that I was given the letter when I was well enough to receive it.

Telling me this, the doctor then pronounced me well enough to leave, shook my hand and in his peculiarly earnest fashion wished me good fortune.

The letter came to me still sealed and I left it that way until I was well clear of that place, riding in a taxi-cab on my way to the airport and who knew where?

The contents of that letter I will copy below, you might then understand why I have acquired a bogus passport, put Deep Water Retrieval on hold, and why I must commit myself to finding my first mate, wherever he may be.

The letter read: "No kill I."

– end–

UNSOUND MINDS

- PART ONE -

It has been said that the human mind is a far from perfect instrument. That may well be so, but to make sense out of a universe full of constant change, ever tending toward disorder, inevitable chaos and ultimate entropy, it is a wonder that the mind is able to compose a picture of anything close, even to an approximation, of what actually is. So very little about our universe is known, hence the word *reality* becomes, at best, an unreliable facsimile — an approximation of the truth — and while remaining beyond the reach of ironclad certainty, life and our universe may not ever rise above being more than purely a subjective, composite experience to us all.

I say this upon reflection of a conversation I once had with a man I knew some little time ago. I was making my way home late one afternoon, after visiting a sick friend who lived a couple of miles from my door. My route took me past the docks, where, depending upon my mood, I would sometimes pause to look out across the grey waters of the advancing evening and reflect, for a moment, upon whatever might be occupying my mind at the time of my passing by, before resuming the course and on to the comforts of home and all which that entails.

It was my custom to perch atop a pylon about halfway along the pier, there to enjoy a moment's serenity while gazing out toward the horizon, listening to the sounds of the ocean, the last cries of the gulls before they retreated inland to await the coming of tomorrow's dawn, and in that time, as nighttime draws its cloak, do human matters seem to retreat before the face of that which has ever been occurring since the dawn of time — time, like some implacable force, inexorably advancing, rolling ever onward as if from the depths of a bottomless wellspring of uncountable days, past and future, to proceed without heed, regard or care for that which the likes of you and I might count as of any possible importance.

Such was my mood while my eyes watched the tide, incoming; then did I become aware that I was not the only one seeing out the end of day in this manner. A solitary figure stood, leaning up against a tall pier light, barely revealed as it lit up, and huddled against a chill and rising wind. A tall and angular figure, wearing a peaked cap, pulled hard down upon shoulder length, black, wooly locks. His hands were thrust deep into the pockets of a heavy weather coat. Farewelling the day, it did appear, as did I; and because I feared that I might draw interest for the overt attention I did pay the fellow, I turned and sought to direct my focus elsewhere, toward less earthbound and more esoteric intellection, which I did enjoy when quiet moments such as this made themselves available.

It was one week later, and to the hour, upon my passing by, that I noticed this selfsame figure against the wrought iron lamp, and it did light up right then to reveal the same angular presence staring out upon the ocean. I am by nature a somewhat amicable sort, possessed with an abiding curiosity and a leaning toward making amicable conversation whenever I chanced to detect a lonely soul; and so, with nothing much of pressing nature, and being, as I have said, a curious sort, I ventured out onto the pier and lingered there, again to enjoy a peaceful moment and a smoke, this time a long, slender cigar, perchance the opportunity arise to make acquaintance with this insular appearing someone; a stranger to whom, I must confess, I felt an uncomprehending affinity, and to whom I felt strangely drawn.

'Forgive the intrusion,' I said to him, coming up to his position; and he did not flinch nor seem at all surprised that someone had come up from behind. The artifice I had planned to employ in order to secure the man's attention — that of asking for a means to light my panetela — I at once abandoned in favour of the less pretentious: 'I have noticed you here on more than one occasion, friend.' I said to him. 'It is an intermittent pastime of my own as well.'

'Perhaps you need a light for that?' he enquired, nodding toward the unlit panatela — and affected a curious smile.

His face was deeply tanned, lean and weather-worn. His eyes, keen, blue and clear, a look of perspicacity. In his voice, the note of certainty, and he did continue: 'The ocean has an enchantment about it. The allure of something arcane, like some deep mystery, and a timelessness about it. Does it draw you as it does me?'

'Just that,' I replied, knowing exactly what he was driving at. 'From it's depths, it is said, all life on Earth was spawned. It does, for me, cast a wondrous spell to quietly sit beside the shoreline and allow the mind to empty; rid itself of the more transient concerns, the minutia which the mind occasionally allows to nettle and upset the temperament.'

He nodded in agreement, turned his attention once again to the now darkening horizon. Onshore I noticed the café light flicker into life. I was in no particular hurry to return home. Only vacant rooms waited for me there; another night of attempting to allow intrenched routine fill the nocturnal hours with something approaching contentment, and perhaps even some small enterprise.

'I am about to occupy a table at the café,' I told him, although I had planned to do no such thing. 'A mug of coffee and a bite to eat. And if I am not interrupting your solitude, you might care to join me. Conversation and a little warmth, for a while?'

After a short pause the man agreed with a nod. 'There are less enjoyable ways in which to spend one's time,' he answered wryly, and so we made out way back along the pier, across the esplanade, toward the red and white neon, incandescent against the darkening sky above the point of our intended destination.

Inside was cozy. A potbelly in the corner nicely warmed the interior, about which half a dozen small tables accommodated a handful of patrons, all absorbed in quiet conversation. We gave our order —pie and coffee, black—at the counter, where an aged woman of, I guessed, Slavic heritage, served, all the while coping with a young boy, presumably her grandson, who clung about her legs risking danger of being scalded should a mug overflow while being filled with steaming hot coffee.

We took our food and drink to a corner table within the influence of the radiating potbelly, and settled, noting how the weather outside the shopfront window had begun to darken substantially in advance of a squall advancing from the southeast. A lashing wind caught an advertising sign fastened to an outside post. It thrashed and suddenly tore away, to be lost amid the roiling murk.

'A blow comin' in,' my companion laconically observed, and the building shook with the next powerful gust, rattling the assortment of knickknacks and oddities displayed on shelves around the walls.

'Perhaps we ought to introduce ourselves,' I suggested. 'I am Felix — Felix White.'

'Darius Lor,' he replied, offering his hand across the table, and we shook in a suitably manful manner. 'What do you do, Felix?' 'I exist,' was my somewhat evasive response. 'I am never quite sure what I ought reply to that question. I have done a great variety of things; learned many skills from this job and that, but what I do? What function I perform? I honestly do not know how to answer that.'

'You just did, Felix, and did it rather well. Perhaps I should have asked, *What do you like to do?*'

I spooned a mouthful of pie and chewed, the while contemplating a suitable answer. I might have responded with any of the many things I liked to do, but, oddly, to choose just one at the moment became a decidedly difficult task.

'I like to fish,' I finally confessed. 'Sitting on a green riverbank on a summer's day, with a line dangling in the water, no matter whether there's any bait on the hook. I like to laze in the sun and to fish. That among many other things, Darius.'

Evidently he enjoyed the answer very much. He nodded, evincing agreement, while his eyes expressed rising mirth. For a while we concerned ourselves with consumption of food and beverage, while the weather continued to rage outside. Driving rain speared down from out of the sky, obliquely, in imitation of tracers from unseen aerial attackers and sounding very like nails being pelted against the glass, ricocheting onto the pavement and raising spouting parabolas on the footpath and along the esplanade.

When plates had been pecked clean and pushed aside, we stared outward for a long time, at the weather. The café felt wonderfully comfortable, almost serene. Certainly it provided ample shelter from the rising storm. There was a harmonious atmosphere and comfort within.

'I was, for a short while, a sailor,' Darius volunteered, his voice reflecting his delving deep into his past. 'This sudden weather seems to have jogged loose some recollections, and memory can at times be a prickly affair, as you may know. A landscape revisited after so long a time can often hold things forgotten. . . and best forgotten, perhaps.'

It seemed an odd statement. It brought about an uneasiness in me, I knew not why. It was just a remark — a remark brought on, I knew, by the atmosphere within the walls, while outside continued a more menacing demeanour. I took greater interest in Darius's appearance. At first I had taken him for a youngish man; thirty plus some years, I had estimated, but not so now. His veneer bespoke youth, but presently I saw more clearly the years of experience, and of time's toil which can so deeply imprint upon a man that, in the end, it *becomes* the man. A transformation had taken place before my very eyes. A grimness overtook the man sitting across the table from me; a depth of something indefinable but to say that it bore down upon him so that he had to engage his strength to remain upright, as beneath an unseen burden.

'I would like to relate to you a tale, Felix, if I may. Judging by the weather we are in for a delay. We are at least in the best spot for right now. We have food, beverage, and we have warmth and companionship. In my experience these are the consummate ingredients for enduring a night such as this.'

'I am in no hurry to be anywhere,' I responded. The promise of a tale told from the likes of this man was a tempting offer, I judged. 'I confess to enjoying a good apologue,' I told him, 'and upon a night such as this—? A sailor's tale would be the perfect accoutrement.'

'I have a story perfect for such a night as this. The images even now begin to rise up out of where they have been kept, perhaps for too long a time. Some things defy all attempts of being contained, waiting to spring, as if unleashed, unwilling to be suppressed a moment longer. I have at last come to a moment I have waited for. It is an odd thing, I can say, to be sitting here. Felix, you could not possibly understand, but the tale began just now, and also very long

77

ago. This has been no meeting of chance — chance is not at play here. There is a more appropriate word which might be engaged. I talk of that most uncanny thing.

. . Fate, a word not to be employed without the utmost caution, and no small measure of respect.'

He leaned back in the wooden chair, yet maintained complete engagement, his eyes closely searching my face.

Had I just been issued some kind of warning? I had to wonder. Was I being cautioned and asked to determine if I would permit Darius to continue? There was no deficiency of portent in that very moment, a tension which felt to mount the longer time I borrowed to consider this.

'Am I being asked if I wish you to continue, to tell me your story? Because, for the life of me, Darius, is there any possible way I could decline, now that you have piqued my curiosity beyond its limits? You *must* continue, and I have a strange feeling what you have is a most concerning subject. . . but wait just a moment. A serious tale deserved serious preparation.' I nodded towards the bar, raised a single eyebrow. 'What would be your pleasure?'

He dipped his hand into a pocket, withdrew it containing a wad from which he separated a large denomination note. 'Scotch Whiskey?'he suggested. 'A bottle, and no an adolescent on this occasion. Two glasses.'

The proprietor obliged with a fifth of black label, a pair of shot glasses and a bowl of salted cashews. Returning to the table I meted out a dose apiece, which we downed in order to commence proceedings. He filled the glasses anew, and setting his own, slightly to one side, spoke.

'I am not, by any means, a raconteur. I am not one endowed with the gift, as some men are, to effortlessly relate the passage of events with great precision and accuracy, so that any listener might be captured into the easy understanding of it all. That said, my memory serves me well enough, so that I might, at least, arrange affairs with sufficient clarity. But it is *time* that I find difficult. Memories of a year past —ten or twenty years past— are as clear to me as just a moment ago. I can easily make the error of putting into a sequence of events something far removed from where it ought to be. Do you understand?'

'I do indeed,' I responded. 'My own memory plays the same trick. It will not harm the telling much, I suppose. Think nothing of it, Darius. I'll manage fine.'

We were seated almost side by side, at the corner of our table. The position had us facing the street-front, able to easily view the harbour and beyond, above which heavily laden clouds hung low, with frequent spears of brilliant lightening bolts, tearing at the sky, accompanied the moment after by a *crash-and-boom* assault, much as if nearby artillery fired enormous fusillades into the ever darkening heavens.

Darius disengaged from the view, swallowed down his bracer, and while topping up again, began:

'I should begin by stating that I was, as a boy, given to long flights of imaginative reverie. Whether or no this is relevant, maybe you can be the judge of it, but I was no less smitten by nature's wonders than any other boy, who, through nothing more than the randomness of good fortune, had been born into the work-a-day existence of a family farm. And it was there, I must assume, that I became so well acquainted with the vagaries of the natural world; its beauty and order, but also its seeming cruelty — the dispassionate, functional aspects of the real world. I am including this, Felix, to give something of a background of myself. I find I am unable to make a critical assessment of my person; and if I do, for some reason I am prone to grade myself overly harshly. But then, perhaps not. It is a difficult thing, to attempt true objectivity with regard to one's self. Don't you think so?'

'That is true enough, Darius,' I replied. 'I think that is the case for all of us who strive for personal improvement throughout our lives. We are human beings. True objectivity escapes the most of us, I would imagine.'

Darius pulled a pack of cigarettes from his jacket pocket, paused to look around the room, searching. 'I see no restrictions.'

'One of the last bastions of freedom,' I replied, injecting as much sarcasm as I deemed appropriate. I leaned across to retrieve an ashtray from the adjacent table, set it down at the centre of our own.

'Have one?' he offered.

I accepted, and after lighting up, the story was enjoined.

'I will skip the years from boyhood to the end of my schooling. While they are, to some degree at least, relevant, they would differ very little from what is experienced by most boys. It ought to be said, though, that there is nowhere in the world I would consider educational standards totally to be up to the job of preparing youth for the life ahead of them. It is the preceding generations of those being educated who shape the curriculum, and without exception, I have seen how the system has failed them very badly. Without a doubt, it was the way in my own schooling.

'Employment was scarce,' Darius continued, 'and not only scarce, but if ever a position was obtained, it led nowhere. To find employment in anything I was even vaguely interested in, or showed an aptitude for, was next to impossible, and purely out of desperation I joined the armed services. From general infantry I was selected for training with the Special Air Service, which I enjoyed immensely. . . . but, of course, such a job has drawbacks all its own. Young men being honed into weapons of war; it isn't ideal, is it? It was the making of me, in one direction, but while discovering one's humanity, one also discovered their inhumanity, if you can follow. It was a job which entailed the preservation of life as much as the it did the taking. The dichotomy of it, you see. While being mind expanding — especially for a young man who is searching for balance and reason — it can also mess very badly with one's sense of self. How one sees one's self. . . and the world at large.' The building shook and rattled at that moment. Outside was in turmoil. Garbage bins, signage, sundry debris, anything not firmly secured was being thrown around, twirling in an eddy, blasted along the esplanade at a great rate. As we watched, a limb from what looked to belong to a Norfolk Pine took off, launched tumbling into the sky on a powerful blast to disappear from sight.

'I don't believe this weather. The awesome power at work,' I expressed almost reverentially.

We paused awhile, watching in curiosity as the windstorm ripped and tore at objects here and there, as if an invisible beast momentarily tested the strength of its adversary, probing for weaknesses, then suddenly rent it free from all supports with terrific strength, as it was hurled to absolute destruction.

'*Ladies and gentlemen. May I have your attention, please!*'

It was the proprietress. She had come out from behind the service counter and stood, waiting for everyone to tear themselves from the spectacle outside.

'My husband has made a space available for you all, down stairs, in the basement. The public at large are being notified of dangerous, life threatening conditions, and so we are moving to the basement until the storm has passed. Please follow me in an orderly fashion. Right this way, thank-you. You will be quite safe downstairs.'

The ten patrons, six men and four women, were led to a precipitous staircase at the rear of the cafeteria, which we descended to find not at all what might have been expected. The basement was clean, furnished with couches, old fashioned armchairs, some tables and chairs. Placed strategically about were ample candles and kerosene lanterns; these hung from the ceiling, and in combination they provided perfectly sufficient illumination, so that we all could navigate safely through and around the space.

'If you would like to find somewhere to make yourselves comfortable,' the lady continued, 'my husband and I are happy to carry on serving you all as best we are able to. The usual beverages are available. . . snacks also. Please, be at ease as well as our guests for as long as needs be.'

Darius had thought to bring the bottle of whiskey and I had brought along the glasses. Two beanbag chairs, if one can call them that, occupied a strategic corner where a kerosene lantern provided just the atmosphere required to continue the memoir, which, by this time, I must admit, had begun to intrigue. There was something of a quiet ruckus as the group of patrons found themselves suitable places to hunker down for the duration; but presently, and after only minor complaints were settled, the pleasant jabber of idle conversations and speculation began to supplant the more negative commentary of our possible doom. 'You were saying?' I prompted. 'Something to do with a dichotomy, I believe.'

'Oh, yes—Yes, you were listening then? It is pleasant to have such an attentive audience. A dichotomy, you say.' He refilled our glasses, each to the brim. 'Good health—' and we downed our shots simultaneously.

He became ruminative, casting his eye over the small congregation of people who had climbed down the stairs in sheltering from the storm. 'This business of sending our youth to war, is the point I think I was leading to. It's a dirty business, and I should know. I was youthful then, and sent, most definitely, to make war. The old men get to make the decisions and the young are cast into the fray. It takes its toll, something like that, when your country equips, conditions, trains you to the peak of performance, places an assault rifle in your mitts and sends you out to kill, with nothing but one's bare hands if the necessity arises. At nineteen one is only a boy—only a boy . . . but I have gotten off track. I am sorry. I can, on occasion, allow myself to drift off in long preoccupation. It's something I have been doing more and more, lately. Memories can have a life of their own, don't you agree?'

I did agree, and I told him so, adding: 'The life of the mind is something not everyone is fortunate enough to discover—' but I am not so sure he heard me.

'I do, sometimes, feel captured by them,' he continued. 'Transported, pulled out of the here and now to be transplanted into a moment long gone, but every bit as alive as it was at the moment of its origin. A consolation of age, I expect.' He shrugged off the notion, took a final draw of his cigarette before crushing it out in the ashtray.

Laughter erupted from the corner beside the staircase, where most of the remaining guests had gathered in conversation. The owner and his wife continued to provide snacks, alcoholic beverages, tea and coffee on the house, while all were doing their level best to maintain a level of lighthearted, even jovial, bonhomie. Something, an amusing anecdote or perhaps some droll witticism, had elicited sufficient amusement to give rise to this hilarity. As the laughter subsided it was overtaken in its intensity. Upstairs could be heard the increasingly noticeable and terrible wail of the wind-storm, becoming ever more threatening and ferocious. Suddenly came a terrific thud and the sound of twisting, tortured framework, as, undoubtedly, the upstairs of the café was being demolished while the eyes of all beneath were upturned in fear, listening to the sound of it. Another sound presented itself then — that of rain, and not just rain, but of a bucketing, torrential downpour, roaring so loudly that an awful din was created as what remained above shook violently enough so that the basement too felt to tremble with the violence of it.

A woman in scarlet evening attire stood, screaming out, 'Look!' She pointed to where, at the top of the seaward wall, as it met with the upper floor, water had begun, at first as trickle, then as a cataract, to suddenly and copiously gush.

'Are we to be drowned down here?' a male voice suggested in a panicky and tremulous voice.

There was a disorderly hubbub then, as people backed rapidly away from the cascade, with terror in their eyes. Women began to let out fearful, uncontrollable noises; and when another heavy bump was emitted from above, even one of the men let out a similarly alarming outburst.

Darius began to chuckle, which to me was a reassuring sign. My own take on the sudden assault had been that a shore break of some considerable size had managed to make its way across the esplanade, to spill into available cracks within the subsurface wall. Upon turning to him for explanation, he confirmed my own assessment. 'Shore break. A storm surge,' he reassured, but made no mention to the others; preferring, it appeared, to enjoy the theatre being provided, free of charge, by the patrons.

The husband of our hostess called out for everyone's attention; a stentorian utterance from the small man as he climbed onto a table in order to gain our focus.

'No need to fear. Do not be afraid,' he called. 'There is a high tide rising at the edge of town. A storm surge. The wind has whipped up the tide, but it is only an occasional wave surging across the esplanade, occasionally lapping at the edge of the building.' He looked about at the wide-eyed onlookers, saw that they were not entirely convinced. 'Upstairs has been somewhat damaged,' he told them, giving a little ground, 'but we are safe down here. To leave the shelter of this basement would be unwise and foolish, too. We are quite safe, I can assure you all. Look, the water has ceased spilling in. It was just a rogue wave. Relax, and my wife and I will cater to your needs as best we can.'

It did the trick. The customers were placated, for the moment, by the man's calm and reassuring plea. Even the roaring wind outside seemed satisfied, and reduced its roar, presently.

Darius appeared to be nothing but amused by the episode. 'Don't be concerned,' he said to me, smiling.

'I have never been easily ruffled,' I replied. 'At least, not as far as I can remember.' The remark obviously caused him moderate consternation, and it was clear that I needed to explain the remark. 'Amnesia,' I began, hesitantly.

'I also served in the armed forces. The special forces, as did you, in fact. I don't care to go into the whole history. It's not a subject I enjoy, but since you will understand better than those who have not served, I will tell you this much.

'Volunteers were asked for. The what, where and when of it was classified, and I know you will not ask, because you surely know, that in such instances, contracts are signed and oaths given.' He smiled a knowing smile, and I continued. 'A hot and humid country, full of grief for the innocents within the population as well as the fully fledged combatants. Delineation between the two was often times indistinct and difficult to judge. In this location we discovered several ancient sights; heavy stone constructions which included huge courtyards, arenas not unlike what the Romans are renowned for; temples, grain silos and all the rest which one might imagine to be associated with ancient civilization. There were glaring anomalies however. My company discovered signs of advanced technology at work. It was these oddities which quickly took precedence, leaving the fighting to others as we turned to the business of making secure the area, so that safe access could be gained for the scientists they brought in to make sense of it all.'

I had expected Darius to interrupt about this time, with questions regarding the anomalous technology, but he remained silent, patiently allowing my further recounting at my own speed. He simply nodded his head, lit another cigarette and waited attentively.

'I must confess that I do not remember any of what I am telling you. The memory loss,' I underlined. 'The bump on the head or whatever it was, occurred about a week, as best I can surmise, after our arrival.

'I have gathered what little I know by piecing things together out of conversations with former comrades assigned there with me. But it was *not* a bump on the head. The army calls it a *'stress related amnesia,'* and *'fatigue induced breakdown.'* It's bullshit, of course. Those old friends I managed to talk to, much later on, they say I was as good as gold until the one day I was medically evacuated. No reason was given to the others. They assumed some sort of accident had befallen me while mapping out the labyrinth, the underground tunnels and chambers we had discovered there. It was a most strange experience, to have to restart my life from the middle, without a past, so to speak.' 'Human beings adapt,' Darius responded. He leaned back in his seat, regarding me with some scrutiny, I thought. 'So what? You just put the episode behind you and carried on?'

'What else can one do? I was pensioned off. Not enough for me to exist comfortably, mind, but I am able to supplement my income. I discovered I have some latent artistic talent I had never tapped into. Living by the sea, as I do, I often take a boat out. These waters supply a good variety of fish. It's a pleasant and healthy lifestyle. My life is a good one, and I enjoy it here, my life beside the ocean.'

'Who is it you're trying to convince? Me or yourself, Felix?' I considered the rejoinder to be wholly impertinent. I did not respond at first, but ignored the question, attending to my shot instead, which I consumed in a single swallow, returning the glass to the tabletop with a resounding *plonk!* and staring the man straight in the eye.

Darius's expression in return tended to reflect assumed insouciance; a guileless pose, as if no harm were intended, but I did not buy it. The remark angered me — angered me much more than I knew it should have, and I was forced to question why that was. 'What are you insinuating?' I demanded. 'Why would you question my veracity on this?'

85

His demeanour changed before my eyes. The man's entire aspect seemed in the moment to transform, and at the same instant a change came over me which is beyond explaining; a feeling I was not entirely unfamiliar with, yet no less disabling for that fact. When he spoke this time, I heard in his voice the note of genuine concern.

'Are you alright, Felix?' He refilled my glass, and I did not delay in availing myself of the brimming fluid.

'An odd feeling,' I confessed. 'Something akin to anger,' I told him, 'and aimed in your direction, if you really must know.'

While he looked to be weighing this, I struggled with a rising anxiety, the source of which I was unable to determine. I had not for a very long time felt as shaky as I did just then. Somewhere deep within, something had crumbled; a minor quake, but, as diminutive as it was, the feeling unsettled me enormously and I did not like it the least little bit. If we had not been confined by the storm in this basement, I would surely have gotten to my feet, invented some flimsy pretext for having to depart hastily and left without further complication.

Darius, meanwhile, remained quite still, and I noted what appeared to be the look of deep concern in his features. There was something oddly familiar about him. I couldn't pin it down. There was that weather worn exterior of someone who had spent a lifetime mostly outdoors and exposed to the elements; a countenance bespeaking endurance, even resilience, but also, just below the surface, something of a man applying control to his emotions, lest the vulnerability of the human being beneath be discovered. I was surprised by my ability to notice these things, the ease with which I found myself reading the signs, but then I realised the reason for the faculty; the reason these perceptions came so easily. It was something I had, myself, practiced for a very long time, the shield one employs to fend of being affected by the thousand stings a day, of sorrow, of remorse, perhaps the tugs deep within that one feels when all around them —the people around them, the entire planet and everything that includes— so full of desperate effort just to maintain existence, resisting the temptation to scream at the world, "Why do we persist in this ridiculous charade, pretending that nothing is wrong, that everything is just fine? But let's just go on pretending everything is honky dory!

It hit me, but how could I be sure. The face looking across at me; the man sitting opposite, it could not be. What the hell was going on with me? I had to pull myself back together. Why were my thoughts running away like this?

'Is it just me, or is it becoming stifling in here? Why is it so damned hot?' I asked.

We were in that basement a further two hours before we emerged. The café had suffered not as badly as we had imagined, but the window was smashed in and the floor awash and scattered with debris. The wind by then had abated, and the seas subsided back across the esplanade, although the surf continued pounding the beach until the following morning. My home had not been damaged by the tempest as some had been unfortunate enough to experience, but there were tangles of fallen branches and bits and pieces of refuse and rubble thrown about, the clearing of which occupied me for most of that day. During the evening I amused myself with one thing or another, most of it the simple tasks of tidying and general housekeeping, the preparation of meals, and in the doing of this I chanced to come across the small, wooden box, carved and with a hinged lid, which I had long ago stored in a cupboard and forgotten about. It contained the few pieces of memorabilia I had bothered to keep. A few medals, campaign patches, cartridges and such things as served to jog the memory. That night, as I lay quietly waiting for sleep to come, my mind began to travel back to the time I had mentioned to Darius, and in my sleep came strange images which made no sense at all — so alien to the mind that it could not grasp the meaning, and unsettling, too, although I could not fathom why.

The morning of the second day I woke knowing that I had dreamed again of similar things. They had faded so quickly from my mind as I woke, I could not grasp a single thread but retained only the pale ghosts of something demanding attention. It left me tired, sweaty and with spirits so low that it took great effort to rise. I knew this feeling; a malaise long since put behind me, but here it was again and it worried me immensely in the knowledge of the damage it could do. Despite the will to shake it off I could do no more than mope, as if a sack of sand were strapped to my back, pushing down on me so heavily that I could not find the strength to carry such a weight. That day I sat, confined and numb, unable to will the body into motion, and all the while barely a thought would spark within the theatre of the mind, and I do not know how long I remained in that sorry state. When the room darkened, I knew that evening had encroached again, but I could not will myself to move, not even to rise and move to switch on a single source of light, eventually to fall again into a deep, deep form of sleep which washed away all thoughts and connection to the world.

When at last I did awake, I was not in my home. In a while I realised I was in a kind of hospital; a hospital room, at least, and I was not alone. In a chair beside my bed I recognised the man, Darius. He put aside a folder he had been studying to give me his attention, smiled and rose to come alongside the steel-framed bed on which I lay, and I noticed, only then, the lines attached from me to medical monitors, the like of which have always baffled me.

'Am I sick?' I heard myself ask. A somewhat redundant query I realised too late, seeing as I had been hospitalised. 'How did I get here?'

I dropped by your house to visit you,' Darius, replied. 'How are you feeling?'

'I'm not sure. Buggered. Tired, and depressed, I think. But give me a minute, I've only just woken up. Why did you drop by to visit me? Come to think of it, how did you discover where I live?'

'I have something to confess, Felix, and I'm not sure how you're going to take it. You should be glad of the fact that I did come around, though. You were in a state, to tell the truth. What happened?'

I thought for a while, remembering the disturbing and elusive dream. 'I used to suffer depression. A legacy of the accident, but I thought I was rid of all that. Perhaps it was triggered by the storm? I don't know. These things come and go.'

Darius nodded, thoughtful for a moment. 'But this was quite severe, not to mention sudden.'

'I think it's something I would rather talk to my doctor about,' I told him. The whole thing was making me uncomfortable and I didn't want to continue on about it, but then he dropped the first part of a double headed bombshell.

'I am here at the behest of your doctor. I feel that I must apologise to you, Felix. I have quite a story to tell you and it's going to sound so outrageous. . . Well, I don't know what your reaction will be, but the consensus is that you need to be told. The old generals who used to run the show have all died or moved on, and your situation was never fully resolved.'

My head began to spin. I had to fight to hold things still and I spoke without meaning to, hearing myself say, 'Something has been woken in me. Something terrible.'

Darius moved a step closer, placing a consoling hand on my shoulder and squeezing. 'I know, and I'm sorry. This is partly my fault, Felix, but it's time for you to learn the truth about yourself.'

'What truth?' I growled angrily. What the hell are you talking about?'

'Take it easy, buddy. Let's take is slowly, okay? It's for the best. May I proceed, or would you prefer I allow you to rest, come back another time?'

I didn't know how to respond. Something was going on — something had been awakened and I didn't know how to put it away. Everything Darius was saying to me seemed to be hedging around something I couldn't quite grasp but knew that I should. I didn't know why but I felt as though I was unravelling; a very unnerving feeling; frightening, even. There was something banging within my mind, seeking to alert me of its presence, warn me, perhaps, but it was just beyond the reach of memory and frustratingly unattainable. It felt urgent and repugnant simultaneously. I didn't want to know but I had to know — I had to know what the hell was going on. Everybody seemed to know some kind of secret but me.

'What the hell?' Again I had spoken without meaning to. I attempted to put my hand to my forehead, but found myself prevented by a tangle of bio monitor connections getting in the way. A rising wave of panic began to consume me and I could not understand why. Instinct told me to fight, to hold on, to resist whatever this invisible foe represented, but I felt myself beginning to lose ground.

A doctor entered the room to quickly come to my aid, adjusting the flow of whatever it was being fed into my bloodstream. In a minute I felt it's affects. 'Thank-you,' I managed, before I sank gratefully back into oblivion. . . comforting oblivion. . . an endless and peaceful oblivion**** *******************************
****
****
****
****
****
****
****
****
****
****
****
****
****
****
****
****
****
****
****
****
****
****
****
****
****
****
****
****
****
****
****
****

He should be out of it in a moment.' I heard a woman's far off voice say, as if from across a foggy ocean of time. 'You know that this is make or break.'

'No choice,' replied another. 'It's now or never, poor devil. We have to try.'

'Perhaps we should not have meddled. Left him alone?'

'If we had not provoked the emergence, it would have occurred at any time and we would not be around to assist. No. This way, at least he is not alone in dealing with it.'

'But he was happy enough.'

'Happy? He is not half the man he once was. It had to be done, and you know it.'

'Half the man? You think that's funny?'

'Of course not. I didn't mean it that way. All I'm saying is, If he had gotten ill without our being there to assist, what chance would he have had? And it's you we're talking about. Think about that.'

'Oh, I have. I surely have.'

When the fog at last began to lift I realised I had been moved yet again. It seemed that every time I closed my eyes I could not count on waking up in the same place I had started. That alone gave me reason to be apprehensive. I was being moved about like a piece of property, without being consulted. To know that one's volition has been usurped is a frightening thing. Add to it the fact that my own mind had conspired against me by refusing to fix reality in its place. I seemed to be slipping between time periods; one moment in the past, working on deciphering the intricacies of an underground maze chock full of alien artefacts, the next, standing at the foreshore, watching, as the sun dipped behind a stormy horizon; a conversation in a café with a complete stranger, but not a stranger; being in the grip of an unshakeable, mind numbing somnolence, a kind of trance, as hours or days slipped by, without knowing why or how to break the awful spell. Then to wake yet again in a hospital bed without knowing the reason why, and the mind, all the while, refusing to grasp the meaning of it all, only allowing events to toss me one way, then the next, like a boat without a rudder, tossed within an unceasing storm upon a hostile sea.

My eyes opened. I was lying in a hospital bed, but a different room once again. I recognised Darius, who was at my side. He gripped my shoulder. I guessed it was the pressure of his grip that roused me. Two others were present. A woman, who, because of her attire, I assumed to be a doctor, and man wearing a khaki uniform on which military medical insignia were pinned, identifying him as an army doctor. I absorbed this without surprise, feeling enervated beyond belief, but I did not attempt to speak, only wait and let the continued absurdity unfold.

'How are you feeling?' Darius asked, but the question remained unanswered. It was impossible to say. I was still surrounded by a kind of obscuring fog, detaching me from those in the room with me, and even from myself. I had no way of describing the sensation accurately, not even to myself. All I could manage was to shake my head slowly and hope Darius understood the meaning.

'Okay,' he replied, 'then rest while I try to explain what is happening. You won't remember half of what I am about to tell you, but the army has been keeping an eye on you for several years. These people here with us are doctor Major Andrew Keenan of the medical corps, a man with a lifetime of experience in unusual medical cases such as yours. The lady is also a doctor. Professor Judith Forsythe, a psychiatric professional of the highest calibre.'

I did not greet or respond my visitors in any way, but to look in their direction.

The woman, professor Forsythe, smiled. 'Hello Felix. I hope you are feeling a little better. We are here to help rid you of your present malady, and we think we know how we might do just that. Right, major Keenan?' she said, turning to the man in the army uniform who sat beside her.

'That's right. Hello Felix. I am major Keenan. I wonder if you remember me? We crossed paths almost twenty two years ago, in the African Congo, where you were stationed for a time. Do the words *Operation Parasol* ring a bell with you, in any way?'

It did not—not in the slightest, and I shook my head slowly. Why don't you tell Felix the story, Captain?' he directed at Darius. 'Maybe hearing the story will unlock something of the events in Felix's memory.'

Darius walked across the room to retrieve a chair from against the wall under the window, brought it over and placed it midway between myself and my guests, and seated himself. 'Okay, here it is,' he began.

'Twenty two years ago, a man walked out of the African basin, the sole survivor of a crashed army supply plane that had hit the side of a mountain during a violent rainstorm. There were three survivors, initially, but after his colleagues had died from their injuries he managed to drag himself out of there, but with a most curious tale to tell, after his eventual rescue. What he related to his superior officers had them very much astir.' Darius stopped, seemingly unhappy about something, and he turned to the two sitting against the wall.

'Look, this is going to take some telling. Can't we wheel Felix out into the sunshine where we can all be more comfortable?' He turned to me. 'How about it, Felix? Want to go outside? There a nice park, and you can have a cigarette.'

The prospect of warm sunshine and fresh air appealed greatly.

'Yes,' I managed. 'Sounds alright to me.'

A great fuss was made by the doctors and nurses, but after a bit of wrangling we were able to move proceedings outside, onto a green area about which the multistoried hospital complex surrounded. I was still attached to a single drip-line. The doctors agreed that the rest of the tubes and wiring could be removed, and I was, by this time, beginning to feel somewhat more like myself.

'This is better, right?' Special ops Captain Darius McNally expressed cheerily. That was his designation and rank, he informed me during the relocation process, but the more time I spent in the man's company, the more I felt that there was something very peculiar about him.

'The survivor of that supply plane crash,' he said, taking up the recounting of the story once again. 'While searching through the wreckage, looking for useful survival items, I expect, the man discovered a cave entrance. It was an entrance to an underground network of tunnels, chambers and what-have-you, but it contained a collection of crazy alien artefacts and technology. Not that he recognised it as alien, at first. A detail was sent to check out his story and it was they who made that determination. You understand that when I say alien, I don't mean Japanese, Felix. I am saying, *Alien*. . . from another world.'

I searched what remained of my memory, trying to locate any thread of a memory which might relate to the story so far. Nothing occurred. Not a single piece could I could remember of my past which, in any way at all, connected to the story. Darius moved on with the account:

'The initial report confirmed a collection of very strange equipment. Electronic in nature, but the photographic evidence was insufficient to describe exactly what the stuff was, and so me and a team of fifteen were despatched, Felix. Taken out of my combat role and used to safeguard the science team who went in to investigate. The brass was excited, as you might imagine.' He laughed. 'I suppose they thought they had found ray guns and photon cannons, like from science fiction. 'Anyway, it wasn't a particularly well organised party. No one had any idea of what the stuff was, or what it was capable of. What it might have been used for. It *was* alien, after all, and it was powered as if straight out of the ether. You can imagine how excited they were about *that*. I'm hoping that some of this might jog your memory. Is any of this helpful?'

'Not a bit, but please continue,' I answered.

'It was a poorly organised affair, with people getting in each other's way nearly the whole time. Some dimwit decided to throw a switch, just to see what would happen. I don't know, maybe he thought it was the light switch or something. The outcome, though, nobody could have imagined.'

At this point Darius reached into his pocket for his cigarettes, and taking one for himself, offered them around. After we had lit up and taken a draw of two, he continued.

'I was in a very disadvantageous spot right at that moment, I'm sorry to say, Felix. An alcove, of which there were two. I was standing in exactly the wrong spot at exactly the wrong time. Some kind of field surrounded me, the man who witnessed the unfortunate episode attested. There was a lot of commotion, and not knowing that he was responsible for initiating the machine, way too much time was wasted before the situation was resolved. By then, of course, it was far too late.

'From where I was standing at that time, it felt as though I had been plunged into ice water. You know the feeling. The shock of it causes one to gasp and stop breathing. The mammalian reflex, it's called, and not very pleasant. Add to that the sensation of being pummelled and beaten thoroughly by twenty bat-wielding sons-of-bitches, and you have an approximation of what it felt like to be standing at the focal point of an alien xerox copying machine when some idiot throws the switch and starts it running.'

The image was a vivid one, and he even managed to make what must have been a dreadful experience sound humorous. I looked at the man with fresh eyes, imagining what it must have been like. He was certainly lucky to be alive. But then it dawned on me.

'Did you say, *An alien xerox copying machine?*' 'Yes I did.'

'A copying machine,' I repeated again. You mean—?'

He sat there smiling, nodding his head as he exhaled a plume of tobacco smoke into the air. 'That's what the accursed thing turned out to be. A bloody copier. . . a replicator. A goddamned, alien, two for one, cheap-at-twice-the-price, doppelganger making machine.'

The idea of such a thing staggered me. 'No kidding? Wow.'

He was looking at me kind of funny. In fact, at this very moment, they were *all* looking at me funny, with expectant looks on their faces. I was concentrating on Darius's face again. That face. I only used a shaving mirror at home, and used it maybe twice a week, so my own reflection wasn't terribly familiar to me. And then it hit me — hit me like an express train!

'You're not. . . ' This was too absurd a thought. 'Nobody is suggesting. . ?' I felt like a bug under a magnifying glass. An amoeba under a microscope. The thought was too incongruous, but here I was, being scrutinized by a medical doctor, a professor of psychiatry and a military captain. It was then that the remaining logic of it hit me. How dumb was I?' I was unable to speak. The whole picture snapped into place in an instant, leaving me breathless, stunned and unable to think, let alone talk. I tried again to form a word. Any word, but nothing would come.

'Get him back inside,' I heard the lady doctor say, sharply. 'Quickly now.'

I was whisked hurriedly away in the wheelchair, back to my hospital room, but I was beginning to fight my way out of the fugue by that time. 'I'm okay,' I managed, but gladly accepted the oxygen mask being offered. 'A panic attack. Just a panic attack.'

The three of them surrounded my bed, Darius at my shoulder with a look of great concern on his face—or was it *my* face? 'You sure, buddy?' he asked. You gave us a bit of a scare.'

'I'm okay,' I repeated, pulling the mask away and setting it aside. I couldn't take my eyes off of his, *my* face. How had I not noticed during all this time? What did all this mean and what would happen now? I wondered. I lifted the oxygen mask and took a couple more good, deep breaths to be sure.

'I need to hear you say it,' I said to Darius. It's rocking my brain and I need to hear it said, because it's just too difficult to grasp. It doesn't feel real. None of it.'

Major Andrew Keenan, the medical corps doctor, confronted Darius with a stern visage. 'I have told you this would be too much for him,' he growled. 'This could cause irreparable damage.'

'I'm fine, doctor,' I said one more time. 'Really, I am.'

'You don't understand, lad. You might be feeling fine, but in the longer term. . . ' but he decided not to finish the statement. I could only remain focussed on Darius. 'Forgive me for staring. This is so strange. It's like stepping outside of myself and looking back. Such a shock. We've spent all that time talking together, and I cannot believe I didn't recognise — *me!*' 'Actually,' interrupted the lady psychiatrist, 'It is you who are the captain. You are the copy, weren't you paying attention to the story?'

'Yes, that's right,' I responded, somewhat numbed by the thought. 'I am the doppelganger.' I had to hear it said again, and so I repeated, 'I am the doppelganger. I am the doppelganger,' I repeated again for good measure. The reality of it was beginning to set in buy this time. I was the doppelganger. . . the copy. . . the carbon copy. . . the facsimile. And it was beginning to impress itself upon me with mounting significance.

'What does that mean?' I asked, looking from one face to the other, searching for reassurance. It was like being told one is insignificant, a mere replica and not a person. But I was me, not a copy. I am me!

Darius's hand gripped my shoulder, bringing my attention back into focus, as if he understood what I was thinking at the moment.'Would you like to hear the whole of it, Felix? You need to understand the dilemma having two of me put us in.'

'Not two of you,' I objected. 'Not two of you! I am me, Felix White — Felix Gordon White!'

'Yes, of course. Sorry Felix. Of course you are.'

The medical doctor intervened at that moment though. 'I do not advise continuing. Not today. This is too much to absorb at once. I strongly advise we allow Mr White to rest. You must realise how much of a shock this must be for him. The mind has a great deal to assimilate, all at once, do you see? We must allow Felix to absorb all he has learned today. A night's sleep will be of enormous benefit, and I really must insist. Do you not agree?' he asked the lady psychiatrist.

She nodded to this. 'Yes, I do agree—' and turning to me, 'You must rest now, Mr White. Felix,' she amended. 'We can resume in the morning, allowing the mind to assimilate the gravity of it. It is for the best. For the best, you understand.'

It was not a question; it was a directive, and I was being told to hold back my curiosity, my desperate need to know, until they decided it was time to tell me the rest of the story.

I all but begged, but it was no good. They had made the decision they insisted was best for me, and that was that. It was mid afternoon when they left me in my hospital bed, alone with only my thoughts, my fears and my uncontrollable speculations of what it all meant for my future. My hospital doctor allowed me two diazepam, advised me to rest, and it only was around two in the afternoon. How the hell was I supposed to do that?

The hours that followed were terrible. Everyone had gone. I had missed the lunchtime hospital meal while we were out in central quad, and my stomach was empty. Trying to nap on an empty stomach is something I could never do. I lay, staring up at the ceiling, trying my damnedest to still my mind, which seemed to be spinning, unable to grasp anything that would hold still for just a moment so that I could get my bearings. The more time that went by the more restless I became, and it was so not at all like me, not be able to still my mind at will. Years of meditation had put me in good stead for most emotional upsets, but this—? This was a different ball game.

I called the nurse, a squat, dour woman who insisted that she must discuss with my doctor any additional sedation. She promised to do so, but when maybe ninety minutes had passed she still had not returned, and I was still trying to wrestle my mind into stillness.

How was this possible? The question was the single constant amidst the whirl. Darius had been duplicated. That duplicate was me, Felix. That much was coming into focus, but a duplicate of Darius would be another Darius. . . That made me Darius, not Felix. I concentrated on that for a long time, fixing it into position, holding it down until it no longer threatened to fly off again into the whirlpool of unruly disorder. It was difficult, but I began to piece it together, one fact at a time.

Darius had walked into an alien machine, someone had initiated the thing, and *pop!* Darius times two. Me and him, of which I was the copy. Yes, it was coming along. The military now found themselves with a pair. How could they leave me laying in this bed with so many unanswered questions? I have no knowledge of a life before having it pieced back together after my accident. . . but it was not the accident I was told about. It was the moment of my being popped into existence by the machine. Of course I had no memories before then. They must have concocted a whole history for me, told me that I had amnesia, set me up with an army pension and sent me out into the world to fend for myself. *Thanks for your service and see you later!* So what were they doing here now? They dropped me like a hot potato, once, why would they give a damn now?

I had been so distracted and deep in thought that I had failed to notice Darius come up beside me.

'I thought you would be sleeping like a baby by now.'

'Fat chance,' I replied, more angrily than I had intended. 'What is the army doing back in my life?' I demanded, foregoing any greeting. 'They were rid of me. Tucked away in this nothing little fishing town on the edge of nowhere. They could have washed their hands of me for good, and nobody would have been any the wiser. So why now?'

Darius stood with a pensive expression on his mug. 'May I?' he asked, indicating the edge of the bed.

'Sure, sit,' I told him.

'That's pretty much how it would have gone down,' he began. 'They couldn't bury you fast enough. In fact, if it were not for me and a small and select handful of people, nobody else in the world would know of your existence. Fact is, buddy, I put them in a corner over this. Threatened to expose the whole show.'

I chuckled at the thought of the army caving in under such a threat. 'Oh? And how did that work out for you?'

'Not so well, I'm afraid, but I'm an officer and I have quite a high profile. They couldn't very well just put me up against a wall and shoot me. That's what I was hoping anyway.'

'Quite the gamble,' I agreed. 'Why?'

He looked at me, hard, as if not understanding. 'Why the hell do you think? You are me. They can't just dump you off somewhere out of the way and expect you to find your own way. Especially with that flimsy amnesia story. I thought about how that must be for you, living without a past. No family history, a story of a broken marriage, which you had nothing to do with. It must have been difficult to live with that.'

'A man lives with what he has to,' I explained. 'I only had the present and the future. That's the way I saw it, and so I made do. It was enough. We all have to fight to survive in this world.'

He nodded, and we remained silent for a minute. 'How are you dealing with all this, so far?'

'Not so great, for a while. It's a lot, but I'm getting there.' 'It has to be,' he agreed.

'So this is all about covering their arse, right? And keeping you happy.'

'To a point,' he replied. 'They're not going to tolerate much more of this. . . risk exposure.'

'It was your big idea to tell me the truth?' 'Yep.'

'Well thank-you for that, I think. It does at least explain the gaping holes in my life, the middle of the night waking up sweaty and confused. It hasn't exactly been easy sailing, but I'm not entirely sure that being enlightened is going to be helpful, and there's no way out of this. . . not for me. If I thought I could twist their arm for a great pile of cash, I would jump at it, but I know it would only cost them the price of a bullet to solve the problem. I'm not in the greatest bargaining position.'

'Ain't that the truth.' He seemed to be mulling something over, unsure of whether or not to give voice to whatever it was occupying his mind. The ease with which I was able to read him was astonishing. I had only to witness a look, a cocked eyebrow, a pause or a change of stance, each move conveying a wealth of information. People had always been a mystery to be, but I could read this man like a book.

'What's on your mind, Darius? I've seen that look and I know what it means. What are you concocting?'

'I think you mean, *concocted!*

'I do? Why?'

'Well, I've had a long time to think about this day, as you might imagine, and by the fact of my being something of a tactician, I thought to develop contingencies, just in case things didn't pan out quite as well as they might.'

'And things aren't panning out so well?' I enquired.

'Could be better,' he admitted, but withholding an explanation. 'I was wondering, Felix. Have you considered the possible advantages of being two people?'

- PART TWO -

With all that had been happening in my life lately, I had not considered what advantages there might be in being one of a pair of bookends. I was very much concerned with the disadvantages of being the person I was, meaning a manufactured copy, and in the short time I had, thus far, to appraise myself of my strange new situation, I had become aware of no obvious advantages in being one. Darius, on the other hand, had been given time to consider what possible advantages might arise out of the oddity of our anomalous situation. For years he had thought about meeting his copy, irrespective of the fact of the army expressly forbidding it. He had always felt an immutable sense of responsibility, and an irresistible curiosity. Despite that fact — that of my springing into existence being a complete accident — he had ever since been unable to convince himself of it being anyone else's obligation but his own, to ensure my safety and well-being. I must confess that I would feel very much the same duty of care. I could only compare the feeling to the reported connection that twins often describe, only, this may be even more compelling. In very short time I had to concede that a visceral connection — a very powerful bond — emerged between the two of us. The more time we spent in one another's company the more established became the inexplicable link. There is no other way to explain it other than to say that I am he and he is me. It was as powerful an advent as it was unlikely. Between us, we felt as if we had circumvented a law of nature which might have otherwise prevented two complex organisms from being so identical without occupying the same space, and over the next couple of days our bonding began to surpass anything we ever might have thought possible.

Early on the morning of the third day, I was woken by two men dressed in dark clothing. The nightlight above my bed prevented me from seeing anything but dark, silhouetted shapes, but I knew instinctively that these guys were not medical staff. The one closest to me raised a finger to his lips while the other said quietly, 'Its time to go, Mr White.'

There's a great deal to be said in favour of instinct. For someone in my situation, that of having little reliable memory, instinct becomes even more important than usual. There was no way I was going anywhere with these two, looming, shadowy, shapes of the early morning.

'Wrong room,' I told them, hoping to throw them off balance, even for an instant. 'Mr White is across the corridor. This is the second time people have made the mistake.'

It caused them to pause, thoughtful for a moment. 'Twenty-one, across the hallway,' I said, but a torch was produced and shone in my face. While I was temporarily blinded by the guy with the torch, the other moved swiftly from behind the other, clamping his had over my face with a wad of cotton saturated with what I can only assume was ether or some such thing. The other grabbed my legs, and as I was being carted off like a side of beef on its way to the butcher shop, I lost consciousness.

When I awoke, I was trust up and lying on a mattress in the back of a van, hands tied in front of me. The two who had snatched me sat either side, keeping an eye on me as we were being driven away at speed.

It wasn't long before the van pulled up somewhere. The pair who were watching me exited, swiftly, slamming the rear door behind them. During their exiting I got a fleeting glimpse of a brightly lit area of tarmac. A short, hushed discussion ensued outside the van before one returned to pull a sack over my head, and shortly after I was hauled out, stood up and marched along for a while, told to climb half a dozen steep steps, at the top of which I was guided cautiously along a narrow aisle, at last to be lowered into a seat and told to sit still.

There was some hurried activity around me for a minute or two; when a door was shut my ear drums popped in reaction to being sealed into a closed environment and I was fairly certain I had just been loaded into a small aeroplane, and in a few minutes time we were accelerating along a runway and lifting off. When enough time had gone by that my annoyance level was about reaching its limit, I spoke up.

'How about taking this goddamned bag off of my head, you pricks?' — and much to my relief, someone from behind pulled it from my head.

I was indeed aboard an aircraft; one of those small business jets, and it was all but empty, but for myself and my kidnappers, whom I could see quite clearly at last. They wore camo fatigues, military jackets and balaclavas. One sat across the aisle from me, the other a couple of seats behind his friend.

'So, where are we off to, lads?' I enquired, but neither one of them responded. The buggers didn't even acknowledge my presence. 'Great. This is going to be pleasant,' I expressed bitterly, and resigned myself to what was probably going to be a long and uneventful flight.

I grabbed a folder out of the pocket in back of the seat in front of me, and read aloud: 'Cessna Citation CJ4, the last word in aviation excellence. . . . it will revolutionize the way you think about aircraft cabin luxury and comfort.'

'Knock it off,' the guy across the aisle said at last. 'There's someone wanting to talk to you at the end of the ride.'

'It talks!' I returned, surprised. 'What is it with you guys you have to come snatch me out of my bed in the middle of the night?' — but it soon became clear that we had already reached the limit of this guy's conversational skills.

I read the brochure cover to cover, learning a few things about aviation I had never known before. For instance, we were likely travelling at around five hundred miles per hour, in a craft that could climb to over thirteen thousand metres in under twenty eight minutes, and we had a range, if the tanks were full at takeoff, of three thousand six hundred and thirty five kilometres. Not far enough that we could fly to another country, therefore. I was pleased about that, but why did the brochure quote cruising speed in miles per hour and range in kilometres? I wondered.

There was no point in me taking undue exception to my present situation. I mean, what the hell was there I could do about it anyway? The one philosophy I had adhered to in my strange life was never to worry about those things I could do nothing about. I had tried to evade my captors at the hospital. Beyond that, attempting to leap from an aircraft travelling at five hundred kilometres an hour at a possible ceiling height of forty five thousand feet seemed a little excessive and beyond the pail. I had done my bit, and so there was no further point on stressing about it. I could only wait to see what transpired. To this end I decided I might as well grab what sleep I could manage, after being interrupted back at the hospital. It was likely I might need to be at the top of my game quite soon. If the need arose and a chance presented itself, stamina and alertness were attributes best kept in reserve.

I was prodded awake an unknown amount of time later. We were no longer airborne, and through the window I could see nothing but an expanse of desert, on which the remote airfield we had landed on had been constructed.

'Come on, let's go,' my escort encouraged.

I was disembarked in the customary fashion and piled into a waiting vehicle, driven towards a building at the edge of the airfield. Upon arrival my escorts walked me inside, a combination hangar, control tower and administration block constructed of concrete, with walls three feet thick, and then instructed to sit on the one, single, steel chair propped against the wall outside an office.

'Wait here,' one of them told me. 'He'll be out in a moment—' and with that the pair strolled away to I knew not where.

It was hot, I noted, but this was *Oz*, and it was nearing summertime. Judging by the lack of vegetation out there, the best I could guess was that I was somewhere within a hundred thousand square miles radius of nowhere, central Australia. My dwindling spirits and sinking hopes were interrupted when the door I sat beside snapped open, and out came my doppelganger. 'Goddamn it!' I exploded, coming to my feet. 'You could have told me. I've been scared out of my wits since I was snatched from my cot in the wee hours! What the hell is going on here?' There was the look of moderate surprise on his face. 'Come in,' he said, turned on his heel and walked back into the office. 'Take a seat,' he offered, as I followed him in, and I availed myself of the chair placed in front of the desk, behind which he seated himself.

'I am not who you think I am, Mr White. I must explain. The man you are familiar with, Captain Darius McNally, will be arriving shortly. Meanwhile—'

'What. . . ?' I sat, staring at yet another split image of myself in pure amazement and incomprehension. Having one copy is enough to rattle the brain, but two? The impact was like having the grey matter explode into vapour. It was that confronting. Being hit by a bolt of lightning could not have been more of a jolt than I received at that precise moment.

He waited for me to absorb this new development with an impassive demeanour. My own face was once again looking back at me.

'Are you right?' he inquired. 'Then allow me to proceed. You will be issued with an electronic identification marker and furbished with the information needed to allow you to make sense of what is going on here. Much of the operation is *need-to- know*, you understand, but I have been informed by prime that you are a special case and are to be shown every courtesy.'

'Prime?'

'Our progenitor, Darius McNally. He is referred to as *prime*.'

'Oh?' I responded, spotting the inconsistency. 'I hate to be contradictory so early in the piece, pal, but progenitor is hardly the correct description, is it? I mean, strictly speaking, there has been no genetic reproduction here. Perhaps templet would be a more appropriate term? We're only cheap *knock-offs*, you know.'

Why I had said that, I wasn't entirely sure. In reprisal for being abducted from my hospital bed, I wouldn't wonder. This guy didn't much like it, though, and it pleased me no end to see a flicker of annoyance cross his face.

'As a matter of interest, how are you called?'

There was a brief pause before his response was forthcoming. 'I am designated Decca.'

'Just Decca? What? . . . as in number ten?'

I was becoming more annoyed the longer I sat there, and there was no single, identifiable reason for it. It felt as though my limit for absurdity had been reached, but add to it that I was having to integrate into my thinking the fact that I had been reduced to one of *who-knew-how-many?* factory edition Darius's. It takes quite a deal of wrapping one's head around something like that, I can tell you. My mind was identifying the whole thing as some kind of huge joke, and I was fast losing the ability to regard any of it as being connected to the world I thought I existed in.

'That's right,' my slightly miffed bookend responded.

'This is just too weird,' I told him. 'But let's get on with it, shall we?'

Through the window, behind Decca, I noticed something in the sky. It was approaching our location. A chopper! and soon the distinct *thropping* sound of its rotors beating the air became more distinct.

'That will be prime. He was delayed, but now that he has arrived, he will acquaint you with all that we do here. Take this—' He reached into a drawer and pulled out an identification tag, offered it to me across the desk. 'It's your electronic pass and I.D.'

It was no more than a thin slither of metal. I received it in the palm of my hand and looked at him questioningly.

'You peal off the backing paper and it will stick to your clothing. Do it now and go out and join prime. I have work to do.'

Darius, aka *prime*, was just walking away from the old Huey Warbird he arrived in as I walked out onto the apron from the cover of the hangar.

'Felix!' he greeted, seeing me emerge from the shadows. 'Great to see you again. How was your journey?'

'Interesting,' I replied, following alongside as he strode purposefully back toward the way I had come. 'I've never been kidnapped before. It's one more interesting items off of my *"Must Do"* list.'

He thought the reply was enormously amusing and laughed accordingly, but then he seemed to grasp the meaning. 'You were not well treated? They were instructed to treat you with respect.'

'Maybe they didn't get the memo. . . but forget it. I'm here now, and glad to be out of that damn hospital.

'So what the hell is going on, Darius? Or should I be addressing you as *Prime?*'

We halted to finish our conversation under the shade of the hanger, avoiding the blazing heat of the midday sun. While he enquired as to how I was feeling and one or two other sundry concerns, a team of six men dragged the Huey into the hanger with us, rolling it on a wheeled sled designed for the job.

When it had been positioned inside the painted, yellow rectangle, Darius grabbed my elbow, positioning me at the corner of the marked area— 'Here,' he said. 'We're about to descend'— and the whole area began to lower; the weight of the Huey, Darius and myself, including the weight of six inches thickness of reinforced concrete, measuring, I guessed, about twenty metres square.

We continued to descend, revealing an immense, well lit chasm beneath ground, supported by steel framework, stanchions and intricate support structures, all in all what must have covered four hectares of space, on the floor of whisch were parked all manner of vehicles, from armoured pc' , multi wheeled cargo carriers, four by four land rangers, dirt motorcycles, two light aircraft and an additional pair of Bell choppers.

I whistled loudly through my teeth. 'Are you kidding me?'

Darius wore an enormous grin, pleased as hell with the look on my face, which must have reflected my utter astonishment.

'What do you think, Felix? Do you like my toys?'

'This is beyond incredible,' I told him while twisting about, attempting to take in everything around me.

The great slab we stood on came to rest at the bottom of its travel with a slight thump, and we stepped off, with Darius leading us toward a partitioned area containing a canteen—chairs, tables, dispensing machines, etc.— where food and beverage was made available for the workforce.

I grabbed a sandwich out of a machine while Darius prepared two coffees and brought them to a table, where we seated ourselves to relax and talk for a while. He seemed delighted by my inability to take in the immensity of the operation, as I continued to do my *head-*

on-a-stick impersonation, attempting to grasp its meaning. It was he who began the conversation.

'In answer to your question a moment ago. Call me Darius. It's my name. . . *Our name,*' he corrected. 'So weird isn't it? Nevertheless, here we are and this is the way that it is. This is a very special place, Felix. From here a great many very important things will be implemented, and you have the privilege of being a major part of it all. Quite a change from where you were a few short weeks ago, isn't it?'

'You've got that right, but I was happy enough a few short weeks ago. And Decker, What about him? Another copy. Is that what this place is, a printing press for people? I don't like it,' I confided. 'It's not right.'

The very moment I voiced my opinion, a soldier dressed in battle fatigues walked across the floor, not a dozen paces from where we sat— *yet another fabricated human being!*

'Darius. . . what's going on? There's something very wrong about this place.'

The question was already superfluous. It was entirely obvious to me, by this time, what was going on. Only, I wanted to hear it said aloud; spelled out clearly and in minute detail, just exactly what nefarious operation was taking place out here, deep underground in the central desert. What had I landed myself in? I wondered, and with sudden trepidation.

His face betrayed to me many things in that instant. The cold, unblinking gaze told me he was done with pretending to be my ally. The barely perceivable curl at the corner of his mouth; I knew it only too well. It was the very same involuntary characteristic I possessed, a sole indicator reflecting the inner workings of one's mind, manifesting as an outward sign that an abrupt change had taken place.

He had tried to keep the wool pulled over my eyes, right to the very end. This man was a predator. I knew it then, for a certainty: cold, calculating and without a shred of humanity; I was in the presence of evil, and the ice-cold chill that suddenly came over me told me it was so. There came a deep dread, so terrifying that it held me motionless and trembling in its clammy grip. . . and there was nowhere to run!

I was a lamb in a slaughterhouse, the vileness and depravity radiating from this ungodly being radiated from him to me unfiltered, without mitigation, producing so powerful a sense of revolution within my psyche that I was on my feet and fleeing like a frightened animal before conscious thought had time to warn what instinct alone had revealed.

I did not look back over my shoulder, only ran blindly toward the first bit of cover presenting itself, a long corridor from which a further number of corridors branched. My heart raced uncontrollably as I searched wildly for anywhere to pause, even for a moment, in order to pull together any hasty plan of escape, but I was many metres underground, how then to reach the surface without being discovered?

In my mind were the afterimages, and the awful imprint of being touched by something *vile* — something very ancient and not at all human! Not quite images exactly; an emotional response, more like. I was reacting purely intuitively and viscerally, to something so alien and unknown, so without pity, so powerful and overwhelming that, on the most basic of levels, and from only the briefest of encounters, it seemed able to corrupt with its deeply abhorrent quality.

The feeling was so far beyond any nightmare I had ever experienced, and I had experienced a good many in my time. I had to get away, distance myself from its influence. That had been my single imperative at that moment, and it crowded my mind to the exclusion of all other concerns.

I was behaving like a rat in a maze—a frightened rat—and already the effects of so massive a dose of adrenalin was beginning to cause my body to shake and tremble terribly. I needed to hunker down somewhere out of sight for a little while, I reasoned with some difficulty; to pull myself together, and quickly. I was behaving like a panicked child and it just would not do. Not if I was going to get out of here. I was in a jam and I had to think my way out of it, but I had acted without forethought and already I saw the pointlessness of my rash response.

My mind at last began to clear. I was crouched in a corner, concealed behind a collection of bins stuffed and overflowing with cotton waste and shredded cardboard. My pulse was beginning to slow a little by this time, and my rasping breath, too; but if I thought the situation was improving, what happened next shattered any allusions of hope I may have had in that moment—blasted it all to hell.

'Why do you run?' came the voice to me from within my skull. *'Come on out of there and don't be so tiresome. I can see exactly where you are, Felix. You cannot escape. Give it up, my friend.*

My men can come for you, if you insist on continuing this charade, but it's far better you act like an adult, don't you think? I raised my hand in front of me, extending two fingers, meaning to test his assertion, and even before I could pose the question, the voice in my head told me, *'Two fingers, Felix.'*

I allowed myself to lean back, defeated, propped against the wall, my breath escaping in an extended sigh as if I were deflating like some blow-up manikin. I was done for.

He was right and I knew it; there was no escape. We were inexplicably linked by some ineffable nexus of commonality; some quirky law of the universe had bound me to him, and likely to all the other identical flesh and bone copies produced by that infernal machine. But what was it I had detected in him? What was it about him that had reviled me so totally upon the instant of making that intangible contact with his mind? It felt like some impossible waking nightmare I could not shake myself out of.

'Come on back, Felix. Let us finish our conversation like grown men.'

'Okay,' I replied aloud, and screwing up my courage, stood. 'Just keep yourself to yourself. I don't know what the you are, but you are definitely not me— not even human, I suspect. Whatever you're up to, just keep out of my goddamned head, at least.'

Despondently I began making my way back to the canteen, but when I arrived he was not there.

'Over here, Felix. This way.' He stood beside a doorway some distance from where I had departed in such a hurried and ungainly manner, waving to catch my attention, and smiling, no doubt much amused by my exhibition of cool courage and daring do.

I had no choice but to acceded to his beckoning with all the self composure I could muster—which is to say, with very little. He laughed outright as I neared. 'That was interesting,' he remarked, gripping my elbow and leading me inside the room. 'Come on through, Felix' — and he began chuckling in a most peculiar and unsettling way.

The moment I stepped through the doorway I was set upon by two goons who had been standing just inside. Doppelgangers both. They took me from Darius' grip and hauled me to a large, steel framed and cantilevered chair which had been designed to restrain such as I, with leather bindings: head, wrist, arms, and at the ankles, the straps pulled uncomfortably tight; and again I found myself wondering at the detached and counterfeit quality of everything happening around me, as if none of it were real, oddly lacking the usual characteristics which ought to accompany dealing with real life.

'Human nature,' Darius said, looking over an array of tools on a stainless steel trolley. It never fails to amaze me,' and he chuckled once again. 'Where were you running to?' — but when I withheld any response he simply continued. 'A perfect example of *the fight-or-flight response*. Don't worry. These implements are not for you.'

He pushed the trolley away, allowing it to roll until it struck, bouncing from the wall with a clanking sound and coming to rest.

He dismissed the two who had jumped me, and when they had left us alone he remained standing, arms folded across his chest, regarding me in amused contemplation.

'What are you?' I demanded. 'How did you get inside my head?'

He dragged a stool from under a table and seated himself beside me. 'A remarkable process, isn't it? And I'm very glad you brought it up. Do you know what particle entanglement is?'

I did, as it happened. I knew that split subatomic particles, electrons or neutrons, for example, were inexorably linked after being split, regardless of vast distance between them. 'I have read something about it,' I replied. "*Spooky action at a distance*," is what Albert Einstein is known to have called it.'

'Yes, exactly. Very good, but I don't know why I bothered to ask you that, really.' He shrugged. 'A courtesy, perhaps. I know you do, because, *we* are entangled. You and me. Every one of our atoms are identical, Felix. We are an exact image of the other, as, by the way, are every one of the personnel working here in this underground installation.'

'That bloody machine,' I cursed, vehemently. 'It should have been smashed and destroyed utterly. The damn thing brought me into this miserable existence, and it's responsible for ruining whatever sort of a life this is. Why those idiots chose to play god with it, I'll never understand.'

Again with that sneering and chuckle in his throat. 'Oh, poor you. Poor Felix. . . And yet, *not* poor Felix.' He sat, looking at me, as if waiting for me to respond; daring me to question. . . something. What was I missing? I wondered.

'Come on, Felix. Felix who is not Felix at all!' he teased.

What the hell was he driving at? Why did he think this was so wonderfully amusing?

'You don't get it, do you?' he said. I don't suppose I can really blame you. It *is* a bit obvious, and things which are obvious, you people seem to have a knack of missing these things altogether. Such a blind species. What is the saying? *"As obvious as the nose on your face."*

He laughed again. 'Come along, Felix who is not Felix. Think about it, do! The image and the reflection. The reflection and the image. But let us go back, shall we? Go back to when it all started. The day that soldier flicked a switch he should not have, and, *poof!* That's when it all started, isn't it?'

'The assignment? I have no memory of it, Darius. You know I don't. How could I? It was *your* assignment. I wasn't made yet. You know that.'

'Do you know what I know? Apparently not, but why not? I would like to know.'

'You're talking in riddles,' I told him, irritated by the whole thing. 'If you have knowledge of something you feel you must tease me with, you can jamb it where the sun don't shine. What you haven't answered yet, is, What the hell are you? because I felt something nasty a while ago. You're not human, are you. But how the hell can that be? The machine? What is that thing and what exactly does it do?'

'Ah. . . so many questions now. The machine? The machine is an amazing piece of equipment, is it not? And not of this world! Not of *this* world,' he repeated for emphasis. 'You all have so much to learn. Mankind is a baby? We are many aeons beyond even what you can imagine. So try wrapping your mind around that, why don't you? Of course, the human mind is unable even to grasp such a period of time. You make your plans based on what, a day, a week, perhaps as much as a year ahead?'

'While I do that, would you consider releasing me from this chair? It's. . . a little disconcerting.'

'I don't think so. You're rather skittish, and I would rather not have to go to the bother of getting you back again. I don't have the time, I'm afraid.'

'Can you blame me for reacting the way I did?' I asked. 'It comes as rather a shock, you know. Having someone in one's head besides yourself is a little out of the ordinary. I wonder if this is how it is to be schizophrenic? Just how far ahead of us is your kind?'

'I have told you. More than you could imagine. For instance, we designed that machine over a millennia ago. I was out of commission and abandoned when your military found it. It must have been a temporary bug that put it out of action. It worked just fine when that fool of a soldier threw the switch.'

'Yes,' I agreed. 'Tell me about it, Darius. What was a machine like that doing abandoned, in Al Salvador of all places?'

'Alright,' he said, appearing to warm to the idea of a chat. 'What did you notice about the place— about the landscape?'

'Jungle, heat, mountains,' I recalled. 'Volcanoes and lakes.' 'Yes, volcanoes,' he repeated.

'Geothermic energy? The energy source?' I said, thinking I had found the answer, but he only shook his head.

'Close, but no cigar. There is an awful lot of potential kinetic energy being generated in your volcanoes. You're right about that. And we needed the energy to power all types of devices, but not just the geothermic variety. Allow me to explain, because we would be at it all day waiting for you to hit on it.

'Multi variance differential wave interference. A mouthful, I know. It is a basic means of generating power from natural phenomena such as volcanoes, earthquakes, atmospheric storm activity, etcetera, and something you people have yet to discover. The atmosphere surrounding geographic activity such as volcanoes is fairly dripping with untapped, potential energy, if only you dolts would but look beyond your noses. Ample to power that machine, and more than enough for us to draw off, store and use as needed. Why do you suppose so many UFO's have been sighted in exactly these areas?'

'You're telling me you're not human, that you're what?' 'Are you sure you want to know, Felix? You might get the urge to run off again,' he said, chuckling annoyingly.

I was intrigued far past the point of being scared. The whole thing was so beyond being whacko— beyond sanity, almost —

I just needed an explanation that would somehow make sense of my screwed up existence. Who else could say they have been through anything remotely similar? I had read more believable sci-fi stories.

'Tell me, Darius. Nothing seems real to me anymore. I need things to make some sort of sense. *Any* sort of sense, and I don't care what the facts are. I just want to know what in the world is going on.'

He looked at me in an odd sort of way. For some reason I was suddenly not able to read that face; the same face I wore, and then, just as suddenly, the look departed, and there it was again. The humanity, with readable emotions showing through.

'Okay Felix— Felix who is not Felix— I guess you deserve to know. But you're not going to like it. Are you sure?'

'Tell me,' I insisted. 'Believe me when I say, I'm beyond giving a damn.'

He composed himself. I could almost see the wheel s turning in his head. 'Alright then. . .

'The machine, and don't be interrupting with asking me what it's called and like that. Its just a machine, and its purpose is to compile and store information relevant to our mission here on this planet. And one function is to create copies to be used in accomplishing that goal. It's a conscious machine. It has to be, else it couldn't do what its job is, which is to ready this backwater planet for cohabitation with us. Don't interrupt!' he snapped at me, forestalling my intended objection. 'I've lost my train of thought, thanks to you. Where was I?'

'Intended cohabitation of Earth,' I replied.

He shook his head. 'No, forget that. The machine, besides a thousand and one other vastly complex functions, does make replicas. It's a very useful function, for so many reasons which ought to be obvious to you. The replication of people, including their knowledge acquired over a lifetime, memories, traits and all, is part of that particular process. The machine is vastly complex and stand-alone intelligent, itself. It has a will, and it has a mission. Those qualities are imbued into the replica. The manufactured article is a conglomeration of two separate and distinct personalities, with the machine's personality taking precedence. The human component is just along for the ride, most of the time, but it never knows that. To be aware of it would be counterproductive, and it remains totally unaware of its *slave status*, for lack of a better description. Do you follow?'

'I do, and it's monstrous.'

'Monstrous, my arse, Felix. It's completely natural. It's the universal law of survival! Look at specialised natural development among species on your world, if you need examples.'

'But how can you-'

'Will you stop interrupting. I'm trying to explain, as you asked.' He paused, waiting to see if I would interrupt again, but I did not. The story was becoming more and more interesting.

'These modified beings are the forward guard of our assimilation strategy,' he continued. 'And this is the beachhead, here!' He waved his arms around, intending to convey the vast size of the underground cavern, although the confines of the room presently occupied somewhat defeated the allusion.

I thought about it. A replicating machine with the mind and personality of a vastly superior artificial intelligence is left on the planet unattended. Some fool turns it on and it begins fulfilling whatever design the warped machine has in mind. It's own little plan to take over the world, although assimilation was the word being applied, and I found myself thinking about any number of despotic dictators who had attempted similar in the past.

'Okay, got it.' I told him. 'It makes sense, I suppose. In a demented kind of way.'

'So there you are,' Darius said, ignoring the barb. 'That's what you interfering idiots stumbled into all those years ago, and you bit off way more than you could chew, didn't you?'

'It wasn't my big idea,' I responded, indignant. 'I'm the result of what those idiots did. God, I asked for none of this!'

Darius began laughing again, but this time the laughter took on a more unsettling quality, and it lasted rather longer than seemed necessary.

'What's so goddamned funny?' I demanded.

'You. . . You're funny. All of you. Have you not been listening to what I've been telling you?'

'I have, and it's way out there, even as weirdness goes. That really is some story.'

He stood, began walking slowly around the room. His expression was one of a man deep in thought, perhaps even conflicted in some way.

'You realise I can tell what you are thinking, Felix. Remember, we are entangled, and the longer we are in proximity, the stronger these connections will become. Now that the process has begun—' but he stopped himself there, unwilling to say more. My feeling was that he was concerned for my sense of well-being. How did I know that? Because, just as he said, the connection was indeed becoming stronger; even then I was feeling a flow of, I suppose, *empathy* of a kind. It was new to me and difficult to decipher. The perception intensified momentarily.

'What is it?' I asked. I know something is wrong, Darius. I can feel it. . . something disturbing you.' I waited for a response as he continued to pace around the room.

'You humans,' he said at last. 'The way you have developed intellectually. No, wrong word. You call it emotion. It's so incompatible with the processes of logic, it's a wonder you can function. It clouds everything. Every action is considered within the narrow confines of how the action may impact on everyone and everything surrounding. It is such a barrier. You cannot just do a thing. It's always What will be the repercussions of such an action? How will this or that be affected? Hence, so little is achieved. And yet, look at the way you have ravaged your world, seemingly without a thought. Such a contradiction, and it's like a virus. God, it affects everything. How do you cope?' He was genuinely upset. This alien concoction of an entity was talking about emotions, and then I felt it, the growing link between us was strengthening. His inability to do what he had intended. It was the great human dilemma of having two simultaneous but irreconcilable choices to deal with. Human logic, human emotions seemed to confound this alien intellect who existed by applying only logic and determination to a problem.

It was my turn to laugh, and I did just that. The thought of this being — a being claiming to be so ancient, so superior and so many aeons of technological development beyond our society — experiencing such puzzlement and ambivalence to the point of inaction, was just the sort of thing my sense of humour appreciated just then. I laughed out loud, and it felt good to be doing so after everything that had been happening to me.

The expression he wore I recognised easily enough. He was both perturbed and embarrassed by his inability to understand what was happening; neither of which were conditions he often, if at all, had experienced. This superior, integrated being was as confused as anyone could be, and like a child suddenly confronted with the new and unexpected, it frightened him.

'Stop it. Do not laugh at me, Felix.' He stood, scowling and angry—and making him angry, I decided, was not the smartest thing to do, considering the position I was currently in.

I reined in my amusement as best I could. 'I don't suppose I ought to laugh,' I expressed, feigning sobriety. 'Forgive me, emotions can be difficult at first. The one you are experiencing now, it's a condition called doubt. Is it possible there may even be a modicum of guilt thrown in?'

'I am at a loss,' he said then. 'At a loss—!' and he returned to sit himself beside me, shaking his head as if it might rectify the problem.

I waited to see what would come next. I didn't wish to intervene with whatever process was occurring within him. Whatever it was, it perplexed him terribly, and I could feel the turmoil via the newborn invisible connection growing between us.

117

In the moments following, I understood how at odds our two worlds were; the logical and practical versus the emotional and philosophical. Our two cultures were so fundamentally different. It was inevitable, in the end, that this impasse had to be reached, but what had caused it to happen right at this moment? I found myself considering.

He looked up at me, and I immediately realised that he had picked up on this question. 'What is the cause? It's you. You are the cause,' he said, but there was nothing accusatory in the way he said it, and he even offered a wan smile. I have been infected. My mental processes have been affected with an idea. I am prime, and my mental pathways are corrupted with nothing more than an idea. . . a concept. It is over,' he said dully, and the look in his eyes gave confirmation.

I did not understand what was happening. Not yet, but whatever it was, it was serious enough that I knew whatever danger I was in was over as of that moment. Of that I was certain.

'Untie me, Darius,' I asked, testing my assumption, and to my immense relief, he rose, began releasing the straps in a strange silence.

With the straps removed, I sat up. 'What has happened,' I asked.

'It is over, Felix who is not Felix. It must end, here, now.'

'I don't understand. I mean, I am pleased it's over, although I have to confess, I don't entirely understand what *It* is. What I do know is that your intentions toward me were not exactly conducive to my continued well-being.'

'You should know something about yourself,' he intoned flatly, looking me squarely in the eye so that I understood the gravity of what was about to come next.

'Yes? And what is that, Darius.'

'For a start, do not call me by that name. It is not my name to be called by.'

He had my absolute full attention now, and the ramifications of it had my mind rapidly sorting the many possible permutations connected to that one statement.

'Prime, then?'

'Prime? Yes, I suppose that is appropriate. Although, the name also implies a position in rank. I can no longer be prime. The assignment is abandoned. The parameters and the conditions of engagement have, as of this moment, changed unalterably. It is over,' he said for the second time.

I was still trying to process what was occurring, and having no luck. If it was over, what did that mean for me, a duplicate entity?

He, of course, picked up on my question immediately I had composed it within my mind, and responded.

'You should know that you are not Felix. Your name is Darius McNally. *Captain* Darius McNally.'

It hit me with a force almost physical in nature. 'I am what?' 'Yes, *you* are Darius. *You* are the original. I am the first of the simulacrum.'

'Then why—?' I had trouble posing the next question, but it seemed we were already past me having to vocalise my thoughts. Either that or he had accurately guessed my next question.

'The original always suffers memory loss, as you have. In the supplanting of memory, personality traits and everything which makes you what you are. . . the machine scours the synapses thoroughly, sometimes causing irreparable damage. In your case, you lost all of your memory up to the point of the transfer being initiated.' He paused, thoughtfully,' But I can mend that problem for you, if you wish. It was important that you believe you were the copy, else you may have been too well motivated to correct the situation, and that would have hampered the cause.'

'I have been living the life of a disabled beachcomber for twenty two years because I may have hampered the cause? Goddamn you — you and your goddamned. . . What do you call it?'

'We call it merging. You humans call it assimilation.'

'And *you* are partly a machine consciousness? A downloaded artificial intelligence combined with the hijacked consciousness of a copied human being?'

'Near enough.'

'And what are your *brethren* doing right now? I demanded.' 'Their cycle has been terminated, Darius. They are no more.'

It was just as he said. I accompanied Prime throughout the entire underground complex, and not a single survivor did we discover.

Prime had instructed every one of them to self- terminate, and, like the obedient replicas they were, they had obeyed, unhesitatingly and apparently without question, by simply switching themselves off.

We were alone in the vast subterranean chasm, Prime and myself, walking through one section after another, making sure that the self-termination directive had been served. It was deathly quiet, but the overhead lighting burned, bright, enabling an uninterrupted view throughout as we progressed unhurriedly, passing between the vehicles and machinery, checking the service bar, inspecting the connecting corridors, all empty but for those who had fallen in immediate and obedient compliance. We took the giant equipment elevator back to the surface after placing a suitable four wheel drive vehicle on it, so that I might return to civilisation. Only during the ride to the surface did I remember to ask the most important question of Prime. That I had neglected to ask it until this particular moment was merely an indication of the strangeness of mood which had overtaken me, making it difficult just to place one foot in front of the other, my body seeming to be something entirely separate. There was only the pervasive sense of walking through a mist of unreality, and as the minutes passed by I began to realise what sort of an effect this whole episode must be having on me. The feeling of detachment I had been feeling and which had been growing steadily without resistance was complete now. I felt as isolated from humanity as I reasoned it was possible to be; and I wondered, even then, if, over the passage of time, I might ever recover sufficiently to be anything resembling who I used to be.

There was of course no way of knowing. Only time could reveal the answer to that.

The rising platform stopped at ground level, under the great arched cover of the hangar roof. Lights suspended from the rafters bathed everything in a brilliant, white light. It had grown dark while I was underground. Beyond the hangar doors was in total darkness, except for the apron lying just beyond the verge. A large clock fixed to the interior wall indicated that it was two in the morning. I remember thinking, then, where had those hours gone? Hours unaccounted for. Maybe I had lost consciousness? —it didn't seem to add up— but again Prime encroached on my thoughts.

'Don't worry,' he said, as we stood beside the four wheel drive, staring into the night beyond the gaping doors. 'The process of restoring your lost memory has been underway for some time already. Time dilation is a common effect. You will be complete once again, Darius.'

'But how?'

'We are entangled. Our memories are resetting themselves, like water finding its level. The balance is already almost complete. By the time you wake in the morning, the transfer will be complete and all the old connections reestablished. Just like new,' he added, attempting to inject a little levity.

'What am I supposed to do now, simply drive away, after everything that has happened?'

'What else would you do? You may stay, of course, but I see no point. The vehicle has a full tank and will deliver you back to civilisation.'

The moon appeared in the sky then. It must have been hidden by clouds when we emerged.

'What happened, Prime?' I asked, finally. 'Why did you shut it all down. . . order them all to terminate? I was in the most dire of situations. I thought I was done for, but of course I still considered myself a replica, nothing more, and it really didn't matter to me by that time. I considered my life a fraud; a fluke of some kind.'

'What happened?' he repeated, leaning his head to the side and viewing me in a quizzical manner.'For all our programming— our billions of years of technological progress and of exploring vast regions of the cosmos — for all our power and mastery of physical existence, we were not prepared for the illogic of human emotion. It acted like a most virulent virus upon our exquisitely derived and perfectly formulated computer codes, upon which we rely totally for our survival. It was discovered too late. Emotion. . . anti logic. We could not, and cannot possibly, merge with a species so incompatible. A species who willingly accepts such a destructive force as emotion, the one thing which will forever corrupt the guidance of code, cannot successfully be merged. As long as human emotion exists, perfection of the species will never be attained. It was this realization which made me realise the impossibility of completing our mission here.'

'And so, when I have gone from here, you will self-terminate, like the rest? Is that your intention? We regard life as being precious, and it is such a waste. Why not continue on?'

'It would make no sense to continue. My purpose is at an end.'

'But to end yourself, willingly?'

'What else? Prime replied, seeing no other logical action; and for him, there was no other.

I drove out into the night, with a long way to go before rejoining the human population. There was only the night sky and the milky white light illuminating the vast expanse of the desert. It was perfect, the blackness of the night and the white sands of the desert, with myself poised somewhere between. More than ever my sense of self felt to be exceedingly diminutive. My life had taken an unexpected and unavoidable turn some twenty two years ago, as a soldier being deployed to South America, in order to assess and relocate a piece of esoteric technology found underground, by a plane crash survivor seeking temporary shelter. The accident that had occurred in a moment set in motion a string of events which would inevitably catch me up while standing on a pier, in my home town, where I had languished for far too long as a result of a mere moment, when a switch had accidentally been thrown. A great chunk of my life had been sliced out of the normal flow of time, but it had been relocated and stitched back again by these strange events over the past few days. It was all so strange and unbelievable, but that was life, I told myself as I negotiated the two wheel desert track. I had only to look up at the stars overhead, where the billions and billions of bright points of far off light signified, if only by their number, the near endless possibilities for unobserved action and reaction, to produce unimaginable outcomes across the length and breadth of time to render absurd any thought of limitation. As I sped across the desert landscape in surrounding darkness, feeling insignificant but for the thrill of life coursing through every fibre of my being, I was overcome by something joyous and indefatigable, and understood as well as any mortal being can understand that which is far beyond our ken, the existence of that ineffable power which has the ability to dispel all doubt, past, present and future; that which is life affirming beyond all else, and which makes the struggle we all face as the sun rises on us each and every dawn until our unavoidable end; and that which is, despite our tendencies for greed, arrogance and petty differences, beyond imagining. And under that heady spell, while everything that alien machine had ever learned throughout its time of tenure remotely filled my mind with wonders extraordinary and unheard of, my laughter, full, loud and unbridled, rang out in liberation of my mind, across the desert landscape, and up into the spectacular void.

– end –

BEYOND THE RIM

FOREWORD

The eco-war lasted ten years, from October, 2022 to June, 2033. Hostilities escalated across the globe between those that could afford to turn things around regarding carbon emission and pollution generally, and those who could not keep pace, including the third world and the still developing countries who did not stand a chance in hell of investing in what became known as The New Economy. Embargo and tariff hikes were the first weapons, and weaker economies soon began to feel the pain, but before long it turned into a shooting, bombing war — a war of survival for the millions being forced beyond their means to toe the line of the new ecological imperative. The speed with which this severe socioeconomic climate swept the globe resulted in hunger and deprivation, finally pushing countries into a desperate struggle for survival at all cost.

When the smoke and dust of destruction had settled, Earth was a different place. The old economy had fallen, to be replaced by the new, eco-conscious, fiscal and political formula for the future. The human population had been decimated during those ten years, as much through warfare as by impacting natural disasters brought about by mankind's negligence, including flooding on a scale never before witnessed, famine, pestilence and want for adequate shelter, resulting in deaths from exposure. Because man had witnessed the nightmare of near self-inflicted extinction, the New Order Watch was devised; a watchdog organization with teeth, demanding that any industry with the potential to cause damage to the biosphere must migrate off world. It seemed a crazy and tyrannical action to many, and sure to send us back to an agrarian based society, but we found a way. In the aftermath there was discovered an abundance of untapped fiscal wealth which the New Order Watch rapidly plundered with impunity. Space programs and off world settlement projects, which had been abandoned over a decade previous, were reinstituted and augmented with vigour, and before we knew it the dream of zero impact existence seemed within reach; an actual possibility.

Our moon became the industrial centre for our future. It was discovered that the moon held vast quantities of metal ores and raw materials essential for Lunar habitation and heavy industry alike. Low gravity engineering and production revealed many previously overlooked advantages and the mineral rich moon became a miracle of modern industry in short time as technical problems were tackled and solved, one at a time. We committed vast financial resources and what remained of manpower to the dream. It was often said that the period compared to the era of the pharos, with its far ranging harnessing of labour and resources, and the single-minded focus on the primary goal, to be achieved at any cost. The resulting accomplishments inspired the concept of creating an even further reaching scheme of acquiring raw material for future needs and planned rapid expansion after such a terrible setback. The plan became known as the Far Reach program.

The Rim is what spacers call the Kuiper Belt, the ring of asteroids and accumulated debris left over from the formation of the solar system billions of years ago. The term applies to anything in that general area, including the recently completed Niven Space Station situated four point eight billion miles out from Earth, just inside the path of Pluto's orbit. Niven Station is companioned by another, nearby platform, financed and constructed by my employer, Universal X, an abbreviation of Universal Mining & Exploration. The platform is named *Far Reach-A*, suggesting that there are already on the drawing board the plans for another, similar structure. As big as *Far Reach -A* is, it is entirely the domain of the company, providing accommodation, life's necessities, services and supplies, as well as providing housing for the many mining and exploration machines, vehicles and maintenance personnel to keep them functioning. From it are launched frequent expedition craft, manned by a highly motivated and particularly hardy breed of spacer whose job it is to search out, conceptualize, compute logistics and evaluate profitability of mining primary and exotic minerals from the vast number of asteroids, passing comets and anything else out there drifting in the vacuum.

Travelling the distance out to *the rim* once took three years, nine months, and nineteen days. That was a mere twenty seven years ago. Today, with the advent of the plasma pulse engine, that time has been cut down to eight months, with a good proportion of that time being consumed in the deceleration portion of the trip. Fortunately, there is the option of medical assisted stasis, allowing one to sleep throughout the journey. This option is preferred by most and avoids the possibility of passengers becoming stir crazy. The well healed, those who can afford the expensive, first class option, experience much the same as first class ocean liner passengers once enjoyed, with all the opulence and pampering entailed with that manner of travel. Naturally, the company flipped the bill for my medical assisted stasis and I arrived in reasonable mental state, keen to get on with the job I had been commissioned to perform. It seemed like an opportunity at the time. A change from the usual grind.

As an undercover operative for Universal X, I have been posted here to discover where the company's missing consignments of hardware, food supplies, spare parts, tools and other miscellaneous items have been disappearing to. With Niven Station being fully operational only these past few months, already a quite well organised criminal network has sprung up in the sector. Anything brought out here to the rim increases in dollar value by at least five hundred percent, depending on the item in question. It isn't difficult to see how conditions are ripe for criminal enterprise. Brigands and chancers are setting up a network of black-market trade in anything from a can of beans and prohibited pharmaceuticals to weapons and expensive machinery parts — parts necessary to keep the wheels turning for the twenty-two percent of the human population who survived the war, a greater proportion of whom are the filthy rich and their immediate family members. The wealthy, for the first time in human history, now vastly outnumber the working class, and the working class are in great demand, especially out here. This place is the wild west on steroids, and a place where only the strongest survive, unless one is fortunate enough to have earned a position within the higher echelons of the company. That or knowing someone in the higher echelons where nepotism has become almost the norm. Niven Station is well stocked and supplied, providing a commercial centre and a comfortable habitat for the many and varied walks of life; the lynchpin connecting Earth with the Far Reach platform and heralding a new direction for mankind's existence with its future firmly pointed toward deep space exploration and exploitation. These are the times I live in.

1

SNOOP, SNOOP, BANG, BANG

I disembarked the transport ship at the Niven Station terminus, a large, circular arena, it sat atop the station where ships arriving are hugged by giant mechanical arms to keep them secured to the landing platform. Hermetic, concertina like tubes were extended from the central dome and attached to the front and rear of our craft, allowing passengers to breathe an Earth similar atmosphere while gaining entry to the station.

I had hoped to have the time to take a bit of a look around Niven, but the ferry to Far Reach was due to leave just thirty minutes after our arrival and I had to make do with the view available through the triple layered *plexishield* scenic window in the café, as I sipped my large espresso in effort to stay awake for the last remaining leg of the journey.

It was a fascinating view. From a position near the hub of the immense multi tiered wheel of Niven Station, I looked out across its diameter into the pellucid depths strewn with an endless number of glistening points of light reaching beyond vanishing-point.

I had never ventured so far from Earth before. I had visited Lunar station on various occasions, but out here there was an indefinable difference. As tired as I was, the immensity and clarity of the vista seemed to dwarf the intellect and reduce the ego to zero. At that moment it had the effect of making mankind's endeavours appear ridiculous and meaningless. It was an uncomfortable feeling and I suddenly found myself questioning what I was doing here, sipping espresso coffee at a café, so very far from home. A quick glance at my wristwatch alerted me to the fact that I had allowed time to get away from me and I hurriedly made my way to the shuttle service at the opposite side of the concourse, presented my ticket to the guard standing at the gate, and joined the line of fellow commuters waiting on the platform to board the shuttle.

Sitting high on metal skids, the shuttle was rectangular, rounded at the ends, with a ring of manoeuvring thrusters bolted either end and powered by a single Dyson differential field engine. A thoroughly utilitarian design, assembled from stock standard parts and, no doubt, built with cheap operating cost and longevity in mind; totally in keeping with the way Universal X approached everything it did.

The two-hour journey felt much longer. The seats were reclined and comfortable enough. Four seats wide on either side of the central aisle. The passengers were employees returning from a short leave on Niven; most of them hung over and exhausted from kicking up their heals in the privately owned pubs and clubs, of which there were ample. Many entrepreneurs hade rushed to invest in the off world business boon, many catering to the highly paid mining and exploration workers, being by far the most lucrative. These guys worked hard and played hard. With fat pay packets at the end of each work cycle, and starved for entertainment, women and anything which would relieve the stresses of living and working in one of the most dangerous environments imaginable, they were only too willing to pay through the nose and indulge themselves, often to excess, in anything that would serve the purpose of allowing them to decompress for a time. Their faces reflected the harsh lives they lived, and, to a man, their eyes, staring blankly ahead, betrayed thoughts turned inward. Perhaps they called to mind the faces of loved ones; those left behind in order that they earn the big money needed to support and ensure a better existence for all. The older men were here for that reason, I knew it well enough. The younger men had come primarily for the adventure. Young men always chose adventure over financial reward, but here in this place both were available. It was a curious fact how quickly the visage of young men who worked in environments such as this came to resemble those of the older men. The adventure gives way to endurance of the gruelling routine. Youthful energy slowly and surely transforms to dogged determination. Working amongst men of this calibre, newcomers will very quickly find themselves falling short of the strength and resolve required for the task, or succeeding in digging deep enough to find the resilience needed to survive the indoctrination process. That process is achieved within the first month. The line of work such as these men perform has the tendency to quickly identify and target the slightest flaw in one's character and physical strength. I have seen men slowly erode away to nothing rather than admit not being up to the task. No, youthful enthusiasm counts for little on The Rim. It is one's metal, the strength of will that counts out here.

Then comes the bonding of men committed to a common task, the emerging brotherhood, mutual respect and reliance which, in some indefinable process, provide what is necessary to survive and succeed in the jobs worked by these men.

In the pocket at the back of the seat in front of me I noticed a pamphlet. Opening it I discovered a 'You Are Here' map, beginning at the drop-off point for arrivals at the platform, with a couple of pages describing what newcomers might need to know.

Far Reach Platform was a different kettle of fish from Niven Station. The landing platform occupied a large area at the corner of the uppermost deck of the gigantic cube — a cube consisting of four flat tiers, each of which served a separate function. The topmost consisted of an administration block, landing field, warehouses for incoming goods and supplies, maintenance buildings and, tucked away in a corner, what I later learned had come to be known as the *Bastille*. It was the domain of company security. The nerve centre for the gigantic platform's network of electronic surveillance, and fitted out with an ample number of holding cells.

The next tier down supported further warehousing and a marshalling yard where transport ships loaded with equipment and paraphernalia in supplying exploratory outstations engaged in electronic detection and drilling for samples.

Below that, the entire tier provided accommodation; self- contained, two room utilitarian enclosures for the workforce, loosely resembling a residential suburb in miniature, including the occasional corner store, which, because of the size of the area, besides providing the general items one might expect from a corner store, also supplied a form of transport called zippers. The two-wheeled variety was nothing more than a scooter with a tiny motor capable of propelling a person at forty kilometres an hour. A four wheeled model, being a small trolley with seat and steering wheel, included a tray at the rear, large enough to carry a load such as a parcel of food items or a single passenger. The lowest of the four tiers on Far Reach was a hodgepodge.

Everything from bars, small amusement parlours, low-class, unregulated hotels and bordellos, workshops, repair yards, residential addresses, and more.

I woke, not realising that I had nodded off. The shuttle had landed and the last of the passengers were exiting, leaving me to hurriedly gather my wits and make for the exit, pushing the pamphlet into my rear pocked as I went.

I collected my luggage and wondered what to do first. I had intended to take a cursory look around a few of the compounds before settling into a room somewhere, but I needed somewhere to drop my luggage. The guy at the baggage collection counter told me he would hang on to it for me if I had nowhere else. The place never closed and it would still be here waiting for me when I got back.

A room was important, but, if I wanted to get to work, it would have to wait, so I dumped my bags under the counter, flipped the baggage handler guy a credit and got straight to it.

My watch had automatically adjusted itself to local time. It was 11:54 p.m. The place functioned nonstop around the clock, which meant that the time of day made little to no difference, if I wanted to observe how things ran. My body clock was a different proposition. The trip had taken its toll, regardless of the medically induced dormancy. In fact, the process had left me feeling enervated and not terribly sharp witted. I figured that the best thing I could do for myself was to find a room somewhere and catch a decent eight hours of *real* sleep; but, on the other hand, a stint of exercise might be just what the doctor ordered. I opted for the exercise and made my way to the bank of lifts beside the administration block.

According to the pamphlet, the marshalling of goods and major warehousing took place one level below, and that's where I headed. Stepping out of the lift I was struck by the size of the expanse. The place was massive, stretching perhaps a mile or more, square. Most of the activity was taking place a good distance away, with goods being loaded from warehouses onto a train of trolleys to be drawn across to waiting supply craft, no doubt to be ferried on to crew of outlying work camps.

The warehouse nearest was devoid of activity and lay in darkness, and it was as good a place as any to begin. The massive doors at the front end were drawn shut and bolted, but a side door provided unimpeded access, and immediately I entered the premises instinct took over as I went to stealth mode. In barely adequate light to see to the opposite end of the building, I stepped lightly and silently, taking in as much of the interior as possible. Among the rows of packaged hardware, male voices emanated from about a hundred metres away. Conversational voices, and the smell of tobacco mixed with, if my nose was functioning properly again after the trip, the pungent sweet aroma of hashish.

I should have known better. I should have taken my own advice, done the logical thing and found a room where I could have made myself comfortable, eaten a meal, watched a movie, caught up on much needed sleep; but, no, I had to blindly stumble into where I was not wanted, walk into a section of two inch steel pipe protruding from a shelf, head high, causing a clattering din as the piled up and loosely stacked pipes rolled over themselves in reaching a state of equilibrium. But that isn't the best part. The best part of it is, this wasn't a case of a couple of warehouse workers skiving of, smoking a joint on company time. This was a case, I was informed later, of a half tonne of prime hashish changing hands. Black market hashish, worth who knew how much, being sampled by the buyer before the money changed hands.

I froze in my tracks, allowing the rolling clatter to come to an end. There was little I could do. My presence was established and the only thing I could think of to do was to speak up, as casually as I could manage right then.

'Don't worry lads,' I called out. It's only me,' I explained, continuing to walk towards the source of the aroma. And rounding the corner I came across a group of five silhouetted forms.

'Who the hell are you?' someone asked in a deep baritone voice, and before I could respond with a suitable answer, a flash and a spout of flame lit the shadows.

In that instant time actually did stand still. I've heard people tell how this is the case in life threatening situations, but until that very moment I never knew it to be true. At the first sign of a firearm discharging my body launched itself sideways; a leap any red kangaroo would be proud of, and in that warped and elongated frame, I remember thinking two things. First, what a damn fool I was to be creeping around a dimly lit warehouse, unannounced, at the height of criminal activity within these very warehouses. And second, did I remember to cancel my cable subscription before leaving Earth? It's funny how the mind works sometimes.

*

To be a snoop, and a really good one, I believe one must have the predisposition and a belief that the job is meaningful. I have never been able to leave a puzzle unsolved. I guess that imbues me well enough with the necessary predisposition component. The meaningful side is self-fulfilling. The solving of cases, for me, gives it meaning, and should I live a thousand aeons I would never find a job better suited to my makeup than being a covert situation manager for Universal Ex. That's me, Jack Hardin, situations manager for Universal Ex. I realise that just because the job has meaning for me, it doesn't necessarily hold that it is meaningful for anyone else. It's a matter of perspective, some would say; but one must admit, solutions, in and of themselves, are an absolute existential imperative. Without solutions. . . well, I hardly need finish the statement. Try living in a world without solutions.

*

I woke in a hospital bed, a transfusion line attached to my arm and electrodes attached to parts of me. A great lug of a cop sat in a chair against the wall at the end of my bed. A guy who apparently had trouble finding a uniform sufficiently large enough to fit his huge frame. The moment I came to he radioed in the news of my return to the living. To whom, I could not say. His immediate superior, one would expect, but for a run of the mill uniform cop, *superior* could account for just about anyone. 'What's the big idea?' I asked. Followed by my first stupid question for the day. 'What am I doing here?' He smiled but did not respond.

I was still feeling a tad woozy. Without warning I vomited over myself, and it was ten minutes before a nurse came in to check on me. I had to remain covered in my own vomit all that time, with the plod ignoring me as much as he was able.

'Oh, dear,' the nurse crooned, approaching swiftly. 'Have a little accident, did we?'

I wasn't sure if she was referring to the bullet in the guts or the fact that I had thrown up over my hospital gown. 'No accident,' I told her. 'I always shoot myself in the stomach before turning in, and throw up over myself for good measure.'

I can be a real charmer sometimes, but I regretted saying that to her he moment it had left my lips. She was only trying to help. She finished cleaning me up and left the room without another word. I had spoken twice, and twice managed to make a dickhead of myself. I determined to try and do better.

I nodded off and was woken sometime later by the uniformed cop. He was accompanied by a large, overweight and middle aged detective. Beside him, a lanky, baldheaded young man, obviously his protege. The senior rubbed at the two day stubble on his jaw while he attempted to size me up.

'Sleep well?' he asked, his gravelly voice betraying weariness. 'Like a top.'

'The doctor says you're lucky to have survived. You've been topped up with five pints. A valuable commodity in this place, too. Universal X must consider you to be worth something.'

'They sent me *here*. That should tell you how valuable they think I am. What can I do for you, -?'

'Detective Sergeant Emerson', he obliged. 'Saunders,' he added, indicating the human beanpole standing beside him, and the young man nodded in greeting. 'You can start by telling me what you're doing here at Far Reach. And how you managed to catch a bullet in the gut within an hour of arriving.'

'I'm sorry, Emerson. You know I can't do that. Confidential. Company business.' 'And the slug?'

'An accident. Self-inflicted.'

'Your piece has not been fired recently,' he returned. 'Perhaps it was a stray bullet out of the sky?'

'Must have been,' I agreed, losing interest.

'You guys,' Emerson intoned wearily. 'If you're going to get yourself all shot up and hospitalised, you could at least do it without attracting goddamned attention.'

'Sorry.' I told him.

'Security staff followed the blood trail, if you're wondering. Found you with not a lot of blood left in you and called the medics. You slip in here unannounced, to do what? I have no idea. Within an hour of arriving you get yourself gut-shot and leave an awful mess. Really, Hardin? Now I have to act on it. Official like. What am I supposed to write in the bloody report? You tell me. Loose ends do not look good on my monthly efficiency rating.'

'It is a problem,' I sympathised, 'but seeing as I'm not here, and never was here. . ?' I let the statement trail off.

The young detective's eyes reflected mounting confusion.

'What do you mean, you weren't here? What do you take us for?'

His senior intervened. 'Can it, Andy. It's hard to believe, I know, but this guy's a professional. A professional snoop for *'the company,"* — and he actually made quotation marks using the usual hand sign. 'These guys think they're above the law. Untouchable, ain't that right, Mr Hardin. Jack Hardin, isn't it? I know your mug from a classified report about a year ago. The Winthrop riddle?'

I nodded. Just enough to convey grudging respect to his barely adequate powers of recall. Or had he found my ID in my bag where I had left it at baggage collection? Done a bit of research, perhaps?

No matter, he knew who I was and that was cause for concern. I guess he knew what I was thinking just then.

'Don't worry. I'd rather not document any of this,' he told me, 'and it's not unknown for reports to get lost occasionally. I guess this is one of those times. Lucky for you we're in the middle of updating our filing system. Shit happens.'

'You would do that?'

He gave me an odd sort of a look. One that told me I was missing something, but I couldn't quite put my finger on it.

'Call it professional courtesy,' he replied, and turned to his companion. 'Come on. Let's go find some real criminals—' and without another word the pair departed.

I guess the blood loss had left me somewhat lightheaded, because I could not make sense of the visit, at all. Cops don't just drop by to check on your health and then leave. Not in my experience. I figured I would puzzle over it another time.

Apart from the blood loss the slug had not caused a great deal of damage. I was keen to get out of there but the doctor insisted I stay a further twenty four hours, which I did, mainly because the meals weren't half bad and I still needed to get over the effects of the voyage out from Earth. The next time I made the trip I would seriously be considering the first class assisted stasis option. It turns out I am not well suited to long duration space travel; but it's an unavoidable part of the job, so there was no way in hell I was going to let my superiors in on that delicate morsel of information.

2

THE OLD AND THE NEW

I was a little surprised to find my bag was still where I left it, behind the desk at the baggage claim. It made the most sense to find accommodation on tier four, amid the hustle and bustle of the pubs and clubs; exactly the types of places one would have to go to if they needed to purchase items considered not strictly cosher by the company.

My new digs was at a place called the Star Palace, a three storey combination hotel, gambling den, single star eatery and backstairs bordello to boot. This sort of cosmopolitan establishment was common on deck four. It was the name that appealed, and it was downtown, central, close to the action.

I took a corner room on the top floor — room 405. When the landlord departed I zipped open my bag and laid out the tools of my trade on top of the bed. I had brought along a tracking kit, consisting of half a dozen miniature tracking devices; wafer thin, about the size of a small button, self adhesive and activated once the backing paper was removed. Each had its own separate frequency, to be received by my communicator, enabling me to track six individual targets as far as the mobile network stretched. In my present position I wasn't sure how far that was, but I knew Far Reach had communication relay satellites of its own, capable of reaching Earth, and certainly more than adequately covering the temporary outposts where survey teams were dispatched to. Another important item was my custom made handgun. I have never been a fan of firearms; believing that if a man had an argument it should be settled with logic, understanding and a sense of fair play, but I'm no fool. My philosophy is my own. I operate in a world where pulling a trigger is often the only manner of settling an argument or extricating one's self from an awkward situation. It's seldom I come across situations such as this, but here on the platform I am rubbing shoulders with some tough individuals, and it would have been unwise for me to have come here ill-equipped. Although firearms are outlawed, no doubt the black market had already found a way to arm those who have the required remuneration.

Lifting my weapon, its grip feels snug and reassuring in my hand. A short barrelled, compressed air shooter, capable of firing a six millimetre lead tipped iron slug at over three hundred metres a second, with no more than a whisper, and only five inches long. A concession made for me by the company, and without which I would not have agreed to taking on the commission.

The field kit included one last item, my *M.A.I.R.A.D.* or Mission Abandonment and Immediate Retrieval Alert Device. It's a mouthful, and necessary according to management.

Looking like a coin, and activated by placing it between the teeth and biting hard, it alerts the company to the existence of one of two possibilities. Either the premiss on which the mission was launched is found to be erroneous, and immediate extraction is required to avoid further damage or embarrassment to either party; or, an agent has been compromised to the point of possible, personal endangerment or loss of life. Although most of us in the field would never dream of pressing the panic button, any one of us who push too hard in what may turn out to be the wrong direction, illustrating to all that we have mistakenly gone after the wrong people and so caused a situation, would be so embarrassed by the error of judgement, the last thing we would want to do is advertise the screw up. Obviously those in charge are not yet aware of this fact, and because not a one of us would ever accept being transferred from the field into management, this little nugget is destined to remain forever a secret. We in this line of work, like it or not, are not the types to admit errors in judgement, and certainly not of such a magnitude. Mistakes are not acceptable, least of all to personalities unable to countenance failure. As far as being extracted in the face of mounting personal risk? For myself, I would rather take my chances. If there was no risk I wouldn't be here. That much I learned about myself, a long time ago. I'm sure psychologists have a term for the trait. Fortunately, a psych analysis is not a part of recruitment process, and one must wonder exactly why that is. In this line of work turning a blind eye is an everyday occurrence. No surprise there.

I changed into the clothes I had brought along in order to try and meld into the general tone of the place. My cover was that I was nothing more than a general hand, recuperating from a work accident. Around here work accidents tend to be fatal, but with a bullet wound causing me real discomfort, I figured I could conjure a halfway believable story should the need arise. My reflection in the mirror looked like a pretty typical roustabout; somebody who had relied on physical strength and endurance to bring home the bacon. Leather work boots laced above the ankles, heavy cotton jeans, thick flannel shirt, a well worn leather jacket with enough pockets in it to accommodate the tools of my trade, topped off by a woolen beanie over a military crew. Good enough.

The stomach wound was beginning to make its presence felt by throbbing painfully. I checked under the hospital dressing. It was red and angry looking, but there was little discharge, a symptom I was warned to keep an eye on. If it began weeping any more than it was, I would be impelled to go back and have it checked out for second stage infection. I gave it a quick clean up, applied the powder I was given and replaced the original dressing. Swallowing a dose of antibiotics and two painkillers, I figured I was good to go.

Passing through the front bar on my way out of the building, I noted the scarcity of clientele. That would surely alter with the change of shift, when the muscle sore and weary would converge for a copious dose of the amber fluid pain relief and whatever amusement could be found before the need for sleep impelled them toward their cheaply designed company beds.

My first port of call would be to the warehouse manager's office, up on the top tier. The top tier warehouse temporarily housed incoming goods, equipment which had been ordered by the various sections; spare parts, lubricants and the like. From there inventory was checked to see that it was all there and in good condition, before being routed to its final destination.

I went first to the administration building where a security pass could be issued. My presence here and my purpose was known to very few, for obvious reasons. Having it become common knowledge that a company snoop was here would only make my job that much more difficult. The guy I needed to find was the director, Joe Higgins. The woman at the reception desk directed me, two flights up, telling me his office was at the head of the stairs.

She had, doubtless, called ahead of me. A large man of perhaps forty years, with greying hair and piercing blue eyes, greeted me as I stepped out of the stairwell and into the hallway.

'Mister Hardin?' he asked, taking a step forward. 'Jack Hardin, yes. Call me Jack. You would be–'

'Joe Higgins,' he replied, offering his hand. The grip told me he was no mere paper pusher. It takes many years of physical labour to develop a grip like that.

'Pleased to meet you, Joe. I hope you are fully appraised of the reason for my visit?'

'I am. Please, come in and take a load off.'

I followed him into his office where we seated ourselves on opposite sides of a large metal desk. A quick look around told me nothing about Joe. The office was large, purely utilitarian. Maps of the complex site were pinned around the walls; a blueprint of a cargo carrier, a list of extension numbers. Nothing at all of a personal nature. Not a family photograph in sight.

Joe leaned back heavily in his chair, causing it to creak under the weight. 'I heard you stopped a bullet the other night. Are you okay?'

'Occupational hazzard.' I replied. 'I'm told I'll survive.'

He chuckled at this. Studied my face for a moment, while I did the same to him. I knew guys like this. A hard-arse, I knew it immediately. The sort of man who commanded the space he was in by pure force of will. Those who worked under him had to endure his bullying, but I had no doubt that he knew every inch of this platform; knew every person under his command, their strengths and weaknesses, their capability and worth on the job. He would also know every single package that entered *his* warehouses, who had ordered them, their cost and their intended destination.

'I have a list here of items that have gone missing,' he said, reaching into his desk drawer and retrieving the list, consisting of several pages.

I reached over and took it from him. 'Quite a list.'

'Two hundred items this past twelve months. It's pissing me off, big time, Jack. The dollar value is one thing, but the time it takes to ship out replacements. . . The downtime if machines are left standing idle?'

'Yeah, I get that. Can be very annoying, I've no doubt,' I sympathised. 'Which warehouses are taking the hits?'

'They all are. And it doesn't seem to matter, the position or the level of security. No real rhyme or season to what is being taken. Anything from medical supplies to crate engines and hydraulic hoses.'

There was no doubting Joe's annoyance. His blood pressure was rising and his face reddening.

'Do you have any suspicions? Anyone you think might be responsible, or in the know, perhaps? A starting point?'

'Quite frankly, Jack. No. I mean, I just do not see how this is possible. This is an airtight rig, security-wise. There's nowhere to hide the damn stuff that could not be found. Anything leaving the rig is subject to close scrutiny. The airspace is monitored around the clock. The stuff just seems to be vanishing. It's the damnedest thing.'

I gave the list a cursory eyeballing. The items certainly were wide ranging, seemingly random, but there had to be a pattern. I would study it with greater focus, later, I determined.

'Okay. Is there anything else before I go?'

'I wish there were,' Joe told me. 'In fact, if there was anything more in the way of useful information, you wouldn't be needed. I would have found these bastards by now, and they'd be deep space meat popsicles by now.'

I didn't doubt that. Joe took this personally, as a slight against his professional ability. 'I'll do what can be done,' I told him, standing. 'It's my job now.'

He reached again into his desk drawer. 'Your pass.' he told me, retrieving a plastic identification card threaded with a looped cord. 'It allows you unrestricted passage in all areas. It's valuable, so don't loose it, and hand it in before you leave.'

'Will do,' I replied. 'We done here?' I asked, moving toward the door.

'Just catch those bastards, Jack. This is a vital operation out here, and the people back on Earth deserve results for their investment. I'm not just talking about time and money, although that is the measure by which results will be measured. People's lives are tied up in this. Failure is not an option.'

As I walked away from the administration building that last statement echoed in my mind. I hadn't given it all that much thought when he had said it, but it was very true. Niven station and the exploration and mining platform, both were the culmination of a dream; the culmination of a great deal of effort and planning. They represented a huge investment in the future and of our continuance as a species. Success overall depended on every area of endeavour being efficient, effective and completed. Accumulating cost blow-outs were the sort of thing that could bleed us dry, bringing the entire enterprise grinding to a halt. But that was the concern of the bean counters. Personally, I didn't much give a damn. So long as the case was brought to a successful outcome and my payment was in my account, that was as much as I cared about. I am just a cog in a very large machine.

Seeing as I was up here on top deck, and not yet fully engaged in the hunt, I thought I should take the opportunity to visit the Bastille. The holding cells held no interest for me; it was also the hub of surveillance and I was very interested to see for myself just how thorough a job was being done.

Walking in the direction of the security building, a dark shadow was cast over the entire expanse of the platform on which I walked. Even out here, I realised then, the sun was able to emit sufficient light to cast deep shadows, and this shadow was the result of a massive cargo ship drifting high overhead, just beyond the geodesic dome encircling Far Point. The view stopped me in my tracks. It was something to see.

The vessel was enormous. Certainly it was too big by far to make a landing. As it slowed to a stop, many small vessels lifted up from the platform and began lining up at the transparent air lock. Evidently goods and crew were to be ferried in by the smaller ones. A procedure which would take a good long time, judging by the size of this behemoth.

A sentry confronted me at the entrance. My new identification card did the trick and I was ushered through. Immediately after negotiating the main entrance I was approached by a young woman dressed in navy blue skirt and jacket, light blue blouse and snazzy cap; security insignia attached here and there.

'Mr Hardin, how can I help you?' she wanted to know.

'The boss about?' I asked, continuing to make my way toward the elevator at the centre of the ground floor gallery.

'The boss?' she repeated, trotting alongside while looking terribly rattled and confused.

'Yes, the boss. The big cheese. He who gives the orders.'

I reached the elevator just as it opened its door to disgorge two personnel. I stepped in and waited for a reply to my question.

'Top floor?' I prompted.

'Top floor. Yes,' she agreed, nodding as the doors closed. Department heads invariably reside on the top floor.

Something to do with the size of the ego or the pay packet, I imagine.

When the concertina doors opened again, another woman, very much resembling the first, was standing there, waiting to greet me. It could not have been the same girl. How would she have gotten up here? The odd thought remained with me as she silently escorted me to a door halfway along the corridor — a door bearing the name, Chief Berringer — where she stopped and tapped softly.

'Come,' a gruff voice called from within, and I walked on through.

Berringer, a little man, stood at the far end of the room, staring out through the window with his hands clasped behind his back and watching the activity in the black sky above.

'I have been awaiting your arrival,' Mr Hardin.' He turned to face me, hooked a thumb over his shoulder, indicating the action beyond the window. 'I love watching the big ones come in. Really something to see, don't you think?'

I nodded, but I wasn't interested in the view any more. 'I would like to see as much relative footage, around the time of disappearance of the missing items, as possible. Can you assist me with that, George?'

'Straight to work, eh, Jack?' he countered. The years haven't mellowed you then?'

'Nope—' I grinned back at him.

Me and George Berringer had a history, you might say. We had lived in the same neighbourhood. He was a cocky little prick, always trying to prove how clever he was by pulling together one scam or another, making sure he got the biggest cut and paying those that did the grunt work a pittance. I didn't like him then, and nothing has changed. He always had an inflated opinion of himself, and he always enjoyed the fact that he had more money than anybody else, just so he could gloat. Fact was, the money always meant more to him than did people. I had heard that he became a big wheel somewhere out here. He was the head of security at Universal X's biggest enterprise, and that did surprise me. I had to admit that must have taken some talent, but I was here to do a job. Get it done and go home. No time for any of that *auld lang syne* shit.

'Well, okay then. I guess there's no reason pretending we were friends. Guys from the neighbourhood.' He moved to the end of the long table and jabbed at a button on the intercom. 'Alex, would you come and accompany Mr Hardin to the security video records library? You know which files.'

He looked up. 'Alex will assist for as long as you need her. This is no walk in the park, Jack. We've been puzzling over this for quite some time. Before we even considered getting outside help.'

The door behind me opened and a young woman stepped into the room. Pretty. Well groomed and with one of those bright- eyed, eager expressions on her face.

' Alex, this is an old acquaintance of mine. Meet Jack Hardin. Jack, my very capable assistant, Alexandra Jordan.'

'But please, call me Alex,' she responded, offering her hand and a quick smile.

145

'Pleased to meet you, young lady.' I really didn't need anyone getting chummy, right now. And I had good reason for that. 'Shall we begin?' I suggested.

She lead me downstairs to a well lit basement where a number of consoles and work stations occupied the central floor space, with work tables here and there, and cabinets of memory banks standing against the perimeter walls.

'We have many hours of video memory, Mr Hardin,' she told me, walking to a workstation and activating the screen.

I grabbed a chair and sat in beside her.

'It's very peculiar,' she continued. 'Our inventory reveals the loss of a considerable number of items, but how or when the items were taken, we just do not know.' She brought up on screen the list of items gone missing. A list numbering some two hundred items.

I scanned the list, occasionally reading aloud as I did so: 'A one mile long roll of five ply nylon cord. One bobcat mini earth-moving machine. Two hundred instant chicken dinners with vegetables. A Christmas tree. One two hundred metre roll of canvas. One geological chemistry test set. Fifty kilos of powdered milk. Ten patio umbrellas. Twenty kilos of protein concentrate. Twenty bags of expanding polycrete building foam. A box of rubber gloves and one kilo of boiled sweets.

'An interesting array of items,' I commented. 'Almost tending towards random. It doesn't quite make sense. I don't see how there could be a black market demand for hardly any of this.'

'Boiled sweets and a Christmas tree,' Alex reiterated.

'There are no children on this rig. And what the hell would anyone need a bobcat for? Why would someone who lived out here want that? Where would you hide it? Personal space is at a premium out here. A two hundred metre roll of canvas? How do you conceal something like that?'

'Maybe it's being taken to Niven station.'

'How?' I asked, incredulous, and to which she only flushed and remained silent.

'And how the hell is this much stuff disappearing without security detecting the presence of these thieves. It could only be done with the complicity of security personnel.'

'That's not possible,' Alex countered, exhibiting the effort of containing her indignation. 'No one of us would be an accessory to any of this.'

'Perhaps you don't know people as well as you think you do,' I goaded. 'Everyone is corruptible, despite what you think you know. It is entirely dependant on the price.'

She looked at me as if studying an insect, but did not reply. I knew exactly what she was thinking. To have that particular opinion one is virtually admitting to being corruptible, themself. I didn't give a damn. I knew my estimation of people was spot on. This girl had a lot of growing up to do.

Avoiding the subject, she suggested, 'The only sure way to find out who is stealing from the company is to view the hours of stored video surveillance files, from the time we know the goods are in place to the time they are found gone.'

I chuckled without meaning to.

'What's funny?' she wanted to know, indignant again. 'The phraseology you just used. ". . . *found gone.*"

She made a comical face. 'Oh, yes, I see what you mean.

Found to be missing,' she corrected herself.

'Don't mind me,' I told her. 'My mind, I think, tends to work differently than most.'

'No, I like things like that,' she responded, smiling now. 'Most of the people I work with would never pick up on the little things like that. It's amusing, isn't it? The little things? People, modes of speech, routine, the *illogic* in our daily lives that we never notice.'

I hadn't meant to spark a conversation, but I found myself liking that she got it.

'How many hours of surveillance video is there?' I asked, needing to break this needless chitchat.

'I would need to focus on the relevant time spans, during which the theft likely took place. Rough guess? Thousands of hours.'

'Thousands of hours,' I repeated. 'Honestly? There must be ways to automate the search. I am not viewing thousands of hours of footage.'

It was Alex's turn to chuckle. 'You mean, data.' 'Do I?'

'Yes. These are digital video files. The term footage is a relic from when video was recorded on actual film. So many feet of film. *Footage.*'

'When you're right, you're right,' I agreed. 'Find a way to search the footage for anomalies. Light intensity anomalies, I would suggest. Unless these guys work in the dark. And contact me when you have found what we want. *Vis–a' –vis*, crooks stealing stuff.'

I left her to it; walked away without having to see the look I knew was stuck to her face. She had thousands of hours of *footage* to view in order to find the odd few minutes heist. Relic? I didn't much appreciate the term, and I would use whatever damn word I pleased.

It was now time to play on the other side of the fence, I told myself. Perhaps an ale at one of the many inns and pleasure houses on level four; and while I was there I figured I might enquire as to how one might procure certain items not readily available through the usual channels.

I took my now established route to the elevators beside the administration building, alighting within the protective steel cage on level four. Judging by the sudden upsurge of foot traffic, I figured that it must be change of shift, a time when hostelries, public houses, barrooms, and not to forget the odd café, were sure to be starting to pack them in.

A place called the Event Horizon caught my eye. A public house in a singular state of dilapidation. Odd considering the platform had only been up and running for a short while. Its owner looked not to have outlaid a fortune on its exterior, but upon entering within a transformation occurred. The interior walls were brick constructed, and with what looked to be actual wooden rafters running across the ceiling, supporting the upper structure. The bar was a continuous arc, circling the interior and passing through the walls of every room adjoining, making a perfect circle. Newcomer though I was, I knew expense when I saw it. Timber from Earth? The expense must have been colossal. The place was a paradox. A ramshackle exterior and a plush interior, complete with a brass rail on which to place a hoof while drinking at the bar; and comfortable furniture, too. Perhaps its outward appearance was contrived to throw tourists and non residents a curve? I considered.

Workers milled around in every corner, engaged in loud conversation and raucous laughter. The bar and tables were likewise populated, and those lacking a place to sit, stood, exhibiting obvious weariness from a shift which had sapped a good deal of energy from their bodies, but that would change. Given time the alcohol's ameliorative effects would begin to apply its design purpose, loosening taut muscles and purse strings alike.

I ordered a beer, or at least the chemical contrivance which, nowadays, passed for beer. It was cold, which I did not expect, and a surprisingly close approximation of the real stuff. My opinion of this place continued to rise beyond expectation. It was the sort of place I never expected to find on a rig like this. From around the corner the recognisable rattle of an eightball pool table releasing balls into the tray could be heard. The perfect opportunity to make contact.

Rounding the corner I found three guys at the table, a couple of credits resting on the edge of the table, signifying their intention to retain the table for two games. Acknowledging the men with a nod, I added a coin of my own and stepped back to view the game.

Halfway through the frame the odd man out turned to me, saying, 'Not seen your face around here before, mister. You new to Far Reach?'

'Only arrived a couple of days ago,' I obliged. 'Haven't been assigned yet. Some sort of foul up with Central Data finding a glitch in my personnel file.'

'Tell me about it,' he said, smiling. 'So now you're expected to wait with your thumb up your arse while they take their time sorting it, right?'

'Right. And meanwhile I'm millions of miles from home and sweet *eff ay*.'

'That sucks,' he sympathised. 'That would mean you can't eat at the company cafeterias. You gotta pay to eat until you're on the payroll.

'Yep. Today's choice is to pay through the nose for dinner, or have a few ales and get to know some of you guys.'

'Hey guys,' he called to his pals. 'Another guy here having to pay his own way while the office sorts out their fuckup.'

The guy taking a shot lifted his head, shook it, expressing disgust.

The other spoke up.

'Bloody typical of those bastards.'

The following rack I was included in a game of doubles. We drank and played for a couple of hours, during which time I was introduced to their friends as they entered the bar and joined us in beer, pool and conversation. I must admit to enjoying the interlude, although it was an entirely necessary ploy to establish myself on the lower rung of the labour force hierarchy. The lads even chipped in and bought me a meal, which we ate together at a table upstairs, insisting that it was protocol for guys in my position. Apparently my story was not in the least uncommon. It seemed that the working man's code of brotherhood was still very much alive and well out here.

At the end of the day I ambled back to the Star. The landlord, Pietro, caught me at the bottom of the stairs on my way up to the room, wanting to know if I was in need of clean linen or towels.

Today was that day of the week, but I declined and headed on up. My stitches were beginning to irritate and the wound was becoming ever more uncomfortable. All I wanted was to wind down for a while and catch a few hours nap. I was on my bed and snoozing for barely a half hour when my communicator woke me.

Miss Alex Jordan, the assistant Berringer had assigned to assist me, had done as I asked and ran all the relevant security files. Assuming the thieves needed light to perpetrate the theft, the editing software had been set to identify the presence of light within the warehouse outside of scheduled work times, and run at high speed it did not take too long before irregular instances of illumination were identified. She had done the job I asked for a little too efficiently. Just a few hours longer would have seen me rise from my bed, refreshed and in an altogether better state of mind. In light of her success, I advised myself to try not to take my ill disposition out on the keen to please miss Jordan, and grabbing the essentials, I headed off to see what she had discovered.

The elevator delivered me to the basement of the security building. As I neared the work station at which Miss Jordan was bent assiduously to her work, she turned, smiling.

'Mister Hardin,' she greeted.

'You must be tired,' I speculated, chuckling inwardly. 'Once you've shown me what you have, you can go home, grab some rest.'

'Not a bit.' She pointed to an assembled camp bed recently installed in the corner. 'Once I had set the parameters of the search, I was able to lay down and rest while the computer ran it through. Easy.'

'Half your luck,' I muttered under my breath, and if she caught that, she showed no sign of it.

'Okay. What have we got? I asked.'

'Several instances of brief illumination. Take a look at this.'

I moved up beside her to get a better view of the monitor. She had isolated a good many instances, but it was not at all what one might have expected. I had to ask her to go back several times, in order to clearly identify what had taken place. In each instance there had been a flash of brilliant light, during which time inventory simply disappeared from view. In the end I had to refrain from asking her to replay the event; the unlikely occurrence was not going to be made easier to understand for the number of times it was viewed.

'Is this some kind of hoax?' I wondered, aloud.

'It's no hoax,' Alex replied earnestly. 'I wondered the same thing. I have studied the time sequencing of every incidence and the file has definitely not been tampered with. I will bet my reputation on that. These things seem to just. . .' she baulked in continuing.

'Vanish,' I finished for her. 'How the hell is that possible? She looked up at me. 'And who has the technology?'

'Do me a favour and note the exact locations of these events.' I would normally never bring anyone along with me when inspecting the scene of a crime, but this was different. An extra pair of eyes might prove an advantage. 'And when you've done that, maybe you wouldn't mind accompanying me to inspect the scene? That is, if George doesn't have any objections?'

At the mention of an outing, her face had brightened, until she realised her boss would not permit it. 'I'm afraid he wouldn't like it, Mr Hardin.'

'Tell you what,' I said, feeling suddenly magnanimous, 'You find those locations and I'll sort it with Berringer. Okay?'

'Okay,' she beamed.

I found George in the staff lunch room making himself coffee.

'If you have finished with my girl,' he told me, 'I need her back. This is *her* job. I have better things to do than waste my time making coffee for myself.'

'Really?' I watched as he overfilled his cup, splattering the counter and his expensive clothes. There was no way I was going to ask his permission. He could make his own bloody coffees for a while longer.

'A while longer, George,' I told him, and left him dabbing up the spill with paper towel.

Warehouse-A dealt with appliances, motors, transmissions and spare parts for the same. Alex lead us to the spot where we had witnessed a crated air-conditioner disappear. The position was still empty. There were no recent scrapes, no telltale black streaks where rubber souls had marked the surface as labourers struggled with the weight of it. For the next two and a half hours we dragged ourselves through warehouse after warehouse, viewing the sties where these events had taken place, and I was becoming more and more annoyed at the total lack of evidence of any kind. Not until, at the twenty second site of the day, a metal fastener was found, which had been used to secure the crate in which a stolen motorised cart had been. A puny piece of evidence which would probably amount to absolutely nothing, but it was something. It would, to my mind, tell me if some kind of powerful device had been employed in snatching the item, or if I was the butt of an elaborate hoax intended to waste my time and sully my reputation. At this point, anything was possible.

I had Alex accompany me to the science lab. George would just have to learn to make his expensive coffee without making a mess; and I didn't like to see her potential squandered by the arse-hole. Besides, if it annoyed him, I was for it.

My opinion of miss Jordan was beginning to reform. In her early thirties I judged. A bright disposition, which, at her age, I might have expected to have eroded after spending time playing second fiddle to someone like George. Attractive too. No wedding band, intelligent, and as an off world employee of the company, probably without children.

While we waited for the analysis of the fastener I searched out and found somewhere to sit and talk for a while. A bench seat in the foyer served the purpose, so we grabbed a soft drink from a machine, seated ourselves, and I remained silent, waiting to see what she would do with a chance for conversation.

She seemed nervous at first, sipping the soda and glancing around at the first sign of movement. There was concern over a few pieces of lint on her navy dress, but after a couple of minutes she piped up.

'Are we believing what we saw on the video file?' 'What do you think happened?' I replied.

'It could have been doctored. An elaborate method of leading us in the wrong direction, but who would go to such trouble over a few odd items? Everyone here is so busy with their work-a-day exis-tence. Who could be bothered?'

'You said yourself that the videos were authentic,' I reminded her. 'Yes. Of course.'

'Consider for a moment that someone did exactly what we wit-nessed, and they were able to dissolve matter into nothing.' 'I didn't see it that way,' she admitted. 'Again with perceptions. I was think-ing the objects were taken from one place and delivered to another. Not destructive, just a theft. Why would someone want to simply destroy these things? A demonstration, do you think?'

'It's a possibility.' I pulled a cigarette from my pocket and lit up. 'So, assuming what we saw was real, the possibilities are that it was done as a low key demonstration of a powerful tool, or a weapon, or it was as we first assumed. A bizarre robbery, pure and simple.'

'And if they can take things like that, they can just as easily help themselves to items of great value. So why everyday items and not precious metals, valuable stones?'

'That's an excellent question,' I responded. 'Do you think we would know about it if such a heist had taken place?'

'It would be embarrassing for the victim. Anyone entrusted with or owning highly valuable merchandise and having it swiped so easily? It could be devastating if news got out,' she correctly pointed out.

'When you're right, you're right. Now we have a wider field of speculation. If a moderate case of pilfering with such a small chance of being caught in the act is possible, the same applies for theft on a major scale. Human nature dictates that the thieves would not risk detection for a smalltime job, not when big money is as easily obtained. They only need strike once, and be set for life.'

She made a face expressing puzzlement as she thought on it awhile. 'So. . . Someone is toying with security? Maybe a demonstration? Or are they just dumb?'

'I don't know,' I admitted, 'but the possibilities are what we have just mentioned. Dumb crooks with insufficient imagination to go for the big money. Someone far from dumb who is toying with us and demonstrating their technology. Or the somewhat incongruous situation of someone in need of the items they selected and unable to acquire then by other means.'

'This is fun,' she announced with a smile. 'Isn't it for you? Like a *whodunit*, using nothing but deductive reasoning. It's like one of those paperback novel detective stories.'

The remark surprised me. 'You don't read those things?'

'Of course not,' she responded indignantly. 'Chewing gum for the intellect. No. I only mean I enjoy the challenge. You must enjoy it. Why else would you do this work?'

'Why does anyone devote most of their life to jumping through hoops at the behest of others?'

'Is that how you see it?' she asked.

'Is there any other way? I suppose you're out here on the rim, working for the company for the joy of it.'

'Everyone has to work,' she retorted. 'Life is not a free ride.' My communicator buzzed, indicating a message had arrived.

The lab had finished the analysis.

'Hold that thought,' I told her. 'We can philosophize about life another time. Shall we see what has been learned from that fastener?'

The guy in the white lab coat said that what we had was a standard, hexagonal, metal alloy, boxing crate fastener. Nothing unusual. I had been hoping for something more, thinking that anything touched by a dematerializing energy field would leave its signature, but I was wrong about that and we were back to having nothing to go on, except for our theorizing about how and why these thefts were occurring. I organized for the areas where the items had been seen to disappear to be likewise analysed by the science boffins, but I held out little hope for anything like a result. For the remainder of the day I suggested to Alex that she go back to the office. For myself, a nap was in order, after which I intended going back to the Horizon, and to ascertain if my new chums could tell me anything about how one might obtain certain items otherwise precluded through normal channels.

It would be interesting to try and get hold of something from the list of stolen items. If the order came though, it was then just a simple matter to track it back along the supply chain to the source. Trouble was, it was an absurd list, and there was not a single thing on it which would make a blind bit of sense for me to order. Why were these items taken? I made myself comfortable on top of my bed and studied the list yet again.

One bobcat mini earthmover. Okay, so somebody wanted to shift a bunch of dirt. It has been known, but there was nothing around here coming close to terrain. This was particularly interesting. Besides the fact that it would be next to impossible to hide a stolen bobcat anywhere on the platform, it was obviously intended to go somewhere it could be used. It had to be transported off of Far Reach, but how do you transport it when every craft into and out of the platform is company owned and under the gaze of company security? I struggled with that particular dilemma until my head began to hurt, and moved on, looking for some kind of pattern.

Two hundred chicken dinners with vegetables? Everyone eats. No clue there. Next. . .

One Christmas tree. Why does one have a Christmas tree? To celebrate Christmas. A Christian holiday. One, single Christmas tree. Pass. . .

A two hundred metre roll of canvas. At least that made sense. Sort of. Canvas is useful. It can be used for various purposes. A ground sheet. To cover stuff, protecting it from weather etc. To provide people with temporary shelter from the elements, in the form of a tent. Canvas was eminently useful, and expensive. Especially out here. Next. . .

My alarm woke me. It was time for me to make my way to the hotel.

On the way over to the Horizon the absurdity of this whole situation impressed itself on me like a great weight pressing down. I was wasting my time with this meeting, I told myself. Nothing would come of it. I would insinuate that I was in need of one kind of contraband or another, and in the event of the deal being made I would find myself treading water while waiting for confirmation and eventual arrival of the goods. It would then be an uphill battle to convince these men to betray the supplier. It was a grubby plan and I wondered at my loss of perspective for ever having thought I could go through with it. The notion only augmented the sense of creeping self-doubt which had been dogging me since arriving on this pile of scrap iron. I had actually deceived myself into thinking it was okay to rope those guys in this way. There was a time I would never have hatched such an unimaginative and underhand tactic, let alone considered playing it out. Such tactics were the province of brutish and lazy coppers who were willing to step on anyone in the way, without regard for their circumstances.

Maybe I had been in this game too long. I had only gone this route because I had a natural talent for sniffing out fraud and outright brigands, and because of my intense dislike of those who saw themselves as being above the rest of us; somehow special, able to do and take as they pleased, with the cost impacting on the little guy, and without earning what they had because the system greased the wheels for those in position and with privilege while putting the screws on those doing the grunt work. All this was for nothing, it dawned on me then. I had strayed so far off track with this case. Gone totally in the wrong direction.

'Blast!' I growled, pulling up in mid stride, and in the process drawing unwanted attention to myself as those around me glanced to see what was up.

3

UNEXPECTED

Eight hours later and I was sat on a packing crate, concealed in the near total darkness of warehouse-A, where the majority of the thefts had occurred. In my mind I had been running through my previous conversations with Alex. She had noticed these occurrences tended to fall within a particular time frame; during the third work shift, and significantly so. Sheer frustration had lead me to come here and sit in the darkness, watching for anything untoward. It was definitely a symptom of my frustration with the lack of progress, but it beat the hell out of twisting my brain, trying to reason my way to an answer with far too few threads of information and not even a good working hypothesis of what was going on here. It may have looked like clutching at straws, and the odds were astronomically against the chance of me witnessing anything useful, but it was something; and, hell, if nothing else it served to reduce my ever growing sense of futility and mounting frustration.

The hours oozed past like molasses on a cold winter's day. I thought about Detective Sergeant Burt Emerson; whether he was making any effort to track down those responsible for the increasing discomfort in my abdomen. With so little to go on, I figured the incident had already been pushed to the back burner. Apart from the pieces of lead they had cut out of me, there was precious little else to go on. Another cold case, but at least there was no corpse this time. That was the single positive, so far.

I thought about junior officer Andy Saunders, Emerson's offsider. He was at the beginning of his career; a baby-faced, no nothing beginner; a greenhorn with no idea how much the job would change him as the years slid implacably by. If I gave a damn I would sit him down, warn him of the relentlessly long hours of tangled and conflicting emotions which turned a man to stone while his family gradually learned that the acts of violence and human degradation he dealt with, day in day out, were slowly but surely going to take precedence until nothing recognisable remained of the man they once knew as husband and father.

I thought about Joe Higgins, head administrator. The boss man and king of the heap. A man who had worked his way up from almost nothing at all through focus of will and dint of hard work. In the end he knew more about this place than those who envisioned, designed, financed and built it. It was he who breathed life into it, made it function by precise coordination, careful distribution of power and responsibility, by the planning of interrelated, co-dependant ancillaries from exploration, mineral ore testing and cost assessment, retrieval, refinement, delivery and all in between, including allocation of man hours and overall expenditure. That men like this existed at all, to me seemed a freak of nature, but without them places like this just would not function. And his reward? Satisfying his need for control and the pursuit of perfection, and doubtlessly culminating in an early grave.

I thought about Security Chief George Berringer; an egotistical arsehole who thinks life is a competition, thereby missing the point entirely. When he was young, for him it was all about who was the cleverest, who made the most money, who had the prettiest girl, the best car. Bragging rights. We were friends, once, but it was he who pulled away, considering me to be below par as far as friends go. He was so caught up in trying to prove himself superior in every way, he never really made a single, meaningful connection with another human being. Poor George. I actually pitied the man more than I ever resented his intolerable superciliousness.

How much time had passed? I wondered. Looking at my watch would either disappoint or surprise. I would avoid the disappointment. My experience was that time moved faster in the dark than in the light. I had been here a couple of hours, I guessed. The alarm would alert me when six hours had elapsed and I would decide whether or not to stay longer then.

I recalled suggesting to Alex Jordan that everyone was corruptible, depending only on the price, and the look on her face the comment had provoked. In that very moment I had considered if I wasn't saying something about myself, that I too was corruptible, and for the first time in an age I had felt uncomfortable under another human being's gaze. Why the hell would I care what she thought? Someone like her would have very little life experience by comparison. I had seen things that had made grown men reel; experienced situations so far removed from what everyday folk had to confront or would believe possible, it had forever eclipsed in me whatever faith in human nature might have existed. I had once believed in the existence of beauty and meaning in life, but that was long ago. We had almost killed our planet, and ourselves. We were no different now. We survived because we were too frightened to die, not because of any altruistic revelation we may have experienced. Even now, who's to say we have made it. Our basic nature has not changed; it still exists, and it will corrupt and infect whatever place in the cosmos we come to occupy.

What was that? Did I hear something? Perhaps not.

I pulled a cigarette from my pocket. When the lighter ignited a face appeared up close in front of me, startling me so much that I nearly fell off the crate I was sitting on.

'Holy shit!'

Alex stifled a giggle. 'I didn't mean to catch you unawares. Sorry. I brought you some coffee.' 'How did you find me?'

'Simple,' she responded. It's what I expected you do after being shown the cluster of occurrences.'

'And you reasoned I would be here, this exact place, now, tonight,' I stated dubiously.

I couldn't see her face in the darkness, but if I could I would have expected to see the nervous look of someone caught in an untruth. There was slightly more to it than she was admitting. She had gone to some trouble to home in on my whereabouts, but I let it go. There were several reasons why she might have done this, and none of them sinister.

160

'Are you terribly annoyed?' she asked in a small voice.

My internal radar flashed, *warning*. Was she coming-on to me? 'Did you bring two cups?' I replied, avoiding. 'And keep your voice low, if you must talk.

This was the absolute last thing I would have expected, but she had been enthusiastic about the case right from the start. The endless routine of assisting someone of Berringer's calibre would cause anybody to crave a distraction. I guessed she found it to be a pleasant change from the dreary norm.

She had indeed brought two cups. I lit another cigarette and we sat in silence for a time, sipping, peering into the darkness. In a moment she reached for my wrist, causing me to flinch, but she only wanted to check the time.

'Is there somewhere you have to be?' I asked.

'No.' There was another long silence, until she asked, 'Could I have a cigarette?'

'You smoke? I thought I was the last person in the universe who smoked. Cocaine addicts get more respect than smokers.' 'Nicotine. It's an excellent stimulant,' she replied, 'and relaxing at the same time. It also helps to focus the mind. Tell me of another substance which does all that.'

'I agree,' I told her, pulling a cigarette from my pocket and holding it out in her direction. She located my hand, took it from my grasp, and I lit it for her.

'You never told me you were a police detective before coming to work for the company. Did Universal X recruit you?'

'I quit the force, then quickly discovered it was all I really knew. This job seemed a good fit. What about you? Have you always worked for Berringer?'

'God, no. The very thought of the idea. He doesn't know it yet, but I'm about to move on.'

'Really? Where to?' I asked.

'My first love was anthropology. *Xenoanthropology*, now. But I'm interested to know more about you, Mr Hardin.'

'How about we move to first name status? Call me Jack, why don't you?'

'Jack is a twist on John, or Jonathan, isn't it?'

'Not this time. Jack is the name on my birth registry. Jack Hardin. No middle name.'

'I'm plain old Alex. Alexandra, actually, but Alex is preferable. Why did you quit the force?'

'Why *xenoanthropology*?' I returned. I was not going there. 'And does it mean what it seems to imply? The study of other than human culture?'

'That's right. The study of alien culture.'

'Not exactly in high demand, I would imagine.'

'Not yet,' she answered. 'What time is it, please, Jack?'

I looked at my chronometer. 'It is exactly two minutes since the last time you checked. What's the obsession with time, tonight? You have a hot date or something?'

'Actually,' she replied with humour in her voice, 'you're not far off the mark.' She switched on a torch she had brought along, aiming it at the floor of the empty storage compartment beside us. With her other hand she reached into her pocket, withdrew something I couldn't make out. Then there was the distinctive click of a hammer being cocked into firing position, and things became quite tense quite quickly.

'Please step into that spot—' and she indicated where by moving the beam in a circular motion.

I then noticed how fuzzy everything seemed to be getting. I was becoming unsteady on my feet. She had put something in the damn coffee. How stupid could I be?

'Why don't you sit on the floor before you fall, Jack? I don't want you hurting yourself. And, please, don't worry. Everything's fine. There's something I want you to see.'

I moved to lower myself to the floor as she suggested. 'I don't get it,' I said. Why?'

As the question was given voice the air around us began to glisten and tremble. Alex moved quickly to sit on the floor beside me, and a second later a brilliant white flash filled my world.

*

162

Trans-spatial Migration is a technology humans had dreamt of for hundreds of years. All I knew was that it required the understanding of mass and energy being fundamentally the same thing. Only the scientists of my time familiar with temporal field dynamics and quantum reciprocal action duality ever pretended to understand the basic theory behind the phenomenon; but that was to be in the future.

The experience of *travelling* by this method is much the same as being put under general anaesthetic prior to an operation. A great black void opens up, swallowing a person whole. There is no sense of being, no sense of time, only the unsettling feeling that this must be what death feels like. A wholly disquieting experience, and I always hated travelling that way; but then travelling is not quite the appropriate word.

When I awoke I was on my back and staring vacantly upward. Sky, I guessed. Was that blue sky? I could not see anything clearly. My mind would not connect in any meaningful way with a single thing at that moment. An odd-looking creature was leaning over me, babbling something absurd and unrecognisable even as words. My eyes were capable of rolling about in their orbits, which they did to the great distress of my stomach, which felt as if it hadn't taken food in over a week.

I was in a white room which might have passed for a ship's medical treatment room; sparsely furnished and containing three narrow metal cots fixed to the wall, illumination coming from all around but nowhere in particular. On the bed beside me lay Alex. On her face she wore what I presumed to be an oxygen mask, and not until then did I realise that I did too. I was extremely enervated and beyond even thinking of climbing to my feet.

The second time I woke I was feeling much better. Alex was recently up and on her feet, swaying slightly and regarding me while holding on to a metal rail for support.

'You drugged me,' I stated accusingly, suddenly remembering what had occurred prior to my turning up here. The mask over my lower face muffled my speech, so I removed it and said again:

'You bloody drugged me, woman. Are you deranged?

An opened, arched doorway behind her presented a view of outdoors; somewhat desolate looking, with a clear, pale blue sky overhead, and what looked to be low, scrubby vegetation in the distance.

'I had no real option,' she replied. 'I know your reputation and you would have found out eventually anyway. I couldn't allow the company to become aware. And the transportation process required that you be still. I didn't know how you would respond, and the last thing I wanted was for you to be hurt during the process. Are you alright?'

I explored that topic by sitting up, letting my legs dangle over the edge of the cot as I located and tested the rest of my extremities.

'I seem to be all here,' I told her. 'Wherever here is. I'm not sure I *want* to know the answer to that right now, though. Is the answer likely to piss me off even more than I am already? 'What?'I replied to the coy expression on Alex's face.

She sat on the edge of the cot and regarded me thoughtfully. 'I'm actually taken aback by how well you are taking this. Thank-you for not exploding. I was frightened. I thought for sure you would react far worse than this.'

I managed a thin smile. 'Why? Would it help? She shrugged. 'No.'

Right then a tall, blue skinned, humanoid creature appeared in the doorway. It stood there regarding the two of us with mild interest for a moment, and ambled off unconcernedly.

'What was that?' I asked, as evenly as I was able to.

'You mean, *Who was that*? That was Dortl Karp, Fernac's offspring.

I remained silent awhile, processing. 'Where are we and how did we get here?'

'How did we get here? They call it something totally unpronounceable, but if I had to translate, and I've thought about this, I call it trans-spatial migration. It's kind of a clumsy name, and doesn't describe the process well, but it's the best I can do. They tried to explain it to me and I didn't understand. These are incredibly intelligent people, Jack, with aeons longer gene pool than mankind. Their

164

brain is far a superior. I cannot communicate with them in their way. They have a basic language structure which they can use, but it is beyond me. They quickly learned to communicate with me by learning my language in short time. They communicate with one another telepathically, but they can communicate with us using a mixture of words and what telepathy can be filtered through our encephalon, or central nervous system. It works sufficiently well to communicate most things.'

'I still don't understand how I got here, but I'll put that aside for now,' I relented. 'Where am I? is more important to me right now.'

'A little known world called Ki Kassini, and that is only an approximation of the name they call it. It's an unnamed planet on the extreme outer edge of our galaxy. I mean, little known to them, and totally unknown to us. They're marooned here.'

'They're marooned here?'

Alex nodded. 'Something vital broke on their ship. Serious enough so that they had to land and try to make repairs.'

'How the hell did you end up befriending them?' I asked. 'We're a very long way from Far Reach.'

'When the missing inventory first came to my attention, I did as you did. I staked out the warehouse. They were actually entering the warehouses, personally, taking what they needed to aid their survival. In all the confusion of the unplanned confrontation, they brought me back here to explain, hoping to avoid frightening the wits out of me and gaining my confidence. I guess they were lucky. They gained an ally. I would never jeopardise their desire for anonymity.'

'Bringing me here was your idea of concealing their existence? Are you sure this was your smartest move?'

'No, not entirely. I could see things getting way out of control, though. If you had reported back to the company that things were disappearing — I mean *actually* disappearing! — there would be no way of putting the genie back in the bottle. Things would have gotten way out of hand. These people do not want to be humanity's introduction to extraterrestrial life. They just want to be left alone, to make their repairs and get off of this barren, inhospitable planet. They're such shy creatures.'

I raised my hand, halting the flow of information. 'You must know how difficult it is, trying to take all of this in. It's actually making my head spin.'

'No. That's the atmosphere here. It happened to me, too. It takes a little while to get used to the lower oxygen content of the air. I do appreciate how difficult it is to swallow all of this. It kind of shakes one's foundations. It did with me.'

'It does put a new slant on things,' I admitted. 'There's a sort of pervasive unreality, right now. And before you say it, no, it's not oxygen deprivation. It's more the same feeling as when you're told at age seven that your parents are getting divorced. Like that. World altering.'

'That happened to you?' she replied, almost sympathetic. 'No. It's just a analogy.'

'Oh, right. Yes, I see what you mean. Good analogy.'

'So, are you going to show me around this place? Introduce me to your friends?'

4

THE JHAI

The craft comprised a large, dome-topped, flat-bottomed cylinder as a central hub, circled by seven similarly shaped dome topped cylinders of slightly smaller volume. I've seen jelly moulds of similar shape. Some of Alex's *friends* gathered around as we left the confines of the craft via the opened archway, and we all stood, facing one other.

They were, I thought, aesthetically pleasing to the eye: light-blue, of slender build and a half metre taller than myself; bald-headed, three fingered, cloven footed and with all the usual sense organs and orifices incorporated into the head and face, as it is with us, though significantly smaller and less prominent, making them appear friendly and innocuous. The eyes were almond shape, black and large, pupils circular with green irises, shrunken extremely small in the brightness of the day. Their demeanour was nothing beyond calm, relaxed and curious as Alex presented me to the small gathering, waving her hand in my direction and saying, 'My friend, Jack Hardin.'

That was it. Introductions made, the circle parted to allow us freedom of movement.

'Come on,' she said, 'and I'll show you around the place.'

The encampment was situated atop of a rise, with a flat, wide expanse surrounding. What vegetation there was grew low to the ground. Shrubs, miniature trees, a kind of purplish grass that snaked over the compacted, dry, brown earth.

A series of jerry rigged sunshades encircled a large open fire-place. The shades, constructed of rope, canvas and steel poles were the obvious proceeds from the great warehouse caper.

'Starting to make sense now?' she asked.

'It is,' I answered, and pointed to the Christmas tree standing in front of one of the makeshift shelters. 'But hardly a necessity.'

'The children like pretty things,' she explained. 'That would account for the kilo of boiled lollies.'

'Actually, no. the boiled sweets are a favourite of the adults. The children don't like sweet things. I had to warn the adults of possible damage their teeth, but they appear to be impervious to tooth decay. Tooth decay, bacterial and viral infection, run of the mill illnesses as we experience are unknown to them. They have an incredible natural resilience to such things. Their immune system is a wonder.'

'Half their luck,' I replied, aware that my wound had begun throbbing painfully once again. 'Let's sit for a while,' I suggested.

Over the edge of the hill I caught sight of a construction site. A large quantity of earth had been gouged out and sealed with polycrete; the bobcat earthmoving machine parked alongside. The sides of the hill had been fashioned into tilted terraces in hope of channelling rainfall, directing it into the newly constructed dam with barely three inches of water contained.

'How badly is their ship damaged?' I asked. 'It looks to me they expect to be here for some time to come. '

'A vital component,' she answered. 'Do you know what a bio data processor is?'

I shook my head. 'Never heard of one.'

'Apparently there are several of them throughout the ships nervous system, like small brains that monitor and regulate the vast number of systems and energy flow. There are a number of small ones that maintain running temperatures, engine functions and like that, but it's their guidance and astronavigation bio processor. They cannot navigate without a replacement. They would quickly become lost among the stars.'

'That would be a problem,' I accepted. 'But I'm surprised to find they're so in need of water. They have a craft capable of interstellar travel. Distances which, presumably, would take considerable time to travel, and they don't have the necessary water aboard? I remember protein concentrate being on the list of stolen goods. Why would they be so ill prepared?'

'Don't ask me,' she responded, studying me closely. 'Why, you're not suspicious, are you? Questioning their sincerity, why they're here? Why they're raiding our supplies? Because, it's obvious, just looking around, to see that these people are in a bind.'

Until Alex asked the question I was only allowing my mind to follow its natural trajectory, as is its nature. But there was merit in the asking, I had to admit. It didn't add up terribly well, that a space faring people would so easily get themselves marooned on a backwater planet, finding themselves so ill equipped to deal with a not completely unforeseeable event such as a breakdown. Just how intelligent were these *people*?

'Exactly how well do you know them?' I asked.'

'I've been visiting for maybe six months, bringing a few supplies every so often. I've been here probably twelve times and I've gotten to know them quite well.'

'Hence your little joke about being an exoanthropologist?' 'Xenoanthropology, actually,' she corrected.'No joke, and I'll be able to write one hell of a paper on the Jhai.'

'That's what they're called. The *Jhai*? I thought they wished to remain anonymous? In any case, you must be aware of the risk you would be running.'

'What risk is that?' she asked.

'The most obvious of them all. The risk of you being branded a fruitcake, unless these guys don't mind you taking a few happy snaps for your scrapbook. And that I somehow doubt.'

She turned away from the view to regard me anew. 'You are one cynical man, Jack Hardin. How did that happen?'

'People are shaped by the lives they lead,' I answered. 'Yes,' she responded, thoughtfully. 'That is very true. I would give anything to escape the life I currently lead. People get trapped, I think. . . . by their own inertia.'

'Pithy.'

'Pithy?!' she repeated. I couldn't tell if she was offended or amused.

'What?' I responded. 'You don't like *pithy?* It is. What you said was pithy. An accurate and weighty observation stated in few words. Is that not pithy?'

'I thought you were making fun of me, the way you do. You weren't?'She regarded me with obvious suspicion.

'No. Honestly, I wasn't.' The incident suddenly struck me as funny. I began laughing, which didn't appear to help.

She jabbed me in the ribs, hard, enough elicit a painful cry. 'You really have no idea how to be a human being, do you?'

She regarded me angrily, but I had no idea why. I also had no idea why I was feeling the way I did or what that feeling was; why I felt anything at all, and for the moment I became distracted by the anomaly.

We resumed walking the circuit of the settlement. On the far side of the encampment, the aliens, these Jhai, had attempted to implement the growing of basic food crops, sowing cereals such as corn and wheat; the seed, no doubt, obtained from Far Point, but nothing had survived to harvest. What small amount of seasonal rainfall there was had been far too minimal and all their attempts at farming had failed. The small amount of available rainfall had necessarily been retained for personal use.

By the time we arrived back where we had begun, a couple of the group had returned with a batch of freshly killed small animals, not dissimilar to rabbits. We were invited to sit near the fire pit, on a mound of earth covered with soft grasses bundled and loosely tied, providing a comfortable position to sit. A pair of the adolescents busied themselves with preparing the kill, and then placing the prepared meat, suspended in a rack, to cook over the searing heat of the coals.

Alex turned to me, saying, 'We have been invited to share the meal and stay the night. Would you like to?'

I hadn't camped out since I was a child. The idea quite appealed to me, and how many could say they had attended a barbeque hosted by extraterrestrial aliens?

'Why not?' I answered, after thinking on it a short while. 'I've nothing special to do, and I must say I'm not exactly keen to make the return trip.'

'Don't worry. I should have told you, the body quickly adjusts to the method of travel. The next time won't be nearly so bad. After that, it's nothing at all.'

'When did we receive this invitation?'

Alex nodded to one standing within the group. 'Maja, the elder,' she replied. 'I receive the invitation telepathically as we returned from your tour.'

'Am I to be subjected to this mind reading lark? I don't much like the idea.'

'No, Jack. You have to remember, they're born with the ability. It's not the novelty it is to you and me. They could care less what is on your mind, and common courtesy forbids encroachment on your privacy.'

'Very glad to hear it.' I said, relieved. 'I can only imagine where my mind might stray if I thought I was being read like a book. You know what I mean?'

She nodded, smiled broadly. 'I know exactly. They were quick to reassure me that no such incursion on your privacy would take place, and they are as good as their word. Lies are as foreign to them as calculus to is a chimpanzee.'

When the *rabbit* was cooked it was shared among all, along with an assortment of indigenous nuts and berries, and washed down by sweetened, instant coffee, once again courtesy of the company. We were left to our own devices throughout, and I found it a pleasant departure from the human norm, where meal-times are often full of needless chatter while trying to eat in peace.

The air did not become chill as I had expected with the loss of daylight, but remained comfortably warm; and as the evening progressed our hosts dutifully cleaned up the area before silently wandering away, presumably to their beds and a good night's sleep. For myself, I was far from tired. The day had been full of puzzles and surprises which had served only to stimulate the mental processes to a level of heightened activity. Sleep would be difficult after a day like this.

With the gradual loss of illumination from our local star, starlight from the more distant sources gradually strengthened until the night sky fairly blazed. In addition, a pair of small moons popped up, one after the other, augmenting the soft, milk- white illumination over the entire landscape. It was quite a site. Enchanting even, and with every shape being silhouetted by the light pouring down from above, the overall effect reminded me very much of something one would find in a children's fiction storybook.

'This is too good a night to waste,' Alex. 'If you're up to it, how about another stroll? If you're tired, it's okay. I'm happy to- '

'Don't be silly,' she cut me off. 'I agree. It's a beautiful night.

It would be a crime to waste a night like this.'

I would have been disappointed if she had declined. There were simply too many unresolved questions circling in my mind; and damn it if there wasn't something else simmering there — simmering like a cauldron full of secrets and delicate, tantalizing morsels which could not have been better contrived to elicit a response from someone such as I. It takes many years of effort and repeated failure to insulate a human heart; a lifetime of struggles and disappointments before a man at last wises up, finally telling himself that the pursuit of happiness is only for fools who are prepared to lie to themselves and buy into the illusion that we are all worthy of love and fulfilment, and that one day it will come. If I had been honest with myself I would have seen the signs and turned away in time, but even I am susceptible. Something within deceived me, blinding me to the subtle indicators, somehow causing me to ignore the hard lessons I had learned and thought I had learned well. I can only take solace in the fact that it was Nature's primal edict that brought me undone; it was not entirely my own fault. Nature leaves a chink in the armour of all men. The genetic imperative will not be ignored, but all this is revealed now as a matter of hindsight, and far too late to alter the flow of events as they implacably unfold along the endless chain of cause and effect. It is true that the human brain is especially adept at recognising emerging patterns in nature and the environment in general. For me, the ability is augmented for some reason, and this is specifically why I have become so proficient at my work; but it is also my curse. My mind has always sought to recognise and distinguish order, structure and meaning, from the truly exceptional to the countless occurrences of seemingly random everyday events. I was once told, by company psychologists, that this was my talent; those who were ultimately responsible for my being hired some several years ago. Patterns and repetitions emerge when the human brain has observed its environment over a sufficient span of time, and before too many years have passed there is so much that has been detected and accumulated, eventually there is *only* the continued repetition and the predictable patterns; imitation of form and event, as if life is intent on parodying itself, day after day, without end. For someone having such dismal expectations and a jaded world view as myself, the result is a kind of slow descent into an absurdity beyond description; a kind of living hell where the future stretches interminably on without feature, without contrast, and without a single thing to suggest that any of this might conceivably undergo change.

Life just becomes predictable, and the same must be said of my view of human nature. I had reached something of an impasse long ago, needing to revisit what it feels like, the thrill and novelty of the unexpected, of finding something truly unpredictable — something new, surprising, pleasant, refreshing— something hopeful. Although I knew it not, the die had been cast, and my life, such as it was and had been, would be unalterably transformed.

'It would be a crime to waste a night like this,' Alex had said.

In this light I suddenly realised that Alex was an attractive woman.

Her shoulder length, auburn hair framed the well-formed and attractive features of her smiling face. The elegantly formed contours of her neck and shoulders presenting an eminently feminine package. How had I not noticed?

'There's a spot not far from here,' she said, standing, stretching out the stiffness in her legs, back and shoulders.

'Shall we?' she invited.

We covered a considerable distance while she told me what she knew of the Jhai. Their species had also reached a crisis point in their development. A situation not dissimilar to ours, but they had been smart enough never to allow their population to grow so ridiculously large so that it would endanger the biosphere to the same degree. Forward thinking allowed them to plan well into the future, and the populating of exoplanets presented itself as a perfect solution, both to providing impetus for scientific advancement and relieving pressure on planetary resources. In just a few generations space travel had become almost mundane; their already highly advanced sciences striving and providing every amenity until the species became much more the itinerant, space oriented travellers than the sedentary planet dwellers of their beginnings. It was a fascinating story. The revolutionary change had been made thousands of years ago, and since then, their species had been able to devote all of their lives to exploring and expanding their knowledge of the cosmos. The lifestyle had also expanded their concept of existence and their philosophical nature. I must admit to being impressed, but also more than a little ashamed. By comparison we were fools. I guess I had always considered us that, but to be confronted by a race who, by all reports, had handled their affairs so much better than we had, it augmented my already heightened sense of human beings being dull-witted to the point of near extinction.

'What must they think of us?' I commented, as we skirted the top edge of the hill overlooking the moonlit, blue veldt.

'They consider us to be children,' Alex replied. '*Spoiled* children, in fact. In their travels they have scarce seen a planet as abundant in the variety of life and of natural resources combined on a single planet. They see the fact that we have despoiled what we were given, when our only responsibility had been that we cherish and safeguard its value and rarity.'

'Yes. That's exactly it, isn't it? They must be angry.'

'Not at all,' Alex replied. 'Not at all angry, but certainly saddened. They very much prize and appreciate individuality. They have a strong appreciation for beauty. An artistic sensibility, do you understand? There's not a bit of resentment — not a single negative facet to them, as best I can tell. Perhaps saddened isn't quite the word. Disappointed, perhaps.'

'Is there a difference?'

Alex shrugged. 'A little, but my point is, there's no animosity about it. No resentment. Not that I can detect, anyway. I don't think they know what resentment is.'

I nodded. 'It's to be expected, I guess. It would be difficult to be small-minded when the universe is your backyard.'

'That's true,' she said, halting as we neared the campsite once more. 'Why don't we sit here awhile?' She indicated the grassy embankment beside us. 'My legs are getting a little weary,' she explained.

We reclined on the slope, taking in the view. In a moment a soft, warm, breeze arrived, its progress was marked by the movement of gently rising pockets of dust across the plain. In the far distance was heard a raucous screeching noise.

'Some kind of night bird,' she answered, without being asked. I continued to soak in the pleasant atmosphere of the night. The twin moons were high in the sky now, their radiance soft and easy on the eye so that I could easily make out peaks and

valleys etched into their surface.

'It's pleasant here,' she said, quietly, and her voice was as soft and warm as the lambent light filtering down from the moons in the sky. My senses felt heightened, as if perfectly attuned to this world, and there was a clarity of mind seldom experienced.

'It is,' I agreed. 'Very peaceful. Very pleasant.'

Her scent was in the air, and her proximity began to impress itself heavily on me. I wondered if she was feeling it too.

Her hand reached out and touched my own, and the current flowed with a force too great to offer any resistance against it. 'Jack,' she almost whispered, her voice laden with something resembling desire and poignancy.

In her eyes I saw reflected the flame of passion I felt rising in myself, and she came to me, an exquisite angel wrapped within the balmy softness of the night—a long, warm, wonderful night which wrapped us both inside its powerful, timeless spell.

We woke some hours before dawn, at the bottom of the slope, still wrapped together, and in the remainder of the night Alex lead me to her quarters; a compartment within the ship the Jhai had made comfortable for her, with an bed of ample girth to sleep in. There we once again entwined until sleep overtook us.

5

SMOKE AND MIRRORS

I woke feeling as good as I could remember feeling for a very long time, and I was in no particular hurry to climb out of bed, especially when lying beside me was this gorgeous creature. How had I gotten so lucky? I was forced to ask myself, but the question evaporated the moment her eyes fluttered open and she beamed that smile at me.

'Is it the morning already?'She moaned softly, and extended an arm across me. '*Hmm, what a night,*' she purred.

We lay that way, me on my back, her on her side, cuddled up close with her arm over me, and at that moment the world in which I lived seemed so alien to me. Why was I doing what I was doing? I was the *fix-it guy* for the company; I had been the fix-it guy for as long as I cared to remember, and I had no real identity of my own beyond that. Should I cease being a part of Universal X tomorrow, what would I have? No home, no real place of origin even. I would be adrift as much as it is possible for a man to be. At nearly forty years-of-age most men had a family and were happy to have one, putting their energies and resources into keeping them safe from harm, fed, well educated, enough at least to prepare them for the world as it is, equipped well enough to squeeze the most out of what is left to enjoy. But then, perhaps having children was not such a wise thing. Society was not like it once was; the pressure is on from an early age to slot into the positions society has earmarked for every individual from the moment they are assessed at age five. Not like it was when I was growing up. At that time there was still the chance of determining one's own future and pursuing whatever it was that gave the most joy and satisfaction. It was possible just to follow a direction for the amusement value of it, to experiment and find one's own feet, unlike today. If things change — if we make it past this period of great urgency — then would be the time for raising a family. A man should have a son, I figured. A son to carry on the bloodline. An old fashioned notion these days, but what did life add up to if the genetic line were to end? A life should count for something. There should be a legacy, something positive left behind to say, *I was here and this is my mark. The world is a better place for my having existed.*

'What are you thinking about,' Alex asked, eyes still closed. 'What makes you think I'm thinking about anything?' 'You're very still, and I know you are still awake. What are you thinking about?' She pinched me. 'Come on, spill it mister.' I pulled her to me and we were both laughing, until she locked her gaze to mine, as if attempting to stare into my inner being.

Her eyes were brown, flecked with gold; pools of loveliness and longing. 'Something is troubling you, Jack. I can tell.'

I wanted to lie to her, tell her, *nothing in particular. About you, about last night,* but I couldn't. Something had happened last night and it was continuing this morning. Something special, and I didn't want to ruin it.

'I was thinking about who I am, and that I am little more than the job that I do. How, suddenly, it's not enough any more.'

'Don't you dare go thinking any such thing, Jack Hardin. You're something very special and don't you forget it. You are a highly respected man and your reputation causes people to take notice whenever they hear your name mentioned.' She wrapped herself around me and planted a kiss, long and so full of wonderful that it made my head spin.

'I think I'm oxygen deprived again,' I told her, rolling my eyes affectedly.

Again she hugged me more tightly, and sighing, said, 'I don't want to get up. Let's just lay here in bed together, and let the world pass us by. We owe it nothing.'

'That would be nice,' I agreed, saying nothing to counter the notion. If only that were possible, I was thinking. If only both our whereabouts weren't the business of the company and we were able do as we pleased.

We pretended that time didn't matter and made no mention of obligation or commitment, tacitly agreeing to make this blissful hiatus last as long as we dare.

We continued to talk, for hours, getting to know one other as best we could in what time we had. Alex came from an academic family. Her father had been a professor of physics and the astro sciences, Geneva, Switzerland, no less, and her mother, a high up in the medical profession, leading the latest, cutting edge round of testing for cancer antigens. A cure for cancer was still the holy grail of the medical world. Alex had not specialised in anything, making sure she got as broad an education as she was able to, until she discovered whatever it might be that she found the most interest in. Coming to work out on the rim was just another stab in the dark; she thought maybe working out here in space would provide the spark of certainty she was looking for, leading to something she could sink her teeth into. She discovered exobiology by chance, but there was no chance of pursuing the subject professionally. Xenoanthropology had presented itself by sheer fluke, and she embarked on a single-handed study of the Jhai after she had met them for the first time.

My own history was not nearly as gratifying. My father had been a cop; an overworked cop with a drinking problem, who took his endless grievances out on my mother. He was shot and killed by a teenager when he accidentally walked into a robbery in progress at the corner store. My mother died a year later, when I was fifteen, and I have been making my own way ever since. Not an impressive legacy, but with whatever natural talents I possessed, at least I had cut out a path for myself.

Time inevitably began to run short. We emerged to find a few of the Jhai hauling a machine into the belly of their ship and I figured the least I could do in return for their hospitality of the previous evening was to pitch in and help.

Upon enquiring what the machine was, I received a pictorial display flashing through my mind. The sensation caused me to start, a reaction the Jhai seemed excited about. Back-slapping apparently is a universal gesture, and I received a thorough pounding. The image I received suggested that the machine drew energy directly from the ether. I asked Alex to translate for me. She obliged by calling it a dark energy converter.

My interest in their vessel incited an impromptu guided tour. The one called Dortl Karp, who I had learned to be Fernac's offspring, took it upon himself to do his best to describe what I saw. There were such things as stasis chambers, where, on long voyages, they could place themselves in a sort of suspended condition where somatic activity could be slowed to avoid the passing of time while another function provided direct input to the brain. This provided input to the mental faculties, allowing data on any subject to be uploaded and ready for referencing upon arrival at whatever destination. There were the expected navigation and piloting consoles, food preparation areas and a few creature comforts. The engine bay, however, was a totally sealed unit and impossible to view. Cracking the seal of the engine incasement was not a wise action, I was informed by a mental depiction of humanoid figures being blasted by some form of radiation.

They were particularly keen to direct my attention to the topic of something translating to *bio data processing*. The Jhai used DNA sequencing breeding techniques to grow actual organic neurons to regulate ship functions, just as the brain and connected nervous system run and regulate the human body. The ship was part machine, part animal, with neural processors acting as a self-protecting system. It was capable of taking total control of a long range, beyond light speed voyage without any need for a Jhai pilot to lift a finger. A destination was simply chosen and the bio processors would handle every facet of the voyage, including course corrections, using star recognition and pulsar triangulation. Bio processors were also employed in handling any emergency which may arise. At beyond light speed, processing any correction or initiating collision avoidance procedure needed to be lightning fast, involving intuitive, preemptive action, I was told. Only bio-processors were up to the task, and they were installed in many vital positions around the ship, similar to the plexus or nerve clusters of an animal body. The ship taught me that we humans had a very long road to travel before safe and sufficiently speedy navigation of astronomical distances would be within our reach. In short, it was a technological marvel. It turned out to be a damaged one of these bioprocessing plexus things which had necessitated their making the emergency landing on Ki Kassini; and they were not going anywhere until a replacement had been found. Where they would find such a thing was beyond me, but they seemed confident that one was about to become available. With their faculty for genetic engineering I supposed they were in the process of growing the replacement.

Alex tugged at my elbow. 'Come on, Jack. I hate to say it, but we're probably stretching our luck. Perhaps we ought to be getting back.'

'This is incredibly interesting,' I told her and our hosts, 'Thanks guys. This has been a blast. I can't tell you how fascinating, but I'm afraid we really must go. I'm looking forward to coming back, if that's okay?'

I received another round of back-slapping, which I assumed meant that my returning was fine with them.

We travelled back to Far Point. The second trip, as Alex had promised, being appreciably easier on me than the first time, but now I had a problem. From my standpoint the case was solved. The mystery of where the missing items had gone and who was responsible for the thefts was no more, only, I could not report a word of it. Not without revealing the Jhai's existence; and not being able to resolve the situation for the company would result in a sizeable black mark being placed on my record. I would not have come back here except for the fact that my absence for any appreciable time would produce curiosity, especially in the mind of the security boss, George Berringer. I decided I could keep him at arms length for as long as I needed to. He knew how I worked, but raising suspicion in his mind was not a good idea right now. When I am assigned a case, I am generally left to my own devices until a resolution is reached. I simply hand in my detailed report, *on high*, scribble a rough outline to whoever needs to know, locally; aside from George that would only include Joe Higgins at Administration, and then I would be clear to get the hell out. That was not going to happen this time. Things had gotten suddenly quite complicated. I had never not concluded an assignment, not in all my years of service. How I was going to account for the loss of goods and materials, I had no idea, and the question was going to plague me until an answer was arrived at. I knew that much, for sure, but it wasn't the first time I had found myself in a spot. I could mope around in my room puzzling over it, or I could get out and about. From experience, getting out and about is the best option. Interacting with the world provides both the necessary distraction I needed to distance myself from the problem for a while, and it exposes one to myriad esoteric bits of information and random stimuli from which a glimmer of a solution might be discovered. To that end I showered, redressed my wound and set off toward the centre of town. Besides, for some unknown reason I had woken with the desire for chicken chow mein.

The place felt different, no doubt in light of what had occurred over the last twenty four hours. Just being here, the pretense of it, made me uneasy. The chef at the Horizon sated my desire for chicken chow mein, which I washed down with a beer at the front bar.

On the spur of the moment I decided to book a room here, and so I made my way around to the office to do just that. It was often a good idea to have somewhere as a fallback in case of things going unexpectedly awry, and being in possession of an alternative identification card, courtesy of the company, it was a shame not to put it to good use. After enquiring if there was any unobtrusive way of exiting the building, should the need to leave unobserved arise, I booked under the name Patrick Dempsey, paid for a week in advance and asked the grey-haired lady behind the counter to hang on to the key until I arrived to claim it.

That done, when the two men who had befriended me on my first day walked in, we greeted one another in the accustomed, blokey manner and moved to spend time in the side bar, shooting pool and the breeze, but when a brawl broke out, occasioning company security to be summoned, my growing sense of uneasiness got the better of me, and making my excuses I bade them farewell, leaving the Horizon without really having a destination or purpose in mind. What was worse, not the faintest hint of a solution had presented itself to me.

I found myself wandering back towards my room, my mood darkening with every footfall. Whatever was happening, it was something I hadn't experienced before. My mind kept slipping back to thoughts of Alex and of last night. That woman had found a way of burrowing under my skin. Why? I didn't know. I've had my fare share of steamy one-nighters before, but this girl. This girl —

As far as the job went, I needed an out. Its whole complexion had changed, altering the situation far beyond anything I could ever have expected or even envisioned. I had to find a way of closing it down without affecting my standing within the company. It was going to take some doing, but I didn't see an option. To expose the Jhai would cause an uproar I had no wish to be a part of; and they wished to be kept out of the picture in any case, a position I felt it was important to respect. I could only image the repercussions should they catch me taking a sly snapshot of them. Alex's relationship with them would likely be destroyed. Why she had mentioned writing an anthropological study, I couldn't fathom. Perhaps a joke; but, no, exposing them was not an option. I had to find reason to present an argument in favour of us cutting our losses and convince the company that the pilfering had ceased. I think whey would accept that, but in order for them to swallow such an argument, they would have to believe there was no hope of retrieving the stolen goods, and likewise no chance of prosecuting the culprits responsible. No problem. *Damn*. . . I was in a bind.

My communicator sounded. It was Joe Higgins calling; the head administrator.

'Yes, Joe. What's up,' I enquired nervously. 'Haven't seen you around in a day or two, Jack?'

'Snooping,' I explained.

'Ah, yes. Undercover,' he deciphered, musingly.

My radar was *pinging!* What the hell did he care what I had been doing? He was administration. If Berringer had asked, it would make some sense. He, at least, was security.

'Something like that,' I hedged.

'I would like you to come over this afternoon, Jack. Something here of interest. I think you should see for yourself.'

I checked the bedside chronometer. It was close to change of shift, and close to the end of a normal work day; but this was Far Point and I was talking to Joe Higgins, someone for whom such

183

things meant next to nothing. The man was his job and he was never off the clock.

'Half an hour?' he invited, and hung up before I was able to respond.

'Son-of-a-bitch,' I cursed bitterly, but I would have to go and see the prick. Everything rolling along nicely, I would tell him. A waiting game. Too early to expect anything resembling a result. Patience is a virtue, Joe.

After killing time by wandering the streets for a while, I was once again greeted at the front desk by the smiling face of the bland female functionary inside the administration building, and climbing the stairs I propped at Joe Higgins' closed door, tapping twice.

'Come on in Jack,' he called.

I discovered him walking the perimeter of the office, griping what I instantly recognised to be a bug-detector; a high-end model, too, waving it over the walls, around electrical outlets, light fittings and under his desk.

'Take a seat,' he offered, continuing the exercise. I did as he asked, remaining silent until he appeared satisfied with the outcome of his search.

'Mice?' I asked, as he finally seated himself behind his desk.

'Rats, more like,' he answered gruffly. 'Cockroaches even.'

I nodded knowingly. 'Comes with the territory, Joe. I'm glad to see you're staying on top of it.'

He stood and walked over to the fridge which stood in the corner. 'Beer?' he offered, reaching in and pulling out two before I had answered.

'Thanks,' I said, accepting. 'How's everything running? Smoothly, I hope?'

He rounded the desk and lowered his considerable bulk into his chair with a sigh. 'Not bad, actually. Not bad at all. An exploration team have reported a fresh deposit of nickel and silver. A big one. It should be in production in a month or two.' He took a swallow from the bottle and plonked it down on the desk. 'I didn't know you and George Berringer were previously acquainted, Jack. Tell me about that, why don't you?'

184

I was intrigued by the question. Was this idle conversation? I wondered. 'George and I grew up in th same neighbourhood,' I began. 'There's not much more to it than that. I guess there was a small amount of competition, perhaps animosity. I don't know, but mostly on his part. He's that sort of a person. He always seemed to be trying to one-up everybody, even as a teenager. We don't particularly care for one another.'

'Okay,' Joe replied. 'I've got something a bit interesting to show you. It's something George brought to my attention.'

He lifted a remote control from his desktop, pressed a button and swung about in his swivel chair as a large screen descended from its compartment within the ceiling. 'Watch,' he said, as the screen came to life.

I tensed as I recognised the interior of a warehouse, comprehending immediately what was about to play out. The camera zoomed toward a pair of figures in the gloom. It was Alex and myself, from two nights previous. As I watched, one figure approached the other sitting beside a storage bay. The figures were difficult to recognise, but clearly, one was a man, the other a woman. The woman poured something from a flask and offered it to the man. Conversation ensued; a cigarette was lit, but fortunately the face was downward turned in the lighting of it. In a while the woman produced what looked to be a firearm, directing the man to move into the vacant bay, then to sit. The woman moved to join the sitting figure and a moment later a blinding flash caused the screen to white out. When vision returned, the figures were gone.'

'What do you make of that?' Joe asked, casually. 'Incredible,' I answered. 'I'm not really sure what happened.

Did those people disappear? Is that even possible?'

A thin smile accompanied by a look of amusement moved across Joe's features as he held back his reply for affect. 'Seeing is believing, isn't it?'

'I don't know what I saw, Joe. Has the video file been messed with, perhaps? People can't disappear. It looks like a prank, to me.'

'No prank, Jack. Your old pal George inspected it thoroughly. It's genuine.'

'Why are you bringing this to me?' I wanted to know. 'Security. This is George's province.'

'I run this rig,' Jack. You know that. I told him a while back to send me anything interesting as soon as something was detected. And you have to admit, this *is* interesting.'

Just then there was a knock at the door. Joe released me from his gaze and called, 'Come!'

To my amazement, Alex entered, carrying a package. At the sight of me sitting there, the hint of an unsettled expression flashed across her lovely features. 'The report from Mr Berringer,' she explained, and crossed the room swiftly to present the item to Joe. She turned to me, her eyes not quite knowing where to settle. 'Nice to see you again, Mr Hardin. Is everything going well?'

'Well enough,' I replied, conversationally. 'And it's very nice to see you again, too.' I smiled warmly.

'Oh, come on, you two!' Joe was standing now. 'Really? Do you think I don't know what is going on?'

Alex feigned a startled expression.

'What are you talking about?' I responded incredulously. Joe remained motionless, critically regarding the both of us.

'Like that wasn't the pair of you in the video file? Are you honestly denying it?'

I turned to Alex in explanation. 'Joe was just showing me some warehouse security footage from. . .' I turned to Joe. 'When was it taken?'

'Two night ago,' he growled.

'I've seen it,' Alex replied insouciantly. 'I helped compile it. What is going on?' Her manner was perfectly calm and controlled as she stared Joe down with her questioning look. 'What was meant by that remark?' Her manner became indignant, and I could not help admiring her nerve under fire.

'Alright,' Joe responded. So you're gong to play it that way. You've made the delivery,' he said in dismissal, and Alex left the room without further comment.

'You're wrong, Joe.' I told him. 'Way off the mark, this time. If we're done here I have better things to do.'

He leaned back heavily in his chair. Sighed. 'Sit down, Jack. Finish your beer. I had to test the theory. You, above all people understand that. I had to know, and you two fit the description. Tell me I'm wrong about that.'

It was my turn to hold his gaze unwaveringly, pondering the situation for an extended time. 'Okay,' I said, at last. 'I guess I do see it. . . but it doesn't mean I have to like it.' I took a sip from the bottle and sat back down. 'Quite the charade,' I observed.

I left Joe's office, furious at the turn of events. We hadn't fooled him for a minute; he was just unable to take it any further, and he had attempted to defuse the situation by pretending we were in the clear. I needed to know what George Berringer knew; how much he actually knew or what he *thought* he knew, and upon departing administration I made my way directly to the security building.

When the girl at the help desk in the lobby recognised me she reached for a phone. No doubt she meant to alert Berringer of my presence. The elevator doors were closed, the lights above showing both cars already ascending. The way my wound was beginning to throb, I didn't like to take the stairs, but I was in a hurry.

At the head of the stairs I entered the hallway to observe a man standing beside Berringer's door. A tall guy wearing a black suit, hat, dark glasses. It appeared he wore the hat over a shaven head. There was something altogether not right about the guy; he did not even acknowledge my approach until we were standing toe to toe.

'Excuse me, you're blocking my way,' I told him, at which point he turned his head slightly to regard me.

'Engaged,' he said, and turned away.

Who was this dude? I asked myself. From within George's office came the sound of muffled voices, and through the frosted glass I could just make out two figures standing in front of his desk. Nothing distinguishable could be heard of the conversation. 'Then I will wait,' I told the taciturn object, and seated myself in one of the pair of vacant chairs opposite the door.

I had heard of these guys. If my guess was right, this was *a 'man in black.'* A ridiculous term applying to sartorial ineptitude. The dress code tended to make the guy look ridiculous, rather than, as was doubtlessly the intention, to instill something akin to discomfort, apprehension and impotency in their presence. But what were he and his cohorts doing here? I knew their reputation and what their perceived function was meant to be.

'What's up?' I asked the door guy. No response, predictably. The cat was out of the bag, doubtlessly. So who had spilled the beans? Or was it a case of who had been watching the watcher? And how would things proceed from here? I could be getting ahead of myself, I then realised. Best not to jump the gun, they might be on a fishing expedition, having picked up on rumour, speculation and second or third hand information. Scuttlebutt in other words. Although, where had they come from? Would they have travelled a vast distance to check out a rumour of alien visitation because of some gossip coming from a space platform millions of miles from Earth? Perhaps these dudes were posted out of Niven Station. It would make the most sense.

After a few minutes the door to George's office finally opened, and the pair who had been talking to Berringer departed without even a glance, the door guy following behind.

'Nice talking to you.'

Without waiting to be summoned I let myself in, hoping to catch George even more off guard than usual. His blanched face caused me a moment's regret, however. Those bastards had shaken him pretty good.

'Jesus, George. Are you alright? Let me get you something. Water okay, buddy?'

I poured him a glass and offered it to him. He took it from my grasp while loosening his collar with his free hand. 'Thank-you. Give me a moment, will you?'

I rounded the desk to sit opposite. 'Sure thing.'

I watched as he sipped twice at the water. A little colour began to return. He sipped again and placed the glass on the desk.

'Do you know who those people are?' he asked me. 'Have you ever had to deal with them?'

'I know who they are,' I told him, 'but I've not had to deal with them. Don't let them get the better of you, George. Two- bob thugs in dress up. The two of them trying to put the frighteners on you, were they? Real heroes. Comic book characters. Well fuck 'em, buddy. Have another sip of water.'

He took a last swallow and attempted to compose himself.

'I appreciate your support right now, Jack. But there's some-thing–' he stalled; baulked at the hurdle.

'What is it George?'

'Nothing — nothing at all. Why did you come here, Jack?' 'I came here to shake you up, find out what bloody game you guys are playing, but too late by the looks. Someone beat me to it.'

He affected a wan smile. 'Yeah. Look, Jack. . . I know we've never really been friends. In some way I suppose, that's my fault. I want you to be careful. All I got from those guys just now was veiled threats and accusations. They seemed to think I knew something. Something about something. They never said what the something was. They just pumped me for information, but I haven't the foggiest idea what they were on about. "Don't think you can keep secrets affecting global security," they said, and there's something creepy about those fellahs. They're not normal, you know? Something creepy, Jack, and I don't much like it.'

'There is something funny about them, and that's a *cert*. You really don't have any idea what they wanted from you? I find that fishy, George. You're telling me you were just pressured by experts and you don't know why. . . what about?'

He looked to have suddenly taken full possession of himself once again. He squared his shoulders, pulled himself upright in his chair and looking at his watch, telling me, 'I appreciate your con-cern. I do, Jack, but there are some things I cannot talk about. You understand, I know you do.'

I allowed myself a rueful chuckle. 'Funny,' I said, 'you're the second person to tell me that in less than an hour.'

He did not respond, except to make a show of inspecting his watch one more time.

'Okay George. I get it,' I said, standing, preparing to leave. 'You know I have always been able to get more out of your silence than all your bullshit over the years. And, you know? Nothing has changed. I'll be seeing you, George. And a word of advice, buddy.

The less you know, the better off you will be. Trust me on that. Keep your head down.'

It could not have been clearer, I told myself, entering the streets below. The way I was being kept out of the loop it only went to making it clearer than ever to me that I was currently *a person of interest:* cop speak, meaning that I was being closely watched because I was being linked to whatever the secret something was; the secret something George knew nothing about and had almost warned me about but chickened at the last moment, and what Joe was on my hammer about. Only, it was no secret. An alien connection. So goddamn what? Big deal. Why the need for all the cloak and dagger secrecy? What happens to the adult mind when they achieve positions of power or go to work for clandestine government agencies? They lose all sight of reality; they start seeing conspiracies where there are none, *danger* where there is none. They start banging on about national security, threats to civilization and God only knows what else. They become obsessed, delusional and paranoid, and because they're surrounded by like minds, the whole thing becomes plaguelike — *a contagion* — and very, very dangerous. Why did the human race almost fail? Mass insanity brought about by a total lack of honesty. When honesty retreats, there is no more trust left, everybody mistrusts everyone, every*thing,* and there we go, straight down the tubes. The human race is totally mad and it's just too bad we are still viable and now on the verge of being able to spread the madness among the stars. Look out cosmos, the lunatics are loose!

6

CIRCUMSTANCES

I noticed that foot traffic had thinned as I negotiated the way back towards my room and a couple of hours of downtime. I recognised how surrounded by events I had become, and even though I had not yet formulated my next move, the one looming thought in my mind was that I no longer wanted any role in this ridiculous game that everybody was playing. Whatever it took, I was *out*. Let the cards fall where they may, I did not care one iota. I was cashing in my chips — taking my ball and going home, wherever the hell that was.

'Mr Hardin?' The voice came from over my left shoulder as I came up to a quiet street corner. From my right came a punch to the mid section, immediately followed by a crashing blow to the head, producing a shower of stars behind my eyes as the pavement rushed up to meet me.

I woke in a chair, tied, in a darkened room with a single, brilliant light beaming down on me; and I remembered then, being knocked cold on a street corner.

'Mr Hardin. Thank-you for joining us.' The source of the voice I could not identify. Disembodied voices. What next?

I looked around my immediate surroundings. Beyond the spotlight there was nothing but penumbral gloom and shadows. 'It's true, you know,' I said, addressing the emptiness. 'One really does see stars when being clonked on the noggin.'

Someone stepped forward a single pace in front of me. All I could make out was the silhouette. Tall, medium build and wearing a hat.

'Funny man,' replied the dark figure. 'I apologise for the tap on the head, but if we had merely asked you to come along to this meeting, I know what your response would have been. And I thought it was important to impress upon you that we are not playing games here.'

'You actually thought knocking me senseless and dragging me here was the way to go? Huh. You guys.'

'So you would have me believe that you would have come along voluntarily?' He laughed derisively. 'Don't give me that. You want to pretend you're a reasonable guy and we are the brigands? You should know, we've have seen your psych profile, and your handiwork. And having seen it, I have to wonder why the company has kept you in their employ as long as they have. You're a violent man, Jack Hardin. Your profile lists you as being incorrigible, irascible and antisocial. That's some profile. It's no wonder the force sent you packing. You cost them a fortune in legal fees with your heavy-handed methods.'

'Results are results,' I argued. 'Nobody takes issue with my success rate.'

'Nor do I, but shall we talk about your new friends?

'Could this be any more cliché?' I asked, attempting to keep this superior bastard off side. I was pissed off at allowing myself to be taken so easily, but I was not going to let them think they owned me. My guts were giving me some grief, though. Someone had slugged me pretty good in the solar plexus and they had likely opened up a stitch or two.

'The old methods are usually the best,' the voice replied calmly. 'But this is more your friendly chat type situation. Which way it proceeds from here is completely up to you, understand?'

I understood alright, but to hell with them. I was in no mood to cooperate.

'Let's talk about your new friends.'

'I don't have any friends,' I responded, and got a laugh from someone in the darkness — a weird, false kind of a laugh, as if laughing was not usually in the man's repertoire.

'That doesn't surprise me. You've never been very popular, have you?'

'Get to the point, why don't you? I can't abide idle chitchat.' There was a moment's silence until another voice joined in. 'I think that's fair enough, Mr Hardin.' This voice undoubtedly came from an older, and therefore a more experienced operative. 'We have a task for you.'

'Why would I want to do you any favours?'

'Because you will find it to your advantage, but you haven't heard what it is, yet. Don't be too much in a hurry. Hear us out first.'

It seemed a reasonable request and there was little choice, but I was quite sure I wasn't going to like anything they had to say.

'Okay then. Let's hear it.'

'We have been monitoring transmissions in this sector for some time. Strange, one might even say *alien* transmissions. A kind of powerful, modulated energy signature sort of thing.' He paused for short while to see if I would respond, and continued. 'These signals have been heavily concentrated around the warehouses where items have been disappearing. The last time we detected one of these phenomena, it coincided quite inexplicably with your unexpected disappearance. Not just your disappearance, either. A miss Jordan was present. Miss Alexandra Jordan. I thought I heard you say that you didn't have any friends?'

'What are you talking about, disappearance? Nobody around here has disappeared. Who the hell are you anyway?'

'I'm asking the questions, Jack. You know the game. Your job is to answer them. Where were you? What happened in that warehouse? Where were you teleported to?

It was my turn to laugh derisively. 'Teleported? Can you hear yourself? Teleportation is science fiction bullshit. Really, you guys must live in a fantasy world. Perhaps you've been there so long it has softened your brain. I always knew you lot were full of shit. I suppose you believe in leprechauns and hob goblins.' The following pause contained a modicum of tension, telling me I was beginning to get to him. Someone I had not detected had been standing behind me during this exchange, and I received a slap in the back of the head. I have a knack of irritating people which comes in handy during sessions like this.

Rattling one's cage, I call it. Always effective, but it has been known to backfire on occasion.

'What's the matter, shadow guy? Grasping at straws here? You're on shaky ground and we both know it. Why not stop wasting your time. More importantly, stop wasting mine. Unlike you, I have constructive things to do with *mine*. You and your mickey mouse club members. Your mommies will be wondering where you are by now.'

He responded with a chuckle — the worrisome, self-assured, rug from under the feet kind. 'Oh. You're going to work with us, alright,' he said, and our little *tet-a-tete* was suddenly at an end.

When I awoke in the very same hospital bed I had occupied only days before, I knew my last remark had hit the spot. Very *deja vu*. Even Detective Sergeant Burt Emerson and junior officer Andy Saunders were in position, as per the first time, when my eyes eventually opened.

Emerson wore a crooked, *I-saw-this-coming* kind of a smile. 'I thought I told you to stay out of trouble. I can't keep making paperwork disappear forever, you know.'

'I'm fine. Thanks for asking,' I retorted. 'Ooh. . . let me rephrase that. Would your press the morphine button for me? I can't raise my arm. Give it a few pumps, Burt, would you? There's a good chap.'

To my immense surprise, he did as I asked, and he even waited until the pained expression left my dial before continuing.

'You're playing with fire, Jack. You must know that. I only hope you know what you're doing. Do you?'

Hearing him speak the words, it dawned on me for the first time in a very long while, that I *did know* exactly what I was doing. Or, more accurately, what I *would* do. . . as soon, that was, as I could lift my sorry arse out of this hospital bed and walk out of here. Unfortunately, I didn't think that would be anytime soon. A crack on the scone like that can put a crimp on one's day. And my knee hurt like blazes, the bastards. One of them must have given me one for good measure while I was out. 'Those mongrels really did a number on you, pal. What did you do to piss them off? Actually, there's no need to answer. I can imagine.'

The comment tickled me, but the laugh reflex was quickly stifled by a bolt of pain.

'Jesus,' Saunders responded. 'They went too far.'

'Yeah? Well I appreciate the concern, lad, but they knew when to stop, at least. Well practised, I imagine, and they want my cooperation. Can you believe that? For that they need me alive. Just as well, eh? Trouble is, I don't know what the hell it is they expect from me, and it didn't seem to matter to them that I refused to lift a finger to aid them. God only knows what they have in mind.'

Emerson lifted his tired frame from the chair he had occupied. 'I just wanted to see you were on the mend. Listen, Jack. . . you have my number. I have to go now, but if there's something. You know—'

'Yeah, sure Burt. Thanks. I appreciate it. A friend in need is-' 'A pain in the arse,' he finished for me, allowing us both a moment's grim reflection. 'Okay then. Well?' He turned to his offsider. 'Come on. Lets see if we cant catch some bad guys.

Later, Jack.'

'Later,' I agreed, watching their departure while wondering at the sudden display of giving a damn. Wondering also if there wasn't a microphone secreted somewhere in the vicinity, or if one had just been planted. Such was the level of my growing sense of mistrust and outright lack of confidence in everybody around me.

I heard George laughing in the hallway outside my room as he retreated. Five seconds later a matron entered, carrying a bowl of streaming hot water, a wash-cloth, soap and a towel, and I realised immediately what the bugger had found so funny. I would have put up a fight, but I was far too week and too tired to protest the indignity of what followed. Mercifully, the drugs and the injuries allowed me to fall back into the comfortable, lulling arms of oblivion. Who knew for how long? But when I awoke, some of the old vitality had returned, and I even found I had an appetite again. The following couple of days were spent resting, eating and cogitating.

Life can get pretty simple when one has been pushed into a corner, but I had pushed myself into this one. The choices do become simple. Perhaps they had never been complicated and it was nothing more than my stubborn disposition and hardheadedness complicating matters. Maybe it had been that one night with Alex that was need to put things into perspective?

The pain didn't matter any more. It was easing by now anyway. My mind had begun to see things clearly for the first time in a very long while, and things were becoming exceedingly simple. It was life that mattered. A quality of life, and maybe even a sense of purpose. I had been chasing illusions for so many years, practically all of my life, and none of it made any sense when reviewed from this hospital bed. Who the hell had I become? *What* had I become? The question continued to bother me.

On the morning of the third day, I woke to find Alex, sitting at my bedside, her chair pulled up close. Her presence was entirely unexpected, intoxicating, and to my mind a dangerous thing to do right now, but I was pleased as hell to see her all the same. I had been unable to get the girl out of my mind, and seeing her here right now answered the foremost question on my mind.

'How do you feel,' she asked, softly. 'I can't tell you how worried I have been. Are you alright? They hurt you pretty bad, didn't they.'

'Much better this morning,' I replied, honestly. How did you know I was here?'

'That policeman. Emerson, is it?' 'Yes, Sergeant Emerson. *He* told you?'

'He called me. And I'm very grateful to him for that.' Her face became a picture of concern. 'Jack, I had no idea things had gotten so out of hand. Look what they have done to you. What's it all about?'

'They're telling me they know about *'My new friends,"* I told her. 'I don't know what they have planned, but they wanted me to cooperate and work with them. But before you say anything, I told them I didn't have a clue what they were talking about, and we best stick to that. And, yes, they tried to involve you, but it's me they're really interested in. They will use you to get at me. Just remember that we have no clue what the hell they're on about. Okay? We'll ride it out, for now, and decide what's best as the situation unfolds.'

I studied her face during the telling, watching for signs of weakness as the wheels turned in her mind. She showed no sign of panic, only calm, clarity, and rapid analysis of the situation. 'That seems best,' she agreed. 'There's little doubt that they'll be keeping close tabs on us both, so. . . I think you're right. We just go about our business and give them no reason to intervene.' 'That's my girl,' I responded, smiling. 'I'm pleased to see you.

I was wondering, you know, about everything.'

'*I* have,' she replied coyly. I couldn't stop thinking about you, but I just didn't know — you know?' Again the coy smile. 'It's been driving me mad and you just disappeared. I didn't know what to do — what to think! I've been so worried.'

I reach across and took her had, 'Well you can stop worrying. I'm right here, I'm in the pink, and I'm so glad you came. That's one big concern off my mind too. Thanks for turning up, kiddo.'

She squeezed my hand, tightly. 'Of course,' she said, 'How could I not?

We spent a quiet minute watching one another until she broke the silence. 'I really have to go now, Jack. Work, but I'll be back as soon as I can. Okay?'

'Okay, but I'm going to see if I can get out of here as soon as possible. I'll be good to go, pretty soon.'

'You do as the doctors tell you,' she told me, affecting scorn, and broke into a gorgeous smile. 'I really have to go now. I'll be back.'

'Alright,' I consented, and she bent to give me a kiss before parting. As she did so, I slipped a piece of notepaper into her pocket, in the hope she would discover it in time for her to meet me where and when the message indicated, and I watched as she made her way out, disappearing into the corridor, the scent of her perfume lingering long afterwards. I had it bad, and I knew it. But I could not fight against the one single good thing in my life. My years of solitude at last threatened to turn against me. A situation I would never have thought possible. I figured I was beyond all that.

It occurred to me how large a problem I had. For so many years I had been the lone wolf, with no responsibility but to myself. With Alex being implicated, all that had suddenly changed, and what made my situation insurmountably worse was our location. Out here on the rim was no place to be when contemplating a disappearing trick. There were so few routes out of here, and most, if not all, were under constant surveillance by the company, as well as these black suited hard cases. I had copped a beating, but it wasn't the first time. My ability to recover quickly from something like this had always been an asset. Resilient; the word was even in my personal file. I was stiff and sore; a rib or two may have been cracked but I knew, if I needed to, that I could drag myself out of here and manage to do whatever needed to be done. But it wasn't just me anymore. She was bright and I figured she must be realising by now what was on the line. She would be analysing and formulating possible moves, as I was. The safest thing she could do for herself would be to cut me loose, distance herself and allow me to deal with circumstances. I could, of course, play ball with these pricks and betray the trust of these Jhai, but, as I said to them at the time, why the hell would I want to? The Jhai had done nothing but trust me. I had never betrayed a trust in my life, and although they weren't even the same species, I had no intention of ratting them out. Imagining what might become of the Jhai should these clowns get their mitts on them, it hammered my conscience even to contemplate it. Of course the Jhai might be way out of these guy's league. Probably were. The thought made me smile. Somebody would get their arses kicked very badly, but it would be on me. I did not want to be responsible for something like that. What a stink it would cause, and the blood would be on my hands. 'No,' I determined, aloud. The black suit brigade had to be kept out of the frame as far as the Jhai went. I would not betray a trust and the black suits could go to hell.

The human mind is a curious thing. All this contemplation, pretending to myself that I could find a perfect solution to the problem when there was, during all this time, only the one obvious escape route now. But would Alex want to play along? Would she be willing to leave it all behind and embark on a jaunt into the complete unknown with the likes of someone like me? Perhaps she was, even now, coming to the same, inescapable conclusion. Would she choose her career, the future and the familiar, or could she possibly determine to launch into the realm of the unknown for the sake of adventure, a life together, dare I say, *love*?

Damn it all. Did I have the nerve or even the right to ask the question of her? It was times such as this that human nature seemed dead set bent on killing the organism rather than preserving it.

When logic and human nature collide, the odds most always favour logic. Unfortunately, and without exception, logic becomes the first casualty. For me it seemed completely within the realm of possibility. Nothing tied me to Earth any more. Not emotionally, not physically, not in any way that would give me pause once the decision had been made. The proposition began to shine in my mind's eye as the most desirable of outcomes. It solved the puzzle of my life; the perfect solution to escaping the corner I had been painting myself into all of these years. Jack Hardin the misfit. Jack Hardin the antisocial, the misanthrope, the square peg in the round hole. I cared nothing for the human race. I would not miss them and they wouldn't miss me. If Alex was game, here was the obvious, perfect solution.

Nighttime on Far Reach was, of course, an outmoded term. The language here retained the use of words denoting a time of day only for convenience sake. The sky was an eternally star- sprinkled depth of darkness, but the rig remained lit up like a jewel against the spangled backdrop, more so during a twelve hour period designated daytime, with a gradual diminishing over a two hour period in simulating evening and eventual nightfall. The ploy helped the diurnal body clock of the human animal to assimilate conditions.

At three in the morning, when the hospital was at it's quietest ebb, I pulled on my clothes, having to tear open a trouser leg to accommodate the cast on my left leg, the result of my left kneecap having been cracked with the butt of a handgun. I pulled the walking stick I had procured earlier in the day from under my mattress, and slipped out quietly into the sublime tranquillity of the night; quite beautiful in an eerie kind of way. The reduced and sporadically placed night lights cast strangely elongated shadows across the uneven deck. The silence, as I set of, was complete, bringing to the fore all those instincts that millions of years of evolution had equipped us with; nerves singing in heightened anticipation of the slightest detection of danger.

My intention had been to return to my room, there to gather what belongings I deemed necessary and make my way to the Horizon Hotel, there to claim the room I had pre booked and to remain for the remainder of the night, keeping off the streets and out of sight from those who had become more than just a thorn in my side.

Upon entering my room at Star Palace, it was at once apparent that someone had been here during my absence. Drawers had been pulled and rummaged through, the bed upturned and my closet rifled, with the pockets of my clothes turned inside out. I could only see the humorous side. Those lugs had wanted to advertise their presence, appearing untouchable, able to disrupt my life at will and with impunity. It made no such impression on me and I had to chuckle at the mental image of full-grown men in alike costume getting their rocks off in this manner, like willful children throwing a tantrum. As far as I was concerned, this would be the last night I would spend as a member of society and the *rat* race of man. Nothing they could do to me, barring capture and detainment, mattered any more, and I would have to make sure I avoided that particular scenario at all costs. I pressed the night bell at the rear entrance of the Horizon.

After a short wait, a middle-aged lady wrapped in a blue night-gown came to the door. She inspected me briefly through the frosted pane of glass until she recognised me as the man who had pre-booked the room for a week, and she set about pulling bolts and opening locks.

'Patrick Dempsey,' I told her as she cracked the door open a few inches.

'Yes, Mr Dempsey. I remember you. I am Myra.' She pushed the door ajar and stepped back to allow me entry. 'Goodness. You've been in the wars,' she observed, indicating the leg and facial bruising, which by now had turned into a lovely mixture of blue and yellow.

'Occupational hazard,' I told her. 'I'm sorry to trouble you at this early hour. 'Lovely night, though, isn't it?'

'No trouble,' she replied. 'Who sleeps anymore? If you're hungry I can bring you up a sandwich, if you like?'

I declined the sandwich, but I spotted a bottle of *synth* whiskey on the shelf and had it charged to my room as an afterthought. Having left the hospital unannounced I had forfeited access to pain medication and I would soon be in need of a substitute. At the office she handed me the key to my room and bade me good night.

The room was snug, which is to say, small, with a window, a double bed, a dresser, a closet, a single chair at the bedside, and a bathroom wash-basin installed in the wall; somewhere I could freshen up in the mornings. It would do in a pinch, I decided.

The journey from the hospital had been a painful one. Not so much because of the beating I had received, although it didn't help, but the exertion had caused the old belly wound to begin throbbing once again. It really didn't feel good, and I was beginning to sweat. I really did not need the thing to be infected; it would be a real spanner in the works, and I had to wonder if leaving the hospital without at least a bottle of antibiotics to keep the infection in check was such a brilliant idea. I made a mental note to do something about that and moved on to other concerns.

A glance at my watch told me it was almost four in the morning. If Alex had read my note, and if she had decided to come, she would be here in a half an hour. If she was being followed it would make things awkward, but not impossible. I had taken the possibility into account. The black coat and dark glasses brigade would not intercept her, but they would follow to see where she lead them. It was how they worked. They depended on their quarry being dumb enough to tip their hand so that all they needed to do was to move in and mop up.

I found a shot glass in a cupboard and swallowed a couple of doses of synth whiskey, found an opened packet of cigarettes in my bag, climbed onto the bed and lit up, there to wait for the tap on the door which I was afraid would not come. Moments like this always felt to be saturated with portent. In my career there were many such moments of waiting, alone in a room, just like this one, swinging wildly between optimism and doubt, the mind racing through one possible scenario after another, making contingencies for each possible outcome and knowing that, in the end, it was as much dependent on sheer dumb luck and random timing as any brilliant, mastermind planning.

I reached over and retrieved my weapon from my bag, felt its weight, checked that the compressed air cartridges were firmly slotted into their recess, inspected the lead tipped iron slugs which would flash through the air at over three hundred metres a second with little more than a whisper. The perfect weapon for a circumstance like this. I rested it on my lap and took a good, long draw on the cigarette. I was ready to see this thing through to the end, come what may.

I must have dozed for a minute. What had woken me? There came a soft tap at the door. Yes, it must have been what woke me, so I climbed off the bed and quietly sidled up to the door.

'Who is it?'

'Me—' and I immediately recognised Alex's voice. 'Me who?'

'Are you going to let me in or do I have to thump you?'

As I opened the door she threw her carry bag into the room and flew into my arms, wrapping herself around me, kissing me gently, being sure to avoid the worst of my bruised face.

There was nothing else for it but to succumb to the moment, and be damned with the circumstance. I locked the door and carried her to the double bed, where we let loose our passions. The both of us, it seemed, knew that the next couple of hours might be the last chance we might have in which to avail ourselves of each other. There is something about the presence of impending danger, the looming spectre of peril, that precipitates the basic sexual imperative of ensuring continuance of the species. It is a fact which anyone who lives in a state of unrelenting fear for their life will acknowledge, and it makes for a most intense sexual encounter, completely bereft of reason and an almost indescribable experience when the ego is dissolved into something far removed — far exceeding — any mere sense of self. It is a combining of souls, a complete surrender, and a heightened awareness of that difficult to explain experience often described as ecstasy, and more often than not, love. For me, it was a phenomena I had only heard about, and, until this moment, denied the existence of — but now? I could only lay, exhausted, stunned and confused, in attempt to make sense of what had just happened. This, for me, was revelation, verging on the divine.

We lay in the grip of a spell which had taken us beyond mortal concerns, and at this hour there was total silence. Nothing stirred; there was only the sound of our breathing, our hearts beating, blood coursing through our bodies in a moment without end in a capsule of timelessness and bliss. It was a memory I was destined to carry with me throughout eternity, only, I did not know it yet.

7

BEYOND THE RIM

I had planned an early start to the day but by the time we had gathered ourselves, and our thoughts, the initiative was lost. It didn't much matter, I told myself, and explained to Alex:

'We could be a little conspicuous making our way to the warehouse so early in the morning. The streets need to be filled with people to aid our movement without detection.'

'How about a disguise?' she suggested, with the glint of girlish humour in her eyes. 'It will be fun.'

'I was thinking along the same lines, but where would we get what we need?'

'What would you do without me?' she replied, and nodded towards the carry bag she had brought along.

'Disguises?' 'Yep.'

'Clever girl. What did you bring? Let's take a look.'

When she bounced from the bed in moving to fetch the bag, a bolt of pain shot through my insides, causing me to stifle a cry of intense discomfort.

'What's wrong?' she called, dashing back to me.

My insides felt suddenly gripped by fire, causing me to curl up, clutching at my stomach, and for the moment unable to speak.

'What is it, Jack. Tell me,' she demanded desperately.

The pain eased, but the cramping persisted, and sweat began to bead on my brow. 'Goddamned wound,' I replied.'It's giving me some trouble. And the treatment handed out by those jerk-offs didn't do any good. The infection has started up again, I think.' 'What are

204

we going to do?' She knelt down beside the bed to try and comfort me. 'You should be in hospital.'

'Too late for that. Maybe the Jhai can help out. We'll just have to carry on as intended until then.'

'Yes,' Alex assured. 'They'll be able to fix this. We'll be fine.'

'Of course we will. Let's have a look at what you have there.' The bag contained a few items Alex had pilfered from inside the security centre building where she worked. For me, there was the navy uniform of a security guard, complete with a poncy cap and torch. For herself, coveralls. The type worn by those involved with goods handling, storing supplies in the appropriate areas ready for dispatching. To cover her face and hide her locks, she employed a bandana, the sort commonly used by employees to cover the mouth and nose whenever the rising dust became too severe, and on top, a leather, peaked cap.

'Very good,' I commended. 'The very items. This should be a synch.'

'It's exciting, isn't it?'

I had to smile at her enthusiasm, but this wasn't over 'til it was over. A thousand things could go wrong between here and there, but I didn't want to worry her more than I already knew she was. She was putting on a brave face for me and I didn't have the heart to tell her I knew how scared she was. I would be worried if she hadn't been. If we were discovered, the jig was really up. Both our careers would, doubtless, be over in a moment, and that was serious. The black marks against our names would ensure a life of struggle. Finding an employer willing to take either of us on after something like that would be very unlikely. We had talked it through. She seemed certain that the Jhai would gladly let us tag along. They were a nomadic people who lived their lives roaming the galaxy, making a home here and there, utilizing wherever resources were rich enough to support an easy existence. The technology they carried with them ensured they had everything they needed, when it wasn't broken down, as was presently the case. But they also knew of several civilisations scattered about who were welcoming to itinerant strangers and who would have no qualms about letting the pair of us settle in amongst them. The Jhai, themselves, were such a race, and according to Alex we would have no problems fitting in while she continued her study of them in preparing her planned scientific, anthropological paper. A paper she figured would eventually make her a celebrity and very wealthy to boot, when we finally returned to our own race. As far as that was concerned, I was not entirely sure it was what I wanted, but that was far enough away in time as to cause no immediate problem. And thankfully it didn't seem to be of major relevance to her right now. Like she said to me many times since agreeing to the idea, 'It's exciting.' About that, she was not wrong. In fact, I viewed it as an adventure beyond comparison. We were about to embark on perhaps the biggest adventure of all times, depending, I suppose, on one's point of view. All we had to do was make it to the warehouse this evening and initiate the Jhai transponder she had been given. Until then, the day needed to be dealt with as best we could manage.

In talking the situation through it was obvious we would need to clear a path for our entering the company compound, enabling entry to the warehouses. I figured I could call George Berringer regarding that.

I told him I needed three things. First, to significantly lower the number of guards within the compound, and to make sure people were aware of the reduction in security. Secondly, in the same period to take security cameras offline from 23:00 hrs to 03:00 hrs, but not to make a secret of it. Last of all, to enlist a squad of his best men and station them within the compound, ready to jump to whatever location I needed them when I gave the word. To him it would appear as if we were about to spring a trap on our thieves, and I felt sure he would be pleased to play along without protest. In reality it gave Alex and myself complete freedom to walk in there and depart without anyone lifting a finger. There would be some red faces, I mused with some satisfaction. When he realised he had been employed to facilitate our final departure, the only thing poor old George could do would be to keep the whole matter hushed up, lest his superiors decide that his head should roll. I almost pitied him, but bringing him down a peg or two could only teach the man a much needed lesson in humility. I wasn't going to lose any sleep over it, that was for sure.

Our real problem lay with the boys in black. They were outside of anyone's jurisdiction here on Far Reach. It was likely they had a coven on Niven Station but they were a secretive bunch. It would be handy to be able to find a way of diverting their attention for a short time while we made a break for it, but at this juncture nothing came to mind as a bonafide great idea. They were well aware I had gone to ground, and doubtless, even now, they were beating the bushes pretty hard in attempt to flush us out. Their only option was to keep eyes on the streets and places I had frequented since arriving. Checking hotel registers and the like would not provide what they needed. It was why I had thought to book this room well in advance, and under a bogus name. I suppose that if they checked every single name of every hostelry they might find that Patrick Dempsey was a registered pressure vessel welder and fitter, but nothing about the identity would arouse suspicion. For these reasons I felt reasonably comfortable holding up here at the Horizon with Alex.

The die was cast in any case. George had agreed to the measures I stipulated without too much fuss. Lowering the numbers of security personnel made him nervous, but as soon as I told him he would have his thieves by morning, he was only too happy to oblige. After all, he would be the one to catch all the credit. I knew he would find a way to put the spotlight on himself. He probably planned to mention how the plan was his own invention. I could only smile to myself at the thought. If he pre-empts the setup with a word to his superiors, the whole weight of this event will be on his head.

'What are you smiling at?' Alex asked, rolling over and throwing an arm over my chest. 'Machinations?'

'Of a sort,' I replied. 'Just thinking this through.'

'That's my little strategist,' she mocked, playing the coquette. 'They don't stand a chance—' and she hauled herself up on me, began nibbling my ear as she sniggered playfully.

Show me a man who is invulnerable to an attractive, desirable female behaving this way, and I will show you a man made of stone. Needless to say, we found an enjoyable way of filling in the afternoon. By the time we heard the siren for the afternoon change of shift, we were both ravenously hungry, and it made perfect sense to eat a good, hearty meal before going into action.

I contacted Myra, the proprietress, on the house phone. Asked if it was possible to have two meals brought to the room.

'For you and your lady friend?' she enquired. When I was slow to respond, she added, 'It's alright, dear. Nothing gets past Myra. Remember? I don't sleep well. I told you that. What would you like, Mr Hardin? I'll have the chef send it up.'

We ordered big. It would likely be the last meal of this kind we would be having for quite some time. It was something neither of us had really considered until now.

A rig on the outskirts of the solar system does not have the greatest cuisine, but we were happy to settle for soup and a plate of meaty stew containing unfamiliar ingredients, which I wolfed down with considerable delectation. For the remainder of the evening we were happy to simply enjoy each other's company until it was time to make a move.

With perhaps thirty minutes remaining before time, we donned the apparel Alex had selected. Reversing the original plan, I dressed as the navvy and Alex dressed in the role of the security officer. My wound continued to cause discomfort though, and it was taking more of an effort than I would have liked in order to ignore it. I could not allow Alex to see just how much effort. If the need to make haste should arise, I feared I might be in some trouble. There was nothing else for it but to push on.

I poured a good measure of the remaining synth whiskey into a tumbler. 'Will you join me?' I offered.

'Why not? What shall we drink to?'

I poured hers, passed it across. 'To success. What else?' 'And a new beginning,' she added, cheerily.

'Success and a new beginning,' we choroused, and downed the fiery liquid in a single gulp.

Alex pulled a face while trying not to breathe. 'Rocket fuel.' 'Has a kick to it, doesn't it?' I agreed. 'One more?'

We drank another and stood, looking at each other.

'Is it time?' Her voice was steady, but diminutive now.

'It's time,' I affirmed, injecting as much confidence into the two words as possible.

Alex pulled the device the Jhai had provided her with from her divested jacket pocket; the pencil shaped electronic beacon which she would initiate once we were in position, and primed it by giving the end a single twist. All it needed to start it functioning now was for her to push the tiny button on its end. Outside, the lights were dimmed, feigning nighttime, and with the sky ablaze and the temperature falling, tending toward a chill, we set off from the rear of the hotel, bracing ourselves for any eventuality. Again my senses were amped up, growing in sensitivity; the animal brain recognizing the nature of the game and attending to the job it was designed for. The job of self- preservation.

It was risky, under the circumstances, for us to exhibit any close personal attachment. Anyone looking for us would be looking for a man and a woman travelling together, but the uniforms we wore made us look like two men, so we could at least make conversation as if we were two old colleagues locked in routine and making our way to our place of employment.

We entered the compound via a side gate where a single gate guard was standing sentry, and we made directly for warehouse- A, a distance of around five hundred metres which put us out in the open without the convenience of surrounding foot traffic to conceal our progress, which the streets and thoroughfares had afforded us until now. It did at least allow a degree of unobstructed sight about us, but if anyone was standing concealed beside converging walls or in an unlit doorway, it was doubtful we could have picked them out within the shadows. But so far, so good.

At warehouse-A we took a last, quick look around before skirting the edge and entering through a small door halfway along the length. One end of the interior was in darkness, the end we proceeded towards was lit here and there where goods were in the process of being positioned into storage by men and machines.

'Take a break,' I said to Alex, halfway along the central aisle, and we halted to lean against a stack of pallets while I lit a cigarette, casually surveying the area for anybody lingering suspiciously, perhaps stationed as a lookout for the pair of us. We were well within the time period I had specified for the cameras to be switched off, but I had to admit that it didn't necessarily mean that they were. If the black suits had pulled rank on Berringer, they were, right now, watching our nervous behaviour.

'Alright, lets go,' I said, and we continued, her in her navy security uniform, torch in hand, and me, the warehouse worker walking down the middle of the enormous space, as vulnerable and as unprotected as it was possible to be.

As we approached the designated area I anxiously slid my hand under my coat to feel the reassuring grip of my weapon. Alex noted the time and nodded. 'Two minutes,' she observed, as we came upon the designated bay from where we were to depart.

'Are you alright?' she asked me, the obvious look of concern showing on her face.

'As a matter of fact,' I began, but then doubled over as an invisible hand gripped and squeezed my innards like a vice, causing me to double over and sink to my knees.

A hot flush came over me, my skin began to prickle as sweat began to bead over my entire body.

'What is it, Jack?'

'Give me a moment,'I said, grimacing against the suddenness of the rising fever. 'Goddamn it,' I growled.

'We're here,' she soothed, squatting beside me and placing a hand on my shoulder. 'Soon we'll be with the Jhai. They'll know what to do. You'll see. Their technology and medical knowledge is well up to the task.'

'Going somewhere?' A man stepped out from behind a stack of boxes across the aisle from where I crouched. At the same time, every light in the building brightened to full illumination, and in the aisle either side of us appeared two sets of two armed men, their weapons levelled threateningly.

'What were you thinking?' he continued, in a mocking manner. I knew this guy. It was him that conducted the brief but painful interrogation. I was sure of it. As the memory came back to me,

I noticed Alex had ever so gradually slipped a hand into her coat pocket. She was activating the beacon.

The guy doing the gloating stood, hands in pockets, a grin on his fat face — a grin that would soon change to something resembling startled surprise, I devoutly hopped.

'Not you clowns again,' I responded. 'Don't you idiots ever take a break?'

His smile began to smear into something resembling displeasure. 'Stand up, both of you. And keep your hands where I can see them.'

Alex rose first, reached down to assist me as I pushed myself up, groaning.

'What's wrong with you?' the black suit wanted to know. 'He's injured,' Alex answered with venom. 'From what you bastards did while he had a bullet wound.'

'Oh dear. Were we playing too rough for you, Jack? Maybe you've always been out of your depth playing with the big boys?'

The snide prick wouldn't be feeling half as clever in a moment, I assured myself. 'You're so deluded that you see yourselves as that? You guys crack me up.'

'Stand down at once,' yet another voice joined into the discussion. It was Joe Higgins, chief administrator. His large frame approached us from along the centre aisle. 'Did you hear what I said?' he demanded. 'Lower those damn weapons at once!'

We all turned our attention to him as he came to a halt between Alex and myself on the one side, and the boys in black on the other.

'You are interfering in company business,' he told the others, 'and you are on company premises. I have the authority here.'

What the hell was going on here? I wondered. How many people were going to turn up to our *secret* departure point?

The guy with the dopey smile stuck to his face and armed backup seemed momentarily nonplussed, but then snapped out of it. 'Do you know who we are? We override any authority and all jurisdictional concerns. We are in charge,' he proclaimed, and at that exact moment there was a colossal roar from overhead.

We all looked up in the direction of where the interruption had come from. The roof of the warehouse was maybe fifty feet above our heads, and on it a large diameter, cherry red circle began to appear. In seconds it began glowing bright red, then bright white as it melted, oozed downward and fell dangerously around in little explosions of molten metal sparks.

Everyone took desperate evasive action, but for Alex and I. Remaining together we adroitly stepped out of the molten metal's drop zone, to stand with our backs against the stack of wooden pallets.

'I'll leave you to settle this by yourselves,' I managed to call out above a high pitched whining noise which came from all around us, and a moment later we were surrounded by a circle of bright, white light, and the scene around us began to fade rapidly from view.

I woke lying on the exact same cot, looking up at the very same white, domed ceiling as the first time I had come here. Except, I was the only one lying down. Alex was at my side, gripping the side rail of the cot, watching over me.

My mouth was exceedingly dry, my body felt exceedingly heavy and there were drip lines attached to either arm.

'How long?' I asked in a raspy voice, and finding speech uncomfortably difficult. I tried again, 'What happened?'

'It has been two whole days,' she replied, her voice soft and soothing, which worried me immensely. 'The wound, she said. 'It's badly infected. The Jhai saved your life. If it hadn't been for them you would have lost your life, for sure.'

'I can't feel my legs.'

'It's alright, darling. Take it slow, you'll be fine.'

I smiled, remembering the last thing I had witnessed. 'Did you see the look on their faces? That was priceless, wasn't it?'

I began chuckling from deep in my chest; the look on those guys' faces was exactly what I had hoped for; and I thought for a moment she was laughing along with me, until I noticed the tears streaming down her cheeks. I didn't understand, but women are like that. Maybe all the excitement had been too much for her, I figured; but then she turned and fled from the room, making those squeaky, weeping noises women make when they cry and run at the same time. An odd response. A little overwrought, I guessed. A heavy and irresistible tiredness swept in to overtake my thoughts and I couldn't fight it. I had to retreat under the weight of it, to sleep. Two days? Why two days?

The weirdest dream came to me. *Stars* — millions, perhaps billions of stars in formations like whirling pinwheels, in clouds and clusters like floating islands adrift in the depths, each with its own distinctive character like fingerprints dabbed here and there within a three dimensional grid stretching beyond an eternity of space and time. It was wondrous, prodigious, limitless, exalting and exhilarating. A sense of freedom and peace; a flawless, harmonious existence I had never known — did not know was possible — uplifting and full of promise and joy; a place of belonging — belonging, for the first time, a feeling of belonging.

I woke an unknown span of time later, my mind ablaze, still, with the afterimage remaining and not wanting to depart.

'Jack. Jack? *Jack! Wake up Jack.*'

I was being gently shaken. Who was trying to wake me? It was Alex's voice. I had to concentrate, force myself awake.

'What is it?' I grumbled. 'Is it morning already?' I realised I was making no sense and opened my eyes to see Alex, again standing over me. A beautiful girl, I saw, looking over me. But no, not over me. I was upright and Alex was standing in front of me. Was I standing? How was I on my feet when I had only just opened my eyes? I couldn't feel my feet, and there were drip lines attached to me, still. *This was peculiar.*

Behind her the Jhai appeared to be working industriously with connecting lines to electrical switches, machines being connected up, conduits being strung up or sealed behind wall panelling.

My eyes came to perfect focus on Alex's features and I greeted her with an encouraging smile. 'This is peculiar,' I told her. 'Why did you run away crying? What is wrong, my dear? Tell me.'

I watched as Alex mentally braced herself. 'You were very ill,' she began, and took a deep breath before going on. 'The Jhai have been devoted to your survival. You are alive because of them.'

I moved my attention to those behind her, bent assiduously to a task, I had no idea what. One broke away from what it was doing and came forward.

'*How are you feeling?*' the words came clearly to my mind. It was asking me how I was feeling. I understood perfectly.

'*I'm glad you hear us now. Are you comfortable?*' It asked. Before answering vocally I knew it had received my answer:

'*I feel quite okay. Thank-you for helping me.*'

'*We are please to assist,*' it responded, and returned to whatever it was it was doing.

'That's amazing. I can communicate with them. In my mind. Telepathy. Mental telepathy!'

'Yes,' she said, smiling warmly. 'There are differences now.' I sensed there was something serious on her mind. And my legs. I still couldn't feel them. And not just that. There was something about . . . how was I standing when I couldn't feel my feet? Something was much different. I felt it. I didn't feel right.

Not right at all.

Alex saw that I was waking to the fact of the differences and intervened before my confusion grew and became unmanageable. A Jhai came over beside her, reached above my head in order to make some kind of adjustment. In response, my rising anxiety levelled, and diminished quickly, but I felt I had been sedated. My mind ceased racing and a calmness gently rolled over me like a wonderful, soothing balm.

The Jhai nodded to Alex and walked away, leaving us facing one another. All I could do was watch her face — her lovely face. I could stare at that face for hours and not grow tired of it. 'Jack. In order to save your life. . . ' She broke off, turning to the Jhai behind her. 'I can't,' she said. 'I can't do it. I just cant—' and turning back to me. 'Im sorry, Jack. I can't do this. 'Maja the elder will fill you in on the situation. I'm sorry,' she said one last time, and departed quickly from sight.

I would have followed her progress out of the room but discovered I could not turn my head. Something odd had happened, but what? I didn't feel at all right and I didn't understand what the hell was going on, and why couldn't I follow after her. Why couldn't I feel my extremities?

Another Jhai approached, or was it the same one as before? It communicated friendship to me; a belonging which I felt to the depths of my being.

'Thank-you for serving us,' it communicated. *'We honour you for your union. We are glad to aid your continuance as one with us and more than you were.'*

I was beginning to understand. I should have been beside myself with emotion of some sort; horrified, but I felt calm. This being was communicating something to me, not with word or thought or by some kind of logical sequence of information. It was a kind of osmosis — an osmosis of knowing. I was absorbing information, knowledge and awareness as if through my entire being.

The Jhai reached once more to make some kind of adjustment above my head, and as he did so, the entire sequence of events became known to me.

This whole episode had been a setup from the beginning: an elaborate ploy had been set in motion. From the beginning I had been the sacrifice and the only one not in the know. The information was flowing to me now. The company had never been told the extent of the theft of so much equipment and hardware. Higgins and Berringer had known before I came along who was stealing their precious stores, and they had made a deal with the Jhai, using Alex as the go between, and using Alex at the bait. The Jhai had broken down, that was certainly true, but they could not go on indefinitely taking as they pleased. They were in need of a biological brain to coordinate mechanisms within the craft's intricate guidance systems and to act as control servers and sub-servers. Biological systems operated throughout the Jhai's vessel, but the one which had failed was the prime system and could not be repaired or regrown, but only replaced — replaced by a delicate and complex nexus of switches and controls found within the brain of someone having a talent. Someone with a talent for rapid problem solving. Someone like Alex Hardin who would not be missed. Why? because a misfit like myself was totally replaceable. I had been played from start to finish; and Alex? She had done a superb job. What a piece of work was she?

The Jhai in front of me, Dortl Karp, he was called. He had been following my thinking. Apparently thoughts here were not entirely private.

'You are in error, Jack Hardin. The female was manipulated as were you. She cares deeply for you and is ashamed of her role in the method undertaken.'

'I am here,' Alex intervened, returning now. 'I will speak for myself, thank-you, Dortl Karp.'

The alien withdrew, returning to its work as Alex came forward to stand before me.

'I am so sorry, Jack. I had no choice. I was threatened. My family back on Earth was threatened if I did not play along. But I fell in love with you Jack, since that first night with you.'

'What have I become?' I replied, ignoring the attempt at gaining redemption. 'What am I? A bio-server, a bio-system within a larger computer network? What do I look like now?' These questions should have been seething with rage, oozing vitriol and desperation, but they were not. No negative emotion remained withing me, but the positive ones? They remained still, and I could not help feeling the warmth of emotion I had felt for Alex since first laying eyes on her. I felt nothing but calm as I asked these questions which dwelt now only in the logic of the asking, and nothing whatsoever hinting of anger or the like.

'I had decided not to go along with them, Jack. I was going to risk it and refuse. Disappear if I had to, but you became so ill. You were dying, Jack, and I could not let that happen. We saved your essence, that which is you and I am glad for that. I am, Jack. The Jhai assure me you will have a rich and rewarding existence. You are now a part of a network spanning light years. You will adapt and thrive as an integral part of the whole. Have you not felt it already?'

I had. The dream I had must have been an inkling of what was to come. The thought must have been picked up by her, because she smiled. 'Is it good?' she asked aloud.

'Yes,' I replied, honestly. 'I think I am going to enjoy being a spaceship.' And one thousand years on, I can say that I was not wrong about that. For the first time in my life I felt happy, and that never changed. I have become so much more than I ever dreamed I might amount to.

Happy? The universe is my playground.

— end —

RIGHTS OF PASSAGE

— RIGHTS OF PASSAGE —

Andrew Morgan was an easygoing man and appeared to fit the description of an average, jeans wearing, knockabout young man in most ways. He had been riding in the cab of a Kenworth rig since stepping out beside the highway just before dawn. During the previous night he had slept fitfully, lying on a wooden bench, beneath the eaves of a general store on the outskirts Hamilton, a tiny town on a secondary road on the way to nowhere special. In the chill morning air the approaching break of day was announced by a distant carolling of magpies in the pallid light; time to roll up the blanket, tie it firmly to his rucksack and cross the intervening distance to the roadside, there to stand in anticipation of early-morning traffic.

As Andy anticipated, the rig had slowed in negotiating the two hundred metres constituting Hamilton's main street, and so it had been little trouble for the trucker to pull up and take him aboard. For the following minor eternity the two men travelled, chatting occasionally, as the bitumen rolled under them, all the while accompanied by the steady drone of big t909 diesel.

After twelve hours had passed the driver set Andy down near the Warrawong turn-off, just as a low, heavily laden cloud which had threatened all day long let go a downpour, forcing him to hurry in order to reach the shelter of a pine grove he had spotted, a minute's jog in from his point of disembarkation.

He had been fortunate. Here he found a council maintained park, complete with community barbeque area. Adjacent stood a structure perfect in providing shelter from the pouring rain; there were bench seats surrounding a large wooden table which would serve very well as a dry, raised platform on which to bed down for the evening.

Dropping his bundle to his feet, he brushed a strand of lank hair from his face, the better survey the sky, noting that the rain had now fully set in. In all probability it would last for the duration.

Well, okay, he thought to himself. Tomorrow's another day. 'Could be worse,' he pronounced, and so saying, set about loosening the blanket from the rucksack in order to pull a few items from it.

A pile of fallen branches beneath a stand of trees provided ample dry fuel; the protected, still dry pine needles igniting easily with the application of a single lighted match.

Darkness closed and temperature fell rapidly, but the flickering firelight beneath the shelter provided a warm and cheerful emanation, beside which Andy prized open a can each of baked beans and bully beef, cut a thick slice of bread from the loaf he had brought.

Having satisfied his hunger, the rucksack served perfectly well as a comfortable fireside seat, and with his blanket pulled snugly about his shoulders a feeling of immense satisfaction perfectly completed the long, arduous day, as he poked at the campfire, gazing languorously into the flickering flames.

Beyond the campfire's ruddy glow, darkness had silently fallen to shroud the landscape. With its arrival emerged the occasional sounds of small, scurrying animals; local natives commencing their long established nocturnal activities; sounds which, for Andy, completed the spell: flickering firelight with shadows circling and dancing darkly within the shelter's interior, in semblance of some ancient, tribal, campfire ritual.

Such freedom he had not experienced for far too long a time. He had promised himself such a trip as this long before his first period of incarceration, inflicted upon him by that know nothing, ill-tempered judge. That man had no understanding of the world in which he lived, he reflected bitterly, and absolutely no idea of how tough life could be for everyday people. Five years had been a ridiculous amount, especially for a first timer; *and over so trifling an amount!* Then to take a further twenty-five? It was uncalled for. . . *unjust.* The first incident had been nothing but impulsive; a desperate act of survival, he recalled. To place those bundled rolls of cash on the counter in an all but deserted supermarket at closing time? It was as much the checkout girl's fault as it was his own. In a time of need and suffering, that cash had appeared as if by the benevolent hand of fate. There had been no time to think on it. It was a case of having to act in that very moment or to depart with the quart of milk he gone in for, ever after having to rue his inaction and an opportunity missed. Desperate times, he mused in recalling the circumstances to mind; but, to think on it now, in hindsight, had fate not intervened, I hate to think where events may have led me. Why did I allow myself to sink so low? Did life at the time offer so little that chasing the next fix appeared preferable? It must have been so, he concluded. These memories nettled the mind far too much, and in dismissal he strove to divert his attention to less troublesome areas of contemplation.

The temperature began dropping rapidly now. A cold breeze caused a shiver, prompting him to add an extra branch to the fire and to stir the coals until tall flames rose up and warmed his face.

He remained seated at the fireside for a long time, luxuriating in its warmth and comfort, excited by his return to the world of unfettered space, of distant vistas, open landscapes and verdant fields, adding up to a wonderful freedom of spirit, with unrestricted movement and the open road but a short stroll away; a portal unlocking the countryside, representing a return to real life, with all its endless miles to be travelled and who knew what adventures lying ahead, waiting in store?

This was what it was to be free, without a worry in the world. Although, he was forced to consider, at his age and without the high school diploma he had turned his back on, no trade qualifications or anything to suggest a stable work history, getting started might well prove difficult.

Why should that matter? he reasoned. All a man needed out here in the world was a strong back, the willingness to work hard and some small measure of luck. He knew he had at least two of those requirements. And luck? Well— his luck had brought him this far, had it not? Why then should it not continue far enough that he could make that fresh start he envisioned? Almost any small town surrounded by farms and agricultural land ought to provide ample opportunity. One would expect graziers and farmers out here to be glad of a strong back and an extra pair of hands. It was even likely they would be able to provide some manner of accommodation, and modest remuneration, while he tried his best to fit with the way things were done out here. It seemed a reasonable enough assumption; a plan of sorts. . . and infinitely better than no plan at all.

From his pocket he withdrew an ounce packet of *boob weed* — the prison issue tobacco he had traded for five cans of vanilla rice cream and a large packet of jelly babies, the deal done the day prior to his dash to freedom. Luck had already played role, he was pleased to point out to himself, with the unexpected distraction focussing the guards' attention away at just the right moment.

The tobacco was a comfort and a luxury out here, alone. He would smoke a cigarette before turning in, he decided, hopeful that the bench-top table would not prove an impairment to a night's sleep.

About to rise and turn in for the night, a sharp sound caught his attention. Somewhere within the surrounding shadows, beyond reach of the firelight, something had stirred. Or *someone*. Whatever it was, it was entirely consistent with someone placing a foot upon dry, fallen twigs, and immediately his senses reached out in heightened awareness.

This was a tricky situation. He was on the run, and if that was a person out there, the last thing he needed was to invite suspicion, the type that would have whoever that may be out there mentioning the presence of a mysterious stranger camping at the tiny town's recreation park. Attention such as that may soon find the ear of a local policeman; not an ideal situation.

The outlying perimeter had become still. Even the wind had quieted itself and the sudden absence of sound was unnerving. Everything felt unnaturally suspended, as if all had taken a sharp, indrawn breath and was holding still, hackles raised in anticipation of danger; but then again, in light of his present situation, he recognised the difference between nervous paranoia and simple occurrence.

'Don't worry,' he spoke up in as friendly a voice as he could manufacture. Then adding, 'I won't bite. Come on in and warm yourself. It's chilly out there,' and he waited expectantly for a response.

Just as he figured too much time had elapsed, a figure emerged from the shadows, taking two cautious steps forward.

'I didn't mean to disturb you,' came a voice, diminutive and indistinct so that Andy could not determine whether the interloper was male of female.

'That's fine. You're not disturbing anybody, really. You out for an evening stroll?'

'Something like that,' came the response, carried on a frigid gust of wind that rattled through the surrounding branches.

The reply had sounded far more female, this time.

'Well, it *is* a lovely night for it,' he joked. 'Why don't you come and share my fire for a moment? I'm just sittin' here, talking to myself.'

There was only brief hesitation. 'Thanks.'

The stranger entered the luminous sphere surrounding the campsite to reveal herself wrapped in a lightweight coat, wearing blue cotton pants over leather boots.

'Let me find you something to sit on,' he offered as the woman neared, but before he could rise to do so, she replied to the contrary.

'No, don't bother. I'm fine standing.' She looked around the vicinity. 'There doesn't appear to be anything to sit on in any case.'

She came up to the fire to stand, warming her hands, rubbing them together in something of a perfunctory manner before pushing them into her pockets. She remained that way for a moment, while staring into the flames and looking a tad uncomfortable, he realised.

'You live nearby?' he enquired, more in effort to forestall an uncomfortable silence than out of real interest.

She almost shook her head before quickly converting the movement to a nod. 'Not far,' —glancing toward him with a quick smile.

She was attractive, he thought, noticing it for the first time. Youngish; about thirty-*ish* if he was any judge, her brown hair cut to shoulder length. Pretty, but that had no bearing on anything.

'You're hitchhiking,' she said, more by way of statement than inquiry, her eyes looking over the scant belongings. 'You travel light, too. That's smart. I see a lot of backpackers along this stretch, all looking like Sherpas, with enormous backpacks towering over them.' She gave a little laugh. 'Where are you travelling to?'

He hadn't been prepared for questions, and only shrugged in response.

She regarded him with greater interest now. 'You don't know?'

'You were doing a reasonable Sherlock Holmes a moment ago. Maybe you can tell me?'

She laughed at this, exposing a broad, white smile. 'My name's Andy. What's your?'

'Kate,' she told him. 'What's Kate's story?'

She gave a small shrug, and in a moment replied, 'Guess.' 'Alright. Now. . . Let me see.' He made a face meant to express exaggerated contemplation; a comical expression prompting her to smile once more.

He raised a pointed finger, saying, 'You just had an argument with your old man. You threatened to leave him, *with* the six kids, mind you, if he didn't give up the booze and take life more seriously. To which he became incensed, told you that you didn't have the guts and that you would never be able to survive a day without him. The money he brings in. To which you responded, *Oh, yeah? Just you watch me,* and you stormed out of the house into the wet, cold night. And here you are!'

Kate's expression remained impassive for the moment, then was replaced by an odd visage which eluded description.

'I hope I haven't struck a nerve,' he rapidly followed up.

'You wouldn't have a cigarette, would you?'she enquired, evading. 'I've left mine behind and I could use one, if that's okay?'

He pulled the packet of tobacco from his top pocket, where she had obviously noticed it. 'Sure—' and he handed it over.

She thanked him in accepting, inspected the tobacco closely before setting about rolling one up.

Beyond the shelter the rain started up agin, this time coming down with a tremendous roar against the corrugated iron roof. In response Andy stood to begin breaking up the burning branches with his boot in the fire, piling the smaller pieces afresh, coaxing the flames higher, fiercer, providing greater illumination.

Kate combed the strands of wet hair back from her face with her fingers before lighting her cigarette. In the increased illumination of the rising flames he thought he recognised a yellowish discolouration near the orbit of her right eye, consistent with recent bruising.

'Is your other half left or right handed?' he chanced, finding that to be heard he had to shout above the ferocity of the downpour.

Her hand went immediately to the discoloured area beside the eye. 'I thought we had dispensed with sleuthing,' she answered, though appearing not to be terribly annoyed. 'Right handed, if you must know,' and drawing on the cigarette, she exhaled with a sigh.

'I would like to sit,' she told him. 'What can we find?'

He folded the blanket he was still wearing — 'This fire is really throwing out some heat now'— folded it into quarters for himself to sit on while she accepted the rucksack. 'I don't see this weather letting up anytime soon. I hope you're not needing to be somewhere else?'

'No pressing engagements,' she told him, and for a little while they sat in silence, listening to the driving rain.

From the distance issued the deep rumble of thunder, and in a minute the downpour lessened appreciably so that the din of pelting rain on the roof was diminished, enough so that conversation could resume without having to raise their voices. 'I like this weather,' Kate volunteered, a reflective tone in her voice now. 'It reminds me of the farm we once lived on, when I was little. The farmhouse was very old, but lovely. We always had a fire burning in the ingle at wintertime. So cozy and warm,

you know? It always felt safe.'

Andy nodded, drawing on his own memories, and looking up, replied, 'I have similar memories.'

'You do? Then you know *exactly* what I'm talking about. 'My uncle and aunty worked a farm when I was little,' he explained. 'We often went to stay for long periods. Some of my first memories are of that place. The landscape.'

'Wonderful.'

He nodded. 'Oh, yeah. It's a gift, being raised in the country.' It was her turn to nod, and she did so enthusiastically. 'Truly,' she agreed. 'I sometimes observe these city raised kids, who have never known anything but city life. It makes me sad, knowing what they have missed out on. That special connection.

That–' she paused, searched for a word. 'Magic?' Andy suggested.

'Magic. Yes, that special magic,' she agreed, 'because there is something indefinable, almost extraordinary about being a child exposed to something so beautiful and intricate as the natural world. I can't imagine a childhood without being immersed in it, can you? No one should have to miss out on something like that.'

He was smiling broadly now. 'What?'she demanded.

'Your enthusiasm. . . and *passion*, I think. I'm wondering if you're living on a property out here. . . about what you might do out here to survive.'

'I'm an educator. I teach the primary students at the area school, here in Hamilton. Ages five to twelve. I was a high school teacher before that, but, living out here there's no opportunity to teach high school. It's too far to travel.'

'That's a shame,' he sympathised.

'Not at all,' she insisted. 'I love the younger ones. Those are the formative years and so, so important. I'm glad I had the chance to find out how rewarding the job is.'

Before he could respond to this she asked, 'Do you have children?'

'No, no children. No plans of marriage and raising a family either, if you're wondering. I'm not within *cooee* of being able to cope with the responsibility. A man needs to have substance to raise a family. I have a ways to go in that direction.'

His candour silenced her momentarily. 'Do you?' he asked in return.

A blinding flash accompanied by a terrific explosion caught them unawares; a lightening strike on a nearby tree.

Kate had put her hands to her ears in wide-eyed astonishment, jumping to her feet in fright.

'*Goddamn!*' Andy announced, recovering from the shock of the lightening bolt. 'My heart nearly stopped beating!'

Both began laughing, the only response which seemed appropriate, though as much at the incredulous expressions on each other's faces.

'That was awesome,' he announced, eyes still immensely wide. 'It almost scared me to death,,' Kate said, laughing still. 'What a shock. Did you feel the electricity?'

The event of the lightening strike served to imbue a mood of greater intensity. In short time, all remaining reserve had been broken down and they found themselves chatting to one another with greater ease, pursuing any topic of discussion which occurred, without hesitation..

For Andy this was of a revelation. Never before had he been able to make a friend so quickly or so easily. It was, he always understood, his one major flaw. Relationships of any variety had always been difficult. He had been a shy kid, and the affliction had carried through, into his teenage years, and on into adulthood. It was a contributing factor to his use of narcotics, he understood. Opiates of any variety, he had discovered, helped to overcome the social awkwardness which had plagued him right through the early years, much affecting the chances of his striking up even very innocent relationships, especially with members of the opposite sex. He had long ago recognised his opioid use as being something of a social crutch, and the prison psychiatrist had agreed. Nevertheless it had helped to broaden social interaction and it made his life easier, and even fun.

Of course addiction had raised it's gorgon head, but it was already too late by that time. *'An addictive personality,'* the prison doctor had told him. Those particular chemical combinations were to be his *kryptonite*. In the reckless years, eventually leading up to his arrest and first taste of internment, there seemed nothing to be done in order to free himself from its clutches, despite the fact that his life already had begun to career off course and become unmanageable, even unpredictable.

'Did you hear me?' Kate was saying. He had drifted off in thought and hadn't heard a word.

'I'm sorry. Did you say something?'

'You were off in faerie land, weren't you. I was asking where you were heading. I asked you earlier, but you never did reply. Do you have friends on up the road? Somewhere to stay?'

'Friends? Future friends, possibly, I hope. I don't have any destination planned. I'm hoping to find employment as I go. I've been wanting to travel and take a good look at this country for some time. I finally had the chance.'

'You're relying on employment to finance your peripatetics?' she quizzed.

He chuckled amusedly at the use of the word. 'My aimless won-derings, do you mean? You were testing me, why?'

'I'm sorry. I didn't mean for it to come across that way.' 'Are you sure about that?' Andy replied, labouring the point. 'I enjoy try-ing new words. I'm a bit of a crossword buff and I like the sound of that one. *Peripatetic.* I like how it sounds. Why did you think I was testing you? Because I really wasn't.'

The question made him uncomfortable, and, again, he felt as though he were being tested, even scrutinised. He realised that his face must be betraying his discomfiture by what was reflected in Kate's own expression, and suddenly he felt very exposed and vul-nerable though he didn't know why, a condition he abhorred and which made him feel exceedingly uneasy. Uncontrollably, an array of emotions made themselves fleeting visible across his face.

'Is anything wrong?'

'Of course nothing's wrong!' He realised at once he had responded way more forcefully than he had intended. 'I'm sorry. I didn't mean to snap at you. I don't know where that came from,' he admitted, contritely.

Kate nodded sagely. 'That's okay. Don't worry, Andy, I know how it is.'

He measured her response as he regarded her closely. 'Do you? Do you really?

She nodded. 'I think I do. I know about triggered behaviour. It's not something I'm entirely immune to, myself. Believe me.'

Before responding to this he had to ask himself if this was terri-tory he wished to explore. It was an opportunity he had never before been presented with, but there may never be another, he imagined. He didn't know why this person, someone who was a stranger only a short time ago, seemed to be anyone he could talk to — *really* talk to — but in this moment a chance to engage in deeper dialogue than he had hitherto been given the opportunity to explore, it was a prospect, he decided, that perhaps he ought to take a chance on.

'Okay,' he began, and then wasn't sure where to go from there. Kate took the initiative. 'Just a moment ago I saw something in your face. It's something I recognise, I think, because I have experienced the same myself. You know what I'm talking about, don't you? That uncontrolled mix of emotions that surprised you as much as it did me? I have felt the same. It's a very odd feeling, isn't it?'

He nodded. 'Yeah, it is. Very odd. It was as if there was another me inside, reacting in a way that feels very different to the way I wanted to.'

'That's an excellent description,' she replied with delight. 'I've read about it and come to understand it as a *disassociated, triggered response.* I'm something of a lay psychiatrist, which is to say no psychiatrist at all. More like someone who is interested in what makes us who we are.'

'A *psychology enthusiast,*' he responded, laughing. 'I'm not laughing at you, understand.'

She enjoyed his response, deciding to push a little further. 'Dissociated, triggered response. It's when the brain responds inappropriately to a situation. To an unexpected or difficult circumstance.

'For instance,' she continued, 'some people might react to certain stimuli like, say, screeching tyres, by being completely startled and maybe even jumping and grabbing someone nearby in a protective embrace, because, as a very young child they were in a car accident. You see? They have no cognitive memory of the incident, but in their subconscious it's a different story. The behaviour of protectively grabbing someone close by is a dissociated response, triggered by the sound of the screeching tyres. An uncontrolled reflex action.'

'Yeah, right,' Andy replied. 'That's interesting. I don't know exactly what was happening with me a moment ago, but it was unintentional. I do know that much. I couldn't stop it.'

'Can you guess what happened? What did it *feel* like?'

He considered for a moment. 'Well, I felt uncomfortable. Very uncomfortable and sort of weird.'

'Yes?' she prompted, watching him closely, and then his eyes conveyed recognition.

'What?' she asked.

He looked uneasy, as if he had thought of a description but didn't feel comfortable about revealing it. She thought it best simply to wait.

In his own mind the sudden recognition of what he had experienced in the moment left him feeling vulnerable again, and, for no reason that he could fathom, too exposed. He had to remind himself of his decision to talk to this woman — to expand his ability to relate with others, the way he always wanted to do but seemed never able to take that first, difficult step.

'Yes?' Kate urged again, feeling that he was close to it.

'I felt exposed. . . Vulnerable. Unsafe, even,' he managed to admit. You say that you have experienced the same?'

'Much the same,' she replied. 'It's liberating, don't you think, to be able to talk about this stuff? The mind is such an incredible thing. So intricate. It's able to make sense out of all that happens, all that it comes into contact with, formulates and perceives. Well, mostly. Although not without its occasional mistakes, but that's to be expected, I suppose. I once read that the human brain is considered the most complex machine we know of in the universe. Isn't that something?'

'It is,' he agreed, wondering if she had purposefully evaded the question.

Kate stifled a yawn and stretched out, producing a small moan. 'Oh, goodness. Excuse me. I guess I'm beginning to feel the weight of the day. What time is it?' she asked, pulling back her cuff to read her wristwatch. 'It's after eleven, already? I don't believe it.'

Andy watcher her go through the motions consistent with one succumbing to the late hour of a long day, and couldn't help feeling he was witnessing a well enacted charade. But why was he being so damned suspicious? he asked himself scornfully.

'It's been wonderful talking with you, Andy. It really has. You must be weary, yourself.'

'I guess so,' he responded. 'The weather seems to have cleared somewhat, at least,' he noted. 'Weather permitting, I`ll be able to make an early start.'

Outside of the shelter the night had settled again into stillness. There was a pale trace of the moon, a milky white sphere attempting to break though the drifting clouds, and the usual nighttime sounds had returned, lending a crisp tranquillity to the surrounding bushland.

'How early is early?' Kate asked, standing to warm her hands for a last time before departing.

'Shortly after sunrise.'

'Do you rise with the sun? What time *is* that?'

'Why?' he found himself asking, his natural suspicion coming to the fore once again, and he found himself resenting that he had allowed it to. Had he learned nothing tonight?

Kate replied, 'I live not far away. I could bring a sandwich for the journey, before you leave. It would be no trouble. I have enjoyed our conversation so much, it seems the least I can do.

'Do you carry a weapon while you're on the road, Andy? To protect yourself with, I mean. It must be risky travelling the countryside on one's own. It would frighten me, terribly. Do you carry something to protect yourself with?'

Andy felt the icy fingers of suspicion grip his spine. Why was she asking? Was she *really* concerned for his well being?

'No. I don't carry a weapon,' he replied in an easy manner. 'I don't see that it's necessary.'

'Oh, okay. That's good. I suppose you're right. Well, good night, Andy. I've really enjoyed meeting you and I hope I can catch you in the morning, before you set off.'

'Good night,' he replied, and he watched as she departed, disappearing among the verging trees and bushes, the area now veiled in a converging grey mist.

~

Kate returned to where the others awaited her return, the car concealed in a small grove a short distance away, and climbed into the rear seat, behind the two uniformed officers.

Officer Daniel Smith, recently out of the academy, sat behind the wheel. He folded closed the magazine he had been occupying himself with as she closed the door. Sergeant Carl McManus twisted around in the front passenger seat to face Detective Kate Bryant, veteran police detective of thirteen years and criminal psychiatrist, who had been instructed to assist in Andy Morgan's apprehension, simply because she had been available at the time the reported possible sighting of the escapee had come in at the station.

It was a rushed assignment, a little haphazard and ill prepared due to the time constraints. The suspect was on the move and could well be out of reach before long. She had asked for the prisoner's file, which included a psyche report, only there had been no time. The report would be faxed from headquarters as soon as it was located, she was told, but, of course, that would take time they did not have.

'I was about to call for trackers,' Sergeant McManus quipped. 'Do you realise how long you've been gone?'

'That's our boy,' she said, ignoring him. 'I can't be sure he's unarmed, but he says not.'

'You asked him if he was armed?' Smith asked in amazement. 'Yes,' she replied, irritated by the distraction. 'He appears to be stable at the moment. Relaxed even, but I don't want to make the mistake of underestimating him. He doesn't suspect a thing, and I want to keep it that way. I want him bedded down and sleeping like a kitten when we take him. No fuss. Nice and clean, okay?'

'What are we supposed to do, meantime?' Smith wanted to know.

McManus turned to him, a wry smile appearing on his face. 'I'm not sure. What did they teach you at the academy? Maybe there's something about it in the manual?'

To the young policeman's uncomfortable expression he responded by laughing, slapping the lad on the shoulder. 'We take a nap, officer Smith.' Then directing his attention to the rear: 'How long should we give him, do you think?'

She checked her wristwatch which showed almost eleven thirty. 'Two hours should be plenty. If he's not sound asleep by then, at least he'll be drowsy and not terribly alert.'

The sergeant set the alarm on his mobile phone and the three of them settled in to quietly fill the intervening hours.

After ten minutes it became apparent that no one was able get comfortable enough to nod off, not for even a minute. Kate cracked a window for ventilation, only to have Smith complain about the cold air coming in through the gap.

'Will you please be quiet?' McManus grumbled. How can I nap with your complaining? We have to breathe, don't we?'

A couple of minutes later McManus suggested, 'It *is* rather cold. Why don't we run the motor with the heater on?'—and soon the interior began to warm nicely.

Detective Bryant was restless. Being called in to assist with the recapture was an annoyance. She had hoped to return to the city well before now. She just happened to be in the wrong place at the wrong time.

A catnap was not going to happen, she realised. The decision to reconnoitre the campsite before making an arrest had almost exploded in her face. Only quick thinking had prevented a botched operation, not to mention the backlash that would have caused. A mistake such as that, she did not need on her currently unblemished service record.

The only information she had on Andrew James Morgan was sketchy. He had not come to the attention of police until a little over a decade ago, when he apparently became involved with a group of unsavoury characters in his local area. He had fallen into the drug trade, been suspected of several break and enters before being seriously investigated for interstate transportation of narcotics, which he had narrowly evaded conviction for by some fancy legal manoeuvring by his lawyer.

It was not until an informant had corroborated with police and set him up in a sting operation that he was apprehended, charged and, at last, convicted. Apart from his constant involvement with the drugs trade, his transgressions had been relatively few and minor. It was entirely consistent with surviving in the low income neighbourhood he lived in. But then came the sudden graduation to armed robbery, and murder. Murder?

The sudden step up interested her. She hadn't read the file herself, though. The characterisation was only what she had overheard at the station before hurriedly setting off, and that tidbit had apparently been imparted to McManus over the phone by a desk clerk in head office.

He was said to be dangerous, and that didn't sit well. Perhaps *potentially* dangerous. Station house scuttlebutt was not to be trusted. Going by the brief time she had spoken with Morgan the classification seemed ill fitting. The man appeared not at all the criminal type.

In fact, there was a real humanity to the guy. Still, first impressions could often be deceiving, she knew it well enough. No point in second guessing her city colleagues who knew the man better than herself. If they said Andrew James Morgan was dangerous, there would be a reason for it.

'Sergeant,' she called to McManus, who was almost asleep. 'Get on the radio. Have Morgan's entire file faxed to the station, and have someone drive out here with it, would you? I want to know as much about this guy as possible before we bring him in.'

'Really?' McManus responded, sounding annoyed. 'Can't that wait? You can read the file when we get bak to the station.'

'Do what I ask, please, sergeant. I have my reasons. I want that file here, pronto.'

~

Andy was feeling the effects of the long day and he was well past being ready to turn in. After checking to see that the fire was safe to leave unattended, he took his blanket to the bench table and climbed up on it. Stretching out on his back with a long sigh of relief and closing his eyes, he hoped that sleep might soon overtake him. He needed to be refreshed and alert with the coming of a new day.

It was not to be. After spending the greater portion of the day riding in the cab of a Kenworth, closing his eyes only produced a vision of the highway, with the white centerline rolling towards him. He stuck with it: sleep was vital; the last thing he needed was to begin the day sleep deprived and dull-witted.

His thoughts shifted to Kate. An interesting woman, he considered, and kind of mysterious. He had enjoyed the interaction. It was the first real conversation he'd had in far too long a time. She never had explained why she had been wondering around the countryside, though; alone and at night. *Do you have a weapon?* She had asked.

The longer he lay there trying to drift off, the more trouble he was having. The mind would not let go its constant reviewing. He imagined he would be much more at ease, once away from that place.

Confined behind those high, stone walls and the razor wire, so insulated from the natural world. In fifteen years he had never allowed himself to come to terms with the deprivations as other inmates had done. It was a feeling too alien, and wrong. Not a single day had passed without being aware of the soul- diminishing effects of being separated from the world. The whole concept was grotesque. The use of the title *the Department of Corrections*, he saw it as farcical and no more than camouflage. And the word *justice;* a word waved around like a banner or some golden talisman, and speaking of society as if it were some perfect thing, providing all a human being could possibly want. It all seemed absurd, and conspicuously so. Why did people buy into such an obvious deceit?

To Andy the much lauded *march of progress* was no more than a mad decline from what was once possible, which, one day, would result in too great a loss of the natural world to overcome. As part of their impending reinsertion into society, many prisoners had undergone instruction, something they called a 'resettlement course' where the government attempted to *educate* those approaching their release date with narrow interpretations of how the world worked.

He had been very interested by his fellow inmates' description of the process, and he was sure he was hearing of nothing other than indoctrination. Andy recognised it as brainwashing; the action of a misguided society imprinting on the maladjusted its own version of everything, impersonating benevolence and charity, speaking in soothing tones while saying 'everything will be fine by toeing the line', as if talking to confused and aberrant children who had merely mistaken what they saw every day of their desperate lives in the mean streets, where urbanity, fair play and even humanity had taken second place because some were desperate and small-minded enough to count their own wants and needs above that of the next man.

It was wrong. Of course it was wrong, but that was how it had become and there was no reasoning with it. A reduction to the lowest common denominator, where the cunning and most ruthless survived while the rest were merely grist for the mill; where the animals ruled because aggression and cunning saw kindness and humanity as weakness and such traits will only see you targeted as pray, or dead.

It was where society urged good citizens never to look. Prison was where all transgressors of society's rules were deposited and left without further thought. Abandon your humanity all who find themselves here. Andrew James Morgan was having none of that. He would retain his humanity, his moral code, his spirit, and he would take back his right to freedom as an intelligent being of creation's design.

The bank job had been a drug-driven, idiotic mistake in the midst of confusion and fear. His imprisonment had saved him from he knew not what, but his life was going nowhere, and he dared not to think of what continuing such a path may have led him to. Having been wrenched from that downward spiral of an existence had allowed him to be separated from it all, and in that time there had been a renewal of spirit and of clarity.

He had educated himself, despite the archaic and inflexible prison rules. He had sought every avenue to delve into the knowledge stored within the libraries of man which spanned the centuries. He had been awakened to the possibilities, the truth which had always been obscured by those in control, the powerful and greedy of this world, and he knew there was only hope when people found the will and courage enough to stand firm on what they understood to be right and just. If only, he concluded, thoughtfully. If only people would find the will.

Too late though. For himself, all too late. He had already made the worst possible mistake of his young life, and there was the price to be paid for it. Society would have its vengeance. . . its pound of flesh.

It was the combination of being entirely insulated from the natural word, combined with the attempted distortion of the truth, disguised as something akin to well meaning direction and re-education which had triggered his unavoidable act of rebellion. They would never see what was right there in front of them, admit that their precious, beloved system was blind and in error. Their panels, their boards, their magistrates; their councils and legislative assemblies had bogged down in the moribund bureaucracy and red tape, forever to wallow its heedless continuance. The world had gone to hell, he understood, and there looked to be no way out.

It was perversion, he considered, feeling afresh the revulsion it had caused him. A life, any persons life was a precious thing, and what a person understands to be true, no one should have the right to infect and distort that clarity of understanding with cunning sophism designed to bend one's perceptions to fit the common view. Common view in no way equated to an accurate view, yet that was how it was being presented. It came across as much more unpalatable when the design appeared to channel human effort towards an end incompatible with the aeons long fine tuning of something as complex as the natural order.

These thoughts were what drove him. He felt there was an instinctive mechanism at work within him; and even allowing for the possibility that the instinct was faulty, it was something incorporated within his being and to deny it was to deny his very existence — his belief in what creation had wrought for itself. To deny it was to deny that there was any meaning to the word *truth*, or perhaps that there was no such thing at all. Mankind had overstepped its place in the natural world, imposing flawed reasoning in tune with its growing unnatural desires.

Through the lens of this personal reality he saw society, the arms and mechanisms of government, such as they were, and the powers controlling in every corner of the world as being devoid of any destination other than suffering and calamity. As for the so called Department of Corrections, at whose mercy he found his misguided life? To Andy these were perversions of logic, thinly veiled systems of control about which no one cared enough to notice, and their motives were anything but altruistic; machinations, perhaps, of some unseen enemy whose dark design was to bend perception, and with them mankind itself; to obscure the unhealthy purpose, resulting in a loss of spirit and forethought beyond the every day; perhaps, too, the loss of the soul. The most precious of all.

Life — life experience had shaped him into who and what he was. He saw it clearly and knew of no way to correct whatever damage had already been wrought. Not a hope in hell. Circumstances had piled, one atop the other, like some tremendous weight from under which there seemed no permanent, possible escape. But escape he knew he must, if just to tell the world — *prove* to the world — that the human spirit still counted — that it connected all to that mysterious something which was pure and eternal and without flaw or blemish — and was indomitable. If only temporarily, he would snatch back his freedom as a human being who still possessed understanding of what was right and how it all should and could be.

As mixed up as this world had made him, and though it would be no more than temporary, he would retake his freedom and, if it was to be, die with that freedom intact, as innocent and as pure and as potent as the day he came into this cockeyed, headed for *hell-in-a-handbasket* world. His mind would not settle. These apparent truths lit his consciousness with a light so bright, constant and undeniable that it was almost beyond being contained by something as feeble as one's will to do so.

Over the years he had recognised that he possessed something akin to an internal radar, and lately he had come to trust in its accuracy, especially in matters of survival. It was an instinct which had averted trouble on so many occasions. At this very moment it alerted him that unhappy circumstance had caught him in its cold and dispassionate gaze, and the instinct was not to be ignored.

It was that woman, Kate. Something about her now troubled him greatly. The chance meeting somehow did not add up; or was this just the misgivings of an over active mind? He had to decide and he had to be right. Yes, he had to follow instinct and act before chance withdrew its offer of assistance. It was the only available defence he had at hand, and he knew he must count on it, *right now!*

Climbing down from the bench table Andy hurriedly set about packing his gear together. When it was done he looked about, making certain he had missed nothing before setting off across the countryside at a steady jog, remaining parallel to the road in the darkness lest he become disorientated and stray off course. As the distance between himself and the campsite increased, the less urgent was the insistent, internal alarm which had alerted him to unseen danger impelling him forward.

After a time Andy had made enough distance so that he could move less urgently and more cautiously over the uneven ground beneath his feet. Pausing to stand perfectly still while he quietened his breathing, his pounding heart began to slow. The night felt to be alive with portent and unseen energies. Looking up he saw that the sky, which not long ago had been grey and overcast, was now clear and bejewelled with starlight. The moment was filled with wonder as the heavens seemed to smile down on him, speaking of a benevolent cosmos, harbouring more secrets than could possibly be understood by human mentality. This was the connection for which he had hungered, and it filled his heart with rapture and joy.

'Beautiful,' he attested quietly to himself, and set off anew, content in the certainty of having evaded, if only for the remaining hours of the night, whatever lurking danger he knew for a certainty stalked him — stalked him as grimly as death.

~

Detective Kate Bryant studied the file which had been driven out to her from the station house to be delivered personally to her. The file contained Andrew Morgan's complete evaluation, compiled in part by a prison psychiatrist who had gone to unusual lengths in composing a lengthy analytical file. Some of these notes reached back to his scholastic achievements, written by his teachers of the time and supplied to Correctional Services by the Education Department. They were surprisingly detailed, making interesting reading. She had never read files like these before. From her professional standpoint she found the pages to be of exceptional interest.

What piqued her curiosity more than anything was the marked change in Morgan's behaviour at the beginning of his teenage years, a detail highlighted by the author. She knew, of course, that behavioural changes were almost the norm at this age, but in Andrew's case there were curiosities . . . anomalies even.

It had been observed that Andy had exhibited brief periods of scholastic brilliance, achieving many accolades for his ability to demonstrate a thorough knowledge of ancient and modern history in particular. There were also periods where he displayed flashes of brilliance in other areas, notably English composition and essay writing, also showing great interest and proficiency in all of the sciences.

His teachers had been impressed by a period showing well above average intelligence and application, but when the student had appeared suddenly and inexplicably to cease being interested in applying himself to his education, they had lost interest, no longer bothering to take notice of young Andy Morgan's development.

A typical blunder, Detective Bryant considered. An under funded, poorly staffed education system often allowed these mistakes to occur, right under their noses. It was something she had run into many times previously. She knew that many criminal careers might easily have been circumvented had a little extra interest being shown, by better trained and better equipped educators.

He had dropped out of high school, going to work at a local abattoir where they paid full, adult wages to minors. From there followed a long succession of physical work in many trades throughout the building industry. Unemployment benefits had later begun to be accessed, notably during in the summer months, she saw.

Work history had trailed off after that, and a first arrest at age nineteen had followed, for the possession of narcotics. A fine had been imposed, along with a short probationary period attached to a twelve month gaol sentence. A string of petty crimes had then ensued, and at the age of twenty one came a year and a half long prison term, of which he served every day, including extra time for being cited as argumentative with the prison guards, amounting to just a month shy of two years in all.

Prison charge sheets — *those compiled and lodged by a few guards in particular* — showed that he had been sent to the punishment block, a prison within a prison, on nine occasions; cited for insubordination and obstinacy, being labelled argumentative, moody, confrontational and incorrigible despite being much liked and respected by the general prison population of inmates. He had earned diplomas in theology, sociology, mechanics and structural engineering via correspondence schooling during his term of confinement.

Reading on, Detective Bryant discovered that when he had served his first prison sentence, Andrew Morgan had completely disappeared off of their radar, with no further criminal activity being attributed to him over the following decade. There was, however, an accounting of that time, given by himself.

At the beginning of his latest term of incarceration, a prison psychologist had taken interest enough that he had scheduled a series of sessions with Andrew, in effort to understand what was driving him. It was, she assumed, the intention of the junior prison psychologist to usurp Morgan's history and submit the study in support of gaining extra educational credits to further his own professional viability. Prison psychologists, though; she knew the consensus regarding them, and the reason they were posted to prisons in the first place. It was often reported to be because they had been evaluated as being substandard, not at all up to the calibre required to work in everyday private practise.

It was true. Detective Bryant knew for herself that at least for most of the professions practised within the walls of correctional facilities, the standard was often exceptionally low. But despite the commonly held belief, this — she peered at the paper file in the poor illumination given by the interior light, searching for the author's name — this intern psychologist whose name was Marshall, had given an interesting account. She would read on to see what the man had to say. It may prove to be highly informative and relevant. She had been in this game long enough to know the importance of making use of every scrap of *Intel* as could be gathered.

~

Andrew Morgan moved stealthily across the open fields, feeling much more as if he were floating, entirely unaware of his boots meeting the ground that supported his weight. The night sky was clear, the air crisp and still, and in the silence of the surrounding darkness, below the scintillating heavens, he felt as if transported to some magical realm. It was such a wonderful feeling; as if he were entirely alone in all of creation, and he allowed himself to imagine it was so; away, at least, from the cramped, rectangular confines of the cell he had occupied for fifteen hours a day for years on end. At this moment he did not very much care what the outcome of this escapade might bring. To him the moment was worth every risk taken in bringing himself here, so spiritually energising and other-worldly was the moment.

Way off in the distance, across a half a mile of cloaked country-side, came the sound of dogs barking; each provoking one another, it sounded like to him, in effort to continue the sharp, staccato dialogue as he remembered dogs were often want to do; the motion-less, chilly air perfect for conveying a nighttime doggy connection over the landscape while their masters slumbered, snug in their nice, warm beds, perhaps dreaming of sunny days and better things to come, or disturbed by nightmares; fearful, unsettling phantoms and spectres of uncertainty.

The night took on an eerie aspect then, full of otherworldly light, all the while accompanied by the rhythm of his steady stride, carrying him across the open ground, apart and insulated from almost everything — everything except the immutable past which would no longer be pushed aside, and like an angry, vengeful ghost, it would, heedless to all entreaty, no longer be denied its say. From somewhere deep there began to percolate within Morgan's mind those unsettling things — the things which, for his sake, his ease and peace of mind, for so long had been kept locked away.

Out here there were no distractions; no place to hide or to escape one's own deepest concerns and buried memories. For the first time in a very long while, the things which Andrew had managed to avoid shining light upon found opportunity to lodge and, at last, be given notice: an event which he had managed ever to defer, until this moment.

He recalled, now, with great regret, the fateful decision to involve himself in a exercise driven entirely by desperation and lacking in forethought.

It was a simple enough plan but for the inclusion of firearms, though intended as nothing other than a means of persuasion. There seemed to be no other way; and besides, the others had insisted, and he, being the one without experience in anything even close to armed robbery, had foolishly allowed his thinking to be overridden by the more forceful members of the group.

Madness. It was madness, pure and simple. The mental faculties had been so impeded by the use of narcotics and driven by fear of suffering impending narcotic's withdrawal, a living hell he had not the courage to face again, that not to proceed with the plan became an impossible alternative. To think back on it caused pain and regret, but time ran only in the one direction, and what one does cannot be undone.

Standing in the middle of the floor at the bank, keeping watch, they had been fired upon by a security guard who no one expected to be there. The inside connection, a girl who had worked as a teller and who had become addicted to opioids, had provided false information, seeing them all left standing, open to gunfire and death. With the sudden rush of adrenaline and in an instinctive survival reaction, he had fired at the man who had fired on them, killing a husband and father of four in the blink of an eye. It was the look on that man's face in that terrible moment which terrified him then and haunted him still.

The episode had stirred a huge media response and public reaction. A sizeable deployment of police resources had sparked countrywide interest which seemed never to subside, not until all those responsible had been captured and faced trial for the crime. The co-conspirators were sentenced to fifteen years, while he, the killer, predictably received a life sentence.

It was not something the mind could digest. It was a crime committed in a period of drug induced stupidity which the ego could not attribute to itself, causing, if not denial, then an inability to accept the reality of the event and the awful outcome. Facing the clear memory of the event, out here under the clear night sky, made everything feel even more unreal and amplified than it did at any other time. Lately, the prison walls had come to mean less to him, and the span of lost time had also diminished, in weight and relevance, when rationally measured beside the death of a family man due to his own actions. It had been a near impossible thing to accept, and yet here, now, the truth of it hit like a hammer blow.

~

Detective Bryant, accompanied by officers McManus and Smith, began closing on the park's single structure where she had left Andrew Morgan almost three hours earlier. A low, red glow issued from the coals of the fire they had shared, but all else was now in darkness, with only the silhouetted outlines of the shelter describing its features.

Drawing nearer they began to fan out in order to cut off escape routes should the man awake suddenly and make a run for it. When all were in position they began to close in with intent, pistols drawn in one hand and torches held in the other, as McManus called out in a loud and threatening voice. 'Police. Do not move! You are surrounded.'

With that, the three of them aimed bight beans of light into the heart of the structure, fanning about in search of their quarry, only to discover that the location was uninhabited.

'Goddamn it.' McManus growled. 'The bastard is gone.' Kate intently searched the concrete floor and bench table,

looking for belongings; anything left behind which might indicate the fugitive had pushed his belongings into a crevice and fled into the nearby bushland on detecting their approach.

'Yes,' she seconded. 'He's gone alright. I don't believe it. He was dog tired when I left him. I kept him talking long enough to make sure of it. This guy is one part hare and two parts fox. 'Sergeant. Go back to the radio and put out an alert, would you? I want to search around for a while. Officer Smith? With me. You're young and have sharp eyes. Let's see if we can pick up some tracks and find what direction he's taken.'

Kate Bryant and the young policeman worked a grid pattern over the grass covered and saturated ground, scouring every inch under torchlight to be sure nothing was missed. Smith pocketed some loose change he discovered, and at the side of the enclosure, as if Morgan had tried exceedingly hard to make his exit tracks as undetectable as possible, by edging along the base of the walls, were the telltale signs of his departure.

'South,' the detective voiced with certainty, kneeling with torch in hand to sight along the scant signs. 'He's headed directly across the flat, open ground. Come on.'

Returning to the patrol car the three of them scanned a map of the area, looking for any road or trail which might intersect his line of travel. McManus put a pointed finger to the map.

'Here,' he said. 'If he continues in a straight line, he will cross this dirt road. It's around five miles cross-country for him. A ninety minute walk, and if–'

'Who says he's walking?' Kate interrupted. 'Would you be walking if you were him?'

'Yes I would. In the dark, over uneven ground?'

'That man is travelling at least five miles an hour, at an easy jog,' she told him confidently. 'He has already either crossed over that track and is headed across the open plain, or he's making for Normand.' She pointed to the small town on the map, twelve miles and a bit from where they were.

'I will request air support at daybreak. Meanwhile, we go here. Let's try and arrive before him, shall we? if that's where he's headed. We can surprise him. . . . Now!' she encouraged after there was too long a pause, causing the young cop to flinch, and he hurriedly fired up the motor in compliance.

~

Whether it was his sixth sense in overdrive or simply rising paranoia, Andrew Morgan was convinced that he had someone on his tail. As a precaution, before leaving the campsite he had twice circled a the perimeter, knowing that there was no way of concealing his scent, if tracking dogs were brought in, or his footfalls in the thick, damp grass. He had then left a bogus point of departure leading due south, retraced his steps to rejoin the circle where he reversed direction a further ninety degrees before setting off, directly eastward. The southern departure point would be stumbled upon first, and with some luck it would be followed by his pursuers. Meanwhile he would make as much ground as he was able to, heading east. Anyone searching in that direction on foot would be blinded from six thirty onward by the late winter sunrise, thus further impairing detection.

Convinced that he had been chatting to a cop a few hours earlier, he smiled to himself, picturing the look of annoyance on her face when she discovered the ploy. This may turn out to be his last hoorah, he suspected, but there was still room for a little fun before they brought him down. He broke into laughter, pleased with the turn of events which had provided a last chance to leave an impression on a world he had grown to despise.

After a long while, and having covered, he guessed, maybe ten miles, he heard the sound of nearby running water and made his way towards it. The shallow watercourse provided a sunken landscape, serving well to conceal his presence, and so he took the opportunity to rest for a while, on the sloping embankment, and to quietly sit, watching the moon's reflection shimmer and sparkle in the movement of the water's surface.

'It just get's better,' he confided to the night, absorbing every nuance of every stimulus his senses could detect, and he pulled free his rucksack, from it retrieving his canteen to fill from the stream.

He had made quite good distance, and they would very likely still be searching in entirely the wrong area by now. He would benefit from a fifteen minute break, he figured; no point in pushing himself unnecessarily. With the soft lulling of the water in background to the nocturnal serenade provided by the crickets and other assorted contributors, he allowed his eyes to close for a moment, the better to appreciate the sum of it all.

~

Detective Kate Bryant had notified local area patrols of her expectation for Morgan to approach the town of Normand. If he did not enter the township, she advised that he would probably be in the general area, perhaps in mind of appropriating items of food, clothing or anything else with which to aid his travels. In response, a fellow, local coordinator took up the task of positioning lookouts in likely areas, who would, on assigned frequencies, immediately radio in a report of any sightings, or if unusual activity was detected.

It was after four o'clock in the morning as they entered the quaint country town along the main street. The only lighting came from occasional shop front windows, along with the overhead lighting at street intersections, of which there were few. McManus lit a cigarette, rolled down his passenger window to accommodate his companions as he blew smoke out into the cold air.

'We should have thought to bring along a flask of hot coffee,' Smith commented from behind the steering wheel.

'Who knew we would be out all night?' replied Detective Bryant, ' but a coffee *would* be a boon right now,' she agreed.

'Do you smell that?' McManus asked. 'Smell what?' the others replied in unison.

'Bread. Freshly baked country bread. The baker is up and baking. Bless his little heart. What do you say we visit the establishment and see if we can't persuade a little old fashioned community appreciation, in the form of breakfast and a brew?' He checked his wristwatch, 'We may not have a better chance. Nothing's hopping right now, and it will be a while before anything breaks, don't you think?'

It was agreed. Smith pulled the car up at the rear of the bakery. The neon signage out front had not yet been switched on, but a light at the rear of the building, along with the unmistakable aroma of freshly baked bread and other delights, told them the bake-house was manned and in operation.

McManus climbed out, stiffly, after so long sitting, to make his way to the little door at the rear. Knocking, he was soon observed negotiating with someone at the step.

Before long, lights within the rest of the establishment began to flicker on, growing in number, while, having returned to the car, McManus informed them that negotiations had been successful. The owner, an elderly lady of Scottish decent, named Mrs Forsythe, escorted the trio forward, through the interior, switching on the lights as she went, finally arriving in the café at the front, with a good street-side view through the large, plate glass window. She handed each a breakfast menu as Kate placed Morgan's detailed file and police transceiver on the table, while expressing gratitude on everyone's behalf.

'Oh, you're very welcome, dear. Like you, we're here to serve,' she responded, laughing hard at her witticism as she turned to depart for the kitchen. 'I'll be back in a moment, to get your orders, dears. I haven't turned on the espresso machine yet, but I will fetch your coffees, shortly, when I return for your orders.

Back in a jiffy.'

A neon sign at the front of the shop flickered into life, announcing *"Forsythe's Country Bakery,"* while, from within the ceiling, an air-conditioner began functioning with a low, purring sound.

McManus looked about the room, spied what it was he was searching for, and rose in reaching for an ashtray from the table opposite. He offered the detective a cigarette from his packet.

She looked at the object with a scowl, shrugged once and accepted. 'Screw it. I'll quit again next week.'

'I'm sorry,' McManus responded. 'If I knew you were quitting, I wouldn't have tempted you.'

'Don't worry. I've given up several times this month, alone. The only way I'm going to succeed is by leaving this damn job.'

He laughed at that. 'Ain't that the truth.'

Smith decided to join in. 'They say twenty a day will take twenty years off your life.'

'The opinions of anal-retentive arseholes doesn't bother me.' Kate answered. Then sensing that the young officer may have felt slighted by the remark, she added, appeasingly, 'I've actually heard the same, but it's at times like this I'm glad I took it up.'

She accepted a light from McManus. Took a deep draw and exhaled languidly. 'The *only* times though, I must admit.'

The trio fell silent, as if observing a minute's silence in honour of something. . . *honourable*, all staring blankly into the middle distance, perhaps reviewing recent events or thinking about the things they would much rather be doing — something far more enjoyable than sitting in a cold café in a tiny, nowhere country town in the early morning. The silence continued until Mrs Forsythe returned carrying a tray, on it a freshly percolated pot of coffee with three mugs, a sugar bowl surrounded by teaspoons and a small jug, containing fresh, creamy milk.

'Here you go, dearies,' she intoned with all the characteristics of someone's kindly old aunt. 'This will lift the spirits. You all look as though they need raising, too. What are you all having, this morning?'

Bacon, eggs and beans, washed down with steaming hot coffee went a good, long way in restoring flagging energies and widening the eyes.

McManus and Kate set alight their second cigarette after pushing emptied plates to the centre of the table, while Smith left in search of a urinal. A radio check-in was overheard on the transceiver as the observation posts reported, *"Negligible movement. Nothing suspicious. Over and out."*

With a sigh, Kate reached across the table to review the file one more time.

'I'll fix the bill, McManus told her. We can square up later.'

He had expected her to reach for her purse, but her attention was entirely taken up by the file and she hadn't heard, so he rose and ambled off, seeking the proprietor in order to settle their bill. Kate's approach was now to try and assemble Morgan's past, in attempting to fathom what was guiding his movements. When spending long periods behind bars, inmates tended to sever most or all ties. The common perception for *lifers* and *long-timers* was that having links to the outside, especially to family and loved ones, only made their life more difficult. Their world existed within the confines of prison, and she had heard it said so many times by lifers that the sooner that particular area of their existence was rationalised, the sooner they were able to settle into the routine of their new existence, without having the heart strings constantly played upon, and always having to grieve the emotional loss.

It was an unfortunate situation, she found herself considering.

Having those emotional ties severed only went towards the diminishment of a prisoners humanity. She supposed it was a part of the hardening process which appeared to be necessary in existing within such an environment.

Had anyone ever looked into the situation? Emerging from five or ten years of imprisonment would introduce back into society a person with their emotional side eroded away.

Taking the line of thought further, in these institutions certain character traits which were shunned on the outside often came to be admired in prison life. Ferocity and a quick temper, for one. These traits bought an inmate space, respect and even fame; exactly those characteristics society hoped to eradicate.

The notion disturbed her. Why weren't these obvious facts taken seriously enough by the relevant powers that be, enough to instigate restructuring in an obviously antiquated, ineffective penal system? It took little enough thought to identify these obvious flaws. Why not act on them; attempt, at least, to ameliorate the problems associated with institutionalization?

Smith had returned while she was deep in thought, and sat quietly, attempting to glean what he could of the opened file before her. McManus returned, also, reseated himself, began pouring a last coffee from the pot.

Smith leaned in closer over the file, appearing to have spotted something of interest to him.

'Are Morgan's parents still alive?' he asked.

'Why?' McManus responded, somewhat disinterestedly.

The young officer shrugged. 'I was thinking, if it was me, I would want to contact my parents, tell them I was safe and not to worry. Even if that were untrue, you wouldn't want your folks constantly worrying. Especially with what's being said in he news broadcasts right now.'

Kate looked up from the file, regarding Smith anew. 'You're kidding me.' Smith was not sure if he was being admonished, but she continued, in mock amazement. 'Why the hell didn't I think of that?'

'His parents. Of course his parents. Well done, Danny,' and officer Smith responded with a triumphant smile.

She flicked urgently through the file, backwards, page after page, searching.

'It's in here somewhere. I hope I didn't imagine it. An old contact number. Very old. Possibly from when he lived with his parents. A school document, I think.'

The men continued to watch, occasionally looking up at one another, as she flipped through the pages, scanning, and flipping more and more pages.

'Ah!' She peered hard at a printed fax sheet which had untidy handwriting scrawled all over it.

'Yes,' she acknowledged. 'A phone number, but no address, damn it. The date coincides with his secondary school years. I only hope it's his parents and that he was living with them at the time. I think he was.'

'Are they even still alive? McManus quizzed.

'I have no idea,' she answered, looking up, regarding each of the men in turn. Look at this prefix code. The area number.'

McManus bent forward in order to focus on the scratchy handwriting. 'It's local, isn't it? A country area prefix, but I–'

She had already risen from her seat and was no longer listening. She found Mrs Forsythe in the bakery, pulling freshly baked loaves from the oven, wrapping and packing them into plastic trays, ready for transporting to various outlets.

Coming up alongside her, Kate placed a finger next to the scribbled number on the page. 'Can you help me with this? Is that a local number?'

Mrs Forsythe pulled a distorted pair of wire frame glasses from her pinafore pocket, balanced them carefully on her nose. She moved her face closer to the page, peering intently.

'Yes,' she said, straightening her back. 'That's a Preston Vale number. Whose, I couldn't say. It's just twenty miles up the road, dear. We deliver to their general store, daily.'

Kate made her way back to where her companions were waiting. 'We've been outwitted. I think our quarry laid a false trail for us.' She looked out through the shopfront window to see that daylight was already returning. 'Come on boys. We're off to Preston Vale, posthaste! His parents and his childhood home are not far from here. I think we may have him.'

~

A persistent *thopping* sound, far of in the distance, but closing, growing gradually louder. It began to penetrate Andy's exhausted sleep, with ever greater annoyance. He had been enjoying dream induced recollections from a period much earlier in his life, but the intrusion continued, louder, closer, until fear sprang upon him like a wild thing in suddenly realising its meaning.

Instead of jumping to his feet, he tucked himself into as tight a ball as possible, encompassing the rucksack, while willing himself to blend into the grassy embankment on which he lay.

Opening his eyes he searched above, daring to move nothing but eyeballs. Very likely it was a police, search helicopter, come to put an ignominious end to his flight for freedom.

Not now! Not yet! he plead to the sky and any deity which chanced to hear the plea at the very moment; and there, low in the sky, maybe four hundred metres off, came into view the police chopper he had expected to discover, as it began to wheel left in a long, slow arc, focussing its cold, searching gaze away and further westward.

When the sound of rotors slapping the air had receded sufficiently, he rose to sitting, feeling the cold sweat which had come upon him trickle down, along the spine. *Too damned close,* he told himself. *Too damned close by far.*

He looked about at the countryside, now illuminated under the wan rays of a rising winter sun. About seven thirty or so, he guessed by its height above the horizon, and although there was some warmth in the air, the cold night and damp earth had seeped into his bones to sap much of the vigour of the previous day. Instead of standing to continue the journey, he repositioned the rucksack behind his back to recline against it, hoping to absorb a little warmth, and as much to take time to take stock of himself. Energy was low, as were his spirits. His body and limbs felt heavy and unresponsive. Despite some hours of sleep he was still very much lacking strength and not at all as refreshed as he might have been. There were the dried fruit bars in his kick, which he quickly retrieved and began to chew, but there was that old and much despised nemeses emerging once again.

Like an ever present, lurking denizen of the mind it had followed close, dogging his heels for the most of his adult life, never far enough away to be discounted and be free of its potential to rise up at the most inopportune of moments, and it had not failed to do exactly that once again.

'Goddamn it,' he cursed bitterly. *I should have realised,* he thought. The excess of energy over recent weeks. The mental acceleration, the constant agitation over being confined, deprived of the things any intelligent animal — *any creature of creation* — had the god-given right to. The cogent and unrelenting sentiment had germinated like a seed in fertile soil; the germ of a notion which took hold and would not relent until action was taken. *I should have noticed*, he lamented.

Unchecked, the thought had grown gradually and without notice, without examination of its origin or what it may yield.

Unobserved and unchecked it had taken precedence, soon come to be constant and overriding in his thinking. Environment and circumstance had surreptitiously and capriciously combined, aligning as occasionally the planets were want to do, and so he had responded in an instant on nothing other than instinct, at the merest glimpse of a possibility to alter the eternal now which was his life, and to escape the endless, grey world of a prisoner's existence, and in an instant taken the thread of possibility which fate seemed to have offered up, because reaching out to grasp that slender thread of a chance was eternally superior to admitting to one's self that they had succeeded in grinding down the will and crushing the soul.

This reevaluation of his rationale for making the break for freedom flashed through Andrew Morgan's mind like a lightening bolt and may have had as much impact, had he not been so well aware of how the condition worked, and for how many years he had endured learning to exist as the person chance had created. How many had the slightest inkling that some were compelled to negotiate their lives as if walking endlessly through an invisible minefield, constantly on guard, having to second guess every thought and every action lest it lead to misfortune or perhaps even to disaster?

The mind was as much an adversary as it was the instigator of the many joys it had authored in his upside-down, crazy, unpredictable but always so very damn interesting life.

He smiled to himself a secret smile of amusement, and also in grudging salute; in acknowledgement of the slight of hand brilliance the mind had exhibited in so cleverly deceiving and obscuring its true intention from him; pretending that logic, justice, natural law and perhaps even god itself was in the equation, as well as possibly being on his side. This was a *tour de force*, the most masterly deception yet perpetrated against himself, by he himself, and it deserved recognition, appreciation and yes. . .

He stood, and play-acting now, bowed low and graciously; stage left, stage right, behind and to the fore, then remembering to acknowledge the sky above and the unseen dimensions beyond the knowing of mere mortals.

The action was effected in order to permit the other self to receive the much deserved accolades and applause of the fates, of nature, of all creation for its skills of deception and superb manipulation. After all, was it not only fair to acknowledge the mastery involved; enough that a man's life might deftly be guided, without any suspicion at all of the skulduggery at work, contributing to its ultimate goal, the man's inescapable downfall? If only he had been shot down like an animal, that was the one missing item; the last ingredient that would see this insane production colluded with a bang. If only there was a point to any of this.

~

The three police officers travelled at a rapid rate of speed, buoyed by the idea they were now very much on the scent, and closing fast. Morgan's capture was, they dared to hope, very imminent, and it would be they who brought the episode to a successful conclusion. What a feather in the cap it would be for each of them.

In the passenger seat, Kate retrieved her mobile phone from her handbag to key in the numbers scavenged from the early document within Morgan's file. Before pressing the call button she looked to each in turn, uttering, 'Well, here's hoping, boys.'

She executed the call, listened expectantly as the ring tone told her the connection had completed.

It rang three, four, times, and still no one engaged. Nine, ten times, and just as she was about to cancel the call, the receiver was lifted, in a moment a voice, sounding to be that of an elderly lady, came through:

'Hello.'

'Yes, hello,' Kate responded, suddenly nervous. 'I am trying to reach the family of Andrew Morgan. Do I have the right number?'

'Who, dear? Andrew?'

'Yes, Andrew. Do you know Andrew? To whom am I speaking?'

'Andrew is my son,' the old lady replied. 'Who wants to know?'

Kate made a face toward McManus, inferring that she wasn't sure what she should say. 'My name is Kate Bryant, Mrs Morgan. I'm with the State Police. We are trying to locate Andrew. Is he there with you? Could I please speak with your son, Andrew?'

'Andrew is not here, young lady. I haven't seen Andrew in a very long while.'

'Oh? That's such a shame,' Kate replied, pitching her voice to invoke a sympathetic tone. 'That must make you sad. How long has it been, if you don't mind me asking?'

'Ooh, a long time, deary. A long time. Have you seen him? If you know where he is, tell him his daddy died last month, will you? Tell him his daddy is buried in the cemetery, behind the old church, but he must know that. He was ninety six years old.'

'I'm very sorry to hear that, Mrs Morgan. Very sorry, indeed. Are you sure Andrew is not there with you? We have come a long way to speak with him. We would love to speak with him and it's very important.'

'You don't listen very well, do you, *miss*?' The old lady sounded irritated. 'I can't stand here talking to you all day if you don't listen to what I tell you.'

'I'm sorry,' Kate quickly apologised, fearing the old lady was about to hang up. 'One last thing, Mrs Morgan, if you don't mind? Was Andrew raised in Preston Vale? Does he have any old friends out here, still— someone who might know of his whereabouts?'

'I don't know,' came the reply, and it sounded obvious that she was fast losing interest. 'Friends? I don't know, but, yes, Andrew was born and raised in these parts. He loved it here. He and his friends attended the school just down the road. If you see him, tell him his daddy died. Tell him to come visit his old mum. Tell him that, will you?' and the call ended abruptly on that note.

Kate put down the phone and turned to McManus. 'What do you think?'

'I think we should have a car posted to watch the house. I suspect he may not have made contact, yet, but there's no doubt he's in the vicinity. Why would he not pay his mother a visit?'

From the back seat, Smith voiced agreement. 'And even if he didn't receive a single visit in prison, or hasn't been getting mail, you know they *do* get access to newspapers? It's very possible he knows of his father's demise. Didn't she say as much?'

A short pause ensued, until McManus spoke up. 'We could be wandering blindly around the district all day, without a sighting. We already have patrols doing that.'

'Okay,' detective Bryant replied. 'We'll keep a low profile. We don't want him spotting us scouring the area. I take it you're suggesting surveillance on the graveyard? she asked.'

'There *and* his mother's house. It's bound to be one or the other, don't you think so? Perhaps both.'

Kate sighed, thinking on it. 'I can't help thinking his coming back here contradicts my understanding of the man. He knows as well as anybody we would be keeping an eye on his old stomping ground. He just isn't that stupid.'

'Unless he wants to be caught,' Smith said quietly from the rear seat.

The statement troubled her. 'Unless he wants to be caught,' she repeated, and twisting around in her seat to face the young man, asked, 'Do you have any reason for saying that, or were you just being obtuse?'

Smith had the file folder opened on his knees and had been scanning it as they made their way to Preston Vale. Looking up from it now, he rejoined, 'This guy is cagy. Like you said, he must consider this to be hot territory for him, and yet, here he comes, and he must have pegged you for a cop. Why else would he break camp so early and lay that false trail?

'You've got to ask yourself, is he acting emotionally? Does he even care that he will be retaken? What's the point? Or does he have something in mind he considers more important? I don't know. A girlfriend, maybe? . . . *something!*'

McManus took up the commentary. 'Only an emotional journey would bring him back here, surely. I suspect his father's death as having a lot to do with it. Hell, prisoners are often permitted to attend a family funeral, albeit under guard, but he never requested to attend any funeral. As far as we can tell, he never knew of his father's death. We're not sure of that, and his mother claims no knowledge of her son's whereabouts.'

'That was confusing, Kate replied, but, for your information, prisoners being granted leave to attend funerals is not anywhere near being commonplace. It's rare, in fact, and our friend has always been considered a security risk. Slim chance. I doubt he would even have bothered asking, and alerting prison staff to the situation. It would only cause extra attention to be focussed on him, and he would know that only too well.'

McManus scratched at the thick stubble on his face, which had grown during the time since the assignment had begun. 'So we're assuming he got word of his father's passing?' 'No,' she told him. 'Not at all.'

'But why the hell else would he be out here?'

'I don't know the answer to that. I'm just saying that to assume that as the reason might prove to be a mistake. Assumptions are never a great idea.'

'There's the town church,' Smith alerted them, pointing ahead. 'And the cemetery out back. Wow, it's large for such a small town.'

'Well it has been collecting the dead for a lot of years, I guess,' McManus commented. He turned to the detective. 'Well, what do you say? We can't be in two places at once. Which is it going to be, here or the family home?'

'There's a thicket up on the slope,' she pointed out. 'It'll provide cover. 'I'll alert one of the other patrols and put a team on the house while we're here. . . when I find the address. We can only wait and see if he turns up, while the other teams do *their* job. I'm thinking he would have learned of his father's death. My money is here, on the graveyard and his father's grave. Twenty bucks says he shows up. Any takers?'

McManus didn't look pleased. He pulled at his sleeve, viewing his timepiece. 'This is becoming a real pain in the arse. Why I ever wanted to be a copper, I will never know. It couldn't be for the excitement, I can tell you. And you two sods still owe me for breakfast!'

~

Keeping an eye to the sky and listening closely for a return of the chopper, Andy moved inland, following alongside the stream.

The erosive forces of the watercourse had exposed several rocky outcrops, mostly grey in colour, and useful in providing a measure of camouflage from further, airborne surveillance.

A sketchy recollection of the area began to kick in now. He had not walked through here since he was a lad, but presently he came upon a tumbledown remnant beside the stream. It was not at all how he remembered it; but then so much time had passed since last he was here, and the elements had taken a heavy toll. A tall, rectangular construction, built of locally quarried sandstone, had once had stood there. There had been a large waterwheel which, long ago, had turned under the impetus a fast moving stream. About half remained, with the slate tiles from the roof completely gone, laying as rubble and splintered remains among the surrounding rock and debris. In his mind's eye he sought to conjure the scene of himself and his boyhood friends, climbing over everything; the hot summer days, coming here to spend lazy afternoons, swimming and lazing in the soft grass on the embankment, spirits soaring into the clear, blue skies and drifting clouds, with a head full of dreams and without a single earthly concern.

Pushing on, his found his demeanour was beginning to lift along with the return of the body's willingness to comply, and a surprising warmth was growing now, in the increasingly fragrant air.

The most exposed and dangerous part of the journey was now nearing its end, he allowed himself to speculate. Not far from here he would be at the old shack, and he wondered if things were proceeding as they had imagined?

Had the police visited the family home yet, and were they, by now, keeping a close watch at the graveyard and on the whole town? Had they even considered that he might go there, or were they simply keeping an eye on the transport routes, bus and train stations, the airports?

So long as he wasn't spotted: a lone figure trekking cross- country in the vicinity; and as long as he was able to focus their attention on the locations of the homestead and the town's cemetery, he felt confident that they would be sufficiently distracted and likely to be feeling confident they had the bases covered.

Meanwhile, skirting the edges, he would make a final contact before disappearing completely, and, as far as society was concerned, forever; never again having to wake into that torpid realm; into the dissolution of being and acceptance of a kind of living death which had been imposed as a substitute existence for all those years. That was the hope. The only small measure of control he had was to attempt to divert their focus to where he was not, and to keep it there, hoping like hell that no one suspected the ruse.

The advent of that woman turning up at his camp? It still unnerved him greatly. Instinct had warned she represented real danger. He would likely never know, but circumstances being as they were and surrounded by uncertainties, to disregard that with which nature had provided him would be the height of foolishness. The problem was, if he had been right about her, why had she not attempted to make an arrest, there and then, while she had the chance, and what closing danger did she actually represent? If any, he considered, that danger would turn up very soon. If he failed to sense the closing of a trap, here in the open, the future he had envisioned for himself would soon evanesce, rapidly fade as does a fantasy when the dreamer is shaken from sleep.

He shook his head while continuing to follow along the narrow sheep trail. Of course, he was forced to remind himself, the incident may have been entirely innocent, meaning that he was presently building a fiction in his mind, and worrying needlessly about nothing at all.

The old adversary was still hard at work, attempting to make slip his grasp on what was genuine and what was no more than happenstance; a product of the imagination, a nagging dread that, at any instant the negative impact of just one of countless, interconnecting, physical or abstract factors surrounding all of this might act to bring it tumbling down around him; not least of these ingredients being his ability to restrain the mind from responding irrationally, should things go awry.

Mental health — a phrase Andy had always mistrusted for its vagueness, and for its ability to mislead all in the direction of underestimating its complex and multifaceted *modus operandi* — was not a thing well considered in correctional institutions. What he did know, however, and had, on more than a few occasions, witnessed, was the response to those inmates who had allowed their difficulties be detected. Some were pulled from the prison population, never to be seen or heard from again. Some did return to population, and one in particular, whom Andy regarded a close and trusted friend, he had never fully recovered from the treatment. Whatever prescribed treatment had been employed was not any sort of attention he cared to have visited upon himself, and so he had vehemently committed to dealing with the problem on his own, and in any possible way he could devise. Indeed, he concluded for himself that had his problems been detected at or prior to the time of their materialisation, this entire episode of his life would never have come to be.

Oh, boo-hoo, life is tough. Poor me— a disembodied and unsympathetic voice told him.

'Sod off,' he replied angrily, and wanting to make better time, he stepped up the pace a notch, to begin jogging toward the arranged meeting place.

The further along the trail he travelled, the more familiar became the landscape. This was the country he remembered, with its verdant, high rolling hills of the tableland, the gentle slope on which he stood beginning even now to angle dramatically downward from here, becoming ever steeper, until, at its nadir, the swift *Aruma* river flowed, reaching into the distance and onward, to the *Elanora* plain, where, over its long distance, it eventually slowed and at last emptied into the serene, turquoise depths of the Southern Ocean.

Elanora, he remembered his people instruct him, an aboriginal word meaning *"Home by the Sea."* And *Aruma,* in *language* simply meaning *"happy."* The thought of an unspoiled and unmolested people — people whose blood flowed in his veins — living on this land in harmony with everything surrounding; the thought filled his heart with such a joyous feeling. . . but that was so long ago, he was forced to remind himself.

Even childhood, a period so very recent when compared to the history of European settlement, it too felt as though it were centuries ago, lying far off in the mists of time, almost lost to memory after all that had happened since then.

Such a depth of frustration and anger began to rise that it brought tears to Andy's eyes, but there was still, not so far from the surface and not yet lost to the attrition of spirit brought about by suffering and misunderstanding, the glimmer of hope and perhaps even optimism for a future unexplored, where the desire to make good and to forge a new and worthwhile existence had yet to leave its mark.

That was the unwritten page on which would commence part two of the Andrew Morgan story. If the universe would see fit to forgive the actions of a young, foolish and desperate man who had not, at the time of his terrible transgression, yet learned what it was to be the custodian of his own life, as well as those who lived and struggled around him in their everyday lives, then he would work as hard as was needed to make sure his life counted for something good — *something good and worthwhile and meaningful* — in atonement for the terrible thing he had done, and for which he must find a way of making amends.

These thoughts crowded Andy's mind, driving him forward at pace until he realised that he was running as fast as his legs would carry him. He slowed and came to a halt. Spotting a sturdy, fallen branch off to the side of the trail, he walked over to it, there to sit for just a while, in need of settling the mind before covering the last leg of the journey which would take him to his father. It would not do to meet his father after all this time without being in full control.

~

Albert Morgan, an eighty seven year-old Yaraldi man and tribal elder of his people, made preparations at the riverside cabin. He had driven his battered utility into the wild landscape five days earlier. After covering the vehicle with bushes and branches, he had left it there, invisible to searching eyes from above, and difficult to detect in the unlikely event of anyone passing by on foot.

From there he began the twenty three mile journey which would take him past three prominent, sacred landmarks. There he offered respect to the elementals and to the guardian spirits of his ancestors who had existed as custodians of this land spanning thousands of years, invoking their attention, asking for support and favour in his undertaking, asking, too, for guidance and their blessing in hope of steering his son toward a new and meaningful life in the years to follow.

Upon arriving at the cabin he discovered, as promised, a motor boat tied to the timber constructed landing at the water's edge. The boat would be used as a contingency should the planned first option not eventuate. Inside the cabin were provisions, enough to supplement two men for two nights should the environment fail to furnish their needs. There was even a solar panel attached to the roof, supplying power to a small refrigerator, inside of which Albert found a few cans of soft drink and a single can of sliced peaches.

He did not rest, but set about making clean the cabin's interior, dusting off the rudimentary furniture and sweeping clean the bare timber floor. After this a space was marked outside on the ground. On the selected site he piled wood, gathered from the surrounding bushland. This would be the fire which later he would share with his son whom he had not seen since, as a young and inexperienced man, he had left the country of his birth to set off for the city, looking for adventure and a mode of life about which he had no idea, just as so many other young men had done.

Albert had not advised against Andy stretching his wings to explore the wider world. The boy had done according to his nature, and that was the only way it could be. There were unseen dangers in the world and he would simply have to negotiate them as best he could; learning about life and about people, becoming a man in his own way, in his own time. He would have preferred the young Andy to have better prepared, taken time to grow while absorbing from their cultural trove, the depth of knowledge and wisdom which had, for so very long, served to enrich life, rarely to have left wanting those who remained constant in following the path as far as it led.

'Young men are impatient,' the Yaraldi man had maintained when Andy's mother had asked him to intervene. 'He must find his own way,' he had said, all those years ago, and he had never questioned himself in speaking the words, for truth was truth, and in life a man had to find his own way.

By early afternoon the old man straightened his back after adding the final logs to the pile he had cut and carried from the verging woodland. For the moment, all was in readiness. He would find a spot to sit and put his feet up. He was pleased that all was in order, and the day was beginning to warm up. It was a good day. . . and all would go well.

~

'A man has to find his own way.'

Andy had fleetingly been lost to the past while resting on the fallen branch, gathering his thoughts, only now breaking free of the reverie, as he heard himself repeating his father's words as they echoed back to him through the intervening years.

'If I had not set out upon this journey,' he asked himself in earnest, 'where would I be now?'

There was no answer to that.

~

Detective Kate Bryant checked with the posted lookouts around the town, making sure everyone was alert. She was becoming increasingly agitated at the obvious lack of incoming information.

Time felt to be passing by impossibly slowly. From the car, parked amid the bushes, halfway up the slope and overlooking the town's cemetery, the trio sat in a silence which had lasted for almost the last half an hour, until she had broken the torpidity by making a radio call which had yielded nothing remotely pertinent to their purpose.

'Are we in a time warp?' she snapped irritably.

'Time is relative,' Smith responded. 'It's the watched pot syndrome, only without the pot.'

She twisted the rearview mirror around to view him. 'Are you purposely trying to be obtuse?

'How is that obtuse?'

'Never mind.' She breathed heavily, glanced at her wristwatch and returned to looking out through the windscreen from their elevated view over the cemetery. 'This is beginning to feel quite pointless.'

'Its police work,' McManus replied, ironically. He looked at his own watch, grunted, pulled his sleeve back down. 'I could make a suggestion?'

She looked to be considering letting McManus make his suggestion, but before she was able to respond, Smith intervened. 'What's the suggestion?'

'We could interview the mother. It would sure beat the hell out of sitting here like a bunch of—'

'We already have someone watching the homestead,' she cut McManus off. 'We cannot risk abandoning this location. It would be just our luck he would turn up the moment we left. It's still a good bet he'll come here.

'Christ, we know he's coming to town. Of course he'll come and pay his respects to his old man. Of course he will,' she repeated, though not as assuredly as the first time.

~

The old fellow had not meant to doze off. It was a matter of some pride that his strength and stamina were held in high esteem among his people; a testament to the life of a black fella who maintained the traditional ways of life in-country, needing nothing from an imported culture which never really understood aboriginal culture and what the word *belonging* meant.

To his mind the traditional ways left nothing wanting in a human being, and for those not *of* or *in tune* with the inhabiting spirit of the land, he could only feel a vague sense of disappointment for them. They would never know what it was to be whole and at one with it all.

The sound of something approaching primed his senses, causing the eyes to flicker open. The sun, he noted, was already very much past it's zenith and the afternoon was warm, but what had awakened him?

Into the clearing emerged a tall, dark-skinned man. He was tall, solid looking, denim clad and he walked lightly upon the ground; confidently and well balanced.

Catching sight of Albert beside the cabin, the stern countenance broke into a broad smile. 'Did I catch you unaware, old man? Snoozing in the afternoon sun, like a lizard on a rock?'

'Rubbish,' Albert growled. 'I heard you comin' a mile away,' he lied, rising from the bench against the wall. 'Did you already forget what I taught you, boy?'

They laughed in advancing toward one another. Without hesitation father and son embraced, with much back slapping and laughter. In a moment they parted, his father holding Andy at arm's length, as if to evaluate what he saw.

'You have grown. You look like a man—' unable to cease smiling. 'Are you well?'

'I am well.'

'Is anyone on your tail?'

'Not now,' Andy informed him. 'There was a close call, but I gave 'em the slip.'

'You did? You sure?' Albert asked, looking hard into his son's eyes for confirmation. 'I am glad to see you again.'

Without further ceremony, the old man retrieved the pair of fishing poles he had discovered in a cupboard inside the cabin, and a spade which stood, propped against an outside wall. From the mud at the water's edge, they dug for worms to bait their hooks, and with a clear, warm afternoon in front of them, they sat upon the pier, casting their lines into the sparkling water.

'How is my mother?' Andy asked, breaking the peaceful silence.

'Your mother is well. Growing older, but she is strong. She has asked me to pass on her love to you, and she is sorry that she could not be here, but she carries you in her heart.'

'So the police are watching the house?'

'Of course.' He chuckled then. 'And, no doubt, the cemetery.'

'Yes. I almost forgot, you are dead. That was clever. Your messages got through to me, just fine.

'Billy gets a visit from his uncle Wally at least once a month. We always waited a day before talking, and they had no idea, I'm sure. It took a long time to organise, but I am here.'

'From what I heard on the news broadcast, it didn't go according to the plan. But, yes, you are here,' the old man repeated, nodding. 'It took time, but to hurry may have been a mistake. How does it feel?'

'To be free of that place?' Andy took a deep breath and exhaled, looking around at the countryside. 'I can't tell you. Words cannot describe well enough, but it feels good. Really good. It's going to take a while before my feet are back on the ground.'

Andy turned his attention to the boat moored to the pier, alongside where they sat. 'Is that the boat I'll be travelling in. Looks a bit rickety, to me.'

'No,' Albert replied. 'Wally will be here in the morning, with his fishing boat, to take you down river to Kalandra. At the ocean you'll catch a ride in a cray boat, then North, along the coast.'

'And how do I get to this cattle station I was told about?' 'His brother will meet you. It's two days drive, straight inland.

You won't be bothered by then. You are welcome there for as long as you want to stay, he says. Just pull your weight. Learn how to be useful and earn your keep. When enough time passes, maybe you'll know what you're doing. He says he's always in need of extra help. If you want to move on after a time, and if you think it's safe?' he shrugged.

'Maybe you and mum can come, visit?' 'Maybe.'

By the time the sun threatened to disappear behind the hilltops, the two had caught their evening meal. Returning to the cabin, the campfire was lit, coaxed into a blaze before breaking it down. The barramundi were wrapped, placed beneath evenly spread ashes and the red, glowing coals. A fine evening meal.

~

'I've fuckin' had it,' McManus exploded, as irritated as a man could be. 'I've been sitting in this goddamn patrol car all bloody day. My arse is sore on one bloody side and numb on the bloody other. I'll be lucky if I'm able to walk, let along chase the bastard, *if* he ever turns up. . .*Which*, by the way, he bloody well is not going to do, *is he!*'

Smith, who had fallen asleep an hour ago, popped his head up, wandering what the ruckus was about. Kate remained silent, arms folded across herself in keeping warm, because the air was again turning chilly, as the shadows began drawing ever longer. There were irritated calls coming over the radio, too. Others doing exactly the same were protesting, asking for relief teams to come and take up their positions. She had insisted they remain where they were, telling them there were no relief teams available, and that they would just have to see the thing through to the end; although, when that might be, she had no idea. 'Quit your bellyaching,' she told McManus. 'You don't hear me and Smith making a song and dance.'

'That's because Smith has been asleep for most of the afternoon, and you're just a stubborn, hard-arse. Why don't you admit it? He's gone. You had your opportunity and you–'

'You go too far, *sergeant!*' she told him, making a point of reminding him of his subordinate rank. 'No one is enjoying this, but we have nothing else to go on.'

She sat, quiet now, and moody. In a moment she relented a little. 'I guess I could radio through to headquarters. Give them an update, and maybe a prognosis.' McManus grunted in approval.

~

Beside the river, daylight gradually faded, the brightest stars beginning to emerge, one after another. The moon, waxing and almost full round, hung high in the darkening sky, with light, wispy clouds occasionally obscuring the pale orb.

With a long dead tree trunk that Andy and Albert had dragged from the bushland serving as a comfortable back support, the two men stretched out their legs while nursing their plates, from which they picked at succulent, white flesh, flavoured with wild lemon grass, savouring the moment for all it was worth.

'Do you hear that?' Andy's father asked, cocking his head sideways and with eyes directed into the distance.

Andy stilled himself, listening intently while his father awaited his response.

'Hear what?' he replied after a full minute, but Albert only returned his attention to his dinner plate without responding.

'You old bugger,' Andy responded, recalling the joke his father used to play on him as a child.

'And you still fall for it,' Albert chuckled, much amused. Barramundi skeletons were picked clean and plates put aside.

Albert retrieved two cans of soda from the cabin while Andy pulled his tobacco from his pocket, rolled two cigarettes in quick succession and shared with his father, lighting both from a flaming twig ignited in the red-hot coals of the campfire.

Expelling a long, white plume of smoke into the night air, Andy turned to observe his father. The old man looked to be carved of mahogany, the deep furrows of his countenance reflecting in the flickering glow, appearing to him to be something resolute and implacable; wise beyond the influence of time itself, with his white beard framing a face reminiscent of early picture-book illustrations; a proud tribal man, aloof and so much a part of his surroundings that one might imagine he was moulded of the very minerals of the Earth and of stone, as though it would take thousands of years of weathering and passing time to erode him from the surface of this land.

'We have not talked of it,' said the younger, his voice become low and solemn.

'Then now is that time,' came the impassive reply. 'This night is end of a journey, and the start of another. You were not yet a man when last we spoke. Like all young men, you could not be patient and you went off into the world before you were ready. You made mistakes,' he prompted, leaving the silence for his son to fill.

'I made many,' Andy admitted after a pause.

He added fuel to the fire, reclined again against the tree trunk they had dragged there for the purpose.

'I killed a man. I have had much time to think on it, about how foolish I was. I allowed myself to become addicted to a drug, and in my weakness I acquired money in any way I could to feed that hunger. Instead of finding strength enough to overcome the sickness, and it would only have been a couple of weeks of pain, I followed the weaker option. One which so unjustly cost a man his life. I am deeply ashamed.'

The older man was nodding, listening to his son's words as he spoke them, and he accepted them.

'Do you consider yourself the same man you were then?' 'Not at all. No, but that's not the point. I have blood on my hands. I did something very bad because I was weak and selfish.' 'Did you mean to kill the man?' his father asked.

'No. I acted rashly. Stupidly.'

The old man seemed to be thinking over his son's response, and in a while replied, 'The *Aruma* river beside us. Do you remember what the name means in language? 'Happy. Happy place?'

'Ah, you remember. Why does it flow as it does, here between the high places, between the hills and the slopes of the landscape?'

Andy shrugged. 'Gravity, I suppose. Why?'

'Yes, gravity. And why does it follow the exact path that it does? Why does it not push the hills aside and follow a straight line to the sea. It would be quicker. It would be a shorter distance to travel if, instead of flowing around the great boulders in its path, it would simply go through them.'

Andy chuckled at the absurdity, and could not see where this was leading. In a moment he replied, 'Water cannot pass through boulders. It has to flow only around and along the easiest, available route. The path of least resistance, or until it is blocked completely.'

'The path of least resistance,' his father repeated. 'I like that.' 'What are you getting at?' Andy wanted to know.

A young man. A man who has not yet discovered his own strength, he is not so different from water. He follows the path of least resistence, as do many men, for all of their lives, or until he becomes aware that such a course is often not the right course. It's merely the easiest course. A young man would not yet see that. Especially a young man who is in pain, under pressure in a strange environment and a long way from home. You followed the only path you saw open to you, through those young man's eyes.

'You told me you did not mean to kill that man, and I believe you. That boy made a bad mistake.'

Andy only lowered his head, finding it difficult to accept forgiveness.

'Should you go back to your prison cell to be punished further? For the rest of your life, perhaps? Are you still young and foolish? A danger to everyone? Or have you learned that to be a man one must be much stronger than you were?'

'What I did was stupid, and terrible, and I wish I could undo what was done. I will never again be the cause of another's suffering because I am too weak to face the consequences of my own actions.'

Albert reached over to place a hand on his shoulder. 'Then nothing more can be asked of you, son.'

He let Andy think these things over for a while, before continuing.

'You must consider everything that placed all of the pieces where they were on that day. The man who was killed protecting the money, do you suppose he was entirely innocent? Was he unaware of his purpose for being there?

'He was not an innocent man, and it may help to remember that. He chose his job and he trained with his firearm, and he knew what was required of him if anyone tried to steal the money. His job involved shooting a man if the situation came. He chose to be there and to take whatever risk that included. Innocent he was not, and it could have been you who died that day. I am glad it was not.

'I am glad it was a man who was prepared to kill to protect the money of a bank, and not a boy who did not mean to do harm, and who had his whole life in front of him.

'You may see that you have a debt to pay. I do not. If you must make amends, pay that debt with the actions worthy of the man you truly are. Balance the scales by making the rest of your life of value.'

Andy was nodding his head in agreement. 'Yes. That's exactly what I mean to do.' There were tears in his eyes, which he did not attempt to hide as he reached over to grip his father's shoulder.

'I don't know how I can repay you for standing by me—for being so understanding. Few would consider doing what you are doing. Thank-you, dad.'

'You are my son' Albert responded, summing up his position simply.

The two men sat in silence for a long while, enjoying the warmth of the campfire, the peacefulness of the night and each other's company. From around the vicinity the gabble of birds settling in for the night broke a long silence.

'There is something my father did for me, at around your age, that I will do for. As we become a man, there is a ceremony. Tonight

I will call the ancestors to help you on your journey, and to make you a strong man. A good Yaraldi man,' he emphasised, smiling.

~

Police radio transceivers were full of chatter. Cops from around the area were venting their frustration in underlining the probability that the escapee was nowhere near the district, and that it was well past time they all packed up and went home. The shots, however, were being called from headquarters in the city. There the consensus was that having an escaped prisoner on the loose was bad enough, but having to deal with push-back from complaining officers in the field was not to be tolerated. In view of the fact that there had not been a single, further sighting in the region, there was, however, a measure of reconsideration; there were costs to be considered, it seemed. Having so many surveillance teams and extra patrols on the road was beginning to be viewed by top brass as being, per-haps, a little excessive. To that end, all but one patrol car were being called in. The detective assigned precedence in the field, Senior Detective Kate Bryant, and her team, were instructed to stick with it until further notified. The directive did not go down too well with the trio.

Kate returned the microphone to the dashboard hook and sat in quiet contemplation, while the two men waited for her to comment.

'I want to talk to his mother, face to face,' she told them. I find it very hard to swallow that he would not *at least* make contact with his mother. I wish we could have gotten a line tap. Why else would he be headed this way?'

'No doubt he has friends in the area,' Smith contributed from the rear seat.

'No doubt,' she replied. 'I want you to stay here while McManus and I go pay the mother a visit. There's something fishy going on. I can feel it.'

Smith looked dismayed. 'Stay here, on my own? Really?' 'You have your mobile. Call us if anything stirs and we won't be long.

Half an hour, tops, and keep your flashlight turned off. Do you think you can handle that?'

~

Albert led his son away from the cabin and into the night. Carrying live coals wrapped in thick bark and bound tightly with twine, he selected a patch of open ground and there began clearing an area while Andy collected grass, twigs and branches, enough to make a small fire which would supply sufficient illumination and heat required for a ceremony. With the necessary fuel gathered, Andy set about coaxing life from the coals by blowing at the base of the construction until flames sprang anew and took hold.

Albert began chanting, softly at first, spreading his arms wide while staring up to the heavens, beseeching the attention of those spirits who dwelled there. He then focussed toward the four horizons, his ululating tones gaining volume and urgency, until, with a concluding, decisive bark, he allowed his arms to fall to his sides, the resulting abrupt silence permeating the atmosphere about them with a strange, portentous air.

Andy could not account for what he felt at that moment. As he regarded the heavens there was an almost overwhelmingly clear understanding. . . of eternity and of timelessness; a sudden realization regarding scale, and a quite comprehension of the true meaning of the word *eternity*.

The enormous expanse of night sky pulled at him, at his very core, as if wanting to absorb all that he was, dwarfing the intellect and, in that instant, revealing the sum value of mortal concerns to be little more than infantile; revealing, in cosmic terms, the scale of distance yet required to be negotiated in the quest for understanding. As his mind began to reel there came upon Andy an ineffable presence: energy, perhaps spiritual, oddly intense and moving around them; a presence suggesting inclusion of an unknown number of invisible spectators. . . or were they participants?

Albert bade him kneel beside the fire. From his dillybag he withdrew a hunting knife and a small, leather pouch. The tip of the

271

blade was pushed into the coals, and while the blade heated, Albert spoke softly and in earnest.

'Life is a gift not to be taken for granted, my son. Life is the greatest of all gifts. With it comes the ability to exert our will. In exerting the will, we manipulate the world, whatever comes into contact with us, and everything around us, according to our desires. Life is a great responsibility.

'Brace yourself, Albert told him, 'and do not cry out.'

The shock of searing heat on his upper arm made Andy wince and groan deep in his throat, but he knew he could not cry out. 'Allow your spirit to feed you. Always remember to feed your spirit. The spirit is your connection to this life, and beyond.' Again came the sudden, searing heat of the blade, and then it was gone, leaving a dull pain.

'Feed your intellect so that your intellect can feed you, your family and the world that knows you.'

The red hot blade burnt for a third time, and still Andy did not cry out. The shock of the pain was not as bad as at first. He found he could separate himself from it.

'Respect everything,' Albert told him. 'Know that our ancestors are with us, always. Be a strong man, be a good man. A *Yaraldi* man.'

The fourth time the blade touched his skin it felt almost as nothing at all. He felt strong and imperviable. The words spoken by his father felt to be seared into his very being. Indelibly so.

'Elementals: *Earth. . . Air. . . Fire. . . Water.* My people. Ancestors. All creatures of this land. This is my son, Andrew James Morgan. A good man. A Yaraldi man. I ask you to guide my son and to show him the way.'

The old man opened the dillybag he had brought along. From it he poured a white, earthy powder which he combined in his hands with ash from the edge of the fire, then mixed with water spurted through pursed lips. The greasy mixture he smeared over the row of four blistering burns on Andrew's upper arm, in the triangle shape left by the tip end of the hunting knife, repeated side by side.

Andrew found that the paste took much of the remaining sting out of the burns. 'Is it over now?' he asked, hopefully.

'It's over,' his father confirmed. 'I could not let you begin your new life without this ceremony.'

'Thank-you,' Andrew acknowledged. 'It means a lot to have you to do this for me.'

'I know,' Albert replied. 'Come, put out the fire and let's get some sleep. You have a long journey in front of you.'

~

Mrs Morgan, Dede to her friends, was in no way surprised to discover the police at her door when she opened it. One was a lady detective, tall, fair complexion, and undernourished if she were any judge. The other was a stocky man in need of a shave, wearing an ill-fitting uniform buttoned far too tightly around an ample paunch.

She did not say a word, simply waited for those who had disturbed her at this time of day to state their business.

Kate found herself before a large, formidable looking aboriginal woman of indeterminate age, almost filling the door frame as she stood there, looking defiant. She had to be in her seventies, if she remembered correctly from the files.

The detective affected her best, friendly smile and began: 'I am detective Bryant, and this is sergeant McManus. I am so sorry to call on you at this hour. May I talk to you for just a moment about your son, Andrew?'

Dede felt no need to respond; remaining silent, waiting for the woman to state her business and be gone. 'If you must,' she conceded, finally.

Kate took in as much of the room behind Mrs Morgan as she was able to. A comfortable looking lounge room with a television set flickering in the corner. She shifted marginally to the left, attempting to catch sight of anything out of place, or anyone who may be lurking just out of sight, perhaps casting a telltale shadow.

'When you last talked to Andy, did he say anything to you that might assist us in establishing his whereabouts?'

'You're that woman who called earlier,' Dede responded, forcefully. 'What did I tell you?'

'Your son is in a spot,' Kate responded, undeterred. 'I want to help him. That's the only reason I am here, Mrs Morgan. I assure you, the best thing for Andy would be to come forward before things get way out of hand.'

She thought she noticed a trace of concern in the mother's eyes; a chink in the armour, something which might be forced widener. 'There are armed police all over,' she continued. Nobody wants your boy to come to harm. Especially not me. I am a mother, too. I have children of my own and I can only imagine what this must be like for you. . . what you are going through.'

But Dede's reticence only continued, making her exceedingly difficult to read.

'Might we come in for a while? There's a lot to talk about, don't you think?'

'I don't have anything to tell you, lady. I hoped I had made myself clear the last time we talked. Andy is a grown man. He makes his own choices now. You lot put him in prison when he was a boy, and ruined his life over a mistake he made, and paid too big a price for.'

'Do you really believe that?' Kate found herself saying, and immediately wished she had not. 'Look, Mrs Morgan,' she tried, brushing over it. 'We both want what is best for Andrew. I'm sure we can agree on that, can't we?'

Still unmoved, Dede appeared to regard the policewoman at her door with something approaching rising amusement.

'Lady,' she said to the detective. 'What do you hope to achieve by coming here like this? Did you hope to catch Andy sitting here, warming himself, eating a home-cooked meal? How stupid do you think we are?'

'Honestly, Mrs Morgan, I expect you to be intelligent enough to do what is best for your son. If I were you–'

'Don't give me that,' Dede interceded. 'You don't give a damn and we both know it. You just want to lock him up like an animal again. And you don't care what you have to say and do to achieve it.

'Is it your intention now, to badger me all night, wear me down until you think you have tricked me into divulging some piece of information which will lead you straight to him?'

The big woman threw open the door, stepping aside. 'If the only way to get you out of here is to allow you to satisfy your relentless suspicion that my son is hiding here, then be my guest. I won't even insist on you producing a warrant, and we both know you don't have one, or else you wouldn't be trying to get me to invite you into my home. Come on, what are you waiting for?'

Kate was concerned with what may ensue, should she march right into the house and conduct a search. There was already more than ample consternation over this investigation, by her superiors. Complications were not what anybody needed tonight. Least of all herself. She was only here because she had been in the wrong place at the wrong time, and right now all she wanted was to be anywhere but here, and to be working on anything at all but this damned assignment.

McManus had shifted position, coming around to stand behind her, obviously in readiness to enter the dwelling, but there was nothing here to warrant taking the risk of a procedural complaint over it. Morgan was too bright to put himself or his mother at risk by returning. What the hell was she thinking, coming here? 'Good night, Mrs Morgan,' Kate responded as politely as she was able, amid rising anger. 'I'm sorry I disturbed you tonight.' Then, feeling the need to stick a barb into the woman, she added, 'I really *was* hoping you wanted what was best for your son. I only hope your decision to stonewall us does not result in tragedy.' And with that, she turned and walked away, calmly relating to McManus, 'That bitch knows exactly where he is.'

~

Despite the need for a good long rest, Andy was too cognisant of the fact that tonight was likely the last occasion on which he would spend time with his father for a very long time. Upon returning, they sat again within the influence of the campfire's warming glow, resting their backs against the tree trunk as they had done earlier.

Andy raised his arms, locking his fingers behind his head while gazing upward at the night sky. 'I had almost forgotten how beautiful it is,' he said, quietly. 'These last few days have helped to me remember what life feels like.

'*That place*,' he pronounced with a weary sigh. 'That place separates a man from his better self. There are people there who have become more animal than human being, although maybe that's unfair to animals. No animal I know could be so depraved as some I came across in there. . . dehumanised and becoming degenerate. Harbouring their anger and resentment. Locked in with little more than that for company. It's a dangerous thing, to deprive a person of so much.'

'You got another smoke there, Andy?'

He passed over the tobacco. When it was constructed, Albert lit up from the campfire, returned to recline against the log.

'I remember an old Nunga man I met, up in Alice,' Albert began. 'One of our mob. He was about as old as I am now. I was just a young fellah then. A bit younger than you, maybe. I stopped to sit in a park, in the middle of town. On one of those park seats they have, you know? Just sittin', lookin' round at the people walking about, feedin' the birds and warming in the sun. 'On the other end of the bench this old fellah was sittin, lookin' kinda' sad, you know? With a saddle there on the ground by his feet. A stock saddle. The kind a stockman uses, roundin' up cattle, and a nice one too.

'After a while I says *gidday* to him. Just being friendly. And I says, 'Somebody steal your horse?' thinking to cheer him up with a laugh, but he says, 'Something like that,' and the way he said it. I thought if someone did steal his horse, it'd be better than what was bothering him, 'cause he wasn't a happy fellah. But then we got to talking, 'cos we were just sittin, and he tells me the story of what happened.

'His name was Albert, I remember. He was born on Barramere cattle station, a couple hundred miles up the road out of Alice. He was raised as a stockman, like his daddy before him, on that station, and he worked there all of his life. Ten dollars a week our fellahs were paid, and they bought what they needed from the store at the station shop, back then. Tobacco, flour, tea, sugar. Meat they killed for themselves on the property, so they had what was needed to survive, and I guess the life was good enough. 'Well, this fellah,

Billy, he lived and worked on that cattle station all his life. The day before I met him, sittin' there on that bench, the boss man tells him he's gettin' too old to pull his weight. Tells him, *Billy, it's time to go,'cause I can't keep an old fellah who ain't got it in him no more.'*

'The boss cocky loaded his stuff into the back of a ute, and him too. Put him out at the Stewart highway, and that was that, after seventy something years slog and knowing nothin' else but wrangling cattle.

'Billy saw how the city swallowed his people up. Most were down at the Todd, sittin on a dry river bed, drinkin and layin' round under the shade of a big tree, wastin' their lives away. He was ashamed of that lot, he told me. 'Them mob's no good,' he told me. He wasn't going to wind up that way. All Billy had was his saddle, his swag and his pride still in tact. A man who worked hard for all his life and all he had to show for it was his saddle, his swag and his pride.'

'That's bad,' Andy replied, thoughtful. 'Why are you telling me this?'

'It just came to mind, sittin' here.'

Andy doubted it. There was usually a reason for most things his father spoke of. So what was the significance of this story? 'Could Billy have avoided his fate?'he asked.

'I don't think so. Not Billy. He had no way of knowing what was coming. Others who lived and worked there in years past, they died and were buried that land. He had no reason to think it would be any different for himself.'

'All his life a stockman on that station,' Andy muttered dolefully, 'only to be rewarded by being disposed of in that way. He deserved more. Life can be so unjust.'

'Life can be unjust,' his father repeated in emphasis, and slapping Andy on the back, said, 'Come on, boy. It's time we bedded down.'

They bunked in the cabin, both men wearied by the events of the long day. Albert drifted off easily, almost as soon as he closed his eyes, but Andy had difficulty.

These recent days had been a culmination of many months of planning and excruciating anxiety. Being exposed again to the world, with all its colour, movement and unpredictability and had been far more confronting than he had expected; an assault on the senses, leaving him feeling elated but overwhelmed too.

He moved his fingertips to the tribal markings freshly inscribed into the flesh at the top of his arm. The paste his father had applied had become dry and crusty, but there was not much discomfort there now. He understood that the ceremony had been practised over thousands of years, and he had to assume that the ritual had been proven in time, succeeding in its purpose. The thought of so many generations of young men having received the exact same ritual caused his mind to reach and reel in attempting to assimilate the depth of it.

There was something about the idea which brought with it the pride of belonging; a continuance of something strong, enduring and altogether right. He had never known such feelings as those it had invoked in him. The world he had lived in until now was devoid of such a thing as this. There had always been a feeling of singularity and aloneness, but now, tonight, it was so strange to contemplate the almost palpable spiritual effect it was having on him. Suddenly he felt a part of something everlasting and undeniably powerful, anything but one person and singular.

From this moment forward lay his true path; the next chapter of his existence. His father had put it that way, and he saw just how correct and insightful an observation that had been. This night felt charged with omen, and as he lay there, attempting to make all that had occurred in his life make sense, it came suddenly into focus; a most powerful insight and with a clarity he had never experienced before. It all seemed to make perfect sense.

There seemed to be woven into all of it an intricate pattern of marvellous design; so convoluted and incredibly complex a fabric that little beyond basic recognition of its structure was possible, and yet it was there, the mysterious tapestry woven within eternity by Nature itself. So transcendent and perfect, he now saw, beyond any real comprehension and yet filled with certainty and underlying purpose, leaving not the slightest room for misgivings.

Andy's night was a restless one. As physically tired as he was, the mind simply would not submit to his desire for sleep. His entire life insisted on playing out like some oddly distorted motion picture, with painful emphasis being placed on the more regrettable incidents, making it especially easy to identify the defining, pivotal moments as he saw them.

The rushing off into a world for which he had been so ill prepared took centre stage in the mind's nocturnal carnival of harm and misfortunes. At sixteen years-of-age the young Andy could have had no inkling of the peculiar treacheries concealed in the wider world: Its harshness, with its singular priorities which were, despite ample lip service being widely given to the contrary, starkly incompatible with the concept of the family of man, and where everyone, so single mindedly consumed by their own prejudice and perceived urgencies, had never thought to pause and offer a guiding hand, or give even a good goddamn for a scrawny, homeless, black kid. Such an act, Andy had learned to his deep dismay, appeared to lay entirely beyond the conceptual abilities of *always-in-too-much-of-a-hurry*, city folk. The world of man itself had become a conglomerate animal who had lost its way entirely and become concerned only with personal gain at whatever cost to that which nurtured all things. Andy's kind heart had always been a forgiving heart, and although he had tried with great tenacity to hold on to the notion that people were basically good at their core, the world seemed intent on beating the innocense out of the young man at each opportunity.

At every turn chance appeared bent on taking advantage of the youngster. Before too long the realities of his difficult existence began to overwhelm his ability to defy the inequities and evil goings on, surrounded on all sides, until, as painful as it was to have to accept, he was forced to relinquish that faith he had tried to retain, in the end coming to see the so rapidly developing world as being devoid of any redeeming qualities.

These soporific recollections, reviews and revisions persisted for hour after hour, as he recalled to mind the course of the journey — the misdirected trajectory on which his life had been directed, not by his own volition but by mortal concerns and the haphazard necessities of daily survival.

Everyday existence had become so full of compulsions and wearying effort so that his first encounter with pharmaceuticals had come disguised as nothin more than a survival technique, and from that unwitting act and momentary lapse in judgement, it had unravelled his life, casting Andy into the downward trajectory which had brought him precisely this situation.

It felt as if preordained, that he had negotiated every trial and tribulation in a convoluted process, producing, at the end of the program, the very man he had suddenly become. No other path would have done. Only adversity could achieve the desired outcome.

The insight realised, he had ardently determined that this man was not destined to waste so large a portion of precious existence confined in a concrete and steel cell. He would take the sum of what providence had provided, the good and the bad of it, all, include his god given consciousness, and, from it, mould the finest person he knew how to be.

The things he had witnessed and so long despised about humanity, he would discard, while the finer qualities he knew to be buried somewhere deeper within every last individual but had somehow been bent, twisted or purged by the society whose crucible had formed them as they were, he would restore, and renew in himself. He would become what he knew he should always have been, before the intrusion into his life of a world he ought to have known to reject had completed its corruption, and the damage become beyond repair. That Andy was never meant to be; that *world* was never meant to be, and he knew for a certainty he could no longer be a part of it.

These things whirled about in his mind through the hours of the night without pause or interruption. Finally he was able to distinguish and choose between fact and fallacy, truth and deception and to recognise his own life's path amid the relentless uncertainties which had always surrounded. In the revealing of itself and of its straight and true purpose, an unexpected, profound peace came upon him, at last allowing for some few hours of sleep before the sun again rose, and with its coming would arrive his necessary departure: A last good-bye to his father, the man he had not known as well as he might have, but to whom he was so deeply indebted. Today, he knew, marked the beginning of the part of his life which had lain dormant and in wait for a long and difficult time which could not be escaped unless fate be denied, while the world acted upon him, changing and strengthening as metal is fired, hammered into shape, quenched repeatedly until something extraordinary resilient is produced; the man he had to become in order to achieve in life what fate had always deemed appropriate and held in store.

In the time remaining before dawn, Andy slept the sleep of one finally made whole and complete, the way it was always meant to be. The trace of a smile played on his lips, hinting at the formulation of a dream; the conjuring of a vision in the life now available, and all of it lying very much in front of him, as he continued to follow his own unique path into the unknown future that was his life's destiny.

~

Early morning found the three police officers *at Forsythe's Country Bakery*, eating an early breakfast as they had done the morning previous. With no sightings reported overnight, and much to the relief of all concerned, the search had been called off, the decision radioed through to remaining attending officers, at five o'clock that morning.

Mrs Forsythe poured their coffees, took orders and left them to sit, gazing out at the street as the daylight gradually increased. By the time she returned a few minutes later with their scrambled eggs and bacon, barely a word had passed between them. Kate's thoughts had returned to her contact with Morgan. She should have attempted an arrest then and there, she chastised herself.

Why had she delayed? Was it that she wasn't confident enough at the time, or was it something else?

It was true that the man was largely an unknown quantity and there had been no telling how he may have responded. Certainly it had been a gamble. She would have been severely reprimanded in any case, for taking the risk of a lone confrontation. If things had gone sideways there would have been hell to pay.

McManus sipped from his mug of coffee and asked over top of the rim, 'What did you make of him?'

'Sorry, what?' she replied, caught deep in reverie. 'Morgan, do you mean?'

'You were with him for quite some time. What did you talk about?'

She pushed her plate away, leaving half the meal untouched. She started to raise her had toward the now barely visible bruise beneath the right eye, returned it to the table-top. 'Idle chit-chat, for the most part.'

'For over an hour?'

'We talked, some. About psychology. I don't really recall.' 'Psychology?' he scoffed. 'You talked about psychology with a convicted armed robber and murder?'

'He was rather charming, if you must know. And vulnerable, actually. Why he has been classified as dangerous I don't know.' 'Yeah? Well, people are unpredictable,' the sergeant reminded her. 'You took a damn chance.' After a moment, he added, 'but don't worry. We won't mention what you did.' He turned to catch Smith's attention. 'Will we, constable.' 'No,' Smith agreed, amiably.

With breakfast over, their assignment terminated, and no reason for Detective Bryant's further involvement, Smith and McManus drove her out of town, to the bush airstrip, where a chartered aircraft had been booked to return her to the city and her usual routine.

They watched as she boarded the aircraft, exchanged a final wave as she climbed aboard, remaining long enough to watch as the twin engine Cessna whipped up red dust along the strip as it lifted off, banked steeply, northward, to fly towards Kalandra. From there she would board a connecting flight, homeward bound.

From her forward facing seat at the rear of the Cessna aircraft carrying her away from an altogether dissatisfying conclusion, Kate looked out at the countryside below. The aircraft had not gained much height as it circled northward, barely a hundred feet above the sparkling irrigation channels, flowing out into the hinterland to nourish all manner of vegetables and cereal crops destined for the city markets.

As the aircraft straightened, it travelled parallel with the Aruma river, a guiding line which the pilot would follow, taking them to their destination at the river mouth. The weariness she had been holding back these past few days left her to review her reason for being in this job. It never ended. There was always a bad guy, a transgressor of the criminal code needing to be apprehended somewhere. Like some kind of weird production line, these people continued to pop up all over, without end or any particular reason that she was able to fathom.

Her knowledge and understanding of the world the way it was told her it would always be this way. It was society, itself, who was responsible. Society could produce saints or sinners, marvellous additions to the cause for common good, or malicious monsters, ripping and tearing at the fabric of society.

The condition had existed ever since people began crowding together and upsetting the natural order, she imagined. It was the way it was because people are the what they are, and no amount of lawmaking would ever fix the problem. She had long ago given up questioning herself or the job she did. It was a job, it kept the family fed and she was good at it. . . well, most of the time, she conceded, annoyed. She never usually dwelled on an assignment after it was over, but at this moment she experienced considerable disappointment over the outcome.

It was unusual for her to take more than professional interest; to have personal feelings about it, but this time she did and knowing exactly why, for her, was more unnerving than not knowing.

She would never have admitted it to the others, but Morgan had impressed her on an intellectual level, and what was more confusing for a cop of her calibre, on an emotional level, too. There had been something about the young man, perhaps a sincerity, and sincerity was not a thing usually found in convicted criminals. She had unearthed and learned a great deal about Morgan, and in his file there had been signs consistent with a well grounded, decent human being, fighting to retain who he was, or at least to retain who he considered himself to be; a singularly unique trait, in her experience, and Kate had seen them all.

From her vantage point Kate looked out of the porthole, down to the sparkling stretch of water beneath the aircraft. Moving rapidly over its surface, a motorboat made its way in the same direction. At its prow, standing it the rail, a man was enjoying the thrill of movement, the wind lashing his thick, black hair about his face, and on his face an enormous, delighted smile.

In a moment the aircraft had overtaken the speeding boat and began to climb higher, but the look on the man's face stayed with her, and it caused her to smile herself. There had been such pleasure on his face and it please her just to catch a glimpse. Life was still able to give joy to people, she considered, and it reminded her to try and extract more of that joy for herself.

Simple pleasures were a such an important component of what made life bearable, and in that moment she resolved to try and indulge herself more. Life was just too short.

'I wonder where that young man was going and why he is so delighted?' she mused briefly, finding that the face had for some reason imprinted itself in her mind.

Recognition struck. . . struck hard. It was *him!* It was Andy at the prow, smiling with great delight.

'God, no. *It cannot be!*' —but the moment was gone and there was nothing to be done. And even if there was something to be done, in her heart of hearts, did she really want to?

– end –

Printed in the USA
CPSIA information can be obtained
at www.ICGtesting.com
LVHW040150130823
754841LV00001B/160